The Mother and Baby Home

Sheila Newberry was born in Suffolk and spent a lot of time there both before and during the war. She wrote her first 'book' before she was ten – all sixty pages of it – in purple ink. Her family was certainly her inspiration and she was published for most of her adult life. She spent forty years living in Kent on a smallholding with her husband John, and had nine children, twenty-two grandchildren and eight great-grandchildren. Sheila retired back to Suffolk where she lived until her death in January 2020.

Also by Sheila Newberry

Sheila NEWBERRY

The Mother and Baby Home

ZAFFRE

First published in the UK in 2020 by
ZAFFRE
An imprint of Bonnier Books UK
80–81 Wimpole St, London W1G 9RE
Owned by Bonnier Books
Sveavägen 56, Stockholm, Sweden

This is a work of fiction. Names, places, events and
incidents are either the products of the author's
imagination or used fictitiously. Any resemblance to
actual persons, living or dead, or actual
events is purely coincidental.

A CIP catalogue record for this book is
available from the British Library.

ISBN: 978-1-83877-145-4

Also available as an ebook and in audio

1 3 5 7 9 10 8 6 4 2

Typeset by IDSUK (Data Connection) Ltd
Printed and bound in Great Britain by Clays Ltd, Elcograf S.p.A.

Zaffre is an imprint of Bonnier Books UK
www.bonnierbooks.co.uk

Dedicated to the memory of my wonderful
daughter-in-law, Diane.
1958–2016

I love to write with tenderness
And sometimes tongue-in-cheek,
My characters are all to me
I cannot make them bleak.
Remember them when reading's through?
Then I have made them speak.

Sheila

PROLOGUE

Christmas Eve, 1940

The young woman gazed out of the window of the Mother and Baby Home as the snow drifted gently down, covering the pavement and the sign for Grove Lane. It was the middle of the night and Serena was up once again, seeing to the small baby wrapped in a blanket and nestled in the crook of her arm, slumbering away. She had just drifted back off to sleep and her small, rosebud mouth was moving, dreaming of the feed she'd had.

Serena stroked her baby's head, knowing that this might be for the last time. After the festivities of tomorrow, she needed to find a way to leave. She couldn't possibly give this baby the life she deserved, and she must return to her nursing duties as soon as possible. The hospital had given her a leave of absence on medical grounds, but they weren't aware of the true situation.

Her mind went back to that day in September. She'd been so scared throughout her pregnancy, alone in a strange country, having come to England from Trinidad to help with the war effort. She'd managed to conceal the pregnancy for all this time, terrified that she'd lose her job and be sent back home if anyone found out. She hadn't seen a doctor for the full nine months, but now she knew the baby was on its way.

Serena had seen the sign for the Mother and Baby Home outside the big house when out for a walk a few months previously. As her labour progressed, something told her that was where she should be, so she had set out on foot. As she got closer to her destination, the pains were getting closer and closer together, wrapping around from her back and into her stomach, forcing her to collapse to the ground in agony.

As she finally stumbled onto the stoop of the Mother and Baby Home, the door opened in front of her and a kind face had looked down.

'My dear, whatever are you doing here?' And then the woman had noticed Serena's belly, and the way she was clutching her hands to it. She had quickly called for help and had managed to get the young woman to her feet and inside to a bed.

Serena had laboured all night long, with the kind matron by her side, until with a final push her beautiful daughter had come into the world. At the matron, Nanette's, suggestion, the baby was named Serena after her mother, but always called Sunny, 'because she looks as if she has been kissed by the sun, with her golden skin,' Nan had said, while cuddling the little girl in her arms the next day. Serena had thought then that this kind woman was already a better mother to Sunny than she could ever be.

No, Serena thought to herself as she laid her precious baby girl back down in her cot. *There's no way I can be the mother that Sunny deserves. How can I possibly look after a child alone? The Mother and Baby Home is a much better place for her to grow up, and Nan a much better mother. Tomorrow, I'll talk to Nan and then slip away quietly. It's the best thing for everyone.*

PART ONE

ONE

1956

Sunny took the mid-morning bus from Grove Lane to Croydon, chatting to the cheerful conductor. He clipped her ticket and said, 'You look very smart today.'

'Thank you!' She smiled. She was wearing the new outfit that dear Nan had presented her with as a surprise. Today was a special day. She smoothed down her blue poplin skirt, which afforded glimpses of a pretty petticoat and which she wore with a white blouse with little pearl buttons, cinched in at the waist by a wide elasticised belt. 'I bought it at C & A,' Nan had said proudly. This was one of the newer stores in town, and teenagers, as they were now called, flocked there for Saturday shopping. Wages were around £4 a week for girls in their first jobs, but thirty shillings would buy a lovely frock to wear at Saturday night hops, the informal name for dances.

Sunny was on her way to her first job interview that afternoon, but she had decided to call on her friend

Chrissie first, in the cafe-cum-bakery off the Surrey Street Market where she worked. It was opposite the back entrance to Kennards, their favourite store, where you could buy an ice-cream cornet in the Arcade, and next to Pets Corner where there were puppies in pens and other small animals in cages. Sunny wondered if the stout Shetland ponies were still plodding up and down the aisle. She'd enjoyed a ride when she was small. And was the elderly parrot still squawking on its perch and preening its feathers?

Sunny recalled the first time she and Chrissie had been deemed old enough to go to Croydon by themselves. She'd spent the half a crown she was saving up to buy a puppy from Pets Corner on a device for curling hair from a slick salesman giving a demonstration to a crowd of young women. He must have spotted her as a likely customer. Sunny was in floods of tears once back home, knowing she'd wasted her money, but kind Nan said, 'You don't need it, but *I* certainly do – so I'll pay for it, eh?' She put the instrument, as she called it, in a drawer in her bedroom, and never used it, preferring her steel hair rollers.

* * *

When Sunny pushed open the door to the bakery, she saw Chrissie was behind the counter, in her white apron, with her long hair braided round her head. Sunny preferred to tie her own hair in a ponytail. She waited at the back of the shop for Chrissie to come on her break and gazed at the stacks of bread. No dull old wartime National loaf and no bread rationing anymore, she thought, but loaves of all shapes and sizes and with such an appetising aroma. The shelves were rapidly emptying of small round cobs, family-sized sandwich and long tin loaves, and best of all, in Sunny's opinion, crusty cottage loaves. The thought of a top crust of one of these, spread with butter, not margarine, made her mouth water. Nanette believed that brown bread was best, though. 'Keeps you regular,' she said firmly.

Beyond the closed bakery door Sunny could still just about hear the noise of the market; the vendors had strident voices, calling out to the many people pushing their way through the crowds. Scales rattled, and stall holders added coins to the piles building up in leather bags, strapped round waists. They sold anything and everything. The market was great entertainment, even if you couldn't afford to buy. Nanette shopped at the parade of shops off Grove Lane. Less stressful she said.

Looking at the buns with cherries on top, Sunny decided not to buy one as they appeared smaller than usual. *Just a mouthful*, she thought. The cafe was at the rear of the bakery. Once Chrissie was free, they could go in there and order a pot of tea and a cheese and pickle roll each. Afterwards, they would have ice creams from Kennards.

'Everything is changing,' Sunny said to Chrissie, when they eventually sat down for lunch in the cafe. 'Two weeks ago, we were celebrating freedom from school in The Grove and practising our tennis serves with those wooden racquets from the jumble sale. It was such a lovely afternoon and we couldn't stop laughing and spent more time rolling down the hill than focusing on scoring aces.' They were both silent for a few moments, then Sunny added, 'We won't have much time for fun once we're both working girls.'

From the age of eleven, Sunny had attended a modern all-girls school. On her first day there, when she was wondering how she would ever find her way around all the corridors and quadrangles, she had met Chrissie Ford and they had become best friends. Sunny had immediately felt drawn to Chrissie. Although Sunny had curly hair while Chrissie's was straight and jet-black, they both had dark skin and eyes, unlike the other girls at school.

'We've been going to The Grove ever since we first met,' Chrissie said. 'It's our special place.' She sighed as she thought of how often they had walked along one of the side roads of Grove Lane, which led to a mansion surrounded by the once-beautiful gardens and a rose walk. The house was empty – no one had lived there since before the war – but it still drew visitors every spring and summer and children played on the vast expanse of grass. The house, it was rumoured, would become a museum of local history.

Sunny said, 'I wonder if we will ever feel that carefree again.' Life was full of change and Sunny was excited but also felt a sense of trepidation.

As they sipped their tea, Chrissie said suddenly, 'Did you not wonder why I haven't been in touch lately, Sunny?' Without waiting for an answer, she continued: 'I've given my notice in here. I've enjoyed the job, but there are no real prospects. I'm thinking of going up to London as soon as I can . . .'

'Leaving home, you mean? You're too young for that, Chrissie – your parents will never allow it!'

'They won't have any choice; they *aren't* my parents.'

'Whatever do you mean?' Sunny was bewildered.

'They've finally told me the truth, Sunny. They adopted me as a baby from a mother and baby home – oh no, not a posh one like the one where you were born. Didn't you ever wonder, like me, why I don't look like them?'

'Oh, I never even thought about it. Nan said your mother told her you were like someone from generations back in the family. But if that is true, Chrissie, remember that I was adopted by Nan, and I couldn't have a better mother. And your parents have always been good to you, whether they're your real parents or not.'

'You've known that you were adopted all along, Sunny, but I never realised until I had to produce my birth certificate, before I started work. Mum gave it to me in a sealed envelope; I was curious and opened it. I can't forgive them, Sunny! They should have told me.'

Sunny exclaimed, 'You mustn't feel like that, Chrissie. Your mum and dad love you; I know they do! And now we have something else in common. Where would you stay if you went to London?'

'Oh, at my auntie's flat in Shoreditch – only I suppose she's not really my auntie either.' Chrissie's lip trembled. 'She works in an office and says I should learn shorthand and typing. That's what you need now. Those examin-ations we studied so hard for are not much use in the commercial world.'

'That's why I haven't got a job yet, I suppose,' said Sunny, nodding. 'Nan wanted me to stay on into the sixth form, then go to college and become a teacher, but I would really have liked to go to art college. Now I need to earn some money and help out; I can't expect Nan to support me.'

'Good luck,' Chrissie said, with tears in her eyes, as the girls stood up to go their separate ways. 'I'll keep in touch.'

We're not schoolgirls anymore, Sunny thought sadly as she walked away. *If I get the job, I'll be working too. But my best friend is going away and I don't know when I'll next see her . . .*

* * *

Sunny had a problem finding the Rowland Printing Press along the High Street because it was situated down a side entrance between two big stores. She had walked past the entrance three times before she plucked up the courage to ask a passer-by if they could help her locate it. She glanced anxiously at her new wristwatch, that Nanette had given her as a sixteenth birthday present. Nanette said it was important to be aware of the time when you had a job. 'Crumbs!' Sunny said aloud. 'Only five minutes to go. I mustn't be late!'

Someone came up behind her and an amused voice remarked, 'You sound like the white rabbit in *Alice in Wonderland*. Are you our new Girl Friday? The name was my idea. I'm Alec Rowland-Dixon – I've dropped the Dixon though – Mr Rowland's grandson. Here we are.'

The young man guided Sunny to the entrance to the print shop. He was tall with a thatch of thick straw-coloured hair, horn-rimmed glasses and, as she lowered her gaze, she saw he was wearing fashionable sand-coloured desert boots. He had a carrier bag in one hand. Covered with confusion, she said awkwardly: 'I'll be interviewed first by Mr Rowland before I know, well, if I have the job . . .' To her dismay, Sunny also noticed that she had snagged her new nylon stockings and the left leg had a ladder down her calf. *Why didn't I stick to my ankle socks?* she thought.

'Don't worry about that,' Alec said cheerfully, as he opened the door to the Printing Press office, where the walls were covered in advertisements. 'No one else has applied!' He ushered her in. 'Grandfather, this is – I'm sorry, I don't know your name.'

An elderly man turned, after switching off a cumbersome machine that Sunny would learn later was a guillotine for cutting paper to size. The man was stooped, as if he had spent too much of his life bending over such contraptions. He had a shock of untidy hair like his grandson, though his was white, and he also wore spectacles, with the bridge obviously held together by parcel tape. 'Miss Sunny Cato, I take it? Alec, did you remember the milk when you bought that jar of instant coffee? Could you put the kettle on before you go to get on with your work?' He swept some papers off the top of a desk, pulled out a chair, dusted that with his handkerchief, and then invited Sunny to sit opposite him. He beamed at her, 'Don't look so apprehensive, where's the sunny smile your name suggests? When can you start work here?' He indicated the chaos all around. 'Any questions?'

'Have I got the job?' Sunny floundered and when he nodded, she added, 'And what is a Girl Friday?'

'Surely you have read *Robinson Crusoe*?'

'Oh, Man Friday, you mean? But—'

'He was invaluable, a great help to old Crusoe, eh? You'll be in charge of me, my dear. Tidying up, sorting, etc. But I'll teach you everything you need to know about printing and designing posters and advertising as well. Your letter to me said you were artistic and wanted to use your imagination. We like imagination here! You'll also deal with clients on the telephone or here in the office. You'll need to wear something more practical at work than you have on. Do you object to that?'

'No, that sounds sensible,' Sunny said and the dimples in her cheeks showed. She liked eccentric Mr Rowland.

Just then, Alec appeared with cups of coffee and a packet of biscuits. Sunny wasn't surprised there were no saucers or plates, given the general state of the place. Alec winked at her, but she pretended not to notice.

He's rather irritating, she thought. *Perhaps it's just as well he's only working here for the holidays.*

After they'd all finished their coffee and talked through the particulars, Sunny set off for home. She would start work on Monday morning at 8.30. She didn't realise until she arrived home, and Nan wanted to know all about her day, that she hadn't been told what her weekly wage would be.

* * *

'Girl Friday,' Nan mused. 'In 1940 there was a film with that name. It starred Cary Grant and Rosalind Russell. I didn't see it, but I heard it was very entertaining, cheered folk up when times were tough. They'd go to sit in the cinema, even though the siren might go off at any time.'

They were relaxing after supper in the sitting room, which Nan still referred to as 'the drawing room', even though its original grandeur had faded, and the large pieces of furniture needed new covers. Only the grand piano lived up to its name, being highly polished, but the lid was always firmly closed. As a child, when Sunny had asked to see what was inside, Nan had said quickly, 'Oh, I mislaid the key years ago.' It was a reminder of the man who had played it; and it was not for a child to thump the ivory keys. The piano would never be sold, even in hard times.

Nanette put her feet up on the sewing box with the faded tapestry cushion on top. Sunny mused: 'Man Friday was a man-servant, though, not a girl like me.'

'I don't doubt you'll be just as indispensable, Sunny dear! Mr Rowland didn't mention an apprenticeship I suppose?'

'No,' Sunny said uncertainly, 'but he did say I'd need to use a typewriter and send out bills and invoices; and Chrissie said this morning that as I didn't learn to type at school, I should go to evening classes.' She paused. She hadn't yet told Nan that Chrissie was leaving home or that Mr Rowland's grandson had winked at her.

'Don't worry about that, you've nice neat handwriting. I've an ancient typewriter in the hall cupboard. I'll teach you myself. The whole set-up sounds rather old-fashioned, but nothing wrong with that. Now, shall I mend that stocking for you?'

'Please!' Sunny said gratefully. She rolled the stocking down and tossed it to Nanette. *She looks tired*, Sunny thought, *but it has been her day volunteering at the welfare clinic where she weighs babies. She's getting on a bit, but she'll soon receive her pension each week.*

'Does Mr Rowland's grandson work there too?' Nanette enquired. She made a fist of her left hand and stretched the nylon over it to inspect the stocking. *No time like the present*, she always thought. *Don't neglect the mending!*

'He has been helping out since he finished his National Service earlier this year, and he is about to go to Cambridge University.'

'Cambridge? Must be a clever chap . . .' said Nanette, carefully threading the needle.

'Well,' Sunny returned, 'it seems clever people don't mind living in a mess!'

TWO

Nanette had grown up in London. Her father was a concert pianist, who had died some years before the Great War and her mother, Florence, was a trained nurse and midwife who had resumed her career after her husband's death. She had spent most of her legacy from her late husband on converting a large Edwardian house on Grove Lane, a rural outpost of Streatham Common in one direction, and Croydon the other, which was then part of Surrey, into the Mother and Baby Home – a place for unmarried mothers.

When she was old enough, Nanette was encouraged to follow in her mother's footsteps, and when she was fully qualified, returned to the Mother and Baby Home, where Florence was Matron.

The home was registered with the local authority and closely connected with the hospital where both Nan and her mother had qualified. Nan and her mother vowed they would respect and care for their young mothers, and encourage them to keep their babies if this was possible.

If they could, the Mother and Baby Home would continue to help and advise them indefinitely. Some of the children born there would remain in Nan's care until they were toddlers and life had improved for their mothers. No charge was made for this help which was paid for by a team of generous local benefactors. Florence and Nan had only a modest income of their own and the charity relied on local support.

Perhaps Nan would have wished to marry and have children of her own, but she accepted it wasn't possible while she was caring for her mother in her last years. She was, however, regarded as a mother figure by those who had been fortunate enough to be sent to the Mother and Baby Home.

So, it had been a great surprise to Nanette when a young unmarried nurse from Trinidad, who had given birth at the Mother and Baby Home and feared that she would be unable to care for her daughter herself, had left the baby with Nanette. When Sunny was three years old Nan, now a single woman of forty-two, had adopted her. There was just something about Sunny that meant she could never bring herself to be parted from the little girl.

By this point in her life, Nan looked like a matron, with her starched uniform, and prematurely grey hair almost hidden under her cap, but she was kind and patient and loved her job. But, most of all she loved her daughter. Sunny had never asked much about her mother, but Nan had always told her, from the moment she could understand, that she'd been loved. Nan knew that Serena believed it was in Sunny's best interests to leave her behind. As far as Nan was aware Serena had returned to Trinidad, as many had done after the war, and they had never heard from her again.

Sunny had always had a happy nature, along with curly hair and sparkling eyes. Shortly after her birth, Nan and the other residents of the Mother and Baby Home were evacuated to Somerset. When they returned, the Mother and Baby Home retained its name, but not its duties. Instead, Nan let the top half of the house, and this provided a steady income. Family planning meant that there weren't as many unmarried mothers and young women wanted better jobs with prospects, like men. Those from poorer backgrounds were no longer going into service and like the suffragettes before them who had paved the way, they were independent. If they married, they were often well into their twenties.

The amount of conversion required to accommodate another set of occupants in the big house was minimal; there being another kitchen and bathroom upstairs. They shared the cleaner, Mrs Perkins, with the tenants; she helped Nan two days a week. The vast basement kitchen housed a boiler which provided hot water for the whole house. Shelves were crammed with all the cooking and crockery paraphernalia dating back to the Mother and

Baby Home days, including a plethora of baby feeding bottles. Nan was sentimental like that. Sunny had been very happy growing up there.

* * *

'Taking the early bus, I see,' said the friendly conductor. 'Does this mean you are starting work today?'

Sunny nodded. She was not wearing her new outfit, bearing in mind that she would probably be spending the day cleaning. She actually felt like a schoolgirl again, conscious that her grey pleated skirt was too short, her Aertex shirt tight across her bust and the green cardigan had shrunk in the wash as well. Thankfully, she had discarded the school tie that Nan had fixed for her every day before school as her own knots unravelled. However, she wore the darned stockings, not socks, with her lace-up shoes.

She had a box-shaped black handbag with a mirror inside the lid slung over her shoulder. In this she'd packed a wash bag with a flannel and half a bar of Knight's Castile soap, a comb, a small hand towel, as she didn't fancy the grubby roller towel in the cloakroom, a hanky with 'S' embroidered in one corner, and a purse containing a week's bus fares. She had been told at her interview that she would be provided with sandwiches at lunchtime. She wondered if Nan would permit her to wear a little makeup now. 'When you are sixteen,' Nan had always said.

'Yes,' Sunny now said simply to the conductor. She didn't divulge where she was actually heading. The bus came to the next stop along the lane, where there was a queue of people waiting. Someone slid into the seat beside her, and she shifted up to the window and gazed out. She knew who it was: Rodney Gibson, from the sub-post office. He had been at the Grammar School for boys, and he'd left school that summer too. He nudged her arm. 'Is it your first day at work, too?' he asked.

'Yes,' she said primly, not looking at him. He was more worldly-wise than she was. He belonged to the Church Youth Club, was in the choir and at the monthly social evenings he danced with girls wearing Tangee lipstick, an orange stick which changed colour to pink once applied to lips, flared skirts and silver dancing shoes. She'd declined to join the club when Nan had surprised her by suggesting she might enjoy it and make some new friends. Chrissie had been to a dance or two in the church hall, but she'd revealed she was once bowled over by a pair of energetic jivers. Nan had given a little shake of her head at that and said, 'They're copying the American GIs. They've got a lot to answer for – throwing their partners around!'

Until today, Rodney had delivered the newspapers at what Nan called the crack of dawn, whistling as he poked the bundle through their letter box. 'Nice lad,' Nan remarked recently, 'good-looking, like his dad.'

'Is he?' Sunny said. 'I hadn't noticed.' But, of course, she had; finding his thick chestnut hair, hazel eyes and good white teeth, which flashed when he smiled, attractive. Rodney Gibson was well built and athletic, and clever with it, she thought. Nan said she'd heard he'd secured a good position in a bank, with two days a week at college, a job which he could resume after his National Service, which was why he hadn't joined the sixth form.

As if he could read her thoughts, he said, 'My kid brother is your paper boy now. He can't whistle like me.'

Sunny didn't comment. He tried a new tactic. 'I hear you got good grades in your exams,' he said. She nodded. He was distracting her, while she was wondering how the day would go.

They walked along the High Street together, but she didn't enlighten him as to her destination. They were almost there when Rodney said cheerfully, 'Good luck! I wonder if the bank's staff is standing to attention to welcome me.' He suddenly looked uncertain, as he saw the heavy closed doors of the impressive building before him. He straightened his tie and squared his shoulders.

Sunny felt nervous too, but she said: 'Good luck, Rodney, maybe they'll hoist a flag in your honour.' Then she hurried off and saw Alec just ahead of her as she turned down the little alley. Her heart beat faster as he turned and waited for her to catch him up. Then they walked on together.

'Whoops!' he exclaimed as she stumbled on the stony path. 'You don't want to ladder your stockings again!'

Embarrassed, she blurted out: 'You shouldn't be looking at my legs!'

'Why not? You've got a shapely pair! I thought we'd get on, but . . .'

'I've come here to work, not to – *flirt*!' This wasn't an expression she'd used before.

'I was only joking, trying to make you relax before you become our Girl Friday,' he said, as he opened the door to the printing office and ushered her in. He added, 'I don't flirt with little girls!'

Mr Rowland lived in the flat above his workplace. When he heard them come in downstairs, he realised he had overslept, not having heard the raucous buzz from his alarm clock. His bedroom was untidy so, hastily pulling the bedclothes over the rumpled bottom sheet, he put on his slippers and made for the bathroom. Ten minutes later he appeared in the office wearing a rather grand dressing gown over striped pyjamas and a plum-coloured cravat. He definitely appeared odd as he stood in the doorway for a moment looking at Sunny, who was sitting on a chair, handbag in lap. Meanwhile, Alec, who was a whistler too, Sunny realised, had made coffee for the three of them, and a plate of toast for his grandfather's breakfast. Alec glanced in the biscuit tin, empty as usual, but then discovered a solitary Penguin chocolate biscuit bar in the cupboard. *This would be a treat*, he thought wryly, *for young Sunny Cato*.

'My dear young lady,' said Mr Rowland, 'I apologise for not being ready to receive you, and please excuse my attire . . . I will remedy that after breakfast, eh? Oh dear, I've mislaid my spectacles; can't do much without those!' He located them on the desk, obscured by a bulky parcel. 'Sunny, I sent Alec shopping on Saturday, and I hope you approve of his choice,' he said, handing over the parcel. 'You'll soon be ready for work!'

As Alec came through with the loaded tray, Sunny opened the package. There were two pairs of blue denim dungarees and a pair of thick red rubber gauntlet gloves. 'You must take care of your hands; I have a pair too. I also bought a new plastic pail and mop,' he said. 'It won't clank like the old bucket! I remembered the Vim.'

'Well,' Mr Rowland asked, crunching his toast, which had obviously been scraped having burned while Alec was hunting for the chocolate bar. 'Did the boy get the right size?'

Alec smiled at Sunny. 'I told the shop assistant your age, and she suggested these. They look baggy to me, but I hope you like them . . .'

'Thank you very much, Mr Rowland – Alec – I really will be a Girl Friday in these!' Sunny said shyly. 'I'll just drink my coffee, and then I'll get changed in the cloakroom.' She saw Alec winking at her and thought, *I'm five years younger than him, and he obviously thinks he is superior. I wonder what Nan will think of my new uniform. Or me scrubbing floors! She'll ask if I am really a maid of all work.*

Sunny was glad of the gloves, and the scouring powder, for it was obvious that no cleaning had taken place there for some time. She paid particular attention to the cloak-room and requested a bottle of bleach.

'Well done!' Alec observed when he looked in on her, mopping the floor. He was doing his bit to help, clearing rubbish and sweeping the workshop floor. Mr Rowland was at his easel, busy designing a poster for the new coffee shop along the High Street.

He called out to Sunny, 'You can help with the colours for the posters, but it's a lengthy process as I have to engrave wood blocks before printing. It involves photography too, but young Alec does that at the moment. However, I'll instruct you in using the Letterpress this afternoon. Did you know this venerable machine is still much in use; it is the oldest form of printing. Bread and butter printing I call it. I taught myself as a boy . . . it was just a hobby then. You need a strong right arm because it's cranked by hand. I must also thank you for all your hard work this morning, Sunny.'

Sunny smiled. *It is jolly hard work,* she thought ruefully, *but it's good to be a Girl Friday!*

* * *

Alec was looking out for her the following morning and they chatted as they walked down the alleyway to the shop. She decided he wasn't as brash as she'd first thought. 'I thought you might live over the shop with your grand-father,' Sunny said.

'Oh no, my mother, who lives in Grandfather's old family home in Shirley, near Croydon, insists I stay with her until I go to Cambridge. She doesn't approve of her father working at his advanced age; but when he retired from his office in the City, he bought this place, as he'd never achieved his ambition to go to art school, because his parents wouldn't allow it. He came here ten years ago.'

Sunny hazarded a guess, 'He must be seventy then.' She added, 'I think everyone should be allowed to, well, follow their heart's desire.'

'That sounds rather old-fashioned,' said Alec, 'but I agree. Here we are, another day. Are you looking forward to it, after all the hard graft yesterday?'

'Yes,' she said briefly. *That's rather condescending*, she thought. *I was only quoting what Nan often says. He shouldn't make remarks like that.*

Mr Rowland was up and about today and talking on the telephone when they walked into the studio. He didn't put his hand over the mouthpiece when he greeted his grandson with the words, 'Your mother wants to speak to you, something about a letter?'

Alec gave a sigh. 'From the university, I expect. Thanks, grandfather, pass the phone please.'

'Good morning, Sunny,' Mr Rowland said. 'Get changed, and then we'll start the day with a cup of coffee, eh? Perhaps you will make it, my dear? You can't stop Eleanor when she's talking on the telephone. She used to look at me disapprovingly when her photograph was on the desk, but I put her away in the top drawer and locked it! Her husband left her when the boy was young, but Eleanor has always worked. She is still a part-time buyer at a big local store. Alec went to boarding school but stayed with me in the holidays. What about you – any brothers and sisters?'

'Not that I know of. I was adopted,' Sunny told him. Then she went to the cloakroom to change into her dungarees.

Her arm did indeed ache after she'd cranked that heavy handle most of the day. She also practised placing letters and numbers into the different-sized blocks. The only respite was at lunchtime when Alec came back after delivering some local printing, with a packet of sandwiches from the nearby delicatessen. 'White bread!' Sunny exclaimed.

'Do you prefer brown?' Alec asked.

'No – but Nan – my mum, reckons white bread has chalk in it!'

'That was during the war,' Mr Rowland said. 'I'm not sure what the filling is though.'

'Egg with mayonnaise. I got four cream buns as well for a treat,' Alec said.

'And who is the fourth bun for?' his grandfather asked, tongue-in-cheek.

'I thought I might be awarded it as a leaving present – I'm off to Cambridge next week, remember. It's a sobering thought, that if I was still in the army on National Service, I would probably have been drafted to help deal with the Suez Crisis.'

Sunny bit into her bun and some cream trickled down her chin and mingled with smears of paint on the bib of her dungarees. Will it be the same working here without Alec and his cheerful, but sometimes annoying repartee? she wondered. Would she have to take over extra chores, looking after Mr Rowland? Is that what is expected of a Girl Friday?

Alec put out a hand unexpectedly and pulled the elastic band off her hair. 'There, you look much lovelier with those curls tumbling round your shoulders . . .'

She stopped herself from saying ouch! because now her hair was untidy, but instead, she said primly, 'It wouldn't be safe with all the bending over the machines.'

'Sorry,' he said. 'I didn't mean to upset you.'

She wanted to say, 'You shouldn't tease me then!' But of course, she couldn't, especially as Mr Rowland was regarding her quizzically.

'Where's the Polaroid camera, Alec? I'd like to take a shot or two of our Girl Friday with her lovely hair like that! You don't mind do you, Sunny?' Alec passed the camera and winked at Sunny. 'Smile please!' he told her. 'This will be a birthday picture, won't it?' She was glad he didn't add, 'Your sixteenth.'

'I – I,' Sunny floundered, but she obliged as Mr Rowland clicked the camera. She thought: *Who on earth wants to see a picture of me looking as I do at this moment?*

Mr Rowland held up the instant photograph in triumph: 'Not a colour photo of course, but I might do a painting from this later, design a poster, and then you will appear in glorious technicolour! Stay put, so I can take another photograph or two. You might like one for your mother?'

'Thank you, Mr Rowland, that's very kind of you,' Sunny said. Though she wondered if Nan would disapprove of her with her hair down.

* * *

Sunny caught the bus home after work and Rodney sat alongside her. He folded his paper, *the Evening Standard*, after a few minutes, then took a deep breath, thinking, *well I can only ask, but I reckon she'll say 'no thanks'.*

'We're trying to raise some money for the church roof fund,' he began nervously. 'Several of the local clubs and societies are involved, and there will be a procession of floats up and down the lane on Saturday. We need, um . . . an attractive girl. Our theme is Adam and Eve in the Garden of Eden. The horticultural society will provide floral decoration.' He cleared his throat. 'I'm Adam, I offered because none of the others did, and I'd like *you* to be Eve. What do you think?'

'Well, if I don't have to say anything,' Sunny said. *He'd put the question nicely,* she thought.

'You'd just have to wave a banner, declaiming something like, WOULD YOU 'ADAM AND EVE' IT? WE NEED A ROOF OVER OUR HEADS! Some of the choir will sing in the background and—'

'I wouldn't have to wear just a – a fig leaf, would I?' Sunny knew Nan wouldn't agree to *that.*

'Of course not. The curate, he's in charge, wouldn't allow it. For my part, as Adam, Mum has offered a moth-eaten old rug!'

'Like Tarzan, you mean? And *me*, Jane, I suppose!' Suddenly, they both became aware that their fellow passengers were listening in.

Rodney looked at Sunny. 'Yes or no?' adding, 'No one else has volunteered.'

The conductor came up beside them. 'Go on, put him out of his misery.' He pulled the overhead bell wire. 'Your stop, young man.'

'Oh, all right, Rodney,' Sunny said. 'But I'll have to make sure Nan agrees, too.'

* * *

Surprisingly, Nan was in favour of Sunny joining Rodney on the float. 'How about a sarong – you know, like Dorothy Lamour wears in the films? And you can borrow that big apple from my bowl of waxed fruit. You can't bite into it though, of course!'

'Rodney's mum is going to make a serpent out of old stockings.' Sunny suddenly recalled the photo she had tucked in her handbag. 'This is for you, Nan, Mr Rowland took the picture with his Polaroid camera,' she said proudly. 'You can produce instant pictures with it.'

Nan said nothing for a long moment as she regarded the photograph. She thought, *Sunny looks beautiful with her hair like that, and her happy smile. I hadn't realised she is no longer a child but a young woman now. How can I advise her about what happens in a grown-up world, when I never experienced falling in love myself? I don't want her to follow in her mother's footsteps; I imagine Serena is still affected by what happened.*

'I must find a frame for this. Please thank Mr Rowland for thinking of me,' Nan said.

THREE

On Alec's last day at the printing shop, there was a surprise visitor: Eleanor, Mr Rowland's daughter and Alec's mother. She was tall and very slim and wore a lime-green linen skirt and jacket, with a ruffled white blouse. Like her father and son, she wore glasses, but hers were the latest fashion: scarlet frames with upswept sides, and tinted lenses. Her lips and nails were both painted bright red to match the glasses. Her hair was platinum blonde – *she's copying Marilyn Monroe*, Sunny thought, *but doesn't have her curves!* She gave a small sigh, thinking: *but nor do I.*

Eleanor looked Sunny up and down. 'Hmm . . .' was her response to the dungarees and the curly ponytail. 'Well,' she said to her father, trapped behind his desk. 'Aren't you going to ask your assistant to make me a cup of tea? And where is Alec hiding?'

Alec emerged from the cloakroom. 'I thought I ought to wash my hands before you told me to, Mother.' He obviously wasn't intimidated by Eleanor and drew up a chair for her to sit on. 'I'll get the tea, or would you prefer champagne? A farewell toast, eh, before I leave for Cambridge. I'm looking forward to a few days holiday before I begin my studies.'

'Don't be facetious,' Eleanor said. 'Have you really got a bottle of champagne?'

Mr Rowland spoke at last. 'It was my idea . . .'

'But you didn't know I was coming,' she said.

'My dear,' he said, 'I *knew* you would!'

'Clean glasses, mind.' Eleanor was smiling, then she turned to her son and said, 'I'll miss you, Alec, despite all the mess you make at home.'

Sunny had a sudden thought: *I will feel lonely here without Alec.* She'd got used to his teasing. She'd had a funny feeling inside, one she hadn't had before, when he'd pulled the elastic band off her hair and run his fingers through the mass of curls.

Sunny realised that it was past the time she usually left to catch the bus. She bit her lip, wondering what she could do. She asked, 'Please may I telephone my mother, and tell her I will be in later than usual?'

'Why is that?' asked Mr Rowland. 'But of course, you may ring her.'

'I have missed the bus home.' *Perhaps I shouldn't make a fuss*, she thought.

'I have my car outside,' Eleanor said. 'You can come along with me to see Alec off at Croydon station, and then I'll run you home; Grove Lane, isn't it?'

'Yes, it is. Thank you! Please excuse me, I must get changed,' Sunny said, feeling flustered.

'I've got your bags in the car as you requested,' Eleanor said to her son. 'Say goodbye to Grandfather, Alec . . .'

'Mother, you don't need to remind me,' Alec said mildly. He bent over his grandfather and hugged him, whispering something in his ear. Mr Rowland cleared his throat and said, 'I'll miss you too.' He handed an envelope to his grandson. 'Your wages, my boy, and a little extra – I appreciate all your hard work. Promise you'll write now and then, eh?'

* * *

At the station, the engine was already steaming and carriage doors were slamming. Alec kissed his mother and she said, 'You'll need to wipe the lipstick off your face, I'm afraid. Good luck!' Sunny hung back, but unexpectedly, he gave her a brief hug too, his lips brushing her cheek, then he hurried to board the train. *Now I'm blushing*, she thought. *But he was probably only teasing.*

They waved goodbye until the train disappeared from sight. As they walked to the car, Eleanor said, 'He's spending some time with his girlfriend in Cambridge, her parents live there, and then they'll go together to the university on the first day. They are studying different subjects, though. Alec has chosen music; he plays several instruments, including piano. He was a bandsman in the army on ceremonial occasions. He also loves composing.'

Sunny thought: *he never told me any of those things, but then, why should he? He likes teasing me, but maybe nothing more.*

When Eleanor and Sunny arrived at the Mother and Baby Home, Nan was waiting on the doorstep of the large house to welcome them in. Sunny hoped Nan wouldn't disapprove of Eleanor's heavy makeup as she herself only powdered her nose.

Nan was tactful. She left Sunny's supper in the warming oven, made a pot of tea and produced a plateful of flapjack biscuits, Sunny's favourite, that she'd baked earlier. Eleanor, or Mrs Dixon as she introduced herself, didn't stay long. She did, however, mention to Nan that she was hoping to find a daily help for her father. 'Too much is expected of Sunny; what time will she get for learning printing techniques if she has to do all tidying up now that my son has gone to Cambridge?'

'Our Mrs Perkins has a daughter, Patsy, who is looking for a cleaning job now her two boys are both at school – she lives in Croydon – I'll ask her mother for her address, shall I?' Nan asked.

'You know her? She's trustworthy, I hope.'

'She's a nice, hardworking young woman, like her mother,' Nan assured her.

'Well, I will get in touch when I have her details. I must drive home now; I have a busy day tomorrow in the store, as it's Saturday. Goodbye, Miss Cato, Sunny.' Eleanor shook hands with them both and departed.

'I'm starving! What's on the menu tonight, Nan?' Sunny rubbed her tummy.

'Sausages and mash; I just need to heat up the pan of onion gravy,' Nan said. 'Then summer pudding, made with the last of the raspberries I bottled, with cream from the top of the milk. Sit down do; you look tired.' *My Sunny girl needs some comfort food*, she thought.

* * *

Saturday dawned warm, a welcome change after some chilly weather. The floats would drive up and down Grove Lane from 11 o'clock. Sunny usually worked Saturday mornings, but Mr Rowland had given her the time off, saying, 'Of course you should help raise money for a good cause.'

The participants changed into their costumes in the church hall. Most of them had already set up tableaux on the conveyances. The choir boys were having a final rehearsal, and a gramophone with a loudspeaker would provide the accompaniment, courtesy of the curate. Sunny worried because her cambric sarong fastened over one shoulder, leaving the other arm bare, so she couldn't wear a bra. Nan had said, rather tactlessly, 'Anyway, you don't really need one!' She wore a garland of leaves around her forehead.

Someone poked Sunny in the back. She whirled round and to her delight saw Chrissie smiling at her. 'You're back!' she cried.

'Only for the weekend,' Chrissie said. 'Auntie said I should make it up with Mum and Dad. I've got a job as a filing clerk, it's unexciting, but I do like being in London! Mum said I shouldn't miss the parade today, as you're playing the part of Eve – you don't look much like the illustration in the Sunday School Bible, eh – too overdressed!' She grinned.

'*Overdressed*! That's not what I see in the mirror,' Sunny said. 'I need some lipstick . . .'

'Here you are! A present from me!' Chrissie delved in her bag and triumphantly produced a pink lipstick. 'Max Factor! Let me put it on for you, I'm more experienced than you are.'

'You've made my day,' Sunny said softly. 'You really have, Chrissie.'

They were the only two in the cloakroom now, and still chatting when Rodney knocked on the door and called out, 'Hurry up! We're in the first float and there's only ten minutes to go!'

When they opened the door, the girls burst out laughing at the sight of Rodney draped in the old rug and wearing rope sandals, which the curate had pounced on at the last jumble sale, saying,' 'They're just right for Adam!' The sandals had rubber soles which looked as if they had been cut out from an old tyre and were probably handmade during the war.

'I heard those sandals squeaking as you approached the door,' Sunny said. 'They'll make your feet smell cheesy too, I should think. Have you got flat feet?'

'Stop looking at my feet! I reckon Mum's hoping I'll fail my medical for the army. They don't take recruits with flat feet, but Dad says army life will toughen me up. Anyway, get a move on! Nice to see you again, Chrissie.'

'Nice to see you – Adam,' Chrissie giggled and she and Sunny followed Rodney out of the hall.

'Actually, I prefer that name to mine,' Rodney sighed.

'How *did* you get your name?' Sunny asked, hoping her sarong was not slipping down as they hurried along. The curate was standing beside their float and waving to them.

'I was called after my godfather, a friend of Dad's, who emigrated to South Africa after the war and was never heard of again. Look, you have to climb the stepladder to get aboard, Sunny, so hitch your skirt up or you'll catch your foot in the material.'

'Good luck,' Chrissie told them. 'I'm going to watch from your house, Sunny. My mum's already there. Nan invited us as a surprise for you. We'll have a good view.'

Rodney helped Sunny up into the Garden of Eden, as one of the choir boys waggled the serpent at her and cried, 'Boo!' Sunny thought, *it's good to hear Chrissie say 'My Mum'*. Then, as the cavalcade moved off, the choir began to sing 'On the Sunny Side of the Street'.

Chrissie was perched on the garden wall, while Nan and Mrs Ford watched the parade over the gate. Sunny waved her banner at them and the serpent wound itself round Rodney's neck. They all sang along to the tunes, which included popular hymns, like 'All Things Bright and Beautiful'. Among the floats, a group of local builders were making a model church from a pile of sand and topping it with a large cardboard roof, painted with a pattern of slates.

There was cheering from the onlookers as the procession wound down the road, and then a clanking sound as volunteers went from house to house collecting donations in buckets.

'We'll have a cup of tea,' Nan suggested, 'before the floats come back up the lane. Shall we sit on the terrace in the back garden? I put some chairs out for us.'

The garden was long and mostly down to grass. There was a heady smell of lavender, and washing, including long johns and baggy bloomers, was airing on the line in the sunshine. The tenants did their laundry at weekends. They'd be watching the procession from their window upstairs.

'The grass needs mowing,' Nan observed. 'The gardener retired a couple of years ago and the old mower is too heavy for me.'

'Why don't you advertise for a handyman; put a card in the shop window?' Mrs Ford suggested.

'That's an idea,' Nan agreed. She looked at the untidy flower beds and the hedge that needed lopping. *It's all getting too much*, she thought. *When Sunny leaves home, which she surely will before I know it, this place will be far too large to keep up on my own.*

Mrs Ford had long ago given up trying to be fashionable. Today, she'd discarded her pinafore but was conscious the buttons of a dress last worn on her honeymoon some twenty years ago were in danger of popping open under the strain. She'd wanted to look nice for her prodigal daughter, as she ruefully thought of Chrissie, who was wearing a new outfit, very different from the clothes her mother had chosen for her. The blue and white cap-sleeved dress, with what Chrissie described as a keyhole neckline, was made from seersucker material, and Mrs Ford suspected that underneath, Chrissie wore the cone-shaped bra and waspie corselet which she'd criticised when Chrissie lived at home, saying, 'People will get the wrong idea, Chrissie.'

She'd meant boys, of course. However, Chrissie was now an independent young lady.

Chrissie was picking a bunch of lavender at Nan's suggestion. Nan had advised her to watch out for bees collecting nectar, so she looked hard at the mass of purple. Believing her to be out of earshot, Mrs Ford told Nan, 'I tread carefully with her, you know. We were wrong, not to tell her she was adopted. We intended to, but the years just went by, and she never asked. She says now she'll try to find out what she can about her mother from the details on her birth certificate; there is no father's name on that. We didn't adopt her as a newborn baby, you know. She was two years old.'

Nan suddenly shivered. 'The sun's gone behind a big cloud. Let's go back to the front gate. They should be coming along soon, and then they'll wave goodbye and return to the church hall.'

Chrissie buried her face in the bunch of lavender she'd gathered. She'd heard every word. She felt compunction for making her mother sad. She walked back along the path, skirting a patch of nettles. 'Miss Cato, did Sunny tell you we've both been invited to the social dance tonight? It would be nice if we could go together, as I'm returning to London tomorrow evening . . .'

Nan didn't hesitate. 'Of course, Sunny can go, I never said she couldn't. She decided the socials were not for her.

But she's grown up since she's been working, and I think she may have changed her mind.'

* * *

There were chairs all around the walls in the church hall, and the curtains were bulging on the stage as the band members settled into position, with the drummer at the rear, and microphones on stands along the front. There was the sound of instruments being tuned. These were amateur musicians, in their late teens or early twenties, who took every booking they were offered, whatever the venue.

The band enjoyed sausage rolls and sandwiches in the interval just as much as the dancers but, aware that alcohol mustn't be evident as they were on church property, they closed the curtains because they'd taken a chance and brought along a few cans of lager. The second half of the dancing would be much livelier!

During the interval, the curate stepped forward to announce how much the parade had made. Beaming, he said, 'Three hundred pounds, including several cheques, plus shillings and pence!' Then he went into the kitchen to help his wife with the washing-up, while keeping an eye on proceedings through the raised hatch.

Passing the cups and saucers for her husband to wipe, his wife wondered, 'D'you think you ought to encourage that wild dancing, dear?'

'They deserve some fun, after all their fund-raising efforts,' he said.

'I'm not sure the parish councillors will approve, you know,' his wife replied.

'You'll be called a wallflower,' Chrissie told Sunny, when she returned breathless after being whirled round in a quickstep by a short lad with his hair slicked back, who held her rather too close to him as they danced. 'Hip to hip!' she confided to Sunny later. 'Plus bad breath!'

Sunny said defensively now, 'I don't care if I'm a wallflower. Where did *you* learn to dance like that?'

'My auntie has some dance band records, and she showed me how,' Chrissie said. 'But I prefer *rock and roll*. You could do that. Where's Rodney? I need a partner to demonstrate with.' Rodney was scoffing a sausage roll and chatting to his mates nearby. He answered the call from Chrissie, and together they showed Sunny the first simple steps.

Chrissie recited, 'Face your partner, hold hands loosely, sway backwards and forwards. Tap feet, rock and roll. Whirl your girl round and catch her hands to repeat the sequence. It's all about rhythm. You should have seen Elvis Presley in *Heartbreak Hotel*!' Chrissie said breathlessly. 'Auntie Beryl and I go to the pictures twice a week!'

Sunny stood up. 'I need to go to the cloakroom,' she said, moving towards the door as the curtains swished apart, the band leader's voice boomed from the microphone, and the crowd rose en masse from their chairs, to *rock and roll*.

Sunny closed the cubicle door. She hoped the two ladies in charge of coats and outdoor shoes hadn't noticed she was crying. She dabbed her eyes with a hanky.

I can't remember how to do the steps, she thought woefully. She smoothed out her blue skirt. At Nan's insistence, she had changed into her one and only special outfit. 'Just the thing for dancing, Sunny,' she'd said, 'Go and enjoy yourself!'

No one asks me to dance, Sunny thought sadly. *I'll be a wallflower forever.* She released her ponytail, combed her hair loose, and then applied more pink lipstick.

As she emerged from the cloakroom and was about to re-enter the main hall, she saw Rodney standing by the wall. 'I thought you'd gone home in a huff,' he said simply. 'I've been plucking up the courage to ask you to dance. Will you?' He held out his hand.

Sunny managed a smile. 'You're still wearing those awful sandals,' she said.

He grinned. 'I don't have any dancing shoes!'

Chrissie was already on the dance floor with one of her several admirers. Sunny thought, *I'm glad we're not doing a formal dance; it's much more fun to just hold hands and rock and roll.*

At ten-thirty promptly, the last waltz was announced, and the lights were dimmed. Shadowy figures moved slowly across the dance floor. Chrissie was partnered by a short boy called Henry, while Rodney said softly to Sunny, 'Don't worry about the steps, I'll lead you. Not that I'm an expert, I'm learning from a manual.' He didn't hold her too tightly, and although she stumbled a bit, she was starting to get the hang of it all now.

In the cloakroom, Chrissie said, 'Henry is escorting me home. He lives just down the road from us. He's a drip but he behaves himself. We'll see you home first, if you like . . . '

'I'll walk Sunny home,' Rodney said diffidently. Sunny smiled. 'I'd like that,' she said.

Nan parted the curtains just a trifle and saw with relief that Rodney was just opening the front gate for Sunny. He stood the other side and they were obviously saying good-night. Nan moved away from the window.

'You'll come to the next social evening, won't you?' Rodney asked.

'Oh, yes, I really enjoyed tonight – though I didn't expect to!' Sunny said. 'Well, goodnight, Rodney. Thanks for bringing me home.'

He leaned over the gate intending to plant a kiss on her cheek. She turned her head quickly and his lips brushed her ear. 'I'll be glad to do so, any time,' he said gallantly, and then walked away. *I embarrassed him,*

Sunny realised. *He only wanted a goodnight kiss, nothing more. But I was thinking of Alec, although I expect he hasn't given me another thought. 'I don't flirt with little girls,' he'd said. But I am not a little girl anymore, I'm growing up fast – look at Chrissie, she's already there.*

FOUR

It was Patsy Perkins' first day at her new cleaning job, and Sunny was showing her the ropes. Mr Rowland was up and asked Patsy to make his bed.

'You have to make a good first impression,' Sunny told her, as if she was wiser than Patsy, if not older. *I never had a grandfather, of my own,* she thought, *but I'm keeping my promise to Alec, to look after his.*

Patsy was a single mum, Sunny already knew that, but it wasn't frowned on these days in the same way as it had been. The war had changed all that. So, Patsy was able to keep her two little boys, who had been fathered by someone whom her mother called a fly-by-night, and who had disappeared from Patsy's life. Some girls, Sunny knew, were still forced by circumstance to give up their babies, but Patsy's mum had supported her daughter as much as she could and wasn't prepared to give up her grandchildren.

Patsy had got her name onto the council housing list and now had her own front door key to a flat in a block. She needed to work hard to pay the rent and send her little lads to school in smart uniforms. They were bright boys and good scholars, something which Patsy suspected they got from their father. She'd had her first son when she was not much older than Sunny, so she was only twenty-two years old now, but she no longer thought of herself as a girl. *Life is what you make it*, she told herself.

Unlike Sunny, Patsy didn't wear dungarees. Rather, she shrouded her modest clothes with an oversized overall with capacious pockets, to hold dusters and polish plus a small screwdriver which she said was useful for 'tightening things up'. One of her first tasks had been to give the small kitchen area a thorough clean, so now the coffee cups had a faint hint of bleach, and the teapot, despite much rinsing before use, had a whiff of Vim.

When Mr Rowland referred to her as Mrs Perkins, she corrected him immediately, '*Miss* Perkins, but I don't mind being called Patsy, but not Patricia though – that sounds too posh.'

She knows exactly what needs doing, Sunny thought, *so I can get on with the paperwork. I'm lucky that Nan taught me to touch-type and I'm getting faster every day, though the typewriter here is even older than Nan's machine.* She looked forward to going out to buy the lunchtime sandwiches and also to delivering orders for local businesses.

After lunch each day, once Patsy had finished her duties and left to meet her children from school, Mr Rowland set aside a couple of hours for Sunny to learn more about printing; he encouraged her to choose colours for posters, and to suggest ideas. He had a painting, covered with a cloth, on an easel in a corner, which he promised to reveal when it was completed.

Mrs Dixon called in one afternoon and said to Sunny, 'What's he hiding behind here, eh?' She tweaked the edge of the cloth covering.

'The picture is meant to be a surprise, Mrs Dixon.' However, Sunny was curious as well and anyway, it was too late as the picture was revealed, just as they heard Mr Rowland coming downstairs.

Sunny's hand covered her mouth, suppressing her reaction as she said, 'Oh, my!'

'Trust you to be curious,' Mr Rowland said cheerfully to Mrs Dixon. 'What do you think of it?'

'I'll make some tea, shall I?' Sunny said quickly.

'Sunny, do you recognise yourself?' Mr Rowland asked. 'Take a closer look.'

The girl in the picture was beautiful, the paint appearing almost luminous. Sunny could only manage a faint 'Yes.' Then she cleared her throat and repeated, 'I'll make that tea.'

When she had disappeared into the kitchen, Mr Rowland asked his daughter, 'Do you think she doesn't like it?'

'On the contrary, I think she felt too emotional to say more,' Mrs Dixon said. 'Let's cover the picture up and change the subject when the tea arrives. Is Patsy proving a treasure?'

'She is indeed,' he agreed, thinking that Sunny was too; and like the granddaughter he had never had. 'How is Alec getting on? I haven't heard from him this week.'

'His studies are going well, but his girlfriend decided that things were not the same since he finished National Service. I gather it was more of a romance between pen friends. First love. I suppose he'll get over it.' Sunny caught the end of this conversation as she made room for the tea tray on the desk.

Mr Rowland said, 'I think the picture will make a good poster – that's if Sunny agrees, and her mother would need to give her permission, of course.' Sunny did not comment but just passed the cups of steaming tea.

'A poster girl!' Nan cxclaimed, when Sunny told her about the picture. 'Oh no, Sunny, I don't want to see your image on walls and billboards endorsing products I might not approve of. When I am asked to give my opinion, I would suggest Mr Rowland frames prints of the original picture and sells those. I would be happy to hang one in the drawing room.'

They were washing up the supper things as they talked. Sunny wiped the dishes and put them away. She was relieved by Nan's reaction. *I wouldn't like to see posters of myself all over the place either*, she thought. *Though when I saw the picture for the first time, I could see a likeness to Serena, my real mother, from the only snapshot I have of her. My skin is paler but that's because of my father, I suppose. I wish I knew what he looked like.*

She said diffidently, as they went from the kitchen into the drawing room, 'Nan, do I remind you of Serena now I'm grown up?'

Nan said simply, 'Yes, you do.'

* * *

The pictures sold well, and Mr Rowland realised that for once he was actually making money from his printing. Patsy was asked if she was interested in fitting the prints into the simple gilt frames, and she proved to be very dextrous. Older houses were being modernised by new enthusiastic young owners and the *That Sunny Smile* picture, as it came to be known, added to their bold decoration.

Sunny and Rodney went dancing on Saturday evenings and, although they enjoyed the monthly youth club social, they also went once or twice to the Locarno Ballroom in Streatham. Sunny was aware of covert glances, and there was the occasional approach: 'Do you know you look like the girl in that picture? Everyone I know has one!' Rodney always came to her rescue, sensing her embarrassment and answered for her, 'Oh, they all say that!' before whirling her away in the next dance.

They were fans of the popular Billy Harrison Quartet, whom Rodney remarked would obviously go on to bigger things. The Locarno was famous for its ballroom dancing, so Sunny and Rodney practised their steps in Nan's big kitchen where there was a wooden floor. They played records on the gramophone and learned the waltz, quickstep and foxtrot from the dog-eared dance manual by Arthur Murray that Rodney had acquired at the last jumble sale. This was, Sunny said when he showed it to her, of the same vintage as Adam's sandals. Each dance was illustrated with a sequence of footprints, which made Sunny giggle, but Rodney followed them in earnest.

'Quick, quick *slow*.'

'Be careful where you're whirling her around in here, Rodney,' Nan said mildly, coming into the kitchen to make cocoa and to remind Rodney it would soon be time for him to go home. She didn't want them cannoning into the shelves where her best china was displayed and sending the whole lot crashing down.

Sometimes Sunny wondered if Rodney was becoming too serious and expecting more of their relationship than she was offering. She still only permitted him to kiss her over the front gate when it was closed between them, but he now gave her a quick kiss on the lips. Nan said nothing, but she felt they were too young to be serious about one another. *I hadn't realised*, she thought, *that children grow up so quickly. I suppose because I was always involved with caring for babies when I was matron of the Mother and Baby Home.*

She needn't have worried, because Sunny had read the problem page in *Woman* magazine and was aware what could happen to girls who got 'carried away', and the often heart-breaking consequences. She was determined not to allow this to happen to her. *After all,* she thought, *I was born in just such a situation.*

* * *

Sunny and Patsy decorated the Christmas tree Mr Rowland had bought for the workshop and they put a sign up in the window which read: STEP INSIDE TO SEE SANTA, WHO WILL BE HAPPY TO PRINT ALL YOUR CARDS!

'Who is Santa?' Mr Rowland asked, but of course he knew the answer. He even produced the outfit he would wear. 'I used to wear this when Alec was home from school for Christmas,' he said gruffly. 'Though he says he knew it was me. The cotton wool whiskers tickle your nose!'

'Will Alec be here for Christmas?' Sunny asked.

He looked at her keenly. 'My dear, he won't. He's joined up with other students to form a jazz quartet; it makes a change from classical music studies. The band have been invited to play in a night club in Paris for a month, believe it or not, all expenses paid, so as he is an impoverished student, he can't afford to turn it down. Oh, there's an envelope addressed to you, Sunny, in this letter to me.' He passed it over.

She tucked the letter into her handbag without reading it. *I was so hoping to see him, I thought he might realise I'm not a little girl anymore. I mustn't tell Rodney about my feelings for Alec. I think he hopes we'll get married one day, but I think I see him more like a brother than anything else.*

* * *

Rodney didn't travel on the bus with her now. His parents had given him a motor scooter for his seventeenth birthday in October. Sunny had not yet ridden on the pillion. Nan said that first of all she must acquire a helmet and that Rodney should gain more experience before he took her for a ride.

That evening, she sat by herself on the bus. It was already dusk and the windows were steamed up from the passengers' breath, as it had been a cold day. Smoke curled upwards from chimneys, lights switched on in the houses, and where curtains were not yet closed, she could glimpse Christmas trees, entwined with tinsel, through the windows. Shops were still illuminated, although it was the end of the day for most of them.

Sunny unfolded the note from Alec. There was an enclosure – a photograph slid onto her lap. She retrieved it before it fell to the floor. Alec sat at a piano surrounded by his fellow musicians. They all wore evening dress, dinner jackets with bow ties. Alec had grown his hair and wasn't wearing his glasses. Sunny thought he couldn't possibly see much without them as he was really short-sighted. His friends displayed their instruments – saxophone and clarinet – and the drummer was seated behind his kit. There was a woman in the picture too; standing close to Alec. Even in black and white, Sunny could tell that this woman, in a strapless sheath dress, had long ash-blonde hair. Alec had written on the back of the photo. *Rowland Rhythm and Blues: George, Jack, Ned, me with Janine.*

Sunny compressed her lips. She felt tears welling in her eyes but blinked them away. *Stop dreaming, he still thinks of you as a little girl*, she told herself. *Why am I keeping Rodney in suspense? I know how he feels about me . . . Oh, but he's not 'The One'.*

She crumpled the letter up and stuffed it in her bag. She was unaware that she had missed a PS after the Christmas greetings. *I miss your sunny smile . . .*

'I thought we might invite some guests for lunch on Boxing Day,' Nan said casually. 'It's so much easier when the only cooking needed is potatoes. We can serve up cold turkey and ham, salad and pickles, and if Christmas pud is too heavy, I can soon knock up an apple pie. We won't be too full to play games then, eh? Who would you like to ask?'

'I believe Mr Rowland and Mrs Dixon will be by themselves, as Alec isn't coming home,' Sunny suggested.

'That's a good idea, not sure if we are posh enough for Mrs D. though . . .'

'There's all the best china, and the canteen of cutlery we never use – oh and your mother's silver tea service on that lovely tray—'

'My parents were given that as a wedding present; it was never used.'

'Time it was then!' Sunny told her.

'We could ask Rodney, if you would like that,' Nan suggested.

Sunny thought about it for a moment, and then said simply, 'Yes, I would like that, Nan.'

*   *   *

Chrissie had called round on Christmas Eve, when she and Sunny had exchanged warm woolly hand-knitted mittens, from a pattern in *Woman's Weekly,* with a cry of 'Snap!' Chrissie was due back at work in London the day after Boxing Day, but Sunny had the week off.

Before she left, Chrissie whispered to Sunny: 'I wrote to the home; I have an appointment for the New Year. I needed my parents' permission to go as I am underage. They said yes but would rather not be involved at the moment. Would you come with me? I feel I need some support.'

'If I can, of course I will,' Sunny agreed.

Rodney popped round on Christmas morning with his present. It was large and round and Sunny immediately worked out what it was. 'A helmet! Oh Rodney, how could you afford that?' she exclaimed.

'I have my own bank account now; the bank encourages their employees to save. I almost cleaned it out this Christmas!' Rodney said with a grin. 'Now we can go for a ride on the scooter.'

'When you have learned how to ride that thing properly and taken off those L-plates,' Nan reminded him, but she approved of the helmet.

He'd arrived just after breakfast, which was later than usual owing to opening presents. Sunny wore a black silk dressing gown patterned with scarlet poppies, an unexpectedly grown-up present from Nan, and moccasin slippers, with a furry lining, a present from Mrs Dixon and Mr Rowland. Rodney glanced at Nan, but she was busy at the sink, and being confident now that he would not be rebuffed, he gave Sunny a hug, and whispered in her ear, 'Can I kiss you under the mistletoe?' Sunny had bought a couple of sprigs at the market and fastened them to the ceiling beams in the kitchen and sitting room.

Nan heard this and said, without looking round, 'Of course you can, eh, Sunny?'

Sunny was conscious of the warmth from his hands through the silk dressing gown, under which she was scantily clad and, on a sudden impulse, she reached up, and this time it wasn't just a brief kiss as usual, but a lingering one. 'Happy Christmas,' she managed breathlessly when it ended. *Have I fallen in love with him at last?* she asked herself. But she knew she was wishing it had been Alec kissing her like that.

Rodney went off whistling happily. He turned back at the gate and called out, 'See you tomorrow!'

* * *

On Boxing Day, Nan and Sunny had a special treat for breakfast. On impulse, as well as the mistletoe, Sunny had purchased from Surrey Street Market, two large grapefruits with pink-flushed skin. 'These come from Trinidad,' the stall holder had said proudly. 'The place where I was born. The sweet flesh inside is pink too. Where do you come from, love?'

Sunny had smiled and said, 'Oh, I was born in Grove Lane, but my mother was from Trinidad, like you. She was a nurse over here during the war. My father was from Poland.'

'Have you been to Trinidad?' he asked, as he took a florin for the fruit.

'Not yet, but I hope to visit there one day,' Sunny said. She realised she hadn't thought of this before.

The visitors arrived at midday. Rodney had called first thing to apologise and explain that he was unable to come later as his grandparents were visiting and his mother said they'd be disappointed if he wasn't there.

Nan had prepared large platefuls of sliced turkey and ham, a tureen full of potatoes sprinkled with parsley and glistening with butter, a bowl of what she termed winter salad, crusty bread and giant jars of homemade pickled onions 'as big as golf balls', mustard piccalilli, chutney and pickled red cabbage. The china was Nan's cherished Crown Derby, the cutlery from the best silver service. Sunny carefully folded the red paper napkins and arranged them like fans in the sparkling glasses. Mrs Dixon had brought some bottles of Babycham along with a bottle of sherry, and Mr Rowland asked the ladies' permission to smoke his Christmas cigar. After a lengthy lunch, they retired to the drawing room, where for once there was a log fire, and after acting charades for a while, to Sunny's surprise Nan opened the piano for Mrs Dixon to play. They sang carols and Sunny squeezed Nan's hand and whispered: 'It's been a *wonderful* day.'

FIVE

One day in early January saw Sunny and Chrissie plucking up the courage to knock on the door of the tall Edwardian house a few miles over the border from the City of London in Middlesex. This area was where many wealthy London merchants had built country houses during the last century, but it already seemed part of Greater London. Agricultural elements were dwindling.

The girls had travelled first by train and then by bus to reach their destination on this Sunday afternoon. It was Sunny who pulled the bell on the front door. For a few minutes, it appeared no one was at home, and Chrissie re-read the letter she'd received from a Miss Muriel Sands, who'd invited them to afternoon tea. They were wondering what to do, when they heard shuffling footsteps and the door opened slowly. The small, bent lady with a pale face and protuberant watery blue eyes was dressed all in grey. Her woollen dress hung almost down to her ankles, and she wore a lacy shawl round her shoulders, fastened with a cameo brooch. The shuffling was caused by down-at-heel slippers, that looked too large for her tiny feet. Her voice, unexpectedly loud and clear, made the girls start. 'I apologise, I was having an afternoon nap. Please come in, you must be chilled to the bone standing out there in the cold. Though the wireless tells us the weather is very mild for January. Which one of you is Chrissie Ford?' She indicated they should remove their coats and hang them on the hallstand. 'You'll soon warm up,' she assured them.

Chrissie said shyly, 'Me, Miss Sands. This is my friend Sunny Cato.' They followed her down the corridor where the door to a large sitting room stood open and there was the welcome sight of a roaring fire, a kettle on a trivet, and a small table laid for tea. The plush chairs were comfortable. On another table sat a large book with a marble-patterned cover and gold lettering and a sheaf of papers.

'We'll have our victuals first,' Miss Sands suggested. She looked up at a large portrait of an attractive young woman above the mantle. 'My sister, Mavis. I'm sorry she can't be with us today – she passed away four years ago. Of course, she was younger when the picture was painted. Will you pour the tea, Chrissie, please. My hands are rather shaky.'

The tea was strong but reviving and both girls stirred extra sugar into their cups. 'Thawing out now?' Miss Sands smiled encouragingly at them. 'You are both pretty young girls.' She sounded wistful. 'My sister and I, well, she was the good-looking one. We were twins you know, but not identical. We both followed a nursing career. Mavis became a district nurse and I was a local midwife. We had reached retirement age at the beginning of the war, but we wanted to do our bit for our country, and she had the idea that we would take in young unmarried girls and their babies, care for them until they were ready to leave us and try to help reconcile those girls with parents who had rejected them. We were aware this problem would escalate during wartime. We would also, but only if it was what the young mothers decided was best for their babies, arrange adoptions. Some of the infants remained with us as foster children and were returned to their mothers if their circumstances changed. This was a small undertaking, because we had no official backing, although we had to be registered, but we had the experience, and were allowed to take in four mothers and babies at a time. The mothers came to us late in pregnancy and we delivered the babies here, although circumstances could mean an expectant mother would arrive earlier because she was homeless. This house was as much their home as ours. Would you like another cup of tea? Cake?' The seed cake was rather dry, but the scones were freshly baked.

Chrissie was more relaxed now. 'I think we should get down to business now, please. We mustn't leave here too late in the evening.'

Sunny said impulsively, 'I was born in a place like this, and I was very fortunate, I was adopted by the matron of the home.'

'We would have liked to have done the same for Chrissie,' Miss Sands said. 'But we realised we couldn't raise her like younger parents could. It was the right decision because, look, she is still young, and I am old.' Then she asked Sunny, 'Are you in touch with your birth mother?'

'No – but one day, if I can save up the fare, I'll go to Trinidad and find her,' Sunny said.

'Please – what can you tell me about *my* mother?' Chrissie asked.

'Let's group round the other table, and I will tell you all I know,' Miss Sands said.

She opened the fat ledger and riffled through the pages. 'August 1940 – here we are: your mother was with us from January that year and you were born in the March. We already knew her – she was born during the Great War, in 1915 – I delivered her as well when I was working as a midwife. Your mother organised comforts for the troops . . .'

Chrissie could wait no longer, 'What was her name?' she blurted out, although of course she knew already.

'Christina; she didn't know what to call you, so Mavis suggested Chrissie.'

'She – she was unmarried, I believe,' Chrissie prompted. 'What was her surname?'

'Harding. I don't know her married name.'

'You mean, she married, but didn't want to take me back?'

'Her marriage happened much later, after you were adopted – which was her wish. She thought it best not to keep in touch with you. Her parents, you see, thought she was away on war work and we weren't allowed to divulge the fact that she was here for almost a year before and after you were born. We had to respect her wishes as she was twenty-five years old at the time.'

Chrissie appeared to be choking back tears. She nudged Sunny. 'Will you ask some questions for me, please? You know what I wanted to find out.'

Sunny wasn't too sure if she should be doing this, but she began hesitantly, 'Was Chrissie's mother from a poor family?'

'Oh, my dear.' Miss Sands looked at Chrissie. 'No, she was the only child of a wealthy local family. Her father was a major in the army in the Great War and her mother was a clergyman's daughter.' She added, 'They never knew about you, and I'm afraid they have both passed away.'

'Chrissie's father?' Sunny asked on her friend's behalf.

'Christina would not divulge his identity, but we guessed he might be a soldier from the Commonwealth. Anyway, he seems to have left for the war not knowing about Christina's condition, and she never talked about him.'

'Do you think that – Christina – would be willing to meet her daughter?' Sunny asked.

Miss Sands closed the book. 'She has not been in touch with me since you were adopted, Chrissie. You have good parents, why distress them as well as yourself, if you were rebuffed?'

Chrissie was sobbing now. Sunny stood up. 'Shall I wash up the tea things, Miss Sands? Then I think we should be making our way home.' As she loaded the tin tray on which the teapot already sat, she heard Miss Sands say to Chrissie, 'I'm so sorry I can't help you more, but the only other thing I can tell you is that Christina married after the war, one of her father's army friends, and I read about it in the newspaper. He was a diplomat, much older than her; I believe they live abroad.'

'I don't suppose she ever thinks of me,' Chrissie said bitterly.

'How could she not?' Miss Sands asked.

*   *   *

When they arrived at the local station, Rodney was there to meet them, as he'd promised. He didn't ask how they'd got on, but offered them each an arm and they walked to Chrissie's house first, where her parents were waiting anxiously. Chrissie clung to her mother and wept. Her father thanked them for accompanying her home, and then Rodney slipped his arm round Sunny's waist and they set off for Grove Lane.

'We could have caught the bus,' he observed.

'No, I'd rather walk,' Sunny said. They were suddenly illuminated in a patch of light from a streetlamp.

Rodney looked at her. 'Didn't it go well?'

'No. A nice lady, but she couldn't help put us in touch with Chrissie's birth mother. It just made me think – we never hear from *my* mother in Trinidad either.' They moved on. She added, 'Anyway, Nan has been a wonderful mother to me, and I wouldn't have had a dad anyway, because he died before I was born.' They walked the rest of the way in silence, each with their own thoughts.

Rodney said tactfully that he wouldn't come in for cocoa, as he was due back to work tomorrow.

Sunny and Nan went into the kitchen and Nan said, 'Would you like Welsh rabbit? I don't suppose you had much to eat this afternoon.'

'No, stale seed cake,' Sunny said, and suddenly she was crying. Nan passed her a large handkerchief to mop her tears. 'I'm sorry,' Sunny gulped, 'I know it was much worse for poor Chrissie, but she now knows she'll probably never meet her mother. Miss Sands said that she'd married and lives abroad and that she'd not heard from her since Chrissie was adopted.'

'Her father?' Nan prompted. She carried to the table a plate of what they usually referred to as 'Welsh rabbit', but Nan reckoned was really called rarebit. The name originated from during the war, when the cheese ration was known as 'mousetrap'.

'This is just what I needed,' Sunny said, after the first mouthful. 'Thank you, Nan. Well, Chrissie's father – nothing is known about him. Do you think Serena would reject me if we ever got in touch?'

Nan put her arm round her daughter. 'The young mother I remember – well, she didn't want to part with you, but she was committed to her nursing, and she thought you'd be happy with me.'

'I am, Nan, I am – but I can't help wondering . . .'

'I know, my dear, I know. Just remember I took you on because I loved you, won't you?'

Sunny nodded. 'You'll always be my mum, Nan. If only Chrissie could believe that about *her* mum and dad!'

'This has been a painful experience for her, but let's hope that she does really,' Nan said.

* * *

Chrissie was lying in her bed at home, pressing her face to the damp pillow. Mrs Ford hesitated outside the door, and then entered the room. 'Here are the clothes you changed out of before you left for Middlesex. I've washed and ironed them. You'll have to be up early tomorrow to catch the train to work in London.' She piled the clothes on the bedside chair. 'Chrissie, dear, I am sorry things didn't go as you had hoped today—'

Chrissie sat up and held out her arms. 'Oh, Mum, I need to hug you. I know Dad is outside the door, tell him to come in too. I must tell you how I feel.'

Chrissie's dad sat down heavily on the neatly piled clothes on the chair, but his wife didn't scold him as she would have done normally. It was more important to hear what Chrissie had to say.

'Mum, Dad; I'm sorry I put you through all this today. I know the truth now, and oh, it hurts, but I'm so glad I've got both of you, and I want you to know I'm so sorry for what I've said and done lately. I realise now that you have loved and wanted me all this time, and that my – the person who gave birth to me, would never have done that. Will you forgive me?' she appealed.

'Of course we will, won't we, Stan? We were wrong not to tell you we adopted you, but . . . '

'It was the happiest day of our lives,' her father said gruffly.

'Will you stay at home now?' her mother appealed to her.

'Mum, I don't know, but this will always be my home,' Chrissie said softly.

They were all aware that things had changed, and they would have to deal with that.

*　*　*

One evening, a few weeks later, when Sunny and Rodney had gone to see a show at the Streatham Hill Theatre, Nan settled down to write a letter, something she'd intended to do for some time.

Dear Serena,

I do hope you are still at the same address. I am, as you will see, still at the old Mother and Baby Home in Grove Lane, but it is now a family home, as I have retired. I have often thought of you over the years, and I am sure you must wonder how the little girl you left with me, and allowed me to adopt, has grown up.

Sunny, as she is known, is a beautiful young lady. She did well at school, and is now an assistant in a printing shop, and is enjoying her job, as it involves her artistic talent. She is in her seventeenth year, she loves dancing, and she is always smiling! I have told her about you and the little I knew about her father, and she is proud of the strength of character you both showed during the war years. She has the photograph you gave me as a precious reminder of the mother who gave her up because 'it was for the best'. However, she did say recently she wished she knew what her father looked like – have you a photograph of him to spare, I wonder?

I can understand why you decided not to continue writing to me, as you didn't want to unsettle her.

I believe she would like to hear from you now, to get to know you – she calls me Nan, rather than Mother, but we are very close. I know if it was me, though, I would wonder what my real mother was like. If you feel the same about Sunny, I will welcome you back into her life, and mine.

It may be that you have married and have had other children. Sunny is, of course, my only child. I am enclosing a lovely photograph taken by her employer. He painted a portrait from it, and many prints have been sold. It is called That Sunny Smile.

You will want to consider whether or not to write, but I hope you do. Address letters here. One day, I hope we will all meet again.

Your friend,
Nanette.

SIX

When the summer came around, Mr Rowland decided to 'shut up shop' as he put it, for the last two weeks of August and the first two weeks of September. It was always a slow time business-wise he'd said, so why didn't they all have a welcome break? Patsy's mother was looking after the children during the early part of the school holiday, but now Patsy could be off work with her boys for longer, and then have some time to herself after they returned to school. Mr Rowland had made sure she had her holiday pay, so she wouldn't have to worry about having the time off.

Sunny was delighted and surprised to discover that she was also being paid for the extended holiday. She wasn't aware that Mr Rowland was generously sharing with his staff a small windfall from an insurance policy which had matured. Eleanor knew, naturally, and agreed with her father when he said, 'You can't take it with you.'

When Sunny told her the news, Nan said, 'Why not spend a few days with Chrissie exploring London? She could arrange her leave for then, too, and you could get the bus and visit all the places you are always saying you'd like to see – Regent's Park Zoo, Madame Tussauds, the Festival Hall, the galleries and museums?'

'I'd love to do that, Nan, but I didn't think you'd want me to go . . .'

'I'd worry if you were on your own, but you and Chrissie, well, I'm sure you'd have lots of fun together.' Nan mentally crossed her fingers. *I have to trust her*, she thought.

Sunny said, 'I hope Rodney won't mind . . .'

'Why should he mind, my dear? There's no dancing in the summer, after all, and usually, all he wants is to go for rides on his scooter, with you clinging on the back . . . which worries me, I must admit, with all the traffic on the roads nowadays. Also, he had his two weeks leave in June, and seemed to spend most of it in a convoy with his mates to Brighton. Mods and rockers, don't they call them? Not that I think he would get involved in any of that. What happened to the socials at the church, and the choir?'

'When his voice broke, he didn't enjoy singing any more, and the socials are for younger kids.'

'Kids? Where did you learn that expression?' Nan interrupted.

Sunny didn't answer but continued, 'There's not so much going on, since the curate left for a new parish somewhere up north. Anyway, Rodney has joined a local football team – he was head-hunted because he's big and they needed someone like him in goal!'

'I thought you hadn't seen so much of him lately,' Nan said thoughtfully. She felt relieved that the youthful romance was fading, before it escalated, but she quickly suppressed that thought. It appeared that Rodney's dad had taken her advice and told his son to 'cool his ardour' after a conversation Nan had had with him. The youngsters weren't aware of this conversation.

Nan changed the subject. 'Is Mr Rowland going away?'

'Yes, with his daughter. To Cornwall.' Sunny paused then added, rather too casually, 'Alec will be at home. He has his holiday studies, but he hopes to attend some musical events, Mr Rowland says.'

They were finishing their breakfast, while discussing the holiday, when they heard the postman giving a rat-tat-tat on the door to let them know he had delivered some post. Nan said, 'I'll get it. Probably a bill or two, eh?' She hurried out of the kitchen and went through the hall. There was post on the mat, and she was right, a couple of bills, but not the airmail letter she'd been hoping for ever since she had written to Serena months ago. She didn't really know whether she was disappointed or relieved.

*　*　*

There was quite a lot of walking around at Regent's Park Zoo, but Sunny and Chrissie wanted to see as many of the animals as they could in one afternoon. It was a hot day, and thankfully, they sank down on a bench in the giraffe house. They were so thirsty that they drained the contents of the bottles of lemonade they'd purchased earlier, even though it was tepid. Nan had made the packets of sandwiches first thing; Chrissie's Auntie Beryl had no time for such things before she left for work at 8 a.m.

Chrissie confided, 'She's got a man friend now. Sometimes he stays overnight. Auntie Beryl told me he has to sleep on the settee as I've got the spare room. He's probably hoping to move in – and he could pay more than I do if he does. I'd have to find a room somewhere else.' Chrissie sighed. 'Do you think you might consider working in London and then we could share a flat?'

'Oh, I love my job and I'm not ready to leave home yet – Nan wouldn't want me to. Your Auntie Beryl seems anxious to have a man in her life; luckily Nan is past all that,' Sunny said complacently. Then, as she unwrapped her lunch, she said ruefully, 'Sandwich spread again! Nan said we must finish the jar before it goes off.'

'Custard creams, my favourite,' Chrissie said, helping herself to several all at once. Sunny said nothing; she'd succumbed to temptation on the bus and eaten the Mars bar they were supposed to share. She wrinkled her nose. 'It pongs in here, doesn't it? The giraffes are such lofty characters, but they are keeping an eye on us – we are not allowed to feed the animals, are we?'

'I don't think they'd like sandwich spread,' Chrissie said, delving into the packet for the last biscuit. 'What d'you want to see next? Guy the gorilla? When I saw his picture in the booklet we bought, I thought he looked sad and must be lonely on his own. Or Dumbo the Indian elephant?'

'The bears I think, especially the polar bears,' Sunny said. 'I wonder how they keep their fur so white.'

'Lots of swimming and diving maybe,' Chrissie wondered. 'I wouldn't mind joining them in this heat!'

The next day they visited Madame Tussauds. They found some of the tableaux rather disturbing in content, especially the crime scenes.

'Perhaps the wax figures are too realistic, though they are beautifully modelled, aren't they?' Sunny said.

'I hope I don't have dreams about them tonight,' Chrissie replied.

They had no such reservations about the galleries, where they spent several hours. They sat on the long benches with other visitors, and Sunny attempted some pencil sketches of things which caught her interest. She also scribbled her thoughts into a small notebook. She had to shush Chrissie sometimes, when her comments, although usually complimentary, were rather too loud and caused folk to turn and look at them disapprovingly. 'It's like being in church!' Chrissie exclaimed.

'Shush!' Sunny whispered.

She doesn't see the pictures in the same way as me, Sunny realised. *I could sit here for ages contemplating* Rain, Steam and Speed *by JMW Turner, such a wonderful painting of the Great Western Railway. I can't tell Chrissie that it seems so real; I imagine I can smell the steam and feel the train is rushing towards me. Why didn't I go to art college as they suggested at school?*

'Time to get some fresh air, don't you think?' asked Chrissie. 'You can buy a card of that picture, and study it at home!'

The girls also explored some of the old London streets, like Drury Lane, Fleet Street, and Wimpole Street, where Elizabeth Barrett, the writer, had lived. One day they went to Green Park and sat on the grass, soaking up the sunshine and watching the world go by. 'Were those young men whistling at us?' Sunny said rather too innocently. 'You know they were!' Chrissie said.

The week was one neither of them would forget, but too soon it was time for Chrissie to go back to work. 'We'll go to all the places we missed this time next year,' they promised each other.

*   *   *

The following Monday, Sunny kept the promise she had made to Mr Rowland to call in at the office and gather up any post. 'We don't want a pile of correspondence and orders on the door mat,' Mr Rowland had said. 'That would be an invitation to any shady individual to break in if they knew the place was empty.'

On the way, Sunny stopped at the baker's and on impulse bought a crusty cottage loaf.

'We miss our Chrissie, the customers still ask after her,' the baker said.

The alley was deserted today. Sunny took out the key she had been trusted with, inserted it into the lock, and almost tripped over a pile of letters. *Mr Rowland was right*, she thought, gathering them all up. She took the envelopes over to the desk to sort out and file in the pending drawer. She was engrossed in her task and was startled when she heard the door open and close and then felt a touch on her shoulder, followed by a tug on her ponytail. She turned indignantly. 'Alec! I might have guessed it was you.' He twirled the elastic band he'd removed and tousled her hair.

'Where's that sunny smile?' he teased. 'You might say you are pleased to see me. Shall I make coffee?'

'No milk,' she managed. She rose from the chair and faced him. 'I didn't know you were asked to look in here as well.'

'I came,' he said lightly, 'because I thought it was the only way I could meet up with you. I wasn't sure what your mother would think, if I knocked on her door. Or if your boyfriend would object. Rodney, isn't that his name?'

'Why should either of them mind?' She sounded cross. 'Rodney is a good friend, that's all, but he'll be joining the army in October and he's not on holiday like I am at the moment. Nan invited your grandfather and your mother to our house last Boxing Day – you would have been included too, if you'd been home.'

'I was working, you know that, I'm sure,' he said. 'Don't let's argue, Sunny, please. I'd like to take you to the Prom at the Albert Hall on Saturday. Mother bought me two tickets, for the stalls, not the gallery where I usually lounge.' He looked down at her. 'You've grown up, I can see. Oh, you're not much taller, but . . .'

'I'm not a little girl anymore,' she said firmly. 'But you must ask Nan first if we can go.'

'You are still vulnerable,' he said quietly. 'I have to remind myself of that.'

'You've got a girlfriend haven't you? Janice, isn't it? She was on that picture you sent.'

'Janine? No. She joined us in Paris as our singer. She's married with two small children, about ten years older than me. She's a beautiful young woman who likes to earn a bob or two with her singing, when she gets a chance.'

Sunny was smiling now. She said huskily, 'You mean a franc or two, don't you?'

He was smiling too. 'I like your tartan – trews, don't they call them? More fashionable than dungarees, eh?' Sunny had bought the tight-fitting trousers, together with a sage-green blouse complementing the green in the tartan, last week in London, in a smart shop that Chrissie called a boutique. She had spent the rest of her holiday money on the outfit and Chrissie had bought the same.

'Now people really will think we're twins!' she'd said.

The new blouse had a prim Peter Pan collar but was sleeveless, which prompted Alec to murmur, 'You look beautiful, Sunny.' She gave a little shiver as he stroked her bare arm. It was a brief, but intimate gesture.

'I've another three years at Cambridge, a busy time ahead, by then I'll be twenty-five, and if I study hard, I hope to have a good career ahead of me.'

'That seems a long time,' she told him.

'You might be married to Rodney by then.'

'I know my own mind,' she said stubbornly.

'You're an amazing girl,' he told her. 'I'd like us to be good friends. I'll try not to tease you!'

'There's a lot I want to achieve before I'm twenty,' she said. 'I want to go to Trinidad, and meet Serena, my birth mother. I want to do well at my job, I want . . . '

He looked at her quizzically. 'I'm hungry, aren't you?' he said.

He took his wallet from his top pocket and opened it. Sunny glimpsed a single ten-shilling note. He said ruefully, 'That's got to last until Mother comes home. I've got the use of her car while she's away, and she filled the tank with petrol, though. She also loaded the fridge with all the healthy food she thinks I should eat. Could lunch be sand-wiches, Sunny?'

'Actually, I was about to ring Nan and tell her I wouldn't be back until later but come home with me and you might get something more substantial,' she said.

'Is she likely to ask me what my intentions are, regarding her daughter?' He smiled, as if he was cracking a joke.

'I hope she won't do anything of the sort,' Sunny replied. But she couldn't help thinking, *I wish I knew what he really feels about me. When he stroked my arm like that, he was looking at me in a different way.*

When Nan opened the door and saw that Sunny wasn't alone, she exclaimed, 'Whatever have you done to your hair, Sunny? You might have combed it!'

'Oh, Nan, I'm fed up with that ponytail. It makes me look like a schoolgirl!'

'It's good to meet you, Miss Cato, I've heard so much about you,' Alec said as he held out his hand. He added, 'Sunny and I met up unexpectedly at Grandfather's shop this morning, and she asked if I would like to come to lunch – only if that's all right with you, of course.'

'He missed out on a Christmas visit,' Sunny said, as Nan shook hands with Alec. He smiled at her. 'I heard how much they enjoyed themselves,' he said.

'Well, come in, you are very welcome. You may call me Nanette, if I can call you Alec? How do you feel about gam-mon and pease pudding with parsley sauce?' Nan asked.

'Homemade?' he asked hopefully.

'Of course.' Nan smiled. *What a charming young man. Good mannered*, she thought. She looked in the bag Sunny handed her. 'Oh, you remembered the bread – good!' She didn't add that she'd asked for a brown tin loaf, not the white that Sunny had bought.

Alec didn't only lunch with them, he was still there after supper. In the drawing room, Sunny saw him looking at the piano. 'Your mother played for us, when she was here,' she said. 'I expect you get your musical talent from her, don't you?'

'Mmm,' he said reflectively. 'But she wouldn't let me touch the keys until I'd had a few lessons with a music teacher. Then she sat me down – I was five years old – and told me to show her what I had learned. That's a lovely instrument you have,' he said, turning to Nan.

Nan smiled. 'The piano was my father's. He was a concert pianist. A long time ago. Would you like to play for us?'

'Thank you, I certainly would. Would you like to suggest a piece?'

'How about some of your – jazz?' Nan suggested unexpectedly.

'Gershwin? 'Summertime' – from *Porgy and Bess*? It's a great favourite of mine.'

'Yes please,' Nan agreed. Alec sat on the piano stool, flicking back an imaginary tailcoat, and he sang the lovely lullaby to his own accompaniment. His audience was spellbound.

He has a good, baritone voice, Nan thought, *but no one can surpass Paul Robson's rendition. He's quite a virtuoso on the piano, though.* She glanced at Sunny, and knew instinctively what she was thinking. *She may not be quite seventeen*, she thought, *but she's a young woman and obviously likes this charming young man. He's won me over too. He had second helpings of pease pudding, and said it was the nicest meal he'd had in ages. It's such a simple thing to make, though you have to remember to soak the split peas overnight.*

Alec closed the piano lid. 'I must be going; I am keeping you up. What did you think of the music and words, Sunny?'

'The music was wonderful, the words fitted it perfectly,' she said softly. 'It was sad, too.'

Nan held her breath as Alec told her, 'It was considered racist at one time in the States.'

'Oh why?' Sunny exclaimed.

'The story is about poor black cotton pickers in the South and how they loved summertime when "*the pickin' was easy*," he said. 'It's how it was then, Sunny. Sadly, prejudice still exists. Even here. The lyrics aren't by Gershwin, but perfect for the music. It's always been special for me.'

'It will be for me, too,' she said softly.

SEVEN

Next morning, Sunny smiled at her reflection in her bedroom mirror. She took up her hairbrush and applied it vigorously to her hair. Nan came up behind her and observed, 'Most girls have perms to achieve curls like that. Try a touch of brilliantine. Sunny, I've just had a phone call.'

'From?' Sunny asked eagerly. *She was obviously hoping the caller was Alec*, Nan thought.

'Patsy. Mrs Perkins is staying with her in the flat, having a week off too. That's why I didn't see her yesterday as usual. Last night she slipped over in the kitchen and banged her head on a shelf as she pulled herself up. Today, she has a headache and sounds rather muddled and Patsy thinks she ought to take her to Mayday hospital. She was wondering if you would go over and look after the boys while she's out. She says her mother might have to wait some time to see a doctor. If you hurry, you should be able to catch the bus in ten minutes' time. There's a cup of tea and a slice of toast waiting for you in the kitchen.'

I can't wear the smart clothes I had on yesterday, Sunny thought. Her dungarees were clean, so she donned those over a yellow T-shirt. 'If Alec rings, though he should be busy studying, tell him where I am, please, Nan.'

'I will,' Nan promised. She added, 'He liked my pease pudding, didn't he?'

'He certainly did,' Sunny agreed. She gulped the hot tea, and left the house still munching the toast. 'Keep them amused,' Nan called after her.

Patsy's flat was on the third floor. As Sunny climbed the stairs and looked at the view from the landing window, she saw that the bus from which she'd alighted had collected all the folk waiting at the stop outside the block of flats and was about to continue its journey. The friendly conductor was on the step; he looked up at her and waved. She waved back, and then walked along the corridor to the blue door as directed.

Six-year-old Davey let her in and led her into the living room. Mrs Perkins sat in the only armchair, looking pale and confused. She had a bump like an egg on her forehead and the beginnings of a black eye. Patsy had helped her mother dress and was now seeing to her younger son Roy in the bathroom. 'He's a messy eater, has egg yolk all down his clean shirt,' she called out to Sunny. 'Thanks for coming at such short notice.'

Soon after, Patsy appeared with Roy, and warned her boys, 'No larking about. I've put the Snakes and Ladders on the table, and some crayons and paper. Mother, come on, let me help you up, then we'll get the lift down. Did you use the stairs, Sunny? I meant to tell you about the lift. I hope the boys behave, there'll be a treat for 'em when we get back .'

'Sherbet Fountain?' Davey said hopefully.

'With a lolly, not lick'rish,' Roy added. He was a year younger than his brother. They both had very fair hair and hazel eyes. Roy had a runny nose. Sunny averted her gaze and hoped she wouldn't have to wipe it as she was squeamish. You wouldn't make a nurse, Nan had sighed when they were discussing possible careers once.

'He's got the snuffles,' Patsy said. 'He knows how to blow his nose, so remind him, now and then, Sunny, please, to use his handkerchief.'

She gave both boys hugs. 'See you soon, I hope, but I can't promise. Bye!'

It was almost noon and after an energetic morning of playing it would soon be lunchtime for the boys. Davey opened the fridge door in the kitchen to point out the Pyrex dish of shepherd's pie. 'We never had a fridge before,' he said proudly, 'but it came with the flat. Mummy left a note for you, see.'

Patsy had written on a used envelope, *'If not back by twelve, please warm up in oven, light with gas poker. Takes twenty minutes. Davey will lay table.'*

However, as the dish went onto the top shelf in the gas oven, they heard the front door open, and the little boys rushed to see their mother and grandmother. When Sunny emerged from the kitchen she was surprised to see that Alec was pushing Mrs Perkins in a wheelchair. He saw her look of surprise, and explained, 'I was driving past the hospital when I saw Patsy struggling to manoeuvre this contraption and about to walk home.'

Patsy was hugging her boys in turn. 'Have you been good? I can smell dinner cooking – thanks, Sunny. Mother is suffering from mild concussion; the hospital lent me the wheelchair. I can keep it for a week or so. No, boys, sweets after lunch, not before, you know that!'

'Shall I help Mrs Perkins into her chair?' Alec asked Patsy. They were in the living room now.

'Yes please,' Patsy replied.

'Then I can give Sunny a lift home, if she would like that.'

'I'm sure she would,' Patsy answered for her. She was relieved, because she had been wondering how she could stretch the shepherd's pie to feed two extras. 'It could have been worse,' she added, regarding her mother.

'Is Grandma going to wear a black patch over her bad eye?' Davey asked.

'She can be a pirate!' Roy added. They'd seen *Captain Pugwash*, a new cartoon programme for children, on their grandmother's small television set recently.

'I can still see what you boys are up to,' Mrs Perkins told them.

Travelling down in the lift, Sunny clutched Alec's hand because she said the sensation made her tummy turn over. She said to him, 'I didn't expect to see you today, Alec. I thought we wouldn't meet up until Saturday when we go to the Albert Hall.'

He opened the car door for her, and she slid on to the passenger seat.

'I couldn't wait that long, so rang your mum and she told me where you were. I was on my way to see you, when I spotted Patsy and Mrs P. I wanted to ask you if you fancied a trip out to Shirley, it's a nice day to sit in the garden. I thought you might listen to me reading my essay on nineteenth-century musicians . . .'

'I can't give you any advice, because all I know is a few names,' she said. 'But we'd better join Nan for lunch first.'

'Do you need to ask her permission to go to our house; she knows my mother won't be there?' They were driving along the High Street and they'd be in Grove Lane within ten minutes.

'We-ell . . .' Sunny said, but she'd made up her mind to go anyway.

All Nan said when she opened the door to them, was 'I thought you would be coming for lunch, Alec! No pease pudding today, but I minced the remains of the Sunday beef and . . .'

'You made shepherd's pie, didn't you, Nan?' Sunny said.

'How did you guess?'

'Well, it's what they're having for lunch at Patsy's!'

Alec followed them into the kitchen. 'You sit there, Alec,' Nan told him, 'while Sunny and I serve up.'

'You're a good cook, Nan,' Alec said appreciatively, having wiped his plate clean with a crust of new bread. 'My mother always seems to be on a diet.'

Sunny glanced at Nan, wondering if she minded him using the diminutive of her name. She thought, this is the moment I should ask if I may go to Shirley, when she knows his mother and grandfather are both away. 'Nan, it's all right if I go to Alec's house this afternoon, isn't it? He wants to read an essay to me, so I can give my opinion.'

'Why should I object to that?' Nan said, smiling, and then she added, 'I trust you, Sunny.'

I wish she hadn't said that, Sunny thought, *whatever will Alec make of it?*

In the car he turned to her before he switched on the ignition. 'Nan meant that remark for me, too, I think. She needs to have no worries on that score.'

*   *   *

Sunny had imagined that Shirley would be more rural than Croydon, because Nan had mentioned she'd visited an elderly aunt 'in the country' when she was a child. Since then it had developed considerably, but the Old

Mill was still *in situ* and there was some pastureland. Alec explained, as they drove along, 'After the war when there was a shortage of housing, the golf course became a large housing estate.' He added, 'Building is still going on. No station, but cars everywhere, nowadays.'

They were driving through a less populated area now, with tree-lined streets, and big, individual houses, with long drives, and large back gardens. 'Here we are, welcome to *Sans Souci*. Know what that means, Sunny?'

'I did learn French at school, you know, even though I didn't go to a posh boarding school like you! *Without Care*, carefree, is that right?'

'Sums it up. Now, I think more, *Uncared For*; it's the shabbiest house down our street. Anyway, my boarding school wasn't posh, I assure you. Some of the teachers weren't even qualified. We had a tough old ex-sergeant major in charge of games, which were compulsory, and he once shouted at me, "You'll never make the team, you're bleeding useless." No one noticed I was short-sighted and couldn't see the ball. I went there when I was six because Mother had to work full-time to support us. My father had gone off to live abroad somewhere and Mother got nothing from him until they eventually got divorced. Grandfather bought the house after my grandmother died. She had money but he was a self-made man. He's worked hard all his life.'

Alec parked the car in the drive. 'The garage is full of the stuff Mother brought with her after the divorce,' he said. He opened the front door, 'Well, come in, Sunny, and I'll make some coffee for us to take outside, eh?'

Sunny thought, *this house is large like ours, but it looks neglected*. But then, Alec opened the back door and she was instantly entranced. 'What a beautiful garden!' she exclaimed.

'Mother is Head Gardener. I help with the heavy digging and mowing the grass when I'm home,' Alec said. He filled the kettle and took two mugs from the kitchen cupboard. 'Sit down, we eat in the kitchen nowadays. Like you,' he added.

There were bright cushions on the chairs, and one of them was occupied. 'Oh!' Sunny exclaimed. 'You've got a cat!' The thin black and white cat slithered under the table, mewing.

'I don't reckon Mother will be too happy. I found her on the doorstep. She's obviously a stray. I enquired of the neighbours, and they said she had been hanging around, hoping to be fed.'

'She's got green eyes! I don't think she's much more than a kitten, Alec. Couldn't you give her a saucer of milk?'

Alec said, 'She's had most of the milk already; I hope there's enough for the coffee.'

'Some things don't change,' Sunny said, but she didn't tell him off. She coaxed the little cat out and the next thing she knew it had scrambled awkwardly onto her lap and curled up there.

'Can you think of a name?' Alec asked, bringing the coffee to the table. 'Shortbread biscuit? To eat, not a name for the cat.'

'Thanks. What's that fishy smell?' she asked, hoping he was not making sandwiches from the contents of a tin he'd opened. *It's not long since we had a good lunch*, she thought.

'Pilchards in oil, thought the cat might enjoy 'em.'

'Let's call her Pilchard then, Pilchie for short!'

'That'll do. Not sure Mother will let me keep her, though.'

'Pilchie might be better off with Mr Rowland. She could be the shop cat! Have you got a cardboard box and an old towel? She'll need a bed, if she's staying here for the time being?'

'Plenty of old boxes in the garage,' Alec said. 'Let's take her with us into the garden, eh?'

'I'll carry the mugs.'

There was a seating area on the lawn, surrounded by neatly clipped box hedges.

Pilchie had obviously been in the garden before and had made a little nest of grass clippings in a hollow under the hedge. 'She's listening in,' Sunny fancied, as Alec opened his notebook.

'She's got a rattling purr,' he observed. 'You seem taken with her. Have you ever had a cat yourself?'

Sunny shook her head. 'No, Nan didn't think that babies and pets were a good combination, so never had them. The habit just stuck, I suppose.'

After a while, Alec began reading aloud from his essay, pausing now and again to ask for comments.

'None so far,' said Sunny. 'It's very interesting, but I'm not qualified to give an opinion.' she said honestly.

'Do you think you'll enjoy the concert on Saturday?'

To herself she thought, *yes, because I will be with you,* but she said aloud, 'I know I will!'

Later they shared a packet of Smith's crisps. Alec had a portable radio and that provided entertainment. The sun was warm on their heads, but a little breeze stirred the last roses of summer and a few petals drifted onto the grass. They sat side by side, but Alec resisted putting his arm around her. *When I return to Cambridge,* he thought to himself, *it will be some time before we see each other again. Sunny must be free to learn more about life. I have to concentrate on my future career. Who knows where either of us will be in three years' time?*

* * *

Sunny and Alec didn't meet up again before Saturday, but in the meantime, there were unexpected developments at the Mother and Baby Home. The tenants upstairs decided that, in view of increasing age and infirmity, the effort involved in climbing the stairs was too great and they could no longer live independently. They were arranging to move to a private residential home near their son, in Berkshire.

'I am wondering how we will manage without their rent and whether we ought to be considering moving to a much smaller house,' Nan said despondently, when she and Sunny were having breakfast on the Thursday morning. 'You're not going out today, are you, Sunny? We need to discuss this together.'

'No, Alec has to get on with his work,' Sunny said. 'I will be here for you, Nan, but – I know you don't want to leave here, and nor do I. What would we do with all the furniture and everything else, including the piano, if we have to downsize?'

They heard the post arrive and Nan went into the hall to pick it up. Coming back in, she read aloud from a circular.

'DEAR RESIDENT, YOUR LOCAL HOSPITAL NEEDS YOUR HELP! WE ARE URGENTLY SEEKING ACCOM-MODATION FOR FOREIGN MEDICAL STUDENTS. INTERVIEWS WITH PROSPECTIVE TENANTS CAN BE ARRANGED IMMEDIATELY. PLEASE RING THE FOLLOWING NUMBER.'

'I imagine they are targeting large houses like this,' Nan said thoughtfully.

'Don't delay, Nan, ring the number today. When are the tenants leaving?' Sunny asked.

'This weekend! Their son has arranged for a removal firm to pack and store their furniture until it can be sorted out. They might have given us more notice but they have only just had confirmation that there are vacancies at the residential home.'

'Do you want me to cancel my trip to the Albert Hall, Nan?'

'No, my dear, as long as you can help me over the next two days?'

'Of course I can. Just get on the phone and find out more about those medical students!' Sunny urged.

* * *

It all seemed to happen at once. By Saturday, everything was arranged, and the following Monday, after the upstairs had been cleared, which fortunately would not involve any effort from Nan and Sunny, the four prospective tenants would arrive for their interview and would hopefully be installed in their new quarters shortly afterwards.

'Enjoy the concert first, Sunny,' Nan said, with a sigh, but actually she was happy to be busy again and looking forward to a change.

Sunny and Alec went to the forty-third promenade concert, familiarly known as a 'Prom', which was a tribute to mark the fiftieth anniversary Anniversary of the death of the famous Norwegian composer Edvard Grieg. They climbed the steps to the South Entrance of the magnificent, towering building and Alec remarked, 'A birthday treat for you, eh, Sunny – your birthday is on the 10th, isn't it? How old will you be then?'

'You know,' she reminded him. 'Seventeen, not . . .'

'A little girl anymore,' he finished the sentence with a smile. 'Well, here we are, look, the ceiling is over thirty-five feet above us and there's the gallery.'

'They stand up there, don't they?' She gazed upwards in awe. They had reached their seats, not at the very front, but not too far back.

'They make a racket on the last night of the Proms,' he told her.

The conductor was the charismatic Malcolm Sargent, affectionately known as Flash Harry by the promenaders. He was famous for his theatricality. The star singer of the evening was a well-known Norwegian soprano, Kirsten Flagstad.

Sunny listened raptly to the musical accompaniment by the BBC Symphony Orchestra. When Nan asked her later about the programme, Sunny told her about the 'Overture in Autumn', and the wonderful Peer Gynt Suite, which had been written by Grieg for Ibsen's famous play. But she didn't reveal that Alec had held her hand throughout the evening or that when they drew up outside her home much later, they sat in the car for a few minutes, and when she said, 'Thank you for a wonderful evening,' he replied, 'I'm glad you enjoyed it so much,' and then he kissed her. It took her breath away, and she didn't want him to stop, but he moved away, saying huskily, 'I hope to pop in to see you on your birthday on Tuesday, but I can't promise. Mother and Grandfather will be returning home that day. Then you'll be back at work the following week, of course, and I'll be off to Cambridge.'

Sunny lay in bed that night, thinking, *my first real kiss, but I can tell he's much more experienced than Rodney. He didn't fumble with my buttons like Rodney does. I just wanted – more – but I remembered Nan saying she trusted me and I don't want to let her down.*

Alec had surprised himself with his reaction, too. He wanted to convince himself that it was only a harmless kiss, but he knew it could have led to a lot more. He had had several brief affairs in his time, but Sunny was so young that he needed to restrain himself. His grandfather had warned him about flirting with his Girl Friday.

EIGHT

Chrissie had been home for the weekend as usual and had returned to London on Sunday evening. But she came back unexpectedly on the Monday morning. 'Why aren't you at work?' her mother asked, surprised to see her. Her daughter's face was pale and her eyes puffy. She had obviously been crying. Chrissie pointed mutely to the large suitcase at her feet.

'My dear, what's brought this on?'

'Oh, Mum. When Rodney took me back to London – oh I didn't tell you because I know you don't like the thought of me on the pillion, but I borrowed Sunny's helmet – I discovered that Auntie Beryl's friend had moved into my bedroom and I was expected to sleep on the sofa. Rodney was about to go, but I decided there and then to leave, and he waited for me to collect the things I need now. I'll send for the rest later. It was late when we arrived back, so his mother put me up for the night. I didn't tell her you didn't know. This morning, after Rodney had gone to work, I rang the office up and explained that I wouldn't be able to return to work.'

Mrs Ford interrupted. 'Did you tell them the reason why?'

'Oh, Mum, I had to make up an excuse. I said I was needed at home. Don't look so shocked; it's true isn't it?' she appealed to her mother.

Mrs Ford swallowed what felt like a large lump in her throat. She hugged Chrissie for a long moment, and then said in an almost normal voice, 'Did Mrs Gibson make you breakfast?'

'No, Mum, I couldn't face anything then, but now . . .'

'Bacon and eggs, and a nice cup of tea,' Mrs Ford suggested. 'Beryl, how could she? She was always ruling the roost when she was at home, but then she was the youngest of us girls, and I suppose we felt jealous. She hasn't changed though. Still hoping to meet Mr Right, but it's usually Mr Wrong, in her case.' She looked at her daughter. 'It's so good to have you home, Chrissie. What a nice young man Rodney is; a credit to his family.'

'Don't read too much into it, Mum.' Chrissie was smiling now. 'The first thing I must do is look for another job. Rodney's going to ask the bank manager today if they can help, and I've been promised a reference. I'm back home now.' *And I'm in with a chance now, where Rodney is concerned,* she thought. *Sunny has obviously moved on with Alec, and she never really liked Rodney in that way. I always have though. I'm sure she won't mind.*

Chrissie had no luck with the bank, but received an encouraging letter:

We recruited two school leavers at the beginning of the month, and have no vacancies at the moment. However, we will certainly keep your details on record and contact you when we have a junior position to fill. Wishing you good luck in your search for employment,

Yours sincerely etc.

She called in to see Sunny with a birthday card to add to the others already on show in the kitchen. 'It's where we are mostly, so I can see them!' Sunny said. She gave her friend a hug. 'I'm glad you're home. Rodney will be off to start his National Service in the Pay Corps in Devizes soon; he was encouraged to apply for that by the bank. He has good prospects in the future.'

'I heard that,' Chrissie said, wondering whether Sunny was aware of her feelings for Rodney. She added casually, 'Did Alec send that large card with the red roses?'

'No – his is the one with the cartoon cat. It's black and white like the little cat he's adopted. I think he's broke at the moment. The rose card is rather puzzling, though. It came from London of all places, and just says inside, *thinking of you on your birthday, maybe we will meet up one of these days.'*

'No signature?' Chrissie asked.

Sunny shook her head.

'Where's Nan?'

'She's making the beds upstairs in the flat as two of the students will arrive today. Oh, you didn't know about them, but we have four new tenants, foreign medical students from the hospital; I presume they will be coming and going all the time, but they need a base when they are off duty.'

Sunny thought, *I'm not doing very well for presents this morning, but Nan has come up trumps and given me £5 to choose something I would really like! And the mystery card, that's both exciting and frustrating, when there's no signature.*

'What's cooking?' Chrissie sniffed the air.

'A chocolate birthday cake; I'm supposed to be timing it.'

'Are you going out somewhere for lunch?' Chrissie asked. 'If Nan's busy, perhaps you'd like to come with me to the bakery and have a roll and coffee for old times' sake, eh?'

'I'd like that, after the cake's out of the oven,' Sunny said. 'I might do a bit of window shopping too, and maybe spend my birthday money. I did say I'd help Nan, but she said to enjoy today, before the tenants arrive.' *It would make my day if Alec turned up*, she thought wistfully, *but he did take me to the Albert Hall last Saturday.*

* * *

Chrissie was given a warm welcome by the manager of the bakery and the rest of the staff as she and Sunny walked in through the door. They sat down in the cafe and studied the menu, which of course Chrissie knew by heart. 'Tomato soup, would you like to start with that, Sunny?' she asked.

'Why not?' Sunny replied. 'But please tell me if I have a red moustache afterwards!'

They were giggling like two schoolgirls when Alec turned up unexpectedly, having called earlier at the Mother and Baby Home and Nan having told him where they were likely to be. 'I so wanted to see you on your birthday, Sunny. May I join you?' he asked politely. Sunny nodded, and he pulled up a chair beside her. 'Happy birthday, Sunny! I picked you some flowers from the garden and left them with Nan,' he said. A bowl of soup was brought to him. 'Beef broth, leaves no mark, unlike tomato!' he said, grinning at Sunny. 'I can't stay long, because I have to meet Grandfather and Mother at the station shortly.'

As it was a small table meant for two, Sunny was aware that their knees were touching under the table. She was glad she was wearing her tartan trews and hoped Alec wouldn't notice she was trembling. 'I hope they like the little cat,' she ventured.

'Grandfather will, I know. I'm not too sure about Mother.'

Alec left Sunny and Chrissie after ten minutes, when they were eating sugary doughnuts, with the compliments of the bakery. 'I'm glad I saw you both,' he said, including Chrissie. 'I have more studying to do before I return to Cambridge, but I will keep in touch when I can.'

After he had gone, and they were about to leave to look round the shops, Chrissie whispered to Sunny, 'Like my mum said to me, life goes on. I'm going to ask the manager if I can work here again temporarily until I find another job. What do you think?'

'I think that's a good idea,' Sunny said.

* * *

Sunny arrived home just as Nan, who had hastily removed her pinafore and slung it over the banister of the stairs, opened the door to the tall man knocking. 'Ah, you're the first,' she said somewhat breathlessly.

'My colleagues are on duty tonight,' the man said. 'One of them will be along later.' He turned and smiled at Sunny. 'I presume you are the daughter of the house. After you.' He stood back to allow her to enter and then followed her into the hall.

Nan introduced them. 'Sunny, this is Imran, a student doctor at the hospital.'

'I am from Ceylon,' he said simply. 'My country gained independence from Great Britain in 1948, but we still feel that special link.' He smiled, and added, 'I went to a Church school, so English is my first language. But I will return home despite the unrest there, when I am qualified. My friends, I believe, intend to stay here as the opportunities are good. I am the eldest of our group and I desire to specialise, to become a surgeon.'

He's very handsome, Sunny thought. Belatedly, she said, 'Welcome to the Mother and Baby Home, Imran.'

He laughed and said, 'We are the babies now, I guess, as we have their quarters.'

'Sunny will take you upstairs and make sure you have everything you need,' Nan said. 'I will make a pot of tea, and Sunny can cut her birthday cake when she's back down.'

'An auspicious day,' Imran commented. He followed Sunny up the flight of stairs.

As Sunny checked that all was in place in the room he was to share with his friend, Ravi, Imran asked, 'What is your own background, Sunny? Where were you born?'

She said, 'Oh, I was born here in the Mother and Baby Home. My birth mother came from Trinidad. She was a nurse in England during the war. My father was from

Poland. He didn't survive the war. Nan adopted me. Is that everything you need to know?'

'I didn't mean to pry, I apologise,' Imran told her. 'I will come downstairs in about five minutes' time.'

Nan gave Sunny a long, searching look when she entered the kitchen. Sunny blushed, as Nan could tell she thought Imran was attractive. Sunny thought, *I hope she won't say he's too old for me, as he wouldn't be interested in me anyway. I am seventeen, and I know how I feel about Alec now.*

'We won't see the young doctors much,' Nan stated. 'Their meals are provided by the hospital. They will sleep during the day after a night shift or be studying.'

Like Alec, Sunny thought to herself, as they heard the polite knock on the kitchen door.

Imran didn't stay long, but they learned a little more about him. He spoke of his wife, a nurse in the hospital where he had done his initial training. Sunny wondered how he could leave her. Imran expected to be over in England for some time.

When he had departed, there were more visitors: Chrissie and Rodney, who were obviously becoming close. Sunny couldn't help thinking that last Christmas Rodney had kissed her under the mistletoe and they had enjoyed learning to dance together. But they hadn't seen each other properly in a while, and she had feelings for Alec.

When Sunny had asked Rodney in a quiet moment if he was dating Chrissie, he was a bit bashful at first. 'Well, I realised you and I would always be good friends, but nothing more. I know you are keen on Alec, but I hope he doesn't let you down. Chrissie felt lonely, and so did I, so we started seeing each other. So far, it's good. We have dancing and the motor scooter in common!' Sunny was pleased for her friends, but wondered why Chrissie hadn't told her about Rodney.

Now, Rodney presented Sunny with a card, no doubt from the selection in his parents' shop. 'Mum reminded me I hadn't sent one,' he said. That hurt a little, but Sunny smiled and said, 'Better late than never, eh?'

Nan cut more slices from the cake and made a fresh pot of tea.

'Sunny and I enjoyed our shopping trip today,' Chrissie said. 'Sorry we can't stay long. Rodney and I are off to the pictures, and we don't want to miss the start of the big film.'

'Happy birthday,' they chorused again, as they left.

Nan said, 'You haven't shown me what you bought with your birthday money, Sunny.'

'I haven't spent it yet,' she replied.

'Are you OK, Sunny?' asked Nan searchingly.

'Please don't think I mind about Rodney and Chrissie because I don't,' Sunny told her. 'We are all still friends. I just wish Chrissie had told me.'

'That's good,' Nan said, embracing her. Over Sunny's shoulder she focused on the mystery card on the mantelpiece. She felt a pang of sadness. *Surely Serena could have written more than that*, she thought.

*   *   *

'Good to see you,' Mr Rowland said. He had already cluttered up his desk, and had opened the entire correspondence, she saw.

'Coffee?' Sunny asked. Back in the old routine. Mr Rowland looked well; the holiday had obviously done him good.

'Yes, then I can tell you all my news, and you can tell me yours; I gather you saw something of my grandson?'

'Something . . . he was busy working most of the time. We enjoyed the Prom at the Albert Hall, though,' she said.

He gave her a quizzical look. 'No declaration?' he asked.

Sunny looked puzzled. What did he mean by that? 'No,' she said flatly.

'Alec, um, behaved impeccably, I hope?'

'Of course, Mr Rowland.' She couldn't help wishing he hadn't. She gulped the hot coffee. Time to get changed and plenty to do.

'Patsy will be here soon,' she said. Then she became aware that the little cat was purring and attempting to attract her attention.

'Oh good, Pilchie obviously likes it here then.'

'And I enjoy her company, too. I must confess she sleeps on the end of my bed and keeps my feet warm,' Mr Rowland said. 'She has an appointment with the local vet, Eleanor insisted, she said if not we'd be overrun with kittens, not mice. My daughter says I am an old softy; maybe I am, but I climbed St Michael's Mount while we were on holiday, and Eleanor declined, as she has no head for heights, so I can't be that soft.'

* * *

Patsy had some good news to impart, and she hoped Mr Rowland would agree to her plan. After she'd sent the dust and the cobwebs flying, she waited until Sunny went out to get the lunchtime sandwiches before saying tentatively, 'May I have a word with you, sir?'

'Now, Patsy, you know I prefer Mr Rowland, but fire away,' he said kindly.

'Well, the doctor said Mum has done her bit for Britain, and it's time she retired. The council are allowing her to live with me and the boys, as there's a queue for council houses like the one she lives in, and that means I can work full-time, and I'll need to for the money. I don't know, of course, whether you would like me to work here more hours, or if you think, well, that it's not necessary . . .' She paused to draw breath.

'My dear Patsy, I don't want you to look elsewhere, no indeed. Actually, I've been thinking we could do with more help on the printing side, and perhaps you could work at that in the afternoons?'

'Oh, Mr Rowland, you have made my day! I would love to learn to do what Sunny does. I'll continue with the cleaning in the mornings of course.'

'Excellent. Then stop worrying and we'll welcome you aboard!' Mr Rowland smiled.

'I can't wait to tell Sunny – I'll be her assistant, is that what you mean?'

'You'll be one of our team, Patsy. Oh, here she is! Have you boiled the kettle?'

'No – I'll do it right away,' Patsy said.

'I bought three macaroons – I couldn't resist them,' Sunny confessed. She went to fetch the plates to dish them out, as she put it.

'Guess what?' Patsy cried when Sunny entered the kitchen. 'I'm going to work here full-time now, and help you with the printing!'

'Hooray! I had a good feeling when I woke up this morning that something nice was going to happen – and it has!' Sunny was smiling and so was Patsy. Life was looking up again.

NINE

'I must find another cleaner,' Nan said, when she heard about Patsy's mother retiring. 'Fortunately, the young men upstairs promise they'll keep their quarters clean if not tidy, and the hospital will deal with their laundry, thank goodness.'

'Perhaps Mrs Perkins can recommend one of her friends,' Sunny said hopefully. 'And you must let me help you with more than just washing the dishes.'

'Thank you, Sunny, but you're young, at the age to be out and about and enjoying yourself when you're not at work. I wouldn't mind a hand with the ironing, though. How about that?'

'Yes, of course I'll help!' Sunny said. Now that Rodney has Chrissie and Alec is gone, I won't have anyone to dance with anyway, she thought to herself.

* * *

It was time to say goodbye and good luck to Rodney. He treated Chrissie and Sunny to the pictures the day before he left for his army service. He had passed his medical, feet and all, they'd just appeared flat in the awful tyre-soled sandals, which he had added to his outgrown clothes earmarked for the next jumble sale.

They sat either side of Rodney, but he leaned towards Chrissie and sneaked his arm around her waist. Sunny couldn't help feeling a little pang of jealousy, but she told herself sternly, *despite that kiss under the mistletoe, which encouraged Rodney to think I was ready for romance, I was always more interested in Alec. He and Chrissie are much more compatible. Although I'll miss him too. He'll always be a special friend, the one who encouraged me to learn to dance, and to grow up, I suppose.*

Rodney and Chrissie escorted Sunny home and then continued along the lane and turned off to The Grove. They weren't the only young couple to walk there in the moonlight, to find a secluded spot under a chestnut tree, to lean against the trunk and whisper sweet nothings to each other.

'I don't want to leave home, I don't want to leave you, Chrissie,' he told her.

She tried to cheer him up. 'You'll be so busy polishing your boots and marching you won't have time to miss me, but you'd better write to me regularly, or else . . .'

She peered out and up at the night sky and asked herself, *why am I holding back from saying he's the one?*'

'Or else what?' he teased.

'You know,' she said, and gave him a gentle push away. 'My mum will worry if I stay out too long, and so will yours. Come on, let's go home, Rodney.'

* * *

In the morning he was gone. Not to Devizes, which would hopefully be a permanent posting, but to a barracks up north. A place full of other young men, from all walks of life, crowded into cold, cheerless huts and drilling outside at the crack of dawn. He wrote to his mother:

Fitted with my uniform today, glad Dad gave me all that advice about polishing buttons and boots.

He couldn't tell her that like most of the new intake he'd shed a few tears that first night and that some of the lads had made fun of him because he wore pyjamas, or that he already had a nickname: Gibbo.

Chrissie's mother looked at her daughter keenly the morning after Rodney had left home. 'Not worrying about him, are you? He'll be all right, Chrissie. It'll make a man of him.'

Chrissie's eyes welled up. 'We'd only just got together really, and now he's gone. And I always knew he was keen on Sunny. Am I – second best, Mum?'

'Of course not! Sunny did lead him on a bit . . .'

'Oh, Mum, she didn't! She had someone else in mind, but that appears to have come to nothing. You mustn't say things like that; she's my best friend!'

'Let's not argue,' Mrs Ford said. 'A good breakfast, that's what you need at the moment. I reckon Rodney is enjoying his right now as well, eh?'

Rodney had actually eaten long before Mrs Ford began frying her bacon and eggs. He had toast as hard as cardboard, smothered in baked beans, something he disliked. Tea was made by emptying a packet of Typhoo tea, a full bag of sugar and a tin of condensed milk into a bucket of boiling water. Each new recruit was provided with a knife, fork and spoon, plus a tin mug. 'Guard 'em with your life,' the corporal warned them. 'No replacements given.' Rodney's companion at breakfast, who slept in the next bunk to him, was a puny, pasty-faced lad called Jack, who'd soon been dubbed Jacko. Looking at his plate he said dolefully, 'Gotta eat to keep your strength up, my mum said, but I'm gonna get out of here, as soon as I can. What about you?'

'My dad said to stick it out, and I'll get used to it,' Rodney said optimistically, as he tried to spear the last piece of blackened toast with his fork. It flew up in the air and landed in his mug of tea. He fished it out, sighed, then ate the now soggy morsel. 'Got to keep my strength up. Your mum's right about that, Jacko.'

That evening he wrote to Chrissie.

Not too bad up here, but much colder than back home. We have to keep moving to stop icicles forming on us! Miss my mum's home cooking. Getting used to strong, sweet tea, though – at least it's hot. Hope you are OK. You can share this letter with Sunny if you like. I hope my scooter is under cover. If the corporal catches me sitting down, I'll have to shovel coal, or peel spuds.

Bye for now,

Rod

PS Already got a nickname – Gibbo.

* * *

'Rod!' Sunny exclaimed when Chrissie showed her the letter when it arrived. 'Mrs Gibson doesn't like his name shortened!'

'I like it,' Chrissie said firmly. 'Better than Gibbo – that's *awful!*' She looked thoughtfully at Sunny. 'Have you heard from Alec?'

'No, I expect he's too busy to write,' Sunny said defensively.

They were alone in the kitchen as Sunny was keeping her promise and ironing a pile of freshly laundered clothes.

'Do you mind, you know,' Chrissie said slowly, 'Rod and me together?'

'Of course not. You've got my blessing, both of you! But you could have said something before.'

'The thing is, I'm not sure he's the one for me either, Sunny . . .'

'Oh. And I can't be sure if there's anything for me to look forward to with Alec. He won't let on.'

'It's seems we're in the same boat,' Chrissie said ruefully. 'But, at least we're still best friends!'

They linked their little fingers and chorused: 'Friends forever!'

'Well, there are other fish in the sea, eh? 'Chrissie said, pointing at the ceiling. 'Four eligible men upstairs.'

'Three. Imran is married. The others are younger but they're always either sleeping or studying when they are here. They're even quieter than the old tenants, Nan says. We hardly hear a dicky bird from them. Imran told us that the two who share the other room hope to transfer to a London teaching hospital for further training, after Christmas. Will you help me fold this sheet up, Chrissie, please? Nan said to just press the folded sides, not iron the whole thing.'

'I do my own washing now,' Chrissie said complacently, taking one end of the sheet. 'Well, just undies. Mum won £50 on the Pools last week. She's been doing them for years and it's the first time she's struck lucky! Anyway, she went out and bought a twin tub washing machine. It's marvellous. But Auntie Beryl said to wash lingerie, that's what she calls it, by hand with soap flakes, and dry it flat on a thick towel. She wears camiknickers. Mum says they aren't decent.'

'A washing machine is just what Nan could've done with in the Mother and Baby Home days,' Sunny said. 'The spin dryer has gone a bit haywire; it dances all over the floor if you don't pack the washing in properly.' She unplugged the iron. 'There, hope that pile satisfies her,' she said, admiring her work.

Nan heard this as she came into the kitchen. 'Now I've got my pension, I might buy a washing machine like your mum, Chrissie, but possibly on hire purchase; there's no stigma to that nowadays! The spin dryer has had its day. Well, clear the decks. Are you here for supper, Chrissie?'

She shook her head. 'I'd better get off home. Mum was making a steak and kidney pie. I just came to show Sunny the note – you can hardly call it a letter – Rodney sent me.' She sighed. Then added: 'Absence doesn't make the heart grow fonder, does it?'

'I wouldn't know,' Nan said. She sighed in turn. 'You girls are getting too interested in romance. You're young and you need to have a fling – don't they call it that? – before you're old and grey like me.'

'I'll tell Mum you said that. She reminds me every so often not to get up to what Auntie Beryl apparently did when she was my age. I don't know what she means,' Chrissie said, too innocently.

Sunny said, 'I bet you're crossing your fingers behind your back because you *do* know!'

*　*　*

'Patsy is a quick learner,' Mr Rowland told Sunny on Saturday morning when Patsy was busy printing off some cards for a client. Sunny was designing a Christmas card at the table. 'We must get busy with these cards,' she'd reminded Mr Rowland earlier that morning and he'd said she should go and think up some new designs.

Sunny was wishing she'd gone to art school. *I love drawing but I don't get enough time at it*, she thought to herself.

'Fifty cards ready,' Patsy said triumphantly. Mr Rowland studied the top one of the pile. 'Thank you, Patsy; these are the right size for delivering by hand, or posting through a letterbox, that's good. This will interest you, Sunny,' he said, passing the card over.

*Local artist offers to share her expertise
on Friday evenings in her studio. Drawing
with pencil or ink, painting techniques,
still-life, etc. Materials supplied at low cost.
Fee: five shillings a session. 7-9 p.m.
Contact Helena Brooke on this number.*

'Five shillings,' Sunny said thoughtfully. *Can I afford that?* she wondered.

'I know Miss Brooke; she used to teach at the art college. Don't worry, I will regard it as part of your training, Sunny, and I'll pay the fees; you would just need to pay for the materials. Well, what do you say?'

'Thank you, Mr Rowland, if you are sure you can afford it?'

He smiled. 'It will be a good investment.' Pilchie was draped around Mr Rowland's shoulders, purring loudly. He had a sudden idea: 'Why don't I take some pictures of the cat, and produce a calendar for next year – you and Patsy could be in it, too, if you like, and maybe Patsy's boys . . .'

'Oh, Mr Rowland, they'd love that, specially as they would get to play with Pilchie!' Patsy said, sitting back now she'd finished her task. She looked at the pile of cards with satisfaction.

'Pilchie'll be a star, I know,' Sunny said. She thought, *lots of nice things are happening today; I wish Alec was here to share in the fun and come up with even more bright ideas.*

Mr Rowland was thinking the same. He looked at Sunny as he remarked, 'I miss Alec, especially at this time of year. Probably won't see him until spring now. He'll be back in Paris with his friends at the jazz club this Christmas.'

Nan was excited about the art classes as well. 'Why don't you ask Chrissie to go with you?' *Dark nights*, she thought, *at this time of year. Safer for two girls together.*

'Mr Rowland is going to contact Miss Brooke and tell her about me,' Sunny said. 'Chrissie might say she can't draw a straight line. Art is not something she's interested in, I don't think. Anyway, if the studio is in Croydon, I can always get a bus there and back.'

* * *

Sunny was having a busy morning with telephone calls in the office that Saturday morning. Mr Rowland, meanwhile, was clicking his Polaroid at Pilchie, who was playing around with Davey and Roy, whom Patsy had brought along for the calendar shoot, while she took the opportunity to go shopping for the weekend groceries.

'Hi, Chrissie. We're very busy this morning,' Sunny told her friend when she phoned.

'Well, I'm busy in the bakery as well, so this is just a quick call. I just had to tell you that I had a letter from the bank today. The girl they employed as a clerk has decided to go to college and train to be a teacher after all. They are offering the post to me! I start the week before Christmas. Mum is more excited than I am, I think!'

'Congratulations, Chrissie – what good news! We ought to go out somewhere tonight and celebrate. You can choose where.'

Mr Rowland remarked, 'Good news? You're smiling. Come and join in the fun, Sunny, and ignore the phone.' Pilchie had climbed the Christmas tree and now perched beside the fairy. The cat was already covered in strands of tinsel which she'd dislodged and had enjoyed batting at the sparkling glass Christmas balls with her paws on her way to the top. The little boys were egging her on.

'I've got some good pictures, I think,' Mr Rowland said, 'but I could do with some help.'

'Time for a refreshment break first,' Sunny said. 'I'd love to get a picture of you with Pilchie draped round your neck,' she added.

'I'll show you how to handle the camera,' he offered. 'But I'd rather be in disguise, in my Father Christmas outfit!'

'Mummy's back!' Davey called.

Patsy surveyed the tinsel-strewn floor, put her shopping down on the desk, and went to fetch the dustpan and brush. She didn't tell her boys off because she could see they'd had a wonderful time while she was out. She said to herself, *best thing I ever did, coming to work here with such nice people.*

TEN

Sunny and Chrissie decided on the Orchid Ballroom in Purley to celebrate Chrissie's new job, and Mrs Ford and Nan insisted on sharing the cost of a taxi home. This was fortuitous; it cost five shillings to dance at such a prestigious dancehall. There was a real orchestra playing, but on this occasion, not the Ted Heath Big Band or the Joe Loss Orchestra, who were the most popular music makers at the time. Victor Sylvester, too, was billed there on occasion, but then, 'We can hear *him* whenever we play one of his *Learn to Dance* records,' Sunny said.

They found two vacant seats and sat down carefully because they were both wearing new circular cotton skirts, which Nan and Chrissie's mum had made, spending a couple of afternoons together using Nan's sewing machine. Sunny's skirt was bright blue, and Chrissie's was ruby red. The girls were thrilled with the results. Their white muslin blouses from C & A could be adjusted off the shoulder, but neither had dared to do this so far.

The girls chatted to each other, pretending they were not looking for partners. 'We could have done with Rodney, squishy sandals and all,' Sunny whispered to Chrissie.

'We would have had to share him, you mean!' Chrissie replied.

However, it wasn't long before they were approached by a couple of smartly dressed young men, wearing cravats, which were allowed in lieu of ties, and black patent leather dancing shoes. The boys had been eyeing them from a distance and now asked in unison, 'May I have the pleasure of this dance?'

Sunny's partner was very tall and smelled pleasantly of after-shave lotion. She enjoyed being whirled round and lifted off her feet when the pace quickened for the quickstep.

They found themselves dancing the evening away, and then, like Cinderella, it was time to depart after the last waltz.

The taxi was waiting outside, as prearranged. The driver one of Mr Ford's friends. Chrissie was in charge of the fare and they giggled all the way. Chrissie was dropped off first. It was well after midnight but, like Sunny, she now had her own front door key.

A few minutes later, Sunny was delivered to the Mother and Baby Home. She tiptoed along the drive and cautiously inserted her key in the lock. Fortunately, she thought, Nan had gone to bed, but, as she'd promised, she called: 'Nan,

I'm back!' No answer so Sunny hung her jacket in the hall and was just wondering whether to go and make a cup of tea in the kitchen when the front door opened again.

'Hello, I thought you might be a burglar.' The newcomer sounded amused. 'I saw your shadow through the frosted glass in the door.'

Sunny spun round and put her finger to her lips. 'Shush. I've been dancing . . . '

'And I've been on the wards all evening,' he said. 'I'm Ravi, Imran's friend.'

'I've met you before,' she said. 'Goodnight. I'm about to have a cup of tea . . .'

'Just what I could do with,' he said, smiling. 'We drink a lot of tea in Ceylon. No milk, but plenty of sugar.' Like Imran, he spoke perfect English.

'All right, follow me, but don't turn the light up in the hall,' she cautioned.

The kettle was still hot, so she moved it back on to the hob, and then saw the note on the table.

Hope you had a good time. Have a piece of treacle tart! Love Nan

Sunny put out another cup and saucer on the table and sliced the tart in two. She offered a piece to Ravi.

'I'm always hungry,' he said. 'Often miss a meal; always on call at the hospital.'

He's very handsome, Sunny thought, *and there's something about him; I believe I've made a new friend. I feel at ease with him. He obviously takes care of his hands, like Alec. I suppose because he is a doctor. With his dark eyes and straight, black hair, I think Chrissie would like him. Maybe I'll introduce them. But what about Rodney?*

Ravi smiled at her, and she exclaimed involuntarily, 'You've got a good set of teeth!'

He laughed out loud then and said, 'We don't eat treacle tart at home! But I must tell you, I really like it!'

The kitchen door opened, and Nan stood there, in dressing gown and slippers. She had a chiffon scarf over her hair rollers. 'I wondered what was going on,' she said, but she didn't sound cross. 'Did you enjoy your night out, Sunny?'

'Yes, Nan, I did,' Sunny said. She took the cups to the sink and rinsed them.

'Are you off to bed now?' Nan looked at Ravi.

'I apologise for disturbing you, Miss Cato,' he said. 'Goodnight to you both, and thank you for the tea and treacle tart, Sunny.'

'Goodnight,' Nan said. 'Hurry up, Sunny. Fortunately, we can have a lie-in tomorrow as it's Sunday.'

'I am on the morning rota tomorrow,' Ravi said ruefully, as he began to climb the stairs.

*   *   *

They were busy at the Rowland Printing Press the following week. The photographs had been sorted and the calendar was taking shape. It was already December, and this was a Christmas gift that would be in use throughout the following year. It would make a keepsake too.

'We'll do a run of fifty, and see how they sell,' Mr Rowland decided.

Within two days they were busy printing more. Patsy soon became expert at putting them together. Another winner, like the *Sunny Smile* picture, they thought hopefully. Pilchie was curled round Mr Rowland's shoulders as usual and they could hear her rattling purr. 'She knows she's a star,' Sunny said, tickling the cat under her chin.

Mr Rowland said, 'I'll send Alec a calendar from us, shall I? You can both sign it. I'll ring round a date or two he ought to remember . . .' *Sunny's birthday for one,* he thought.

Sunny offered to go to the bank during her lunch break, with a bag full of cash to be deposited from the Great Calendar Sale, as Mr Rowland called it. She also hoped to get a glimpse of her friend and if they had a chance to talk, to ask what plans she had for their next weekend outing. As she entered the bank, she saw the cashiers were all busy, with customers queuing, some rather impatiently, moving slowly along to the next available bank clerk.

To Sunny's disappointment, Chrissie was nowhere to be seen. Sunny guessed she must be in the office behind the firmly closed door at the rear. She moved along with the queue. *I don't think I'd like to work here,* she thought, *it's not creative like my job. I'm looking forward to the art course tonight, too.*

When at last it was her turn and she passed the heavy money bag over the counter, the pale-faced girl on the other side smiled at Sunny and said: 'You're Rodney's friend, aren't you? Have you heard how he's getting on in the army?'

'I haven't heard personally,' Sunny replied cautiously, thinking the cashier might have asked Chrissie that question. But then, perhaps the other members of staff weren't aware Chrissie was Rodney's friend too. Sunny added, 'He seems to be settling down all right, but I think he'd rather be back here.'

She was not aware that Chrissie, who was actually eating her lunch in the staff room, was at that moment reading a letter from Rodney, that she'd not had time to open before she left for work.

It was longer than the brief note that was all she had received thus far.

Dear Chrissie,

I have had time to think about you and me, and I realise I can't expect you not to go out and enjoy yourself now you have a steady job at the bank. I was glad to hear that from Mum. I did have the feeling when we said goodbye under the tree in The Grove that you were not too sure about you and me. Well, I must admit it is the same for me. When Sunny rejected me, I turned to you. Chrissie, you will always be my good friend, too, but I don't have time for romance now I'm in the army. It's a hard life, but I must make the most of it. They tell me because I passed well in my exams, I have a good chance of a commission later when I am with the Pay Corps.

Please understand, and I look forward to seeing you and Sunny again at Christmas. I have forty-eight hours' leave!

Cheers!

Rod

Chrissie crumpled the letter, then smoothed it back out and folded it before tucking it away in her handbag. She felt a mixture of disappointment and relief. 'Plenty more fish in the sea,' she said aloud, and the male clerk, who was sitting at the table with his sandwiches, looked up and smiled. He said, 'Are you referring to me?'

She'd learned a few tricks from Auntie Beryl. 'I might be,' she said boldly, 'but then again, I might not.'

* * *

Sunny took a deep breath before she pressed the bell on the studio door. There were no shuffling footsteps before Miss Brooke opened the door and said, 'How nice to meet you, follow me!' She had an attractive husky voice, but didn't look at all as Sunny had imagined her. The artist's auburn hair was twisted into a top-knot, her eyes were accentuated with blue eye shadow and mascara and her lips were pillarbox-red, like her fingernails. She was a small woman wearing a paint-smeared smock, with, as Sunny observed, when following her down the hallway into the studio, black fish net stockings and ballet slippers. Sunny took to her immediately. *She's an eccentric, like Mr Rowland*, she thought.

The studio was crowded with colour. Canvases were stacked against one wall, there were two easels, one displaying a half-painted picture, jars crammed with paint brushes, half-squeezed oil paints in an open box by an artist's palette on a long table, pencils, charcoal, a box of watercolour paints, a jug of water, rolls of paper, and a whiff of turpentine; used to clean the brushes, Sunny supposed. She also noted the low chair, covered in emerald-green velvet and with a shawl folded on the seat, that sat in front of the French windows, curtained to match. Miss Brooke indicated it and said, 'A good place to pose for a painting. It's too dark to look out into the garden, not much to see anyway this time of year.' She pointed to a long sofa against the other wall, 'Sit down and tell me about yourself; I'll give the fire a poke, and warm the room up.'

Sunny was given a small sketchbook and encouraged to draw what her mentor suggested, 'A friend' with a few strokes of a 3B pencil. Sunny sketched her lovable employer, Mr Rowland.

Miss Brooke smiled; she obviously recognised the subject. 'It's Alexander,' she stated.

'Alexander?'

'Mr Rowland. His grandson was named after him, but his mother preferred him to be called Alec. You've met Alec, I presume?'

'Yes, I have,' Sunny said simply. She had the strange feeling that Miss Brooke could read her thoughts. She added, 'He's studying music at Cambridge.'

'Musical like his mother,' Miss Brooke said. 'Eleanor and I have been friends since our schooldays. I was a few years older and looked out for her when she was a new girl. My parents worked abroad, and I often spent the summer holidays and Christmas with her in Shirley. Alexander's wife was alive then.' She paused, and then carried on. 'She was a difficult woman, who thought she had married below her station, as they say. He was always unassuming, never reached his full potential, I think.'

'I believe he has now – business is looking up. It's never too late, Nan says . . .'

'And who is Nan?'

'My mother. She adopted me as a baby.'

'Ah . . . well, I can tell from that little sketch you have the potential to progress in art, Sunny.'

'I don't suppose I'll become a great artist though,' Sunny said. 'Mr Rowland encourages me to try, because he would have liked to have studied art himself, I think.'

'Not many of us do achieve greatness – but always follow your dreams, my dear.'

Like Mr Rowland, Sunny thought. *He believes in me, I know.*

*   *   *

'All the post is for Ravi today, some from overseas,' Nan observed, scooping it up. 'He was on duty last night at the hospital, so is no doubt asleep in his bed now, and Imran left for work earlier. I'll leave these on the hall table, eh?'

'Perhaps it's his birthday,' Sunny said, yawning. *I must get a move on or I'll miss the bus*, she thought. She was glad that it was Saturday morning and she was only working a half-day.

When she arrived home at lunchtime, to mugs of hot Bovril and cheese sandwiches, Nan said, 'Ravi asked me just before you came home if he might cook a special dinner for us tonight – a curry. You guessed right, Sunny, it *is* his birthday. His twenty-fifth, he told me. He said he would go shopping for the extra ingredients when he had recovered after last night; apparently they were busy with an emergency admission.'

'Oh, I was about to say that Chrissie is coming round this evening. I said I thought it would be all right if she stayed for supper. She is working at the bank all day.'

'I'm sure there will be enough for one more,' Nan said. She added ruefully, 'I have never cooked a curry dish myself, of course.'

'I hope we like it,' Sunny said, 'I've heard it's an acquired taste. Chrissie did say she'd been to an Indian restaurant with her Auntie Beryl and the food was very hot with lots of spices. They had mango chutney with it.'

'I'll open a tin of peaches and one of Nestlé's cream,' Nan decided. 'To cool us down!'

'Hope you don't mind us watching you,' Sunny said, as she and Chrissie laid the table, and Ravi, looking relaxed in casual dress of slacks, open-necked shirt and a colourful waistcoat, attended to the bubbling pans on the stove. He shook his head; too busy at that moment to talk. Nan wisely kept out of the way as she didn't want to appear to interfere; he'd turned down the offer of an apron and had tucked a tea towel round his middle.

'This is fish curry,' Ravi said after a while. 'Please, could one of you dab my eyes; chopping garlic, red chillis and onions always makes them water. My hands are covered in the juices!'

'I'll do it,' Chrissie offered quickly. She'd let her hair down today and it hung, black and shining, almost to her waist. She gently wiped Ravi's streaming eyes with a clean towel, and he focused on her face, so close to his own, aware that her dark eyes mirrored his. A strand of her hair brushed his face, and she tucked it quickly behind one ear. Ravi smiled and murmured, 'You would make a good nurse; you have a soft touch. You remind me of my sisters back home. They have long hair too.'

She moved away, feeling embarrassed by an unexpectedly intimate moment. 'I'm a bank clerk,' she stated. 'And *my* eyes are watering now – but the curry smells good!'

Observing them together, even briefly, Sunny was reminded of her first meeting with Alec in the alley leading to the Rowland Printing Press. She thought: *I know you can fall in love at first sight even though I didn't realise it at first; I do believe Chrissie may have found her match! Rodney will probably be relieved.*

'What did you say the fish was?' she asked Ravi.

'Tuna – you could call it our national fish. Haven't you tried it before?'

'No, I've seen tins of it, but Nan sticks to pink salmon. Can I help too?'

'If you really want to. Could you slice these tomatoes for me, please?'

'Of course I can!' Sunny smiled.

'I'm going to watch and see what happens next,' Chrissie said. She had a sudden thought and taking out a small diary from her shoulder bag, which was slung over the back of her chair, she flicked to the note pages at the back. 'What spices are you using?'

'I'll call them out to you,' Sunny offered. 'Paprika, cumin, oh, and peppercorns; and Ravi has already sprinkled the fish with salt and turmeric.'

'Just a couple of teaspoons of each,' Ravi added. 'You forgot coriander powder, Sunny, and curry leaves. It wouldn't be curry without those!'

Three cups of water with two tablespoons of coconut milk were then poured into the biggest pan and brought to a bubbling boil. Meanwhile, the other ingredients, including the sliced tomatoes, simmered in a second pan. These were added to the big pan, followed by the cubed fish. Then Ravi announced, 'Now, we cook it for another ten minutes, while the rice steams. Can you warm the plates please?'

'I'll do that,' Chrissie offered. 'You go and tell Nan it's ready, eh, Sunny?'

As she entered the kitchen, Nan thought privately that the smell of the curry was almost overpowering. She was glad she had remembered to buy a new bottle of Milk of Magnesia. She would need a dose afterwards, no doubt. However, she turned to the beaming young man who was ladling the curry on to the plates and said, 'What a treat!

Not too much for me, please. Sometimes my stomach plays up.'

'Thank you for allowing me to cook my birthday meal,' Ravi said, and as he passed her plate he added: 'The rice cools it down, Miss Cato!'

The girls had no qualms: they were game for second helpings.

The dessert was served, and even after that they managed to eat the small iced buns Nan had made earlier and sing 'Happy Birthday'.

After they tackled the washing-up, Chrissie exclaimed, 'It's later than I thought! I'd better go home. Thank you for the wonderful meal, Ravi.'

'Would you allow me to escort you?' he asked gallantly.

'Oh – thank you!' Chrissie said.

When they'd gone, Nan turned to Sunny and hugged her. 'I do believe you're matchmaking, Sunny.'

Sunny smiled. 'Well, you never know; but Chrissie likes him, I can tell.' She turned her head so Nan wouldn't see the sudden tears in her eyes. *If only Alec was coming home this Christmas*, she thought.

Chrissie held Ravi's arm as they walked to her home. They didn't talk much, but she found herself wondering if he would expect to kiss her goodnight, and whether her mother would open the front door before he could. In fact, the door remained closed and looking up at the bedroom window she saw the curtains were closed as well. 'They must be in bed,' she noted.

They were standing on the porch and Chrissie was fumbling for her key in her purse, when Ravi put his hands lightly on her shoulders and said softly, 'Goodnight, I hope to see you again.'

'I hope to see you, too,' she said. Then, 'Aren't you going to kiss me? Or – is it too soon?'

'No, it is not too soon at all, when you know you have met the girl you will marry. However, I promise to observe all the proprieties,' he said, before his arms closed round her. It wasn't like this in The Grove with Rodney, she thought exultantly. His breath smells of curry, but mine does too! 'I will see you after Christmas,' he promised. Then he released her and went away.

'Is that you?' Chrissie's mother called from her darkened room. Her husband was asleep, snoring gently, but Mrs Ford couldn't settle until she was sure her daughter was safely home.

The door was ajar, so Chrissie opened it a little wider and said softly, 'Yes, it's me, Mum. I had a lovely time.'

'Who brought you home?' her mother asked. Chrissie felt a little piqued. She had been looking out of the window after all, she thought.

'A friend. He cooked our dinner. He's one of the medical students Nan has taken in," she said. 'He is very respectable, Nan approves of him.'

'I was reading a magazine until Dad put the light out. It featured a lovely wedding dress . . .'

'Mum, don't get your hopes up! But he's really nice,' Chrissie told her. 'Night, night.'

'Night, night, sleep tight,' her mother said, as she had since the first night when she had tucked her new little daughter into her cot.

ELEVEN

It was Christmas Eve, 1957, and Sunny and Patsy were at work that morning tidying up the print shop, while Pilchie skittered about batting at crumpled-up paper which had missed the wastepaper basket.

'A week off,' Patsy said, 'and I've got instructions from Mum to collect the turkey from the butcher when I leave here, and to buy some new lights for the tree she got down the market, as the old ones were flickering.'

Mr Rowland overheard and said, 'Allow me to pay for those, Patsy. An extra present for the little boys. I hope they haven't been sneaking a peep into the Christmas parcels, to see if they are getting what they hoped for?' Yo-yos were all the rage this year and he'd asked Patsy her advice on what to buy for them.

''Course not,' Patsy said. She didn't seem too sure, though. *Boys will be boys*, she thought, Mr Rowland should remember that. She added: 'Any news from Alec?' She didn't look at Sunny, but Patsy guessed she would also like to know.

'Just a Christmas card; I haven't opened it yet,' he said. He produced a couple of bags and gave them one each. 'A few small gifts for the Christmas tree,' he told Patsy. 'Something edible for you and your mother to share, too.' She peeped inside the bag. 'Oh, a tin of Quality Street! Thank you, Mr Rowland,' she said.

He turned to Sunny. 'You'll have guessed you've got the same, eh? I have had a Christmas surprise myself; Eleanor is taking her aged parent to Paris for four days! Alec has arranged our accommodation. We will be nightclubbing, Eleanor says, to attend a performance by Alec and his friends. I hope they will join us for Christmas lunch in the hotel.'

Sunny managed a smile. 'I hope you have a wonderful time; give Alec my best wishes. What about Pilchie?'

'I was about to ask if she could stay with you,' he admitted. 'Along with some tins of cat food, of course. Eleanor could bring her to you later in the car. D'you think Nanette will mind?'

'Not if I take care of her, and have her in my room at nights,' she assured Mr Rowland.

As they left, Mr Rowland turned the shop sign from OPEN to CLOSED.

*   *   *

'You're very quiet, Sunny,' Nan observed after lunch. 'I hope the cat will behave herself; when are they dropping her off?'

'Sometime this afternoon,' Sunny said. 'It's going to be a quiet Christmas this year for us, Nan. The young doctors will be busy at the hospital, cheering up the patients.'

'You never know, famous last words, as they say, Sunny.'

Nan was proved right. Just after lunch, came the first knock on the door. 'Chrissie, I expect – you go, Sunny,' Nan said.

'Oh, it's *you*!' she exclaimed, as she saw who was calling.

'Aren't you going to invite me in? I travelled overnight on a crowded coach and arrived home in time for breakfast. Mum fussed over me so much, I thought I'd visit you – can't stay long, though.'

'Come in, Rodney!' She smiled to show that she was pleased to see him.

He gave her a brief hug. 'You're still a good friend, and as I told Chrissie, I don't expect more than that from either of you. Last year . . .'

'I know. Everything has changed for you since then,' she said, leading him into the kitchen. *I've grown up, too*, she thought, *but Alec doesn't seem to be aware of that.* 'Look who's here,' she said to Nan.

Nan was pleased to see Rodney too. 'You look very smart in your uniform,' she told him.

'I haven't had time to change yet,' he said. 'I'm sorry I haven't got you a present this year, Sunny, but being paid a pittance; I'm always broke.'

'Chrissie and I play your records, thanks for those. We went to the Orchid Ballroom recently and we weren't wall-flowers as I feared!'

'I haven't been dancing since I left home,' he said rue-fully. 'Well, Mum said not to be long, so I must go. Happy Christmas and a have great New Year!' With a brief hug he departed. Sunny and Nan were back to washing the dishes, when there was another knock on the door.

'I'll go,' Sunny offered, for she knew Nan didn't like to be caught out in her apron with her hands in soapy water in the sink. 'Probably Mrs Dixon with Pilchie,' she said.

She hurried along the hall, opened the door, saw a couple standing there, and as she looked into the woman's face she realised immediately who it was. She was accompanied by a tall man, who removed his hat, and gave his companion a little nudge forward.

'Serena?' Sunny asked tentatively. *Am I dreaming*, she asked herself.

'Yes; and this is Jan. May we come in?'

As Sunny moved back to allow them to step inside, Nan called out, 'Who is it?' as she came through from the kitchen. She gasped and put a hand to her mouth as she recognised Serena, who, like Sunny, was not very tall though a much rounder shape, and wore her hair in a neat coil at the nape of her neck, just as she had in 1940.

Her companion appeared to be European, with short blond hair and blue eyes. Nan said involuntarily when she looked at him, 'You look like . . .' She recalled the one picture she had seen of Sunny's father. Serena had taken this with her when she left the Mother and Baby Home.

'My brother, Nils?' he suggested. 'Sunny's father.'

Nan nodded.

'I am Jan Novak and Serena is now Mrs Novak,' he said.

Nan opened the drawing room door and waved them through. 'Please come in here, the chairs are more comfortable than in the kitchen.' Sunny said nothing as she followed them into the room. Nan had lit the fire first thing, for they would spend time in there over Christmas.

'Is this a short visit? I'm afraid we've had lunch, but would you like a mince pie and a cup of tea or coffee?' Nan asked. 'It's cold enough to snow, I think,' she added, as they sat on the chairs either side of the crackling fire.

Jan spoke for both him and Serena. 'That is very kind of you, thank you.'

Nan busied herself in the kitchen to give Sunny time with the visitors.

Serena spoke directly to Sunny. 'I am so pleased to meet you at last. Did you get the letter we sent advising you of our arrival? We posted it yesterday.'

'No . . .' Sunny said. She realised they were still wearing their outdoor clothes. 'I'm sorry, please give me your coats and I'll hang them on the stand in the hall. Otherwise you won't feel the benefit of them when you leave later. Are you staying in the area?'

'We rather hoped,' Serena said slowly, 'we would be welcome here over Christmas. I have never forgotten my time in the Mother and Baby Home. But I realise you are not prepared for visitors. Perhaps Nan can recommend a place where we might stay, so that we can visit and spend some time with you.'

'Did you send me a card for my birthday? It wasn't signed, but it had a London postmark,' Sunny asked.

Jan answered. 'It was from me. I work in the motor industry. I am a designer. My head office is in the City. Nils encouraged me in my interest in engines. You would be puzzled, I thought, if you saw a name you didn't know, but I thought Nanette might guess.'

'She didn't say,' Sunny said. Just then, Nan appeared with the kitchen trolley, loaded with a steaming coffee pot, a teapot, cups and saucers, a jug of milk and a bowl of sugar, as well as a cake stand with mince pies and short-bread biscuits on it.

Sunny had not imagined that meeting her mother for the first time in seventeen years would be like this. No hugs or tears, just polite conversation. Nan tried her best, and said immediately that the unexpected guests were welcome to join them for Christmas. 'We have lodgers in the upper part of the house, where the mothers and babies used to be.

You can have my room and I will share with Sunny and a visiting cat who is joining us this afternoon.'

'Thank you,' Serena said. She looked at Jan, as if needing encouragement; he nodded his head. She continued, 'Perhaps I should tell you what happened after I left the Mother and Baby Home all those years ago? I returned to Trinidad at the end of the war and have been sister in charge of the maternity ward in the hospital there for the past ten years. Jan discovered my whereabouts after years of wondering where I was when he found out about my connection with his brother. He's visited me the past two summers. We . . .' She looked at Jan.

He responded: 'We were married over here in August and Serena now shares my bachelor flat. We decided to catch up with the past and meet her daughter; and my niece. Serena has spoken about you a lot, Sunny. Thank you for making us welcome.' A pause, and then he added quietly, 'I was seventeen when I last saw my brother at our home in Warsaw in 1939. He was twenty. He asked me to take care of my mother before he came to England. Later, I had to escape as well. Warsaw was occupied by enemy troops and my mother told me to take my chance and come to England. We never saw each other again. I am now a British citizen.' He paused, swallowed hard and continued, 'I heard that my brother had died in action in 1940 and a baby was born just after that, and eventually I learned that Serena had returned to Trinidad.'

Nan looked at Serena. 'Is there another reason that prompted you to come to the Mother and Baby Home now, my dear?'

Serena clutched her husband's hand and looked at Nan. 'You can tell – can't you? I am pregnant. I'm thirty-eight years old and Jan is thirty-five. This might be our last chance to be parents. I said to Jan as soon as I found out that we must go to the Mother and Baby Home and ask Nan to take care of me when the time comes. I should have realised it would be a shock for you both.'

They were all startled by the knock on the front door. Sunny, who'd said nothing during the story, went to see who was calling. Mrs Dixon stood on the front step, cat basket in hand. 'I thought you must be out when you didn't answer straight away. My father is in the car, look, he is waving to you. There are tins of cat food is in this bag. Sorry, can't stop, we've a plane to catch.'

Pilchie gave a plaintive mew and Mrs Dixon handed Sunny a folded one-pound note. 'For milk and anything else you might want. You will need to escort the cat in the garden in the evening after dark. Oh.' She produced a crumpled envelope from her pocket. 'Father said this is for you, from Alec. Happy Christmas!' and she went back to the car.

Sunny watched as they drove off. She didn't go back into the drawing room, but carried Pilchie in the basket, and the other things she had been given, into her bedroom.

She closed the door and sat on the bed. Tears coursed down her cheeks as she opened the envelope addressed simply 'To Sunny'. She read the few lines written in pencil:

Dear Sunny,

Sorry I haven't been in touch before, but I didn't know what to say.

I think of you often. We will meet again, I promise you.

Meanwhile, enjoy Christmas and have fun, as I will, I hope.

Alec

She screwed the paper into a ball, and then smoothed it out. The door opened and Nan stood there. 'Oh, here you are. Is it all too much for you, Serena turning up like this?'

'She's obviously happy to be having another baby after all this time; but she didn't take much notice of me,' Sunny said with a sob.

Nan came in, closing the door behind her. Pilchie was mewing to be released from her basket. 'She says you are my daughter and she hasn't come to take you away from me—'

'Good! Because I wouldn't go, you know that, Nan!'

Nan said softly, 'Thank you. That means everything to me. But I think she'd like to get to know you, to be your friend. So would your Uncle Jan.'

'I can't call him Uncle. I don't know him. He doesn't look old enough anyway! And I won't call Serena "Mum".'

'She doesn't expect you to. Now let that poor cat out of the basket. Dry your eyes, and where's that sunny smile?' Nan said.

Sunny allowed the cat to curl round and be carried on her shoulders as Mr Rowland did. Jan was not in the drawing room, Nan explained, because he was unloading the car and bringing their bags into her bedroom. 'I must help with that,' she said. 'You and Serena need to talk.'

Sunny left Nan and made her way reluctantly into the drawing room and sat down. For some time, nothing was said. Then Serena looked at Sunny and almost whispered, 'Can you forgive me for leaving you soon after you were born?'

'There is nothing to forgive. It was wartime; I can only imagine how it was for young people then. I've had a happy, secure life with Nan. I think of her, of course, as my mother,' Sunny said firmly.

'You must understand, I was grieving for my lost love. We planned to marry, you know, but I lost him before you were born, and I couldn't cope as a single mother; I was committed to returning to my work at the hospital. You know the rest. I have always thought of you, over the years, but I knew you would have a proper childhood and lots of love from Nan, and I couldn't give you that. I see your father in you, and I see myself too. How Nils would have loved you! Jan is very like him, I think.'

Pilchie decided to introduce herself to the visitor. She slithered down from Sunny's shoulder and then managed a wobbly leap on to Serena's lap. She began to purr. Serena smiled. 'Oh, we are friends, it seems!' She looked up at Sunny. 'Can we be friends too?'

'I – I believe we can,' Sunny said. *If Pilchie approves of Serena, well, I can, too*, she thought.

'Jan helped me change the bed linen,' Nan said later to Serena. 'Why don't you go in the bedroom and have a short rest before I rustle up some supper? You look tired.'

'I would like to help you to get things ready for Christmas Day,' Serena told her.

'Well, if you could peel potatoes, or trim sprouts, I would be grateful. I have the turkey, that I will cook slowly overnight, to prepare for the oven. I had been thinking I should have chosen a smaller one as we would likely be eating it all week, so it's good we have extra mouths now. The pudding can wait its turn on the stove until the morning. I've done all the baking already.'

'I have things to sort out later on,' Sunny said. She exchanged looks with Nan. 'I need to pop along to Gibson's before they close at five.'

The Christmas tree stood in a corner, trimmed with tinsel and lights, which didn't work but were pretty ornaments. Parcels were piled round the base of the tree on the small round table. The holly, ivy and mistletoe adorned the beams in the kitchen as usual. Sunny thought, *Rodney won't be here to kiss me under the mistletoe this year – nor . . .* But she mustn't think about Alec, or she might cry again.

'Good idea,' Nan said. 'I'll scribble a quick list for you, eh?' She always had her handbag close by and she opened it and extracted her purse. 'Enough change in there I think to cover everything.' She wrote in pencil on the back of an envelope which had contained a Christmas card: *Suggest chocolates? A couple of small gifts too, please.*

Sunny was glad to be out of the house for a short while, even though it was a cold, dark and dismal afternoon. She was wearing her new cherry-red winter coat from C & A, which had a hood; Mr Rowland had said, 'You look like Little Red Riding Hood, Sunny,' when she had worn it for the first time to work that morning. *How can things change so much in a single day?* she wondered.

She entered the shop and saw Rodney behind the counter. 'Didn't expect to see you again,' he told her. 'Mum and Dad are worn out. They've been on their feet all day. I said I'd tidy up in here and close up.' He could tell from her expression that she was upset, as mutely she handed him her short list. 'What's up?' he asked.

'My birth mother, Serena, has turned up unexpectedly. Nan has asked her to stay with us over Christmas – her husband too. Apparently, he – he's my uncle – my father's brother. It's all a bit of a shock . . .'

Rodney came around the counter. 'I suppose it is. Are the chocolates for them?'

She nodded. 'Sorry – I need a shoulder to cry on,' she said.

He gave her a brief hug. 'You can rely on me when I'm around,' he said awkwardly.

'Thanks, Rod,' she managed.

'Are you seeing . . . you know, Alec, isn't it, this Christmas?'

She shook her head. 'No, I'm not,' she said flatly. 'But it's just as well, with unexpected visitors to cope with.'

'You're lucky, last box of Milk Tray, and two propelling pencils – popular this year, Mum said, but they won't sell in holly-patterned boxes after Christmas! Mum marked them down from ten shillings to seven and sixpence. Will those do?'

'Thank you,' she said. 'I hope I see you again before you go back to the barracks.'

'Mum's got the two days all planned,' he said. 'And you'll be too busy I guess.' He, too, had been recalling last Christmas. So much had changed since then, he thought, but he was glad that he, Sunny and Chrissie were still good friends.

TWELVE

Nan was still sound asleep at five o'clock on Christmas morning, as she had Sunny's comfortable single bed. Sunny, meanwhile, had tossed and turned all night on the old Victorian day bed, in the sleeping bag she'd only used once before when on a trip to the New Forest with the Youth Club. She hadn't had much sleep then either because of the rustlings of wild life in the undergrowth.

Pilchie had refused to sleep in the cat basket and ignored her improvised bed in the scullery off the kitchen – a cardboard box with an old jumper to keep her warm – and her plaintive mewing in the early hours had woken Sunny just when she'd finally got to sleep. She'd gone to find out what the matter was and scooped the cat up scolding her mildly, 'Oh, I suppose I'll have to take you back to my room with me. Nan will disapprove, but what else can I do?' So Pilchie spent the next hour or two at the bottom of Sunny's bed. Sunny had also brought the emergency 'thunder box' as Nan referred to it, just in case. She didn't want to venture outside in the cold when it was still dark.

Nan had woken up: 'Put that box on the far side of your bed, mind,' she said. 'Now, perhaps I can get back to sleep. Don't wish me a happy Christmas yet please.' Fortunately, the visitors were evidently still enjoying the comfort of her double bed and feather mattress, she thought ruefully.

Later, yawning, Sunny pottered about in the kitchen, making up the stove, moving the kettle onto the hob, warming the teapot, setting out two trays of cups and saucers and putting the rest of the packet of shortbread biscuits on a plate. She also turned up the heat on the oven for the turkey.

She didn't hear the door open, when Jan, clad in Nan's old robe, which he'd found hanging on the hook on the bedroom door, padded in on his bare feet. He saw the slight figure bent over the trays, pouring tea into the cups. Sunny was wearing her kimono, her present from Nan the previous Christmas, but she had not brushed her hair and it framed her face. Looking up, she said, 'I was just going to bring you both a cup of tea and wish you a happy Christmas.' Pilchie went over to greet Jan, purring and rubbing her face around his ankles.

He bent over to stroke her. 'That's enough, I think; you are tickling my feet,' he told Pilchie.

'Is – is Serena awake?' Sunny asked him.

'No, she had a restless night. I will take the tray intended for us, if I may.'

'Of course.' Sunny passed it to him. 'Pilchie and I will see if Nan is stirring.' Belatedly, she called after his retreating figure, 'Bathroom's free; breakfast at eight, I hope.'

At the breakfast table Nan noticed Serena looked wan; hopefully, they might be able to have a private chat later on, she thought. Serena was wearing a red woollen dress with a white collar and cuffs that looked Christmassy. When she was handed a bowl containing half a pink grapefruit, carefully cut into segments, and glistening with sugar crystals, she exclaimed, 'Oh, this must have come from Trinidad! So sweet and juicy and just what I fancy! I'm not too sure about a fried breakfast to follow though.'

'Don't worry, I can boil you an egg, or make toast, if you would prefer that,' Nan said. She added, 'The grapefruit will become a family tradition for Christmas, I think. Yes, they are from Trinidad.'

Sunny put in, 'I bought them in Surrey Street Market for the first time last year.'

'Like you,' Jan said, 'I have become a fan of the pink grapefruit!' He smiled at Sunny.

He still seems too young to be an uncle, she thought, *but he's the one who can tell me about his brother, my father, when they were in Poland.*

It was nice to have a man around to chop wood and get the fire going in the drawing room, where they would open their presents later. The young doctors were still busy at the hospital and not aware of the unexpected visitors at the Mother and Baby Home.

Serena said, 'Please let me help! I can wash up . . .'

'Rest up while you have the chance,' Nan advised. 'The first three months are always uncertain, and it's a long gap since you had – your first baby. You can sit and chat to us while we are busy, of course.'

'You didn't say it's not so easy sometimes when you are older,' Serena said.

'Sit in the old rocking chair by the stove,' Sunny suggested. She fetched a cushion and placed it carefully behind Serena's back.

'Thank you.' Serena looked up at the girl bending over her and smiled.

Sunny straightened up. She had a funny feeling inside. *She's a nice person*, she thought. She became aware the cat was scratching at the back door. 'Oh, Pilchie wants to go out!'

'Put your coat on and your boots too; I just looked out of the window and I do believe it's beginning to snow,' Nan told her.

'Snow for Christmas,' Serena said. 'I remember we had lots of snow in 1940.'

Jan had returned to the kitchen, and he remarked, 'I hope the roads won't be too icy tomorrow; we must go back to Brixton then. We abandoned our intention of making the flat look more like home. I am due back at work next Monday.'

'Brixton!' Sunny exclaimed. 'You were so near to us and didn't come before.'

'I had to wait until my wife decided it was time for a family reunion,' Jan said.

'We are glad you came at last,' Nan said. 'Aren't we, Sunny?'

But Sunny was opening the door and letting a blast of cold air into the room while Pilchie was already skittering down the garden. Any reply was muffled by the scarf round her mouth.

Serena looked at Nan. 'She didn't expect any of this. Perhaps it seems like a dream to her . . .' Jan put a hand on her shoulder. 'It certainly seems like that to me,' he said simply.

Christmas dinner was a happy affair. The turkey was succulent, and the roast potatoes brown and crisp. The bright green sprouts were not overcooked, and the buttered parsnips and carrots were perfect. There were individual Yorkshire puddings, bread sauce, cranberry sauce and a good hot 'sturdy gravy' as Jan solemnly pronounced it.

There was a bottle of burgundy and two bottles of Wrights fizzy lemonade. 'We like to mix the two, but please have whatever you prefer,' Nan said.

'Just lemonade for me,' Serena requested. 'No lemonade for me,' Jan said with a grin. Jan was invited to light the brandy glistening on the top of the dark, fruity Christmas pudding, then golden custard and thick cream were added to the slices as they were handed round. Serena had a smaller portion and was the first to discover a silver threepenny bit.

'Please can I have those. They date back to my mother's time; she used the same ones every year,' Nan said, passing a little jar for the coins. 'Make a wish on the coin first!'

Sunny confessed: 'I kept mine, one year, but I didn't spend it.'

'She felt guilty. She was only seven, but she put it back in the jar in the pantry one day. I knew, but I never said; until now,' said Nan, with a knowing look.

After the plates had been cleared, Nan asked Jan if he would help with the washing-up, and he said that of course he would. Nan turned to Serena. 'Why don't you go into the drawing room with Sunny and have a chat? We'll join you later and we can have tea or coffee, whichever you prefer, and then we'll open up our presents around the tree. I see that some mysterious parcels have been added.' She smiled at Serena and Jan.

Sunny and Serena sat side by side on the settee, but a little apart from each other. Pilchie stretched out between them, purring.

Suddenly, Sunny broke the silence. 'I always wanted a little brother or sister, and Nan told me why that wasn't possible, but now – I suppose I feel part of a new family, as well. When is the baby due to arrive?'

'In June,' Serena said. 'I'm glad you are pleased about the baby.' She smiled at Sunny. 'We would like you to choose the baby's name if it's a boy. If it's a girl Jan would like to call her after his mother. Is that all right?'

'Of course it is! How about – Alexander?'

'I like that. Isn't that your employer's name?'

'Yes, it is. His grandson is called after him, but he is known as Alec.' *Why am I telling Serena all this?* Sunny wondered.

'Someone you admire?' Serena guessed.

Sunny said, 'Yes. Yes, I do. But he thinks I am too young . . .'

'Age doesn't come into it, I think. Love is love and means everything at times. I was twenty when I met your father. I don't regret what happened, I never will. I hope your love will be returned.'

'You understand.' Sunny felt choked.

'Yes, but Nan is the one who knows you best, not me. I left you, after all, and have always regretted it.'

'Thank you for saying that,' Sunny said, as they heard the rattle of the trolley outside.

It was time to open presents round the Christmas tree.

'Oh, a new copy of my favourite book,' Sunny exclaimed. '*Pride and Prejudice* – oh, and this edition has some lovely colour plates. Thank you, dear Nan.'

Nan was equally pleased with her warm scarf; she put it loosely round her neck. 'Angora wool, so soft; you shouldn't have spent so much on me, Sunny.'

'Yes, I should,' Sunny assured her, 'and, it's blue, your favourite colour, Nan.'

The tin of Quality Street was unwrapped and opened. 'From Alexander Rowland,' Nan read aloud. 'To us all, wishing us a special Christmas – and it is!' She smiled at Serena and Jan.

They opened their identical parcels. 'Sorry,' Nan began, 'bought at the last minute.'

'It doesn't matter,' Serena assured her. 'No pencil leads to sharpen and something to treasure, eh, Jan?'

'Certainly,' he agreed. 'But I think we should save the Milk Tray for later, eh?' He passed the square parcel from Serena and himself to Sunny. 'We hope you like it,' he added.

Sunny had guessed what the present might be from its size and shape, and she was right. An enlarged photograph, black and white, in a simple silver frame. A young man standing by his plane on an airfield. He had removed his flying helmet and his fair hair was ruffled. He had a boyish, smiling face, and Sunny exclaimed: 'Yes, he is like you, Jan, but younger of course.'

'He was twenty-one there,' Jan said quietly. 'I am proud he was my brother.' He reached for Serena's hand. 'Don't cry, he would be happy to see us all together now at last.'

Serena looked directly at Sunny. 'He was my hero.'

Sunny said softly, 'He will always be a hero, my father, to me as well, Serena.'

Nan's present was a purse in soft tan leather and she exclaimed, 'Just what I needed! The old one dates back to the Mother and Baby Home days. Thank you both!'

Sunny would look back on this Christmas Day and remember how special it was. The rest of the day they talked non-stop, there was so much catching up to do. *My family has expanded, I am so lucky*, Sunny thought.

*   *   *

The following morning, after breakfast, when it was time for Serena and Jan to leave, Nan embraced them in turn and told them: 'I hope you will come often, now.'

'We will, I promise,' Serena assured her. 'There's the telephone too, and I hope you will be with me when the baby is born?'

'You should let your doctor decide that, but I hope so, too.'

Jan hugged Sunny. 'When we have the flat reorganised, will you come and stay for a weekend? We have a spare bedroom.'

'Yes, I will,' Sunny said immediately.

When they had gone, Nan sighed. 'A quiet day watching the television, I think, eh, Sunny? No one else is likely to call in, are they? Our young men upstairs are not back yet.'

'Rodney's on his way to his training camp, I imagine; he should be moving on to his permanent base soon. Mrs Dixon said they'd collect Pilchie before the week-end, maybe tomorrow, and Chrissie and her family are expecting Auntie Beryl for a couple of days with them.'

'Well then, you can relax, as you are still in your pyjamas.' Nan smiled.

'I didn't have time to get dressed; they went so early! You sit down, Nan, and I'll make another pot of tea,' Sunny said. 'Let's have a lazy day!'

There was a loud knock on the front door. 'I can't go,' Sunny said, but she swung her legs down from the couch, and looked round for her slippers.

'Well, I will,' Nan sighed. Then they became aware of a persistent rapping on the window. Nan peered through the net curtains. She turned to Sunny. 'Don't worry, it's Chrissie. I'll let her in.'

Chrissie was dressed in Christmas finery, including a furry Cossack hat with matching gauntlet gloves. 'Aren't you up yet?' she asked cheerfully.

'No – but let's go in my room, and I'll get dressed,' Sunny said, after a look from Nan, which she interpreted to mean, '*Get on with it!*'

Pilchie was asleep on Sunny's bed. Nan, who'd slept there overnight while their guests were with them, had made it up, but the couch under the window was as Sunny had left it earlier.

Chrissie perched on the bed and stroked the cat, while Sunny put on her clothes. At least she'd washed earlier, she thought thankfully.

'Auntie Beryl is on her way; she's been crying down the phone to Mum and me because her man friend got blotto on Christmas Eve and she's thrown him out of her flat. She wanted to know if I was going back to London, but I said no thanks, I really enjoy being home and working in the bank. Mum said if I was going to laze around, I should come to see you,' Chrissie said complacently. 'Anyway, I'm eager to hear about your mum's visit. Mum heard about it from Rodney when she popped into the shop.'

'She's not my mum,' Sunny said quickly. 'But, yes, we got on well, and my uncle is very nice too.'

'Lucky you. And you saw Rodney?'

'Only briefly. Once at home and I had to dash down to the shop before it closed on Christmas Eve,' Sunny said, giving up on her hair and reaching for a rubber band to confine it.

'You know,' Chrissie said reflectively, 'Rodney did me a good turn rejecting me after he left home. I really like Ravi, but I'm not rushing into anything – you just get hurt if you do. I didn't fret because he was at work all over Christmas; I'm looking forward to seeing him again, though. You ought to try to cool things down with Alec.'

'Nothing to cool down,' Sunny said flatly.

'You were a lot happier when you two were just good friends,' Chrissie said candidly.

'We don't even seem to be that now.' Sunny suddenly realised how true this was.

Nan put her head round the door. 'Sounds like you girls are growing up fast,' she observed.

'Nan! You were eavesdropping!' Sunny exclaimed. Then she said, 'Don't worry, Nan, I believe we have put the world to rights this morning.'

They made their way back downstairs and to the front door. Chrissie's parting words were: 'Shall we go to the New Year's Ball at the Orchid?'

And Sunny said immediately, 'Why not? See if you can book tickets! Oh, but we'd need formal dresses!'

'I'll oil the sewing machine, shall I?' Nan said, tongue-in-cheek. 'I was content to wear my nurse's uniform at your age.' She smiled and added, 'That was me, but you are you . . .'

THIRTEEN

The following morning was grey and overcast, but not actually snowing. Sunny was trying to comb Pilchie's fur, which was bedraggled because, reluctantly, she had stepped through the patches of snow remaining on the grass.

'Don't do that in the kitchen, Sunny, most unhygienic,' Nan reminded her.

'I'm grooming her before Mrs Dixon arrives, that's all.'

'And when is that likely to be?'

'I believe they were coming back late last night.'

'Well, someone is banging on the door right now. You'd better go.'

Sunny heaved a sigh. 'I'll have to ask her in, while I put the cat in the basket,' she said over her shoulder as she went along the hall.

Alec was stamping snow off his boots on the mat when the door opened. He looked up, and smiled, taking a step back.

Sunny hesitated and then said, 'Oh, it's you. We were expecting your mother.'

He looked disconcerted. 'Aren't you going to wish me a happy Christmas?'

'No, because it's almost the New Year now.' Sunny ushered him in. She was aware that Nan was standing in the doorway of the kitchen and must have heard every word.

He obviously decided two could play this game. 'Pilchie ready to go home, is she? Well, back to Shirley anyway.' He cleared his throat. 'Grandfather said I was a coward, writing notes to you, not proper letters. He suggested I travel home with them and get on with revising for the exams I have coming up when I return to Cambridge, instead of loafing about, as he put it, in Paris with the lads.'

'Did he send you here this morning?'

Alec caught hold of Sunny's arm. 'No, it was my idea; I wanted to see you.'

'I don't believe you,' she said.

Nan called out then, 'Have you time for a cup of hot chocolate, Alec? I'm glad to see you!'

'Thank you,' he said. 'Sunny obviously doesn't agree . . . '

Sunny turned her face away. *Don't cry*, she told herself. *He deserves this.* 'Pilchie is in my room, we can talk there if you want to.'

'Good idea,' Nan said and closed the kitchen door.

The cat was curled up asleep on Sunny's bed. Sunny and Alec sat side by side on the old couch, though she made sure there was a gap between them.

He looked out of the window. 'Snow hasn't vanished yet.' Then he turned to her and said, 'This is ridiculous, Sunny; I'd much rather have you weeping in my arms than telling me off, even though it's what I deserve.'

She couldn't help it; she was trying hard to hold the tears back. 'Oh, Alec, it's so unfair. You asked me to wait, but you won't graduate for another two years, and you don't write to me, or think of me.'

'That's not true,' he said. 'I do think of you. I have two loves in my life. My music ... and you, Sunny.' Then he added sadly, 'But I know now you are not prepared to wait ...'

'I could, if we were in touch more.'

He drew her, unresisting, into his embrace. 'Will you allow me to kiss you better?' he asked softly.

It was nothing like the brotherly kiss she recalled from the time in the car last summer. This was a grown-up kiss she thought exultantly, full of passion and promise. She suddenly realised that they had slipped into a reclining position on the hard couch and that he'd shifted a cushion under her head. *What has he got in mind next*, she thought.

Sunny was relieved when she heard Nan's footsteps along the hall, followed by a discreet tap on the door. 'Hot chocolate is ready! Have you sorted out your differences?' she called.

Alec grinned, as he did in the old days in the Rowland Printing Press. He sat up, and so did Sunny. He called back: 'Can we have it in here, please? I need to reassure Sunny; we've not quite finished talking yet.'

'Well, I brought the mugs on a tray, thinking you might prefer that,' Nan said. Alec rose hastily and went to open the door. 'Oh, thank you.' Nan smiled at Sunny. *They don't look guilty*, she thought with relief.

'Take your time. If you'd like to stay to lunch, Alec, you're welcome. Your favourite; gammon and pease pudding.'

'How can I refuse that? Thank you,' he said. Nan closed the door as she left.

Sunny and Alec sat side by side again, sipping the hot chocolate. Suddenly he asked, 'Do you still care for me, Sunny? I know I shouldn't expect you to commit yourself at your age, but . . .'

'I know my own mind. If you feel the same, I can wait. I want to study art seriously now I've had a couple of lessons with Miss Brooke and I'd have time then . . .'

'Without me distracting you?' he teased. 'I'm not about to propose, you know; I can't afford an engagement ring . . .'

'I don't need one yet,' she said. 'But I do need another kiss . . .'

'Drink your hot chocolate first,' he advised.

'To get my strength up?' she teased.

'I'd better ring Mother to let her know I haven't blown a gasket on the car,' Alec said, before they sat down to eat.

When he returned, he sat down beside Sunny and smiled at her. 'Mother says to bring you back for tea, that's if you'd like to come. She said make sure you take the cat out in the garden before we leave. Oh, and, Nan, you're invited too!'

'Not today, Alec, thank you – it's been a busy Christmas and Ravi and Imran have just arrived back, so will expect me to be here. Afterwards I'll put my feet up and watch the box.' She smothered a sigh. *This Christmas had been an emotional roller coaster*, she thought. *What will the New Year bring?*

The phone was ringing as Alec and Sunny were about to persuade Pilchie into her basket. Sunny answered it. It was Chrissie. 'Sunny, I'm afraid all the tickets for the ball at the Orchid were sold before Christmas – hope you're not too disappointed?'

'No, in fact I probably couldn't have gone anyway; Alec's home for a while! He's taking me over to Shirley for tea this afternoon. Pilchie is looking very disgruntled to be back in her basket.'

'As a matter of fact, I don't mind about not going dancing on New Year's Eve either. Ravi popped in on his way back to the Mother and Baby Home and said he wouldn't be working then and he'd like to take me out. I don't know if he likes dancing though!'

'That's all right then! See you soon!' Sunny replaced the receiver.

* * *

Sunny and Alec walked to the car and Nan waved them off as they drove away.

'How would you like to celebrate the New Year?' Alec asked casually as they drove along.

'Nan says there are some good programmes on the television. I'm back at work next week, remember. But Mr Rowland did mention having New Year's Day off. It would be nice if you could come round to our house and entertain us again on the piano. I'm sure Nan would invite your mother and grandfather too.'

'We'll see what they think. Well, here we are, *Sans Souci* with icing on the cake, or rather some snow lingering on the roof, eh?'

Mr Rowland came out to carry Pilchie indoors, after greeting Sunny with a Continental kiss on each cheek in turn. 'Well,' he said cheerfully, 'it's what they do in Paris!' He added to Alec, 'Your mother is having an afternoon nap, I believe. Upstairs.'

Alec glanced at his watch. 'Just after three. I'll go and tell her the cat has returned, and Sunny is here, too.'

Mr Rowland ushered Sunny into the living room. 'Sit down, my dear. Did you have a good Christmas?'

She hesitated for a moment; *it will take some time to tell him about the unexpected visitors*, she thought. Then she said, 'Yes. We did.'

'And Alec . . . have you two made up? Are you good friends again?'

'I – I think so,' she said.

'I told him to apologise to you. Did he?'

'Yes, but – perhaps I was expecting too much.'

'I would welcome you into our family,' he said gruffly. 'Well, take it day by day, I think.'

'I intend to,' Sunny said, as Mrs Dixon came into the room and greeted her with: 'How nice to see you! Alec is just seeing to the cat. He'll be with us directly.'

'I put away the shopping you asked for in the kitchen,' Alec told his mother as he came back into the room. 'Plus an extra or two things that I fancied. The cupboard was nearly bare!'

'Well, we were going away for Christmas and you should know by now I don't bake cakes,' she returned.

'Peanut butter,' he turned to Sunny. 'D'you like it?'

'I've never tasted it, although I like to munch nuts and raisins at the pictures,' she said.

'Good. I'll make some sandwiches then.'

They're an unconventional family, Sunny thought; *no wonder Alec enjoys Nan's cooking so much.*

When it was time to go home, and the invitation for New Year's Eve to a musical evening at the Mother and Baby Home was readily accepted, Sunny said, 'Perhaps I can persuade Nan to make a Stargazey Pie.'

'Sounds good, but what is it?' Alec asked, as he helped Sunny into her Red Riding Hood coat.

'I thought it might be something you would enjoy, because it's made with pilchards, and your kitchen cupboard is stacked with tins of them!' she teased. 'Nan said it was a traditional pie in Cornwall; she cuts recipes out of magazines and that's one she actually made. It tasted good.'

'I reckon the original would be made with fresh fish, the tinned ones are mostly for Pilchie,' he said.

It was time to venture outside into the cold but there, the streetlamps were alight, and they were soon ensconced in the car. 'Fancy a little drive around?' Alec asked. 'Any suggestions?' Sunny immediately thought of The Grove. Would it be deserted? she wondered. It was the place for courting couples, she thought, with a tingle of anticipation.

'The Grove – we could just go as far as the trees and look at the night sky,' she said shyly.

'Star gazing,' he said softly. 'But I think it will be too cold to linger there, Sunny.'

When they arrived, they ventured a few yards over the grass and sheltered under the first big tree they found, which seemed to loom up before them. 'A goodnight kiss and then back home for you,' he told her. She stretched up, put her arms round his neck, and he bent over her and hugged her tight. Their faces were cold, but their lips were warm. She murmured something.

'Did you say what I thought you did?' he asked.

'I'll love you forever,' she repeated.

'I must get you home before you freeze,' he said.

'You didn't say the same to me,' she said.

'Can't you read my thoughts?' he asked, as he opened the car door for her. 'Of course I will.'

'Stargazey Pie?' Nan said. 'Oh, Sunny, I thought something simple. We've all eaten too much rich food over Christmas! High tea, I told Mrs Dixon on the phone, and I wondered if she liked Welsh rabbit? She corrected me, of course, and said, "Rarebit?" Then I asked her to suggest something sweet to follow that, and she said, "How about treacle tart? Alec asked me to make one, like you do, but I hadn't got any golden syrup." I'm going to make a chocolate tart as well, might as well use that bar of Bourneville dark chocolate still hanging on the Christmas tree.'

'Sounds like quite rich food after all,' Sunny commented. 'However, we've got your Milk of Magnesia, haven't we?'

'Not much left after that curry,' Nan said wryly.

* * *

The visitors were due to arrive at six and Sunny had already spent a couple of hours trying on one outfit after another. At last, Nan sighed and said, 'Why don't you wear your dungarees? He chose those for you, after all, when you first went to work with Mr Rowland, and there's that lovely picture of you which made you famous.'

'Oh, Nan, it didn't! But it might make Alec remember that occasion, and I'll wear that yellow jumper I knitted, he hasn't seen me in that. Oh, and have I got time to wash my hair?'

'Get on with it, then, they'll be here before you know it!' Nan advised.

Sunny was brushing out her damp hair when she heard Nan greeting Mr Rowland and Mrs Dixon. When she ventured into the hall to join them in the kitchen, there was a tantalising smell of melting cheese.

The front door had been left on the latch, and she turned to see Alec come in. He closed the door and said, 'I had to park the car further up the road; I have a belated present for you. Can we go to your room for a moment, so you can open it in private?'

She turned and he followed her into her bedroom. 'They'll wonder where we are,' she said.

He smiled and sat on the side of her bed. 'No, they won't. Don't stand there looking at me – come here.'

'Someone might come in,' she said, but she sat down beside him anyway.

'Close your eyes,' he said softly. Then he put something on her lap. 'You can look now.'

It was a little enamelled box. Opening it cautiously, she saw it was lined with blue velvet. Then her eyes focused on a small object inside and Sunny gasped.

'It's an eternity ring, not an engagement ring. Mother gave me the box and I went into a jeweller's in Croydon and asked what they'd got. The assistant showed me a tray of rings. It's not new, in fact I was told it was made at the turn of the century. It's a gold band, and that's a diamond, a small one, but it's real. Do you like it? May I put it on your right hand? One day I'll get something more beautiful for your left . . .'

He slid the ring onto her finger; it was a good fit. She looked at it. 'This is beautiful, Alec.'

'A quick kiss then, to seal our betrothal. I think you can call it that. Then we must go for supper.'

She said, as they left the room, 'Oh, Alec, I should have worn something more suitable.'

'You look beautiful just as you are,' he assured her.

Nan sat at the kitchen table, with his mother and grandfather. Nan said, 'Oh good, the Welsh rabbit is in the warming oven, you sit down and I'll pass the plates!' She bustled over to the stove.

Mr Rowland said, 'Well, has she accepted you? Tell us!'

Nan turned and said simply, 'Sunny, I am happy for you both!'

'Oh, thank you, Nan, that means so much to me.' Sunny dabbed her eyes.

'Yes, she has accepted. It's not an engagement ring, but an eternity ring – a ring forever,' Alec said. 'There won't be any wedding bells for a couple of years, but

I hope to be able to offer much more to Sunny in the future.'

'You must get on with your career first,' Mrs Dixon said firmly. 'It could be longer than that.'

Sunny looked at Alec and he said, 'Don't worry, Mother's right, it may take longer than we would like but eventually we'll be together. Sunny, while I'm away do go out and about and enjoy yourself; as Grandfather says, you're only young once, make the most of it. After all, I'll be making music with the quartet most weekends, I hope.'

'I'll be working hard too, at my art,' she promised.

After the others had retired to the drawing room with their cups of coffee, Sunny and Alec tackled the washing-up.

'Do you think they really are happy about our news?' Sunny asked. He was washing and she was wiping the plates and stacking them ready to go back on their shelf.

'Well, they convinced me,' he said. 'They are probably relieved we're not eloping, eh?'

'Me too! You'd need to take a piano with you, and where would we go, anyway?' Then it came to her out of the blue: 'Trinidad . . . though Serena's over here now, and so is Jan.'

'We'll honeymoon there perhaps,' he told her. 'Come on, they'll wonder where we are.'

'You can't play the piano in those rubber gloves, Alec.'

'True. I only put them on to protect my hands, of course,' he said, with a grin, peeling them off.

'I've dusted the piano,' Nan said. 'But drink your coffee first; it'll be cooling by now.' They were grouped around the fire, where a blazing log gave out welcome heat to the big room. Sunny sat beside Mr Rowland, who beamed at her and whispered: 'You've made me very happy today.' Sunny wasn't sure Mrs Dixon felt the same; *she didn't marry the right man*, Sunny thought, *and she doesn't want Alec to rush into things. Not that he would; his career comes first.*

'There are sheets of music in the piano stool, Alec,' Nan suggested.

'If you don't mind, I can improvise. If you request something and it's unfamiliar to me, as long as you can hum the tune and know the words, I can work it out. This is a sing song evening, not a concert,' Alec said, as he took his place at the piano. 'Requests, please!'

'How about "The Galloping Major"?' Mr Rowland asked. He cleared his throat, and boomed:

'All the girls declare, he's a grand old stager . . .'

'That sounds like you,' Mrs Dixon remarked, but she was smiling. They all joined in with gusto.

Bumpety, bumpety, bumpety bump, as if I was riding my charger –

Hey, hey, clear the way, here comes the Galloping Major!

Nan was enjoying herself. 'Flanagan and Allen sang that during the last war,' she recalled.

'I believe it dates from before that,' Mrs Dixon said. 'It sounds like the cavalry in the Great War, doesn't it? Alec, can you play "Underneath the Arches" next please?'

Sunny knew that song. '*We dream our dreams away,*' she added.

'Just right for you,' Alec told her. 'Join me on the piano stool, there's room for a little 'un.'

She glanced at Nan, who gave a nod of approval. As she sat down with her back to the company, Sunny heard Mrs Dixon say to Mr Rowland, 'I hope *their* dreams all come true.'

FOURTEEN

Folk said that 1957 was the happiest year of the century so far. The Prime Minister, Harold MacMillan, declared, 'You've never had it so good.' This was true for many, but not for all.

In January 1958, Sunny resumed the art classes with Miss Brooke, determined to have a career of her own. She told herself, *I need to show Alec I have a talent too. Mr Rowland is thinking of retiring at the end of the year. He says the days of one-man businesses are in decline. New technology is taking over. A client saw the old typewriter on my desk the other day and remarked, 'That's a museum piece!'*

Miss Brooke was an inspiring teacher; she was determined to set her pupil on a new career path. 'You have to learn the basics before you decide on your style,' she said. 'Whether you paint in oils or watercolours, use pastels, pencils or Indian ink, your pictures must be unique, though many artists nowadays take photographs, which they refer to in their studios, rather than spending hours sketching or painting outdoors.'

'Now that my friend Rodney is no longer around to whizz me out to the countryside on the pillion of his scooter, I have to rely on The Grove; the trees are lovely in spring,' Sunny mused.

'You are eighteen this year, aren't you?' Miss Brooke said one evening in March. She had some brochures on her desk which she intended to show to Sunny.

'In September, yes. But that's still a long way ahead.'

'Why not work towards a place at art school then? Not the big one, but a smaller establishment founded by three artists after the Great War. I studied there myself and taught there for a few years as well. I could help you apply for a course in art and design, and recommend you, as you have completed a foundation year with me. Bursaries are available if you need help with the fees.'

'Well, I know I would love to go there, but I can't expect Nan to pay from her pension. She won't have my weekly contribution anymore if I stop working. Also, our last two tenants will be moving on shortly. Imran has qualified and is returning to his home country; Ravi has completed his hospital training and has been offered a six-month contract with a general practice the other side of Croydon in Surrey. I know it's not so far from here, but he has already found digs,' Sunny said.

'And what about your fiancé?'

'Oh, you can't really call him that. He won't graduate for another two years. If I went to art school in September that would be fine.'

'Discuss it with your mother first, and tell me what she thinks,' Miss Brooke suggested.

Sunny hadn't told Miss Brooke about meeting her birth mother and uncle at Christmas, but she thought, *I can't ask them for help, or advice – I don't know them well enough. Nan says I should go and stay with them one weekend soon. Perhaps I will, I don't know . . .*

Sunny decided to impart the news about the possibility of attending art school that evening when she arrived home.

Nan listened and then said, 'Well, why not? I think by then Mr Rowland may have made his mind up about closing the Printing Press. Eleanor (they used their Christian names now) is concerned about his health; she thinks he may have had a minor heart attack while they were in Paris. She made him see the doctor, but he merely advised him to slow down a bit. I have something to tell you too, Sunny. I spoke to Serena on the telephone earlier, and she mentioned that she had been wondering if I would take them on as tenants upstairs; Jan said why not ask me? It wouldn't affect him as he travels around to different places. The flat, she says, is not the place to bring up a baby. She said she would feel happier to be with me here and I said it was fine by me, but Sunny must want it too. Do you want to think about it?'

'I'll tell you now,' Sunny said simply, 'I can see you like the idea, and it would be good for you to look after Serena. I know you still miss the mothers and babies, Nan. I'm grown up now, and you will have a new baby to love.'

'You might have some doubts,' Nan suggested.

'No, honestly, I don't. I'll keep my promise and visit them soon, when I have a Saturday morning off. Is that all right?'

Nan nodded and dabbed her eyes. 'What a lovely girl you are, Sunny.'

'And *you* are a lovely mum, don't forget that,' Sunny said, then gave her a hug.

* * *

Brixton had been in decline since the war, when relentless bombing had led to a housing crisis. There was an acute shortage of affordable privately rented places; in particular those big houses that were occupied by middle-class tenants between the wars. There was a demand at that time for businesses such as theatrical boarding houses, owing to the proximity to the music halls and theatres in London. However, many of these Edwardian houses had fallen into disrepair and slum clearance made way for council housing.

The first immigrants arrived in 1948 and were housed, initially, in temporary accommodation in an underground bunker in Stockwell. There was now a huge working-class population, all needing homes and jobs. Most of the remaining three-storey houses had been converted into flats, like the one Jan and Serena lived in.

It was only a short journey to Brixton, somewhere Nan and Sunny went rarely, for they were more familiar with the shops in Streatham. Nan preferred Streatham to Croydon, as it was good to stroll on the Common. There was a cinema at Streatham Hill with comfortable red plush seats and also the popular theatre.

The Brixton streets were milling with shoppers. Sunny climbed the steep steps which led to the flat at the top of the house. She was aware that Serena was out of breath and clutching at the banister. It had been rather a shock to see her at this stage of pregnancy. Despite living in the Mother and Baby Home Sunny wasn't used to seeing expectant mums.

'Only three months to go,' Serena said, noting Sunny's concern. She pointed upwards. 'Another short flight of steps to the attic. See that door? That's the spare bedroom. The bathroom is on the right-hand side. Jan uses the room as a study, so you'll see a desk in one corner. Mind you don't trip over a box or two. I did ask him to tidy it up for you. Leave your bag in there and I'll be in here.' She opened a door and disappeared inside.

Later, as they sat in the kitchen-cum-living room where there was a view from the window of neighbouring roofs and chimney pots, Sunny remarked, sipping her tea, 'Seems a quiet place to live.'

Serena smiled wryly. 'There are musicians in the flat below. They belong to a steel band and they practise their drumming at weekends. But they are not up and about yet; they were playing somewhere last night, I think. Is your tea all right?'

'Fine,' Sunny said. She supposed she would get used to green tea. 'When will Jan be back?' she asked. It was eleven o'clock in the morning.

'He will be here soon, I hope. He wanted to take the whole weekend off, but had an urgent phone call from a customer first thing.' She paused. 'Ah, one of the drummers below is in action; don't think I am criticising him, because all the members of the band come from Trinidad, like me. These bands are part of our culture, but there are *seven* of them in that flat.'

Sunny asked, 'Is that why you want to return to the Mother and Baby Home?'

'Nan told you?'

'Yes.'

'We've almost completed our six months here. How do *you* feel about Jan and me moving in?'

'I agree, it's a good idea,' Sunny said. 'We are family, after all.'

*　　*　　*

Jan was back for lunch, which he brought with him, wrapped in a large newspaper parcel. 'Fish and chips. I guessed you would be too busy talking to bother about cooking. Am I right?'

'You are,' Serena said. She sat down suddenly on a kitchen chair and sighed.

Jan put plates to warm in the oven and filled the kettle. 'You're tired,' he said simply to his wife. 'Don't worry, Sunny will help me, I know. You do too much, Serena.'

'I can't help it, I've been a busy person all my life,' she said, but she smiled at him.

'This is a real treat for me,' Sunny said, as she tucked into the cod and chips. 'We don't have this very often at home.' She tapped the base of the ketchup bottle and recited: 'Tomato sauce, in a bottle, first a little, then a "lottle" – whoops!' *Bottled sauce is another thing Nan doesn't approve of*, she thought, *so I must make the most of it!*

Later, they relaxed in the small sitting room, which was crowded with furniture. There was one comfortable chair for Serena, and a pouffe for her to rest her feet. She closed her eyes and dozed for a while. It was time for Sunny and Jan to catch up. There was so much she wanted to ask him about his brother, the father she had never known.

* * *

Sunny returned home on Sunday afternoon, but got off the bus a stop earlier as she thought she would visit Chrissie on the way back. Chrissie had phoned her on the Friday evening before she was due to go to Brixton for the weekend and asked if she wanted to go dancing on Saturday evening. Sunny explained she wouldn't be able to, but she thought Chrissie must be feeling down and would need cheering up because Ravi had moved on.

Chrissie was actually home alone as her parents had gone out for a meal with Rodney's parents, which they did once a month. 'Oh, it's lovely to see you,' she exclaimed. 'We can have a private talk, which we can't when Mum is around.'

'You sound a bit down in the dumps,' Sunny said. 'Is it because Ravi has moved away?'

'Well, it's not just that. He warned me he wouldn't be able to see me very often, as he must be ready for emergency calls from patients to prove that he will be up to all the challenges. Then he could be offered a permanent position.'

'We're in the same boat, it seems,' Sunny said sympathetically. 'I don't know when I'll see Alec again; I've only had one letter from him since Christmas. That's when I decided not to mope at home, but go out and about as usual, as he said I should, and I'm glad to have your company again!'

'You mean that, don't you? We can always dance together!' Chrissie said. 'Oh, and we might visit the new London Planetarium and explore more of London like we did before.'

'That's a good idea; we've got a pair of clever boy-friends, haven't we, and we'll show them we're interested in serious pursuits too,' Sunny said hopefully.

'Are you hungry? I could make you a sandwich,' Chrissie offered.

'I had a large lunch and I guess Nan will be cooking up something for supper. I really ought to go home now, or she will wonder where I am.'

'Thanks, Sunny, you have really cheered me up,' Chrissie told her friend. She added: 'Auntie Beryl asked me when she was here if Ravi and I had – you know – and I said "No!" She said if I needed any advice in that area I could get it from her!'

'I'm glad I haven't got an Auntie Beryl,' Sunny said. 'Don't listen to her!'

'That's what Mum said, but luckily she didn't know about *that*!' Chrissie said.

'Well,' Nan said, after hearing all Sunny had to say about the weekend, including her concern about Serena's well-being. 'Serena confided to me she has a problem. She has high blood pressure and needs to rest. That's a tall order for someone who has worked so hard all her life. I hope

Serena won't have problems with this baby, so long after having you. I can keep an eye on her if she comes to live here.'

'She can't wait to come! Jan likes the idea too,' Sunny said, adding, 'So do I.'

* * *

Cleaning was needed after the departure of the young doctors; Nan wanted the upstairs rooms to be ready soon for Serena and Jan. The old nursery, she thought, would make a good sitting room. Would Serena think the baby furniture good enough to be in use again? Mrs Perkins was duly contacted and said she could manage Monday to Friday the following week at the Mother and Baby Home. She would come in after taking her grandsons to school in the mornings, and work through until three without a break, because she must be there to collect them in the afternoons.

'I'll insist she stops for lunch and a cup of tea,' Nan said to Sunny. 'She is such a good worker. It'll be nice to have her back, and perhaps she will oblige now and then again.'

'I am wondering what will happen to Patsy's job if Mr Rowland does shut up shop,' Sunny said. 'She loves doing something other than housework, you know.'

'I'm sure Alexander will make sure she is all right,' Nan said.

Sunny smiled. *Alexander*, she mused. *Could Nan be ready for romance too?*

Nan obviously read her thoughts: 'He asked me to call him that, you know! It doesn't mean anything!'

She said: 'Perhaps you'll help with painting the walls with emulsion, Sunny? It would liven them up.'

'Of course I will, and maybe Chrissie will help too,' Sunny said. 'Will the baby be born here?'

'Well, that would be like old times, but Serena may have to go to hospital, depends what her doctor decides. If it was here, our local midwife is very capable, and I could always help.'

Sunny thought, *Nan sounds wistful. Maybe the Mother and Baby Home will be revived.*

FIFTEEN

Alec came home at Easter. It was the first time Sunny had seen him since Christmas. Chrissie was more fortunate, for she and Ravi were together whenever he had time off. Ravi was rewarded for all his hard work and cheerful manner with patients, with a permanent position at the busy general practice, and it seemed likely that her parents would give their permission for her to marry him before she was twenty-one. They even allowed Chrissie to go away over the Easter weekend with him. There was the stipulation that the couple should have separate rooms in the small hotel in Rye, but Chrissie whispered to Sunny, 'They won't know if we do, or don't, as they won't be there!' All she said later to her friend about the weekend was, 'It was wonderful, despite the weather!' and proudly displayed an engagement ring on the third finger of her left hand. 'We intend to spend our summer holiday visiting his parents in Ceylon,' she said. 'Ravi hasn't seen them for six years, you know. He wants to introduce them to his future wife!'

Sunny and Alec didn't discuss their future together, time was too precious for that, and anyway she knew he wouldn't change his mind. He was pleased to hear about her plans to go to art college and said he was proud of her. She said the same about him. However, he kept his promise not to 'compromise' her. In a way she was relieved, for she didn't want to deceive Nan.

* * *

Later that month, Sunny and Chrissie went to Drury Lane to see Rex Harrison and Julie Andrews in *My Fair Lady*, the musical, courtesy of Mr Rowland, who gave them tickets for the opening night. It was an evening they'd never forget. Waiting in the queue to enter the theatre, the girls were thrilled to see the celebrities arrive; including Dirk Bogarde and Ingrid Bergman. '*Real* film stars!' Chrissie said in awe.

When the curtain went up, they were transported to the setting in Covent Garden where the new singing star Julie Andrews, in her role of cockney flower seller Eliza Doolittle, sat outside St Paul's Cathedral with her basket of flowers.

'Isn't she wonderful?' Sunny whispered to Chrissie, who whispered in return: 'So is Rex Harrison!'

* * *

Sunny was humming a snatch of the tune, 'Oh wouldn't it be loverly!' as she inserted her key in the front door lock. Downstairs appeared deserted and she felt disappointed as Nan often waited up to hear all about her evenings out. Perhaps they'd had an unexpected visitor, she thought, for she'd noticed another car parked alongside Jan's outside the house. The taxi which brought her home had to stop further along the lane.

She had a sudden thought: Nan must have spent the evening with Serena and Jan. As she went up the stairs, she saw Nan looking down at her from the landing, finger to her lips. 'Shush! The baby is on its way. Five weeks early! The midwife is with Serena now. So is Doctor Stringer. Didn't you notice his car outside?'

Sunny reached the top of the stairs: 'Yes – but is Serena all right?' she asked anxiously.

Nan didn't answer for a moment, and then she said, 'I'm helping. We had to call the doctor out and he's sent for an ambulance. He thinks she should go to hospital, but it might be too late. I'll send Jan out to talk to you in the kitchen.' Then she rustled away, and Sunny noticed she was wearing her starched apron and cuffs over her sleeves.

Sunny saw a large pan of hot water at the back of the stove, and at the front, a kettle hissed and steamed. Some-one had removed the cap which whistled when the water reached boiling point. She turned as Jan opened the kitchen door and joined her. His eyes were red-rimmed and his fair hair was ruffled as if he had been running his fingers through it. 'They said I was getting in the way, because I was gripping her hand. She wanted me to,' he said flatly.

'Sit down, Jan, you're shaking. I'll make you a cup of strong coffee,' Sunny said. She suddenly realised that she was taking charge, and that she felt quite calm. 'You mustn't worry, Nan has delivered many babies in her time, including me.'

'Serena wanted this baby but I have to admit I wasn't so keen, because of her age.'

'Women have babies when they are older than Serena, Jan.' She passed the mug of coffee to him. 'Are you hungry?'

He shook his head. 'We had a good dinner, maybe that started it all off. She didn't feel well afterwards. Nan came up and was reassuring, and I rang the midwife. Nan told me not to worry as there is everything here we might need, apart from medication, of course, so then I called the doctor. He said he would come immediately and would decide if she should go to the hospital, but if it was likely she would give birth shortly, she couldn't be moved until after that.'

They heard a scream from the bedroom and looked at each other, but kept quiet, wondering what would happen next. The knocking on the front door below made them start.

'I'll go,' Sunny offered. 'You'd better see what's happening up there.'

She opened the door and the ambulance men came through, propping the stretcher against the wall. 'Anything happened yet?' one of the men asked Sunny.

'I – I'm not sure.' They looked up as another piercing scream was heard.

'Lead the way,' the men said, and Sunny turned and went up the stairs as fast as she could.

Nan came out to speak to the ambulance men. 'The baby has just arrived – the midwife and doctor are with the patient. Sunny, take these people into the kitchen, I expect they would like a cup of tea. I'll be back when it's all over, but Doctor will speak to you shortly.' She went back into the room and closed the door firmly.

She didn't say whether the baby is a boy or a girl, Sunny thought. She realised she was trembling.

'Don't worry, young lady, all in a night's work, as they say,' one of the men said cheerfully.

Jan appeared, looking pale and shocked. 'They are getting Serena and the baby ready now to go to the hospital. The baby needs to be put in an incubator.'

'Jan, what is it? The baby I mean,' Sunny asked urgently.

'A girl. Zosia, after my mother,' he said, pronouncing the name Zoh-sha.

The doctor joined them. 'Time is of the essence, bring the stretcher. The midwife and Miss Cato will go with Serena and the baby in the ambulance and I will follow in my car. You can follow in yours,' he said to Jan.

The ambulance men left the room immediately, but Jan asked the doctor, 'Can't I go with my wife, too?'

'The ambulance would be too crowded if you did. I might need to stop and help if needed. You will be able to wait in the hospital and stay a while with your wife after the doctors there have seen her. I will bring Miss Cato and the midwife home later,' the doctor said.

'What about me?' Sunny asked tremulously.

'Best if you stay here and get a good night's sleep. You will need to help your mother tomorrow,' she was told.

'I – I haven't seen the baby, yet,' Sunny said.

'You can have a quick look and a word with your – Mrs Novak – now.' The doctor was aware of the relationship between his patient and Miss Cato's adopted daughter.

Serena was tucked round with blankets, her eyes closed and the baby was in the midwife's arms. Sunny glimpsed a tiny, red face, and greasy black hair, for Zosia had not been bathed yet.

Sunny said hesitantly, 'I can't come with you, but I will be thinking of you and the baby.' There was no answer and the stretcher was loaded into the ambulance. The little cavalcade set off, one car after another, following the flashing blue lights.

After they had gone, Sunny went to her bedroom and sat on the bed, feeling dazed.

'Zosia,' she said aloud, 'I have a little sister.' She lay down on her bed, still wearing her finery, as Nan termed it. She kicked her shoes off and unexpectedly, she was engulfed by sleep.

It was three in the morning when she woke to hear the insistent ringing. She tumbled off the bed and rushed to the telephone in the hall.

Nan's voice was not much more than a croak. 'The baby is in an incubator in the nursery, she weighs just over four pounds – but she's all right. Serena is undergoing tests and we haven't been allowed in the ward to sit with her. Ring Alexander and say you won't be in to work tomorrow.' The call ended abruptly.

It's Sunday today, she thought, *I don't have to work.* She wasn't aware of the tears coursing down her cheeks. Then she heard a rapping on the door, and a voice calling, 'Sunny, it's me, can you hear me?'

Rodney stood on the step in his uniform. He put his arms round her and hugged her to him, her face pressed against the coarse material of his jacket. 'I'm home for a few days. The coach didn't come out this far and I had to walk from Streatham Common and took a short cut across The Grove. Spooky at night. Mum said they'd heard the ambulance, saw flashing lights, and caught a glimpse of Nan. They couldn't sleep for worrying about you on your own here and I told Mum I would go and see if you were all right.'

'I don't know much yet. Nan just rang and said she'll be home sometime this morning.' Sunny moved out of his embrace and noticed something different about him. 'Rodney, you've had an awful haircut – but you've got your first stripe!'

'Lance corporal,' he said. 'The first step up. And it's the regulation haircut! Let's go into the kitchen and I'll make us a cup of tea.'

'I'm glad you came,' she said. 'I really am.'

'How are things progressing with you and Alec?' he asked. 'I'm told that Chrissie is engaged to Ravi – no ring for you yet?'

Sunny glanced down at her hands. The ring was in its box on her dressing table. At first, she'd taken it on and off her finger when she was washing up, and mislaid it a couple of times, which saw her panicking and asking Nan, 'Where on earth did I put it?' Nan had put it back in the box and advised Sunny to wear it when Alec was home. 'He'd be upset if you really lost it and it's not something you can wear to work when you are printing, really,' she said.

'Mine is an eternity ring, not an engagement ring, Rod,' said Sunny.

'Gives me a glimmer of hope,' he said lightly.

'Haven't you found someone special yet?' she asked.

'Nope. Oh, I took a couple of local girls out, but nothing came of it. I'm thinking I might make a career of the army. More challenging than the bank.'

'I'm going to an art school in September. A two-year course. Did your mum tell you?'

'She did. She still hopes we'll get back together – so do I.'

Sunny went to the fridge and took out four rashers of bacon. 'Might as well have breakfast now, I think.'

The bacon was soon sizzling in the frying pan on the stove. Rodney sniffed the aroma appreciatively. 'It'll make a nice change from beans on toast,' he said.

'You can watch the bacon, see when it needs turning over; there are white and brown eggs – have which you prefer. I really must get washed, well, have a lick and a promise, and change out of this outfit. Chrissie and I went to a show last night.'

'I know,' he said, turning the bacon in the fat. 'I told you, Mum keeps me up to date!'

'Rod,' Sunny said impulsively, as she was about to leave the room, 'were you very hurt when I rejected you that time?'

'You taught me a lesson,' he said ruefully. 'I was too young and eager, I suppose, and you were right to spurn my advances!'

She smiled. 'Thanks!' *It's good to be back on the old footing. We're both grown up now,* she thought.

After breakfast she suddenly felt weary and said, 'I need to rest for a while. You can lie on the sofa in my room and I'll get under the eiderdown on my bed. I don't want to be alone, Rod.'

He yawned. 'I need a kip too, it's still early morning,' he said.

He took his jacket off, and she covered him over with a blanket. 'Like my mum . . .' he said drowsily.

Sunny didn't know what prompted her to bend over him and kiss him. 'Thank you,' she said simply. Then she went over to her bed. It was after nine in the morning before they both awoke with a start, to hear the phone ringing in the hall. It was Jan, to say they would be back for lunch. When she returned, Rod had replaced his jacket and combed his hair. 'I'd better go home and put Mum in the picture,' he said. 'But I'll be back again later.' He paused, and then said, 'You kissed me, or did I dream it?'

'Oh, Rod, I – don't read anything into it.'

'Don't worry, I won't, but it was – good,' he said, and he was gone.

Nan and Jan returned home at lunchtime to find Sunny had food to put on the table, courtesy of Rodney's mum. There were pasties, which Sunny reheated, and four jacket potatoes she'd put in the oven earlier. Rodney had also brought a bunch of black grapes from the shop for Serena.

It was reassuring to hear Serena had been moved to a room off the maternity ward, as tests had shown she had not developed pre-eclampsia, a serious complication of childbirth that might have been caused by her high blood pressure. If the birth of her baby had been delayed, her kidney function could have been damaged. However, she was still suffering from shock and would be kept in hospital for some days until things had returned to normal. She also needed to express milk for the baby.

'Is Zosia going to be all right?' Sunny asked.

Jan said quietly, 'It is hoped that she will. We have not been able to hold her yet, which is hard for Serena to accept.' Serena had said to Jan that she'd always regretted having to leave Sunny when she was so young and this was bringing back memories. He didn't tell Sunny this though.

Jan pushed Serena in a wheelchair as he and Sunny accompanied her to the nursery. A nurse told them that the baby was doing well and added, 'Thanks to Mother's milk, you'll be able to cuddle her in a day or two, we hope. She needs to gain at least a pound in weight, though, before you can take her home.'

'I am permitted to do this,' Serena said softly, stroking the baby's cheek with her forefinger, which she had carefully inserted through one of the windows on the side of the incubator. Sunny thought how tiny Zosia was, her eyes still closed, her dark hair hidden by a warm woollen bonnet. Her face was less flushed today, and Serena, who guessed what Sunny must be thinking, said, 'She will have a fair complexion, like her father, I imagine.' She touched Sunny's face now. 'And you, of course. You are a beautiful young woman.'

'I have your dark eyes and hair,' Sunny said, embarrassed.

Nan, who had joined them, turned away, to hide her own mixed feelings at this exchange between Sunny and Serena. It was time to return Serena to her bed and to chat for a while. Then, when she fell asleep, Nan tucked the blankets round her and they tiptoed away.

What other changes lay ahead for them all at the Mother and Baby Home?

PART TWO

SIXTEEN

1958

This year would certainly not hold the record for good weather, with many summer thunderstorms.

Serena, Jan and baby Zosia were settled in at the Mother and Baby Home, and Nan was now Nana to the little girl she regarded as her first grandchild.

Sunny and Chrissie, like many of their generation, became enthusiastic fans of contemporary music and, in particular, the young singer Cliff Richard after his debut with 'Move It'.

Chrissie and Ravi had two weeks off work in the spring and they went to Ceylon, visiting his family. Chrissie received a warm welcome, and the approval of Ravi's parents, though they advised the young couple to wait a while before they married. Ravi was now a qualified doctor and had been offered a permanent position with the practice that he'd joined several months ago, but he should provide a proper home for his bride, they were told. The bachelor rooms he occupied at present didn't come into this category! If the couple agreed, they would be given financial help.

Sunny looked forward to art school and her eighteenth birthday in September. Meanwhile, she continued her art sessions with Miss Brooke. She dreamed that one day she'd be in the audience at the Albert Hall, listening to Alec performing his debut on the grand piano at a promenade concert.

Rodney transferred to Germany in the spring after further promotion in the army Pay Corps. Unlike Alec, he sent letters to Sunny every week. These were signed, 'All the best, from Rod'.

Sunny didn't hear at all from Alec and when she asked Mr Rowland, he sighed because he had to respect his grandson's wishes not to divulge the reason why he had not contacted her.

He said, 'I'm sure he has a good reason for not being in touch, but he must be man enough to tell you himself.'

Sunny managed a smile. 'I expect I'll hear from him soon,' she said. 'Don't worry about me. Whatever happens, I'll always keep in touch with you!' Pilchie was purring and nudging Sunny, so she lifted the little cat up and stroked her under her chin, whispering in her ear, 'I'll miss you too!'

'That's good news, I regard you as one of my family,' Mr Rowland said, rubbing his eyes after removing his glasses. When he replaced them, a newer pair than those he'd worn when they first met, Sunny noted that they were already missing a leg. He's eccentric, she thought. I wish he was *my* grandfather!

* * *

Sunny was grateful that Nan didn't question her about Alec's absence at Easter, but she received a letter from him a day or two later.

My dear Sunny,

You will have heard, I hope, from Mother or Grandfather about my stroke of good luck! Yes, I am with a youth orchestra travelling to various venues every weekend, so I can't give you an address to write to at present, but will keep in touch, though you will know my intentions are good if my correspondence is lacking! I might try to ring you at some point, but although we are well fed and staying overnight at decent small hotels where we can have hot baths, etc., and this is all paid for, we only get a small allowance for personal spending. A beer or two with the boys, and that's it.

I hope you will enjoy your holiday, and I know you are looking forward to your art course in September. I will endeavour to come home for a week or so around your birthday.

Always thinking of you. One day I will explain why I am as I am. My regards to Nan and to your new family.

Love Alec

She passed the letter to Nan at the breakfast table. 'I don't mind showing this to you, Nan, because it's not a love letter,' she said flatly. 'I don't know what to think of it.'

'Nor do I,' Nan said, as she slotted the letter back into the envelope. 'I've had a letter too, Sunny. I have received official permission to transform the old Mother and Baby Home into a day nursery for babies and toddlers whose mothers have decided to return to work. We will care for up to six young children each weekday.'

This had been Serena's idea. She could be involved as a trained nurse, and Zosia would have playmates when she got bigger. Nan, of course, would be Matron.

'I think it's a great idea,' Sunny said, though she wished she had been involved in the discussion. *Before the family upstairs arrived*, she thought, *it was just Nan and me, and so much has changed. Serena and Jan seem to think of Nan as a mother figure, but I suppose it's hard for them to accept that the baby Serena gave up is grown up now.*

'You had issues to deal with and that's why I thought it best not to worry you about all the changes. We've a lot to do here to get everything up and running by September, and there'll be an inspection by the authorities before we can go ahead. Jan has offered to contribute financially. He would like to install a lift.'

'I could help get it all ready,' Sunny offered. Chrissie was still away, Rodney was not home very often, and it was no fun, she thought, going out on her own.

'You could decorate the playroom with nursery rhyme murals,' Nan suggested. This was the large room overlooking the front garden, the same size as the sitting room downstairs. The playroom was adjacent to what had been the night nursery in the old days. Now, it would be a quiet place with cots for young babies.

'Like Rex Whistler in the Tate Gallery? I'm not that good yet, you know!' However, Sunny was smiling at the thought.

'Before you ask, I might not look like *Whistler's Mother*, but I don't mind posing as Old Mother Hubbard. You could paint me on that big cupboard, where we will store the toys and books for the children,' Nan said.

'I'm getting ideas already,' Sunny said dreamily. 'I know Miss Brooke will approve, and advise me, too.'

Nan gave her a hug. 'You are still number one with me, you know,' she said. 'Maybe Alec isn't "Mr Right", as they say? "Mr Right" never came along for me,' she said, sounding wistful.

'He still could, Nan!' *But Alec is the only one for me,* she thought to herself. *Am I the only one for him, I wonder?*

* * *

Nan's sixtieth birthday was coming up in July, and Sunny had been thinking of a special present for her. She needed to have a private word with Mr Rowland about it. When Patsy went out to get the sandwiches for lunch and to deliver some printing, she seized the chance to ask him a big favour.

'Mr Rowland, please could I borrow your easel and have you a spare canvas you could let me have? I'll pay for it, of course.'

'Hold on!' he said, smiling at her. 'Are you planning to paint your first masterpiece? Why don't you ask Miss Brooke's advice?'

'I haven't got that far in my lessons with Miss Brooke. She probably wouldn't think I'm ready for this,' Sunny said. 'But it's Nan's birthday soon, and I would like to paint a picture from a photograph. It's an old black and white one. I've had plenty of practice painting all over the walls in the new day nursery!'

'I gather this must be a secret, and you would like to do your painting here?' Mr Rowland was already putting a new canvas in place on his easel. 'Plenty of paint around; perhaps you could paint for an hour or so in the evenings?'

'I could paint in my lunch hour too. Patsy will know, of course, but she doesn't gossip.' The snapshot was old, of course, as it had been taken during the war when they were evacuated. The younger Nan sat out in a garden in a deckchair, and baby Sunny was in her arms, holding a little black bear in one chubby hand and smiling at the person clicking her Brownie camera.

'You still have that smile and the curls,' Mr Rowland observed.

'I also have the wonderful picture you painted of me and then gave to me and I thought it would be nice for Nan to have something like that for herself. This photo is a lovely one of her. Her hair wasn't grey then, of course.'

'I believe it was originally dark brown,' he said. 'As it was, when she was "snapped" as a child with her mother; that picture in the silver frame on the top of the piano, eh?'

Mr Rowland encouraged Sunny to paint when she should have been working. He saw that she followed his hints, but this was a portrait painted with bold strokes, bright colours. It was a picture painted with love for the subject, he thought. He wondered if he could persuade Sunny and Nan to allow him to make prints because he had a title in mind: *Mother Love*.

When Nan unwrapped her gift on her birthday morning, she was amazed at the memories it brought back. 'You look like Zosia does now,' she murmured, with tears in her eyes.

She read the card:

'WITH LOVE TO MY WONDERFUL NAN ON HER BIRTH-DAY FROM SUNNY XX'

'Sunny, you are going to succeed, I know, and become an artist. We must get a special frame and hang this in the drawing room.'

* * *

Now that it was July, Sunny was feeling sad that her time at the Rowland Printing Press was nearly over. However, Mr Rowland had some good news for her. 'I have received a communication signed by all my local clients, urging me to think again about closing the business. They say we provide a friendly service and that the advertising works. Anyway, I have agreed to carry on for the next year or two.'

Sunny exclaimed, 'Oh, but I will be leaving you in the lurch! How will you manage?'

He beamed. 'My dear, Patsy will take over your position as Girl Friday! She is bright and cheerful and she is very capable having had, may I say, excellent instruction from you!'

'Mr Rowland, I am so pleased for Patsy; and for you!'

They could hear Patsy humming a happy tune as she gave the cloakroom a good scrub out before the Rowland Printing Press closed for the holidays.

'I've had a great two years here with you,' Sunny said, and she gave a little sigh.

Mr Rowland looked at her quizzically. 'Have you heard from Alec recently?' he asked.

'No, I haven't,' she said slowly, then in a rush she added, 'Only twice since Easter, actually.'

'Well, Eleanor received a letter from him a week ago. He wrote that he had a chance to perform with a small orchestra in the Netherlands for the next six weeks. He has already arrived there. All expenses paid, but he was more interested in gaining experience and hopefully some recognition.' Mr Rowland paused, then said quietly, 'I'm sorry, Sunny, I know how much you were looking forward to being together this summer.'

'He should have told me,' she said huskily. 'I would have said of course he must take this opportunity, but now I wonder if . . .'

'Yes?' he prompted.

'I wonder if he regrets making a commitment to me last Christmas, but he did say the ring he gave me was not an engagement ring, didn't he?'

'You don't wear it,' Mr Rowland said, with a sigh.

'No, I don't, but it's still precious to me. He told me to go out and enjoy myself while he was not here, as *he* intended to do, remember.'

'Have you enjoyed yourself, despite his absence?' he asked. 'I don't blame you, if you have.'

She gave a little nod. 'I still care for him you know.' *I can't reveal that Rodney corresponds with me, but any outings are innocent ones, on my own, or with Chrissie,* she thought.

'I am aware of that. But I thought he felt the same about you, though he wanted to concentrate on getting his degree at Cambridge.' Mr Rowland gave a little sigh. *The course of true love never did run smooth*, he thought. He couldn't tell her that he knew the real reason behind it.

* * *

Serena obviously enjoyed being a mother again after all these years. Zosia was catching up fast, though she was still smaller than average. She was a placid baby, enjoying cuddles with Nan and Sunny as well as her doting parents. 'See her dimples when she smiles,' Serena said proudly. 'She looks like her big sister, doesn't she?'

Sometimes, while she was on holiday at home, Sunny took the baby out in the pram. One afternoon she ventured as far as The Grove, keeping to the pathways because it was difficult to push the pram over the grass. She saw someone was waving at her. The sun was in her eyes, so at first she couldn't see who it was but then as the person drew nearer, she realised that it was Rodney. He was wearing mufti, as he termed it; slacks and a maroon sweater that zipped up the front. The army barber had not 'scalped him' this time, she was glad to see. He appeared to be fit and muscular; no longer a lanky youth, but a good-looking, confident young man.

'You're supposed to be in Germany!' she exclaimed.

He grinned. 'I do get leave occasionally,' he said mildly. 'I hitched a lift on a plane taking personnel back home. Dad met me at the airport in the van. It made a nice change from the long coach journey I've done before.'

Zosia, who had been lulled to sleep by the movement of the pram wheels, now opened her eyes. She didn't cry but gazed solemnly at the young man looking down at her and smiling. The baby smiled in return and waved her hands at him. 'She looks like you,' Rodney said, waving back.

'Nan says that,' Sunny said. She knew Nan was worried about her feeling jealous of the new baby, but she didn't feel that at all. She propped Zosia up with her pillow behind her, so she could look around. 'Shall we sit on the seat over there; we've got a lot to catch up on.'

'You're telling me!' he said, walking alongside the pram towards the empty bench. A ball whizzed by their heads, followed by the girl who had failed to hit it with her racquet. 'Sorry,' she called as she sped back with it to continue the game.

Sunny was reminded of herself and Chrissie batting a ball backwards and forwards on the sloping grass. She'd been fifteen and a half and Chrissie sixteen, both in their last year at school. It was their final school holiday. Now she was almost eighteen and her romance with Alec was waning, she realised. She was not sure of her feelings anymore and Chrissie, well, she was properly engaged.

'You're a good friend, Rod.'

'You sound sad,' he said. 'Cheer up, I was hoping to take you out on the bike tomorrow. We could take a picnic lunch; that's if Nan agrees.'

'Nan lets me make my own mind up now,' she said. 'That would be lovely. I feel I need a break.'

'My parents still say what they think; they don't want me to sign up for two more years in the army. I'm probably one of the last national servicemen, you know. I've another six months in Berlin, in the Pay Corps, and then I'll be back home, working at the bank again and' – he looked at her – 'seeing you, I hope.'

'It must be strange to be in what was an enemy country,' Sunny said, changing the subject.

'The people at home there suffered like we did; like us they went through bombing and all that. I don't think of them as the enemy,' he said reflectively. 'But we're not supposed to fraternise with them ... the girls, that is.'

He added, 'It doesn't bother me; I reckon you know why, Sunny.'

Sunny put out a hand and touched his arm. 'You've grown up, too,' she said softly.

She looked at Zosia, wriggling about in her pram. 'Oh dear, I'll have to take her home, she needs her nappy changed I expect, and' – she glanced at her watch – 'Nan said she'd be due for a feed about now. Hard work looking after a baby!'

'I'll escort you back,' he said with a grin. 'I'll call for you at ten tomorrow and we'll go . . . I'm not sure where yet, so if you have any bright ideas, just say!'

'I will,' she promised. *I'll wear my new white linen pedal pushers*, she thought, *with that pale pink chenille tee shirt, and the white cabled sweater I made last winter. I had plenty of time for knitting then.*

Nan greeted them at the front door. 'I thought you must have met someone and were chatting; nice to see you again, Rodney, come and join me in the kitchen for a cup of tea, while Sunny takes Zosia upstairs to her mother. We park the pram in the hall; no one wants to heave it up and down the stairs, eh?'

'I'll be about ten minutes,' Sunny told Rodney.

Nan passed Rodney a mug of tea. 'Would you like a flapjack? They've turned out a bit hard, but you've got good teeth! Now, how do you think Sunny looks?'

'Just the same,' he said. 'But – she doesn't smile as much as she used to.'

'I'm sure you can guess why,' Nan said gently.

'Things haven't gone as she hoped, regarding Alec? But it's good news that she's going to study art, isn't it?'

'Yes. I'm glad you two are good friends once more. My advice, for what it's worth, is to be patient.'

'I will,' he said. 'But I know that she loves another, and I have to respect that.'

Sunny came into the kitchen and, seeing Rodney selecting another flapjack from the plate, told him: 'Don't eat them all. Nan made them for me – my favourite!'

Rodney grinned at her. 'Mum says my stomach is a bottomless pit!'

'I was just thinking, how about whizzing along to Camber Sands tomorrow? Chrissie went with Ravi a month or so ago and said it was fun exploring along the beach. They did a spot of beachcombing apparently.'

'Good thinking! It would be nice to go to Rye, too, before we get covered in sand on the beach at Camber. That always happens if it turns out to be windy,' Rodney said ruefully. 'Remember how the sandwiches lived up to their name and were all gritty when we went there a couple of years ago?'

'Of course I do, but when the tide goes out and there are miles and miles of wet sand, you can make marvellous sandcastles,' Sunny said.

'You'll need a bucket and spade then,' Nan said, tongue-in-cheek.

'I'm sure Mum's got both in the shed somewhere, she never throws anything away.' Rodney grinned. He was enjoying remembering what pals he and Sunny had been before.

'I'm not a kid anymore,' Sunny said, but she was smiling too. 'But like Chrissie, I count you as my best friend.'

'I've always known that, and I know I must accept it. Alec needs to tell you how he feels, though.'

* * *

'Going to be a fine day after all,' Rodney called back to Sunny as they sped along the road to Rye on the scooter, which he'd cleaned thoroughly the previous evening as it only came out of the shed when he was on leave. He was aware of her arms clinging tightly around his waist and the proximity of her body. They arrived at Rye Harbour, where moored fishing boats bobbed on the water alongside the Salts, grassland that was overwhelmed by the sea long ago. After the flood water had evaporated, the salt deposits were collected and used to preserve catches of fish. At that time, Rye was a small village, and fishing was the main occupation. However, in the sixteenth century the sea had retreated and sheep had been grazing the reclaimed fields ever since.

'Rye was a Cinque Port, wasn't it?' Sunny asked. 'And what about smugglers?'

'There are lots of books written about that time. I'll look out for one for you,' he promised.

They moved on to the famous Rye Pottery in the Old Brewery at the bottom of Mermaid Street. They browsed, entranced by all the amazing pottery. 'I'll buy you something for your birthday,' Rodney said. 'You choose. I won't be here on the day, so I want to give it to you now.'

Sunny decided on a Rye Pottery pig, beautifully decorated by an artist, who, they learned, had worked there for many years. It was well wrapped and stowed away in the luggage box on the back of the bike. Before they remounted their steed, as Sunny liked to call it, she glanced around and seeing no one in sight, put her hands on Rodney's shoulders, stood on tiptoe and gave him a warm kiss on the lips. 'I love my pottery pig, Rodney, I will treasure him forever!' she said breathlessly.

He hugged her in return. 'I wish you felt the same about me,' he said simply.

She moved away then but smiled. 'Didn't I say earlier, you are my best friend, Rodney?' They left the cobbled streets of Rye behind; it was getting warmer by the minute and this wasn't the day for exploring a town full of history and mystery; Camber Sands was not far away. Having parked the scooter beside other vehicles, they carried their picnic box between them. Rodney also had a haversack containing their boots, towels and swimwear. They walked along the beach, revelling in the sensation of their bare feet treading in the sun-warmed sand. The sea was as they thought, almost on the horizon, but the tide was turning. It would be some time before they could immerse themselves in the water.

'I used to ask Nan if we could stay here at Pontins Holiday Camp, but we never did,' Sunny said wistfully.

'Holiday camps sound rather like being in the army, I reckon,' Rodney said. 'Early morning exercises for everyone and contests for the knobbliest knees!'

'My knees aren't knobbly!' she said.

'Mine are.' He grinned. 'Here's a good place to sit and a dune to change behind, but I'm getting hungry, how about you?'

'Mmm. Save the bags, we can collect shells and there's the bucket, too. I've got Marmite and cheese sandwiches – how about you?'

'The usual, spam rolls; here, let's do a bit of swapping! Mum gave me two bottles of pop, one each.'

Two hours later, they changed into their swimsuits in turn. Then they ran, hand in hand, to splash in the water. Rodney didn't stare at her brief two-piece white towelling costume, which left nothing to the imagination, because he knew he would get told off if he did. He wore a pair of rather ancient trunks, that had belonged to his father in his youth. Sunny stayed on the edge of the water, paddling rather than swimming, because she was not very practised at that. Rodney plunged in, and swam around, spraying her with water. At least it cooled them off. Then they heard a distant rumble of thunder and hurried back to the dune to dry off. Sunny found a strand of seaweed, which Nan had requested to hang outside the back door to foretell the weather, and a few shells, but she drew the line at a dead crab. Rodney discovered a coil of tarred rope, which he thought would be useful. 'Should we break down on the scooter and need a tow . . .'

They brushed the sand off their feet, pulled on their boots and set off home.

SEVENTEEN

It was now September and there were headlines in the papers about a race riot in Notting Hill, and scenes recorded by TV which shocked the peaceful inhabitants of Grove Lane. There was a nuclear test on a remote island, and horrific pictures of this too, but public relief at the promise that it would be the final one in a series that had begun in 1948. The plight of the evicted islanders was not over yet, they couldn't return home until decontamination was assured.

Sunny and Chrissie were becoming aware that although the war had ended over thirteen years ago, there were many signs of renewed unrest in the world. When Sunny tried to talk to Nan about her fears, she was told, 'You've got a special birthday coming up. Learn to take each day as it comes and make the most of it! Soon, you'll be embarking on an exciting new career.'

The art course would begin on the Monday after Sunny's eighteenth birthday and the day nursery would open its doors the same day. Two young nursery nurses were already being trained by Sister Novak and Matron Cato. The hallway was cleared to make way for prams and pushchairs, but most babies would be carried in from cars nowadays, by mothers off to work.

Sunny had no idea of the proposed celebrations for her birthday and Chrissie was not divulging any secrets. She was involved with Nan and Serena in the planning, because as Nan said, 'You know what she would like to do!' Chrissie's suggestion was to hire the church hall and invite all of Sunny's friends. They would have someone to play the piano and they'd all bring along party food. 'Will Alec be around?' Chrissie asked.

'Eleanor told me she was planning a surprise for Sunny, so, maybe.' answered Nan.

'Fingers crossed, it's Alec,' Chrissie said. 'I hope she's wearing her ring.' She glanced complacently at her own sparkling ring. She and Ravi were planning their wedding for next spring, following his family's advice during their visit to Ceylon. Chrissie wished so much for her friend to be happy too.

'When Eleanor collected Sunny earlier, she said she wanted to call in at the store where she works and buy something; I wonder if it's a present for Sunny.'

'Oh, and you think that might be the surprise?' Chrissie asked.

'It could be,' but she didn't sound very confident. Alec is such a charming young man, she thought, but I can't help wondering if he has found love elsewhere.

*   *   *

Sunny was in the changing cubicle and there wcre three outfits hanging on the back of the door. She had stripped to her undcrwear and donned a silk slip provided by Eleanor. Seeing her reflection in the long mirror in the small room, she made a face at herself. *Suppose I don't like Eleanor's choice,* she thought. *Which one shall I try on first?* She fingered the material of each garment in turn. *Are these cocktail dresses?* she wondered.

One was in black taffeta, sleeveless with a bell-shaped skirt, patterned with bold bright pink tulips. The next was of softer material, rayon, she decided. This had a slinky skirt, with slits up the sides, a cross-over neckline and again it was sleeveless. The colour was a startling, deep purple. She thought it would reveal far too much leg when she walked around in it. The last frock was much simpler, in a blue-and-white-spotted silky material. She liked the sweetheart neckline and the cap sleeves. She gave a twirl in front of the mirror, and the panelled skirt opened out like petals on a flower. *Perfect for dancing,* she thought.

There was a polite tap on the door and Eleanor asked, 'Have you come to a decision yet?'

'If you can squeeze inside for a moment, you can see!' she replied.

Eleanor regarded her for a long moment. 'Oh, Sunny, it shows off your assets remarkably.'

'My assets?' Sunny asked artlessly.

'Well, that neckline draws the eye to your bosom. You have developed into a lovely young woman. You've made an excellent choice. The black was too bold, and the purple was too sophisticated.'

'Do you think – Alec – will like it. That's if he comes home this weekend . . .'

'You've guessed my surprise. He's probably raiding the larder at this very moment. Right, I'll take the dresses back to the counter, while you get changed, and then we'll make our way back to *Sans Souci*, eh?' Eleanor said. 'You can keep the slip; it'll fold up and fit in your handbag.'

'Is he – is everything all right, or will he say he doesn't feel the same about me as he did?' Sunny had to know.

'My dear, he doesn't tell me anything either, but Father and I hope he won't make a big mistake and let you go,' Eleanor said, as she went off with the armful of dresses.

Alec had been watching out for their arrival and opened the door. 'I thought you'd never come,' he said cheerfully, just as if he'd never been away. 'I've made a bowl of salad,' he said, 'and opened a tin . . .'

At last Sunny found her voice, and her sense of humour. 'Of pilchards I presume?' she asked.

He grinned at that. 'Actually, salmon – you like that, don't you? Shall we have lunch in the garden, Mother?'

'You two can, but I need to have a rest on my bed. I got up too early, thanks to you arriving at dawn and expecting egg and bacon for breakfast,' she scolded him fondly. 'I don't want to spoil the reunion, either.'

'We'll have a picnic, won't we, Sunny? We can sit under the tree and talk of what we've been up to since we last met, eh?'

Eleanor heaved a sigh. 'He hasn't changed, I'm afraid. Is there any coffee in the pot? I'll take a cup upstairs.'

Sunny noted his interested glance at her outfit – her curves were accentuated by the clinging T-shirt over a lacy bra. 'You've really grown up now!' he observed.

'You look more "with it", as they say, in those new specs – round lenses without frames! Are you trying to look groovy?'

'Growing my hair is next on my list!' He grinned.

She felt her apprehension lessen as they talked about this and that, but nothing remotely romantic; it was as if they had never been apart. Suddenly, he said, 'I know this will upset you, Sunny, but I have to explain why I didn't write often – guilty conscience, I suppose. I have been unfaithful to you, since I last saw you.'

She murmured, as if repeating something that had been said to her. 'Out of sight, out of mind.'

'Yes . . . but that's no excuse.'

'You told me when you gave me the ring that it wasn't an engagement ring,' she stated. 'You said we shouldn't stop going out with our friends and enjoying ourselves.'

'And did you do that?'

'Yes, but I didn't . . .' She broke off, turning away from him, so he couldn't see the tears.

'Can you forgive me, Sunny? I wasn't in love with the other girl. She sang with the band and it just happened. Only once. That's all I can say. She's engaged to someone back home. We just sort of came together. He, her fiancé, doesn't know. But I knew I must tell you.'

'There is nothing really to forgive,' Sunny said slowly. 'As you remind me, *we* aren't engaged. But – is it the end of us?'

'I hope not. Mother and Grandfather don't know all of the details but they knew something was going on.'

'I won't tell Nan,' she said sadly.

'They are all expecting us to make an announcement,' he said tentatively.

'I'm not sure if we should – like you, Alec.' Sunny stood up. 'Maybe it would be best if you take me home.' She wanted to leave before she broke down. Once she started crying, she thought she'd never stop.

'You'll have to tell Nan, then. I hoped we could put this behind us, and not upset anyone.'

'But *I'm* upset – don't you understand that?' She was about to go back indoors. Alec followed her, turned her around to face him and then held her close. 'I do love you, please believe me, Sunny. Please,' he begged. Over her head, pressed against his shoulder, he saw his mother silhouetted in the doorway. Had Eleanor heard any of their conversation?

She called out, 'Helena has just been on the phone; she said if I was doing nothing this weekend, why don't we go out on the town together. She'll come and get me, so I'll leave my car for you. I can stay with her overnight – if you two don't mind?'

He murmured in Sunny's ear, 'What shall I say?'

'*She* probably rang Miss Brooke. Tell her of course we don't mind. We need to talk,' she said.

Nothing more was said about the incident that evening. They watched an old film on TV, sitting side by side on the settee, but with a gap between them, until Sunny said, 'I'm tired. Where am I sleeping tonight?'

'In the spare room – top floor, next to my room. Hope you don't mind?'

'Why should I mind?' she asked. 'May I go in the bathroom before you?'

'Of course you can. I don't know if the immersion heater is on. If it is, you can have a bath.'

'I had one this morning,' she told him primly.

'Well, I'll escort you upstairs, but I'm not ready for bed yet. I'll watch a bit more TV, I think. Would you like a hot drink to take up with you?'

'No thanks,' she said.

He went ahead of her to her room. 'You can lock the door, but there's no need because you can always call out to me or knock on the wall.'

'I'm not expecting an intruder. Goodnight, Alec.' She closed the door and waited to hear him going downstairs. Then she ventured to the nearby bathroom, to clean her teeth, and looked at herself in the mirror. She thought, *is this really me? I look so sad.* She was tired, and it was too warm for the pyjamas she'd brought with her, so she felt more comfortable wearing the slip Eleanor had given her. She threw back the covers and snuggled down under the top sheet. Sunny actually fell asleep soon after she climbed into the bed, which had a hard, unyielding mattress, with sheets and a candlewick cover that didn't smell freshly washed. She surmised this had long been in the airing cupboard.

It was around midnight when she opened her eyes to see Alec gazing out of the window at the garden in the moonlight. He let the curtain fall back in place and said, 'Sorry, I didn't mean to wake you up.'

'Why did you come in here?' she demanded, sitting up and fumbling for the switch on her bedside light.

'I wanted to tell you – I need to say sorry for upsetting you earlier,' he said. He came over and sat on the bottom of the bed. 'I'm such a fool,' he continued. 'But – Sunny, I adore you, even though it must seem to you I don't care.'

'How can I believe you?'

'Please . . .' he said, almost inaudibly.

'Where are your glasses?' she asked. She was aware that without them everything would be blurred.

'I thought you didn't like them.'

'Well, I'm used to seeing you with sticking plaster holding the old pair together, like your grandfather's,' she said. 'You want me to say I forgive you for your behaviour, and I can't say why, but I do. Nan always says men are stronger in the arm, but weaker willed than women.'

'She's right.' He was gradually shifting along the bed, and now his head was on the pillow beside hers, although he didn't touch her.

'You want to kiss and make up, is that it?' Sunny asked. She couldn't help herself; she put out her hand and stroked his damp, floppy hair back off his forehead. *He must have had a bath*, she surmised. He was obviously feeling the heat too, for he had not donned his pyjama jacket. His upper body was not lean and tanned like Rodney's, she thought, he obviously wasn't athletic or a sun-worshipper. He was fair-skinned and he didn't have a hairy chest, to her relief.

He nodded, turned towards her and put his arms around her. She didn't resist as he fiddled with the straps of her flimsy slip, which dropped in silken folds around her waist. 'Wriggle out of it,' he whispered in her ear.

She gave a little shiver of anticipation as he caressed her bare skin.

'It's the first time for me,' she whispered, 'but I don't want, you know – to get pregnant.'

'I'll make sure you don't. It's still two years before we can marry, and I promise you I'll be faithful to you from now on.'

'I am wearing my ring. Look,' Sunny said, as she held out her hand.

He slid it off her finger. 'I'll put it on your left hand, Sunny. I think we should be officially engaged.'

It's going to happen, she thought exultantly. *I think Serena may guess but I'll keep it a secret from my dear Nan. Chrissie doesn't say whether she has or hasn't . . .*

* * *

Waking with a start, Sunny stretched out her hand, but Alec had gone. She looked at her watch, which she'd placed on the bedside table. It was after nine o'clock in the morning; the curtains were drawn back, and sunlight was flooding the room.

Last night had been so special. To begin with, it had been painful. She'd not expected that, and then . . . she bit her lip. Was Alec regretting what had happened? He'd comforted her when she cried out and she'd relaxed in his arms as he'd whispered, 'Don't worry, you don't have to.' She thought exultantly, *but I did; and it was wonderful. I don't feel guilty as I imagined I would. We both had something we needed to prove to each other.*

The door opened, and Alec came in with breakfast on a tray, which he placed on the bedside table. 'Only cornflakes I'm afraid. I had the last of the bacon yesterday when I arrived. My mother isn't a good housekeeper like your Nan. There's toast and marmalade too. Is that enough for you?'

'More than enough, thank you,' she said. She sat up and placed both pillows behind her head and then, after realising what she was revealing, pulled the sheet up under her chin.

'Sorry, I didn't think,' he said, and he retrieved the petticoat from the carpet by the bed and handed it to her. 'You're smiling – is that a good sign?' he asked hopefully.

'I believe it is,' she said. *Am I the same girl as I was yesterday?* she wondered. She knew things had changed. 'I love you, Alec,' she said simply. 'You can't stop me doing that.'

He took his glasses off and polished them on his sleeve. 'Now you've made *me* blub,' he said. After she had eaten some of the breakfast on the tray, and he'd helped himself to the last piece of toast, Sunny said, 'What are we doing today? I told Nan I'd return this evening, and I don't think she'll be surprised to see you with me!'

'Well,' he said, 'We seem to um – communicate better in bed . . .'

Sunny giggled. She couldn't help it, she felt so happy. 'Give me ten minutes in the bathroom.'

EIGHTEEN

When Sunny got home Nan guessed the reunion had been a positive one, and if she realised the reason why, she kept it to herself. As Alec had not followed her indoors, Sunny took the opportunity to ask, 'May Alec stay with us tonight, please, Nan?'

Nan answered, 'Well, we don't have a spare room down here or upstairs, but there's the couch in your room. He wouldn't mind that, would he?' Nan wondered if she was doing the right thing, but thought it best to trust them.

Sunny flung her arms round her and gave her a hug. 'You are the best mother in the entire world, Nan. Oh, I'm so happy, I can't tell you.'

'You don't have to, my dear. Where has he disappeared to, I just heard the car start up.'

'He's gone to call on his grandfather, because he hasn't seen him yet, and I hope you don't mind, but he'll probably bring him back here for supper, as Eleanor is visiting Miss Brooke. I've got time to put you in the picture, regarding our relationship.'

'Well, you'd better pop upstairs first to give Serena the good news too, eh? I need to get on with cooking the supper – a bigger dish of macaroni cheese and a Bakewell tart than I thought!' *I don't want to hear all the details*, she thought, *I just hope she won't be too hurt if things don't go as planned.*

Sunny tapped on Serena's bedroom door. She'd guessed she would be in there seeing to the baby.

'Come in!' Serena called. She was sitting in the low nursing chair, with the baby in her arms.

'Zosia's just gone to sleep; she's had her feed, so I'll put her in the cot.'

Sunny watched as Serena settled her baby down. Then Serena said, 'Well, how did it go?' She looked keenly at Sunny. 'You look happy, that's good.'

Jan appeared in the doorway. 'All quiet on the Western Front?' He smiled.

'Yes,' Serena said.

'Supper's ready, when you are.'

'I can't stay long, Alec is bringing his grandfather over, and Nan is busy cooking for us, too – but . . .' Sunny said.

'Give us a few minutes then I'll be with you, Jan,' Serena put in.

'I understand,' he said and closed the door.

Sunny said in a rush: 'I'm properly engaged now, look, Serena!' She displayed her ring.

'You kissed and made up, is that the expression?' Serena looked keenly at her daughter.

'Serena – I can't tell Nan, but—'

'It was more than that, I think. Sunny, I'm sure Nan won't react as you think she might. After all, look how she helped young mothers in my situation for so many years, and never made us feel like we'd done anything wrong. Of course, she hoped you would wait, so did I, and that when it happened it would be with the right person, but that's not always how it goes. I hope Alec is the right person, though. Nan would never condemn you for it, I know, and I certainly understand. I just hope that because you are so young and are looking forward to art school, there won't be – any reason—'

'There won't, Serena. He – he promised me that.'

'Then don't feel guilty but put yourself first. He has certainly done that himself in the past. Well, I won't pass it on, but don't be afraid to talk to Nan about it. She's a very wise woman.'

'Thank you, Serena, you are wise too,' Sunny said. 'See you tomorrow. Alec will be here, he's staying overnight. Nan said he could . . .'

'You see, I'm right!' Serena gave her a hug. 'Don't let her down.'

Sunny was aware that at last she was in tune with Serena. She'd always think of Nan as her mother, but Serena, Jan and Zosia were family, too.

Sunny greeted Mr Rowland in the hallway, when he arrived with Alec and he whispered to her, 'Now you can call me Grandfather!'

She whispered back, 'I've always thought of you as that anyway.'

Later, when Alec returned after taking Mr Rowland home, Sunny was already in bed. He kissed her goodnight, and then settled down on the couch, under the window. 'Turn the light off please,' he said. 'We should sleep well tonight after that lovely meal. I like the jolly pig on your dressing table. Who gave you that?'

'A friend, for my birthday,' she said, but she didn't enlighten him further.

* * *

Alec was already up and about, talking to Nan in the kitchen, when Sunny awoke. It was after eight o'clock, and it still seemed strange to her that she no longer had to hurry to catch the bus to Croydon and walk down the alley to the Rowland Printing Press.

She saw that Alec had folded the blankets on the couch as, yawning, she pulled back the curtains. She picked up the pottery pig and held it for a moment against her cheek, before bestowing a brief kiss on its china head. 'Good morning, Mr Pig – I was going to call you Rodney, but I'm not sure that's a compliment to him.' As she replaced it on the dressing table, she felt the brief familiar spasm which heralded what Nan called, 'the time of the month'. Today she welcomed it with relief, though it was a few days early. *I needn't have worried after all,* she thought. *Thank goodness I should feel better by my birthday on Wednesday.*

Nan looked at her keenly as she seated herself at the kitchen table. 'Just toast, please,' she requested. Nan passed her a cup of tea and pressed a couple of aspirin into her palm.

Alec was spreading marmalade on his toast, having consumed a plateful of fried breakfast already. He asked, 'Did Grandfather say he has decided to sell *Sans Souci*? Mother told him she'd been invited to share Helena's house. They got to know each other again, after you went to art classes in the studio, Sunny. Mother has never felt at home in such a big house, especially since Grandfather decided he prefers to live over the shop with his cat, and I'm happy with dossing down there when I come home.'

'Which isn't very often,' Sunny stated, not looking at him.

'It sounds as if you got out of bed the wrong side this morning. I was going to suggest we might go out for the day . . .'

She pushed her chair back, having gulped down the tea and pills, and left the toast untouched.

'Not today,' she said flatly. 'Jan's just left for work, I'll go upstairs and help bath the baby.'

When Sunny had gone, Alec said to Nan, 'What did I do, or what did I say, to upset her, Nan?'

Nan thought, *he doesn't know as much about the opposite sex as he thinks he does.* She said, 'She just feels off-colour that's all, why don't you give your grandfather a hand today and talk to him about things? He misses you too, you know. Also, your mother may be waiting for a lift home, as you have her car.'

'Good idea,' he said, but he didn't sound enthusiastic. 'Perhaps it would be easier for you if I stay with Grandfather until Wednesday? I'll be travelling back to Cambridge at the end of the week.'

'Do what you think is best, and don't worry,' Nan advised. 'She's still wearing her ring!'

'I'm wondering what to buy her for her birthday, right now. She seems to like pottery.'

'Oh, you spotted the Rye Pottery pig?'

'Who gave her that?' Alec asked, but he had already guessed.

'Rodney – have you met him? He's with the army in Germany, so he won't be at the party.'

'We've not met, though I've heard about him. That's a relief, no competition!' Alec sounded rueful.

'They've been friends since primary school,' Nan said. 'Well, I must get on, good luck with the present buying!'

As she washed the dishes, Nan wondered, *is Sunny confiding in Serena now, not me?*

* * *

On her birthday morning, Sunny found a pleasing pile of cards on the front door mat. She opened them after breakfast. Most of them had words to the effect of *PS I'm bringing your present to the party*! So, there were only two parcels to unwrap, from Nan and Chrissie; who'd brought hers round a couple of days ago, only for Nan to whisk it away. Sunny said, 'I already have the lovely dress from Eleanor and . . . Grandfather . . .' she added shyly.

'Well open them up!' Nan said. 'I expect Serena will arrive shortly with something too, eh?'

Nan's gift was something Sunny was hoping for, a pair of gold sandals; perfect for dancing.

'I couldn't try them on, as I wear size six and you have such small feet, I had to go to the children's section in the shoe shop to find a size three! Glad you like them.'

'Thanks, Nan, I certainly do!'

Sunny opened Chrissie's present, and discovered it was something she and Chrissie had admired in the big window of Pratt's Store in Streatham; a soft, cobwebby, cream wool stole which would be perfect with the new dress. 'Oh, it's super!' Sunny exclaimed. 'I expect she's hoping to borrow it occasionally!'

'You missed this little box,' Nan told her, and handed it over. Inside was a gilt mermaid brooch. There was a small card with the box. It read, 'All the best for your birthday, from Ravi.'

Nan chuckled. 'Oh dear, *she* needs something to cover her up, too!'

'I can pin it on the stole,' Sunny said. 'It's lovely! I didn't expect anything from him.'

Then Serena and Jan appeared, with Zosia. 'Happy birthday!' they chorused. Sunny had another present to unwrap; a large box of watercolour paints, and assorted paint brushes. There was an envelope to open too. Sunny withdrew a card, and they crowded round to read it. Sunny exclaimed, '*The Grove Driving School, Qualified Instructor Major Walter J. Matthews!*' Details were also enclosed of a course of weekly lessons for Sunny which could be booked immediately, as the subscription had already been paid. Sunny was excited, this was a gift she hadn't anticipated, but she couldn't wait to learn to drive.

'I haven't got a car, though,' she reminded them.

Nan put in, 'Serena and I are buying one of the new Mini cars and the three of us will share it. I will need lessons too, but Serena can already drive.'

Serena suggested, 'When you have passed your test, you will be able to visit Alec in Cambridge, eh?'

* * *

There was an exciting day ahead. Sunny guessed that the big tin in the kitchen concealed a birthday cake made by Nan, but she wasn't saying who was providing the refreshments. Sunny had been told the party would begin at seven o'clock in the church hall. 'Who's coming?' she asked, but Nan smiled and said, 'Wait and see! Chrissie made a list of everyone she said you'd want to turn up. Alec and his family will be there, anyway. Wear your dancing shoes.'

'Alec can't dance, apparently,' Sunny told Nan.

'He'll be at the piano, taking turns with his mother, I imagine.'

The party had turned into something much bigger than Sunny anticipated; after all, she thought, *I am eighteen, not twenty-one and I already have the key to the door*!

This party was not just a celebration of her birthday, but of her engagement to Alec and the beginning of her new career in the art world. Also, as Nan said simply, 'Being reunited with your first family.'

Sunny had hugged Nan fiercely when she said that and thought how fortunate she was.'Nan, what about the day nursery? It's a chance to publicise that too!'

Sunny had had her hair trimmed to shoulder length by the local hairdresser and then washed and set. Now she could wear it loose and not pulled back with an elastic band. Chrissie had provided her with a face pack and although Nan shook her head, commenting,'You don't need that!' Sunny's face did glow afterwards. She added a touch of blue eye shadow to match her dress and carefully applied coral lipstick. She blotted her lips with a tissue, not wishing to leave an imprint on all the guests she'd be expected to kiss!

She'd not seen Alec all that day, but he'd phoned her first thing to wish her a happy birthday. He was bringing Grandfather to the party, he said, and he would pick up Patsy, her mother and her little boys. Eleanor would come with Miss Brooke, who'd not yet suggested Sunny call her Helena. As it was a Wednesday, and a working day, Chrissie would come to the hall after work. Ravi was on duty, so unable to accompany her.

Sunny was excited at the thought that she and Chrissie would be able to dance together – just like old times!

Jan drove them to the church hall at a quarter to seven. Sunny sat in the front, trying not to crease her new dress. Nan and Serena were in the back with Zosia, and the carrycot and baby-bag were stowed in the car boot, along with the large cake tin.

Nan had been to the hairdresser too. Her silvery hair had been permed for the first time in her life, and she looked much younger with her wavy bob. She wore blue like Sunny, a two-piece costume, with a chiffon scarf at the neck. Serena was in the dress she'd worn at Christmas, for she still had what she described ruefully, and incorrectly in Sunny's opinion, as her 'baby bulge'. Jan donned a clean white shirt with his grey office suit.

Just as Sunny was thinking that Alec with his grandfather, Patsy and co. weren't there yet, their car drew up alongside them, outside the hall. Alec helped his grand-father alight, and the Perkins family followed one another out of the back seats. They waved to the occupants of the other car, and then went inside the hall, closing the door behind them. Sunny spotted Miss Brooke's car parked fur-ther up. So, she and Eleanor had already arrived.

'They might have waited for us,' Nan said, as the baby was tucked into the carry cot, and she and Sunny led the way to the door.

Sunny opened the door and blinked as she took in the smiling faces of all her guests, the balloons and decorations; then Alec came to greet her, her companions gave her a gentle nudge forward, the door closed behind them, and there was a rousing chorus of 'Happy Birthday To You!'

'Three Cheers for Sunny!' called the familiar voice of the curate who had returned with his wife. Sunny learned later that Chrissie had been in touch with him and he'd agreed to be MC for the evening. 'Hip, hip, hooray!' rang to the rafters. Sunny suddenly recalled the get-together after she and Rodney had posed as Adam and Eve on the Youth Club float. It seemed like such a long time ago.

Then Sunny was greeted in turn by other old friends and taken to the table where her presents were piled up. Alec stood close by her side. The old gramophone was wound up and toes tapped to 'Good Golly Miss Molly!' sung by Little Richard. Chrissie danced towards them and embraced Sunny. 'I knew you'd love the shawl; mind you,

I may ask to borrow it on special occasions!' she said, as Sunny had predicted she would. She still had her long hair, because Ravi liked it, and was wearing an Alice band and lipstick to match her red taffeta dress.

The hatch to the kitchen opened up, and the curate's wife was calling for helpers to carry out the trays for the buffet supper. Chrissie said, 'I'll round 'em up!'

Most of the presents were connected with Sunny's coming venture into the art world. Several sketchbooks, boxes of pencils, sticks of charcoal, pastels, chalks and crayons, and tubes of oil paints.

There was a bouquet of flowers from Mr Rowland, a Lego model of a Rolls-Royce car made by Patsy's boys, and a small Kodak camera from Alec. He had only been able to remove half the sticker on the case which said BARGAIN BUY. The letters BARG remained. This didn't worry Sunny though. 'Oh, just what I wanted,' she exclaimed.

'You can take some pictures this evening. It's simple to operate,' he said, pleased at her excited reaction. 'I love your hair like that, and you look gorgeous in your new dress.'

Sunny suddenly thought of Rodney, and how she had kissed him outside the pottery in Rye not so long ago. She experienced a feeling of guilt; she'd likely given him the impression that his hopes of them getting back together might be realised. She'd committed herself to Alec now, after their night of love, but would *he* remain faithful to her once he returned to Cambridge?

Chrissie was back. 'Come on, we can't begin eating until you two join us. You're at the top table, see? The curate will make a speech after we've eaten!'

The food was familiar party fare, unchanged since pre-war times: small sausage rolls, mini pork pies, various sandwiches, with cocktail stick 'flags' proclaiming their contents: egg and cress, tinned salmon, cream cheese and chives, cheddar and Branston pickle. There were banana sandwiches for the children and cups of tea or coffee for the adults, along with beakers of Coca-Cola for Patsy's boys.

After this, the second course emerged from the kitchen fridge: large bowls of raspberry trifle with cream, small iced cakes, brandy snaps filled with more cream, and in the middle of the top table, there was the large chocolate birthday cake made by Nan, crowded with eighteen candles.

Alcohol was not permitted in the church hall so the guests raised their teacups to toast the birthday girl and wish her good fortune in her new career.

The announcement of her engagement to Alec followed. Everyone clapped and Alec embraced her and planted a brief kiss on her lips. Then the curate cleared his throat and looked over at Nan and Serena. 'Congratulations are also due to Miss Cato and Mrs Novak on the reopening of the Mother and Baby Home, as a day nursery.'

The candles on the cake were lit, then extinguished. The cake was cut, and the tables were cleared. Chrissie, Mrs Perkins and Patsy volunteered to help with the washing-up. Chrissie had made all the sandwiches with help from her mother. Patsy's boys requested 'another piece of cake, please', and sat in a corner wiping sticky fingers on their best clothes; Serena retired behind the curtain on the stage to feed baby Zosia, and Nan sighed because it had been a long day and her new shoes pinched.

Alec entertained them by playing favourite songs on the piano while Sunny sat beside him. She felt as if she was dreaming. *Was all this really happening?* She experienced a sudden shiver – *this should be the happiest day of my life,* she thought, *but I still can't be sure about Alec. I need to concentrate on my studies at art school and not let anyone down.*

'"Summertime",' she requested. 'Please play that for me, Alec.'

Most of the guests had departed by ten o'clock, as tomorrow was a working day. The curate and his wife were among those leaving, promising to visit their old parish again later in the year.

Sunny looked around the almost empty hall just before eleven, the curfew hour. Patsy's boys took all the balloons home, and were warned, 'Off to bed directly you get home, school tomorrow!' Jan took Nan, Serena and the baby home. Mr Rowland left at the same time, with Eleanor and Miss Brooke. 'The cat will be wondering where I am,' he said.

Then there were just three of them. Alec was about to close the lid of the piano, Chrissie had stayed to the end, and she admitted to feeling 'whacked'. Sunny was yawning too, and suddenly realised she'd not danced all evening, because she'd been too busy talking to her guests. 'Alec, can you play the last waltz please?'

'Well, I can, but I can't dance with you at the same time,' he told her wryly.

'Chrissie, may I have the pleasure of this dance?' Sunny asked her friend.

The two girls waltzed round the hall, the lights were dimmed, and Sunny murmured, 'Thank you, Chrissie, for arranging everything. This has been an evening I'll always remember.'

'I enjoyed every minute too,' Chrissie said. 'Even though tonight I'm sharing my bedroom with Auntie Beryl. I hope she's not still awake. She can't stop talking and I need to get some sleep.'

After taking Chrissie home, Alec drove Sunny back to the Mother and Baby Home.

'Are you staying here tonight?' she asked.

'I'm off to Cambridge tomorrow, and all my stuff is at Grandfather's, so it's best I leave from there. Please send me copies of all the photos you took this evening.'

'Goodnight and goodbye then,' she sighed. They exchanged a lingering kiss.

'I'll be home over Christmas, I promise. Busy time ahead.'

'For both of us,' she reminded him.

NINETEEN

The art school was situated in a former private school, attached to a big house. Only one of the three original artists who founded it was still at the helm. This was Miss Guyatt, a lively character, despite her advanced age. She'd painted many landscapes in oils over the years. She'd been joined by her niece, Joyce, who carved beautiful objects from wood, and Greta, who specialised in painting on silk. These three ladies lived in the house.

There was also a new member of staff, a young male artist. At first sight, Sunny mistook him for a girl, with his long hair and pale complexion. He had a deep voice and a strong Scots accent, which came as a surprise. His name was Lachlan, and his subject was photography. He came into work by motorcycle from Croydon, three days a week. An older man with a grey beard, who didn't say much, was introduced as Alfred, the potter. He worked in the old stables, and Sunny guessed he lived there as well.

There were eight new students, only two of whom were men, both verging on middle age, hoping for a change of career. The six female students were aged from eighteen to fifty plus with Sunny and two other girls in the youngest group. Miss Guyatt, who employed Miss Brooke on occasion as a visiting artist, took a special interest in her protégée, Sunny.

'You have had good experience, I understand, with the Rowland Printing Press, and are studying art and design with us. Have you learned silk screen printing? That is on our curriculum.'

'No, but I'd love to try it,' Sunny said shyly. 'I've helped Mr Rowland design posters and other advertising material.'

'I am aware you were the subject of a picture by Mr Rowland. I bought a print at the time. It has been admired by many visitors here.'

Sunny nodded. She felt rather overcome by the welcome she'd been given. She gazed around the main studio, at the lines of easels, sturdy tables for craft work and pictures by former students. Some of these were abstract pictures, with splodges of bright colour; interesting, but not her style. When contemplating, she'd already developed a habit of twisting her ring on her finger, but now it was back in its box in her bedroom. Nan had advised: 'You might get it covered in paint or take it off and forget where you've put it. Best to leave it at home.' When

Sunny hesitated, she'd added, 'After all, Alec doesn't wear a ring.'

'That's because he plays the piano,' Sunny said defensively. 'If – when we're married, he'll wear a ring, I believe.' *Not that he's said he will*, she thought ruefully.

Now, after the introductions had been made, and she'd chatted with some of her fellow students, Sunny was allotted an easel and then joined the others at the work benches for a talk by Miss Guyatt. She shared her bench with another girl, who introduced herself as Jen. She wore a smart new artist's smock over jeans and Sunny wondered if her dungarees, the ones she'd been provided with at the Printing Press, were out of fashion now. They were certainly not as baggy as they had been when she was sixteen. Her companion gave her a nudge and whispered: 'You're wearing those in your picture, aren't you? You're the girl with the Sunny smile!'

'May I have your attention please everyone?' Miss Guyatt requested, and the lecture began.

*　*　*

Back at the Mother and Baby Home everything was in full swing. The day nursery had its full quota with three babies, two at the crawling stage and three toddlers who needed the most supervision. Nan, downstairs in her kitchen, coped with the sterilisation of feeding bottles and filling them with the required amount of milk for each baby. One of the young mothers, who had returned to work when her baby was six weeks old, expressed breast milk and brought two bottles along, which were kept in the brand-new fridge, bought especially for the nursery. These were 'warmed up', as Nan put it, when required.

Nan had a new ledger in which to record attendance and fees and there was more office work than her usual baking to be done daily on the kitchen table. At ten o'clock, two hours after the first of their charges arrived, Nan went upstairs, taking the new lift. She went into Serena's kitchen to make cups of coffee and tea for the busy staff. The young nursery nurses settled the older children with their mid-morning snack and greeted the hot drinks and packet of Bourbon biscuits with enthusiasm. Serena took Zosia to the nursery to join the other small babies having their nap.

In passing, she said to Nan, 'Are you happy with everything so far, Nan? It all went off very smoothly, I thought.'

Nan nodded. 'I wonder how our girl is getting on?'

Serena paused for a moment. 'Nan, she's always been *your* girl, not mine, you know,' she said gently. Then she hoisted baby Zosia on her shoulder and kissed the top of her downy head. 'I am so lucky to have another chance,' she added. She hurried off before Nan saw the tears in her eyes.

Nan sipped her tea and enjoyed watching the toddlers playing with the toys. A little girl plucked at her skirt and Nan put down her empty cup and lifted the child upon her lap. Ayesha was the daughter of an Indian couple from Kenya who had moved into one of the new houses at the end of Grove Lane. Their neighbours were from the Caribbean. Grove Lane inhabitants appear somewhat bemused by all the changes to the old Mother and Baby Home, Nan thought.

She jigged the little girl on her knees. 'Ride a cock horse to Banbury Cross,' she sang to little Ayesha. She thought, *it doesn't seem so long ago I was amusing a small Sunny like this. Everything has changed now she's grown up – so much has happened this past year.*

'More!' Ayesha urged, and Nan obliged. She was looking forward to story-time next. The two young nurses were to take turns at this.

*   *   *

Chrissie had an appointment that afternoon. The chief clerk at the bank thought she was off to the dentist. She felt guilty about deceiving him but told herself, *it's the most natural thing in the world, what has happened to us, and Ravi advised me to go to the Family Planning Clinic. I wonder if I should suggest that Sunny does the same? We could talk about things like that when we were not involved with them, but now I don't know if I can. I can't tell my parents either.*

She took a deep breath before she opened the door she had been directed to. There were rows of women seated on benches awaiting the call into the office. Some of them were girls like herself, and she hoped she would not see anyone she knew. Some had babies and toddlers in tow and looked worried.

A young nurse came over and took Chrissie's details. 'I- I'm not married yet, but I will be, next spring,' Chrissie assured her. The nurse said cheerfully, 'All the more reason to say you've made the right decision.' Chrissie's embarrassment faded rapidly. She was whisked away to be weighed, and to have a few tests to see if she was 'fit and ready'. Then while she was waiting to see the nurse in charge, she filled in a questionnaire about her health, past and present, and chewed the end of a borrowed pencil a bit, wishing her mum was with her, because she couldn't remember exactly when she had all the usual childhood illnesses.

'Bit of a palaver,' the kind nurse said as she scrutinised the paper, 'but everything is changing all the time; there's a new pill for women being tested and when it's cleared for use, though these things take a long time, women will cheer and all you'll need to do then is get a monthly prescription from your doctor.'

Chrissie was relieved at that news. She was not sure she could manipulate the 'Dutch cap' recommended. *A pill was easy to swallow*, she thought.

*   *   *

Sunny listened and learned there was a boom in pop art, a bold, fresh approach to advertising in magazines, on posters and billboards. There were young artists with a fresh new approach to art and design, and many of them came from, or had moved to America. David Hockney was mentioned in particular. Roy Lichtenstein was already famous for his bold colourful comic strips.

The English artist Peter Blake was quoted as saying, '*You can't make art without knowing the history of art.*' Miss Guyatt was determined to get this point over to her new students.

After lunch at twelve, they would have an hour to discuss the morning's lecture, but were told to be back in the studio promptly at two. The students provided their own lunch and as it was a pleasant day ate outside in what Miss Guyatt described as, 'My wild garden. Believe it or not, those are not weeds, the purple flower heads are onions gone to seed. Lachlan has offered to mow the grass though.' She left them to eat their sandwiches and pour tea from Thermos flasks.

They had not been told where the toilet was, which was rather worrying, but Jen said, 'I've discovered it: that small wooden shed at the end of the path! Pretty primitive, but clean and smells of carbolic.'

'Thanks for telling me,' Sunny said. 'I like it here, don't you? And the studio is up to date.' She was suddenly aware that they were being watched from the window of the pottery barn. 'The Pottery man,' she exclaimed.

'He seems rather eccentric, but he's a male; they're thin on the ground here!' Jen said. 'I'm going to give pottery a go! You've already been involved with printing and advertising, haven't you?'

'Yes, but there's a lot more I need to learn. Are you ready for a cup of tea; do you take sugar?'

'I smuggled some sugar lumps in that little jar,' Jen said. She sighed. 'Mum says I should give up sugar because I'm overweight. Dad told her it's just puppy fat. He's not one for upsetting people, but Mum is.' She added wryly, 'I'm not sure you can call it puppy fat when you're thirty.'

'Well, I wish I had a figure like Diana Dors. I didn't need a bra until I was sixteen.'

There was the sound of a lawn mower not far away. Lachlan was obviously busy already.

'I wonder how old *he* is,' Jen said. 'Have you got a boyfriend?'

Sunny hesitated, then said slowly, 'I am engaged, actually. But I want to have a career, and so does he, before we are married.'

'Sounds like a sensible chap,' Jen said. 'Come on, the others are packing up and going indoors.'

Sunny couldn't help laughing. *Sensible chap! Not Alec,* she thought. She realised this was the first time she'd thought of him today.

* * *

'How did you get on with the silk screening?' Nan asked that evening. She was sitting in the kitchen soaking her feet in what she called a mustard bath. They had eaten cold cuts from the Sunday joint with bubble and squeak hastily fried from leftover potatoes and greens for supper. Nan had been too weary for any more cooking this evening. The last baby had not been collected until six, the same time as Sunny arrived home. 'Shall we have fish and chips?' she'd asked hopefully. Then remembered, 'Monday – they don't fry tonight.'

'Before I tell you about my day, what about you? I hope it wasn't all too much for you?'

'Oh no,' Nan said. 'I actually enjoyed being back at work, it was almost like old times.'

Sunny described the silk screen process. 'It's a simple wooden frame, or nowadays it could be aluminium, with a woven fabric, probably synthetic but originally silk, stretched over it. A stencil with a negative image is placed on the fabric and ink is forced through it. The surrounding areas are blocked with cut-out paper stencils covered with photographic emulsion. I hope I got that right, as we will probably be questioned about it tomorrow, and it's hard to scribble notes when you are supposed to be taking in what's going on. We all had a go with the squeegee, which is a rubber blade used to press the ink through onto the material; in this case, it was paper. Greta, we are allowed to use her first name, was in charge and said this is called serigraphy. I was the only one to manage a clear impression on the paper, and she said that was because of my training at the Rowland Press.'

'Alexander will be proud of you, I know,' Nan said. She lifted one foot from the water and Sunny fetched a hand towel to dry it for her.

She said, as she knelt by Nan, 'There, now, let me dry the other foot, then I'll empty the water down the sink. Nan, I believe that of dear Mr Rowland, but I'm not sure Alec will be very interested. Playing classical music on a grand piano is much superior to my small effort.'

'I thought he would have sent a good luck message today,' Nan told her. 'Well, I'm proud of you. You are both using your talents, that's important.'

'Someone at the front door,' Sunny said, hiding the emotion stirred by those words. She added, 'They'll have to wait a moment while I pour this water away!'

There was a second, louder knock and she hurried to open the door. Chrissie stood there. She held out her arms and hugged her friend. 'How did it go? I won't stay long, as I guess you will be tired after your first day being arty.'

'I've always got time to talk to you, Chrissie. Say hello to Nan, she's just going to the drawing room to watch TV I expect, you and I can have a chat in my room.'

Chrissie had decided to confide in her best friend. 'Just between you and me, please. I can't tell Mum and Dad, yet, anyway. They get enough grief from Auntie Beryl.' Sunny listened in silence while Chrissie told her about the appointment that afternoon. She ended, 'Please don't think I'm a bad person, Sunny, but when you love someone like I do Ravi, it doesn't seem wrong.'

It was Sunny's turn to hug her friend. 'It isn't, I know that. But – for us – Alec and me, it's different. I can't be sure of his commitment to me, or even of mine, to him, now. Oh, Chrissie, I'm relieved to be able to tell someone, although I think Nan and Serena have probably guessed, but, well, we had one night of – love. It was just one night, just before my birthday.'

'*One Night of Love*, wasn't that the title of a film?' Chrissie asked softly. 'Don't cry, Sunny, I'm sorry things aren't working out so well for you. Any news from Alec?'

Sunny shook her head. Then she managed a smile. 'Anyway, if it happens again, which I doubt, I'll be sensible like you, and follow your example.'

'Come on, let's go and talk to Nan, I'm sure she wants to know more about your day at art school. Sounds like Serena coming down the stairs to hear it all, too!'

'You're such a good friend, Chrissie,' Sunny said grate-fully. *Like Rodney,* she thought. *He sent me a message wishing me well.*

*   *   *

Sunny had to wait until November to have her first driv-ing lesson. Delivery of the car was delayed due to a union strike for more money for workers on the production line. The Mini lived up to its name. It was small and compact but could reach seventy miles per hour. The long-promised motorway, the M1, was at last a reality, too.

Nan became aware of the costs involved in running even a small vehicle, but decided to join the RAC anyway; as she said, 'Jan is the only one with technical knowledge. He's promised to teach us all how to change a tyre though!'

Serena was looking at the headlines in the paper, which the two households shared. She remarked, 'The Russians have managed to send an unmanned spacecraft to the moon and Luna 2 has landed. Though no one, man or woman, has yet gone out into space!'

There was hilarity at this statement. Sunny said, 'We're not planning to drive that far, Serena!' She was looking forward to the driving lessons. When she told Chrissie about them, Chrissie said, 'Ravi's teaching me to drive, too, but I can only use the car when he's off duty. I won't be able to afford a car of my own; you're lucky!'

'I know I am,' Sunny acknowledged. She'd bought an atlas but Cambridge looked so far away.

TWENTY

The car was bright yellow, the colour chosen by Nan and Serena in the belief it would be visible on a dark night or in a fog. It had to have a name of course and Sunny was asked to choose one. She said apologetically, 'Not very original, I suppose, but I would like to call her – well, Minnie!'

'Easy to remember.' Nan looked at Serena, who nodded, smiling. 'Minnie,' she repeated. 'I like that.'

The instructor, Walter Matthews, was known by Grove Lane residents as the Major, on account of his wartime service in the army. He lived up to his nickname, having a bristling moustache, and a military bearing. He barked out instructions and believed that everyone should 'listen and learn'.

Sunny's first lessons were in the Major's car, a large black limousine, that gleamed due to his diligent cleaning. There were leather straps for nervous passengers to hang on to in an emergency. Naturally, the Major wasn't a driver who swerved or overtook other vehicles, though this did not apply to his pupil drivers. He didn't make small talk but kept up a commentary about safe driving and would ask snap questions. 'Tell me what that sign indicates, Miss Cato.' Sunny wondered whether the whiff of perfume emanating from the Major's portly figure was after-shave or hair pomade.

'You may call me Sunny,' she said, thinking he was not very friendly.

'That would not be suitable,' he said firmly, putting her in her place.

Sunny mentioned the odd smell and this comment to Nan.

'Now, now,' Nan reproved her, but with a smile. 'I expect learner drivers make him sweat when they have near-misses, and he's covering it up. He is formal with young ladies because he has a reputation for being correct. How did you do today?'

'Well, he boomed, "Watch out!" several times,' Sunny said. She sighed. 'I'm not sure I'll get the hang of it all, and I was hoping to pass my test before Christmas.'

'Oh, that's too soon, but I hope you will before the bad weather. Cambridge and Alec, you'll get there, but it might be spring by then,' Nan said. 'Still, I can't talk, I haven't had my first lesson yet!' She thought, *I won't tell her but I remember the Major's wife and their only child, a little boy of three years old, died of TB while he was away in the war. His son would have been about the same age as Sunny. Poor man.*

When it was Nan's turn to sit in the driving seat with the Major close by, she made sure her skirt was covering her knees and she wore walking shoes; the Major didn't approve of high heels apparently. You couldn't be aloof in a Mini though, there wasn't enough space.

The perfume Sunny had noticed was evident giving Nan a sudden flashback to when she was a small child and had watched her father rubbing some concoction into his hair. Her mother had enlightened her. 'It's bay rum, Nanette, keeps hair healthy.' *I didn't realise some men still used it,* Nan thought.

The Major actually paid her a compliment. 'You don't look any older than the last time we met, Miss Cato. That must have been just after the war.'

'Yes, I think it was,' she replied, but she remembered exactly when it was. They had met in the churchyard when she was seeing to the plants on her mother's grave and he was doing the same for the double grave for his wife and son. Of course, he was a familiar figure in Grove Lane, but usually in his car, driving up and down, as it was a good stretch of road for learner drivers.

Nan thought, *it must be my new hairstyle; Alexander commented on the change in my appearance too, at Sunny's party. I suppose my mother didn't encourage me to wear pretty clothes off duty, as I do Sunny – I never felt young really, even when I was eighteen. I certainly didn't have a young man (or two) in tow like my beautiful daughter does. On the other hand, I didn't suffer a broken heart, which I fear Sunny might one day.*

Later, she suggested to Sunny, 'Shall we invite Alexander over for Sunday lunch? I'm sure he misses you now you are not working for him.'

'I know he's getting on well with Patsy, Nan.' She looked at Nan and thought, *gosh, she's actually blushing*! She added: 'It's a nice idea though, but how will he get here? Eleanor brought him before, but we could ask Miss Brooke to come as well.'

'I'm not sure I can cope with a lunch party,' Nan admitted. She was looking forward to seeing Mr Rowland on his own and getting to know him better.

*   *   *

The memory stirred of meeting the Major all those years ago in the graveyard made Nan realise that she hadn't given her mother's memorial stone a good scrub and tidied up the rose bushes in autumn as she usually did. Saturday and Sunday were now her only days off from work.

On Saturday morning she went shopping and bought a rib of beef at the butcher's; she intended to cook a special roast dinner on Sunday. Alexander had accepted the invitation and Jan had kindly offered to be his 'chauffeur for the day' as he put it.

In the afternoon, she changed her shoes for boots and filled a canvas bag with trowel and fork, a scrubbing brush, a flask of hot water, secateurs, ancient rubber gloves discarded by Mrs Perkins, and a rolled-up sack to take any rubbish to the designated place. At the last minute she remembered a mat to kneel on. It was a drizzly day, so she tied a headscarf firmly round her hair.

There was no one else in the churchyard, probably because of the weather, she thought. She got busy clearing the layer of autumn leaves which had blown over the plot and gave the two rose bushes a good trim. She was busy for almost two hours. She was still on her knees scrubbing the moss on the stone, when she heard the crunching of the gravel path, which meant someone was approaching. She straightened her aching back.

'Please allow me to assist you to stand up,' a familiar voice said. One heave from the Major's strong arms, and she was upright.

She wobbled and he held her steady. 'You need to sit down, you've done too much,' he said, sounding concerned. 'It's cold here. Let's go into the church and you can rest for a short while in the back pew. I'm early for the bell ringing practice.' He packed her bag neatly. 'Leave the sack for the moment, I'll dispose of that for you later.'

They sat together in the church and she took off the headscarf, *there's nothing I can do about the muddy boots*, she thought ruefully.

'I'm not a regular churchgoer,' she admitted, 'but I sometimes attend services at Easter and on Christmas Eve.'

'Ringing the bells has been my salvation,' he said, and he wasn't booming now. 'My wife loved to hear them. As you may know, we lived in the cottage just below church hill and I'm still there. You've lived here for a long time as well, I believe?'

'I was a hospital nurse for years until I came here with my mother before the war and we set up the Mother and Baby Home,' she told him.

'You never married?' he asked. 'But you have a daughter, as I know.'

'No, I suppose I didn't have time to marry. I adopted Sunny when she was three years old, but I had looked after her from the time she was born.'

'Your daughter is a credit to you. She is progressing well with her driving. You are too.'

'Oh, thank you, that's very encouraging.'

There were others in the church now, bell ringers both young and old. The Major said, 'I must join them; I have the key to the belfry. I will see you for your lesson next week. It has been a pleasure to talk to you.' He stood up, waiting for her to rise.

He saw her out of the church door. As she made her way to the gates, she heard the first bells ringing. *He's much nicer than I thought he was*, she thought. *I will make sure I go to Midnight Mass on Christmas Eve.*

* * *

Jan called for Mr Rowland just before midday on Sunday. Mr Rowland opened the door with Pilchie draped round his neck. His cravat was askew due to this, but he wore what must have once been a fashionable business suit, navy blue pin-striped with wide-legged trousers and a waistcoat. 'I'll be with you in a moment,' he said, 'I'll just pop the cat in the washroom, the tap drips and she can duck her head under it to get a drink. I put her food bowl in there earlier, which was a mistake, as she ate her dinner there and then.' Jan was left on the doorstep for five minutes before Mr Rowland reappeared.

'Home, James, and don't spare the horses!' He used an expression familiar to those born before the turn of the century but Jan gave him a startled look as he'd not heard it before even though he was familiar with more recent sayings. He thought, *is the old fellow losing his marbles?*

Sunny opened the door when she heard the car arrive. 'Oh, Grandfather, you look very posh today!' she told him.

He beamed. 'You might see a few cat hairs on my collar, though, Sunny!'

Jan was about to go upstairs. 'Enjoy lunch!' he said. 'I'll see you later to take you home.'

Sunny opened the kitchen door. Nan was just taking the joint out of the oven and she looked up and smiled a welcome. Mr Rowland waited while she set the hot roasting tin down, then he greeted her with a chaste kiss on the cheek. Close up his suit smelled strongly of mothballs. He hadn't done much to his shock of white hair, and Nan allowed herself the errant thought that a touch of the Major's bay rum might have helped. Still, he had replaced the broken spectacles with rimless ones, with wire legs which hooked behind his ears. His daughter had forced him to buy these and gone along with him to the opticians.

'Sit at the table, Alexander, and read the *News of the World*,' Nan suggested. 'Sunny can help me dish up.' He was polite enough not to say he preferred *The Sunday Times*.

'Why are there always stories about rogue clergy or doctors left money by elderly ladies?' Mr Rowland refolded the paper neatly and watched what the ladies here were up to. Nan carved the meat, while Sunny decanted the vegetables into serving dishes and stirred the bubbling gravy in the pan. They were aware of his gaze, which made them drop a spoon or two, and there was a bit of panic when they remembered they hadn't made the horseradish sauce.

'He must think we are very clumsy,' Sunny hissed into Nan's ear. 'Where's the gravy boat?'

'Where it always is,' Nan replied, *sotto voce*.

However, when they sat down to lunch, thankfully, the tender slices of pinkish meat, the perfect roast potatoes, the variety of vegetables, including tinned butter beans, prompted their guest to exclaim, 'I haven't had these for years, but then I'm not much of a cook myself, nor is my daughter. This meal is absolutely spot-on!' Sunny suppressed a giggle, when she saw a grease spot on his waistcoat, where he'd dropped a large roast potato down his front. He'd hastily retrieved it, and they pretended they hadn't noticed.

The cook and her assistant, pink-cheeked from the heat of the oven, breathed a joint sigh of relief. By the time Mr Rowland had enjoyed second helpings of beef, and Nan was wondering whether there would be any leftovers for dinner on Monday, Sunny was dashing to the hob, where the saucepan was threatening to boil dry and ruin the jam roly-poly. They served this up with thick custard and Mr Rowland patted his narrow middle, observing, 'This is the stuff to give the troops!' He was the only one who could manage a second helping.

The table was cleared, and Sunny suggested Nan and Mr Rowland have a siesta in the drawing room, while she washed up. 'Are you sure, dear?' Nan said uncertainly, wondering how she could entertain him, but Sunny insisted. She winked at Nan as they made their way out of kitchen, and Nan whispered, 'You're a cheeky girl!'

Nan gave the drawing room fire a good poke and added some knobs of coal. She sighed. 'It would be wonderful to have central heating; but actually I do love sitting by the fire.'

He nodded. 'If we hadn't just eaten the most satisfying Sunday lunch, I would have suggested we make toast for tea!'

'I've got an antique toasting fork, but I gave it a rub-up with Brasso so it's probably best left hanging on the wall,' she said.

They were sitting in the wing-back chairs either side of the fireplace. He had chosen a chair when she'd thought they might sit on the sofa together.

'We've sold the Shirley house,' he said suddenly.

'Oh, that's good,' Nan said. 'Does Eleanor intend to stay on with Miss Brooke then?'

'It appears so. The money will be divided into three, one part each for Eleanor, Alec and me.'

Nan wondered why he was telling her this private information but didn't comment.

He continued, 'I will be able to renovate my shabby abode but will keep going for a while in the business, wind down gradually, I suppose. Eleanor won't need to work for her living anymore. If she invests some of her share it will see her through later on; though she and Helena are planning a trip to Rome soon. Alec, well, his share will be kept until he leaves university and becomes established in his musical career.'

Nan said quietly, 'You didn't need to tell me all your private business, Alexander, you know.'

'I thought you would like to know that Alec will be able to support a wife, as Sunny will be involved.'

'Alexander, he might change his mind – he seems to blow hot and cold in that direction.'

'I have to agree with that, it's true. I suppose you could say he takes after his old grandfather. When I married my wife, I regretted losing my independence. She wanted me to change, to be successful in the City, but I always wanted to do something very different. She found someone who fitted the bill, as they say, and left me. Eleanor was affected badly by her mother leaving, and later she too made the mistake of marrying the wrong man, and was divorced when Alec was still young.'

'Was that when you became like a father to him, too?'

'I suppose it was. We are alike in many ways.' Mr Rowland sighed. 'I never wished to remarry, and I imagine he thinks marriage is not the be all and end all, like me.'

Neither noticed that Sunny was standing just inside the door. She'd come to ask if they were ready for coffee and had overheard most of the conversation.

Nan suddenly realised that Sunny was there with a stricken look on her face. Without saying anything, she turned and went to her bedroom.

'Excuse me,' Nan said, 'I must go and try to explain what we were really discussing.' What Mr Rowland had divulged about his own view on marriage had given her a jolt too. She thought, *I'm a fool, imagining he and I might get together one day. What can I say to my girl to comfort her?*

Mr Rowland followed her out. 'Perhaps it's best I go home now – the cat will be prowling about. I'll go upstairs, if I may, and ask Jan if he can take me shortly. I apologise for upsetting you both.'

Nan didn't answer. She tapped on Sunny's door and then went inside. Surprisingly, Sunny didn't shed any tears. Cradled in Nan's arms, she repeated, 'Why?' but Nan had no answers.

Sunny didn't emerge for supper and Nan went to bed early as well.

Around midnight, Sunny awoke from a short sleep, reached for the sketch pad and pencil kept on her bedside table in case she wanted to record an idea, and she wrote:

My dear Alec,

I have come to the conclusion that we should release each other from the commitment we made in September. We both need to be free to go our own way and concentrate on our future careers. Please don't feel guilty about anything. We may not meet again for some time, and I wish you well. I don't expect a reply.

Sunny

At the bottom of the sheet of paper, she drew a sad little face, but erased it, and then she blotted a tear or two which had fallen on her message. She'd post it first thing, she decided.

TWENTY-ONE

Suddenly, it seemed, Christmas 1958 was only a month away. Since she had sent the letter to Alec, Sunny hadn't heard from him at all. Mr Rowland, however, had rung the day after his visit to say he was sorry if he had put his foot in it and would they forgive him? Sunny passed the phone to Nan and indicated that she didn't feel like talking to him at that moment.

When Nan put the phone down after reassuring Mr Rowland that of course they were still friends, she said softly, 'Perhaps he actually did you a good turn, Sunny. You have been honest with Alec, and he should be the same with you.'

Serena wisely didn't get involved with all this. As she said to Jan, 'We don't know much about Alec; we only met him once or twice because of Sunny's birthday party. Nan will deal with it.'

Of course, Nan did help Sunny come to terms with having been the one to jilt Alec, not the other way around. 'You mustn't feel guilty,' she said at the beginning, when Sunny cried herself to sleep each night. 'If you are meant to be together, it will happen, but you are right, you both need to work hard at your chosen professions.'

Sunny was determined to succeed, so she swallowed her sorrow and learned a great deal about the history of art and the great creative genius of artists, which had survived the centuries. She embraced modern art too, because she realised this was what she wanted to do and she succeeded with the silk screening. Jen, on the other hand, sighed and said, 'I guess I'll be a potter. I'm big and strong. I'm a good cook so I'm expert both with dough balls and lumps of clay!' Sunny laughed and said, 'Old Alfred says you're his star pupil.'

'He's not that old,' Jen asserted. 'Fifteen years older than me, if you want to know. It's that grey beard which makes him look ancient. And, by the way, he's not what everyone thinks he is.'

'Oh, and what's that?' Sunny teased her.

'You know! He likes women. He'd like to be married and have a family – so there!'

'Oh, Jen, sorry, I do like his sculptures; especially that figure Miss Guyatt was praising the other day.' She paused; *I'd better not say that the curvaceous lady in question might have been based on Jen,* she thought!

Jen was blushing. She guessed what her friend was thinking and she had the answer ready: 'You can suppose all you like, but I'm not saying!'

*   *   *

Sunny had not seen much of Chrissie recently, so she decided to visit her one evening after Nan told her that Chrissie was unwell and confined to bed at the moment. 'Food poisoning, her mum thinks – nothing contagious,' Nan said. She was pleased that Sunny was actually going out and not mooning about in her bedroom, as she thought of it.

Mrs Ford greeted Sunny at the door with, 'Oh thank you for coming! Chrissie feels really poorly. She's been in bed for nearly a week now.'

'What does Ravi say?' Sunny asked, as they went upstairs.

'Oh, he's been away on a course, and doesn't know. She insisted I mustn't say if he phoned.'

'Has he phoned?'

'No. He's sharing a hotel room with two other young doctors and there's no privacy if he uses the phone. He writes to her every other day, though. He'll be back at the weekend, and she must buck up before then. I called our doctor, but he was a bit cagey about what it might be.'

Mrs Ford opened the door and called to her daughter, 'Sunny's here, I'll leave you to have a chat.' She closed the door and they heard her descending the stairs. Mr Ford would be home shortly and supper must be on the table. This was an old-fashioned household.

Chrissie was hardly visible under the bedclothes, and Sunny tapped her on her shoulder. She struggled up, her face almost as white as the sheet. There was the smell of sickness in the room, Sunny thought, and she saw a covered bowl on the floor beside the bed.

'Oh, Sunny, I'm so glad to see you. I have to tell someone,' Chrissie said, then she began to sob and Sunny held her hand and said, 'You can tell me. I won't pass it on, if you don't want me to.'

'I – I'm not sure, but I think I might be having a baby.'

'Oh, Chrissie! I thought you went to the clinic.'

'I did, but it can still happen. They told me that, although it's not very likely.'

'How did you find out?' Sunny asked. She felt as if she had a lump in her throat.

'Well, I missed the usual, last month, but then I began feeling sick and couldn't keep anything down. That's why Mum thought it was food poisoning. But I had a "show", you know, and hoped I was mistaken. The doctor called and said I should go to the surgery for some tests. I think he knew but could see I was worried what Mum would say.'

'When Ravi comes home, you'll tell him. You *must*, Chrissie!'

'He's a doctor, he'll know. I need support when I tell Mum and Dad.'

There was a tap on the door and Mrs Ford enquired anxiously, 'Everything all right?'

'Tell her now. I'll support you,' Sunny urged Chrissie. 'Come in,' she called to Mrs Ford.

Chrissie held out her arms to her mother. 'Mum, oh Mum! I have to tell you something. I'm so sorry, but . . .' She broke off as Sunny moved aside to allow Mrs Ford to hug her daughter.

'You're expecting a baby, aren't you? I've never experienced it myself, but I knew in my heart that's what it was.'

'Oh, Mum!' Chrissie choked.

'Did you think I'd turn away from you, call you a bad girl? Because you aren't. You are our wonderful daughter, and these things happen, I know that. We'll call the doctor again, and then, thank goodness, Ravi will be here two days from now.'

Sunny said, 'I must go, leave you to talk. You have a lovely mother, like mine, Chrissie. We'll all support you; I promise.'

As she walked home, she thought, *I'm glad I said the right things to Chrissie. Ravi is such a nice chap. He will make things right. I expect there will be a wedding sooner rather than later, now. But I have lost the love of my life, and Chrissie and I have probably come to the parting of the ways.*

* * *

On Friday morning there was a letter in the post for Sunny. She recognised Alec's handwriting. 'I'll read it when I get home tonight,' she told Nan. 'I'll have the weekend to think about what it says.'

She caught the earlier bus to art school and was in time to see Jen descend from the back of Lachlan's motorcycle. *Surely Jen hasn't got two suitors*, she thought. Jen caught up with her as she went into the studio. 'It's not what you think,' she said breathlessly.

'Why should I think anything at all?' Sunny said, but she smiled.

'I didn't realise he was interested in me; you know,' Jen said smugly.

'Old – sorry! I don't think Alfred will like it.'

'He shouldn't have asked me to pose for that statue then. Lachlan told me then he'd been hoping to photograph me – with my clothes on, of course,' Jen added hurriedly, 'I didn't strip right off for the statue, I wore . . .'

'Never mind,' Sunny said. 'Here come all the others!' She suddenly realised she was smiling at the thought of Jen posing for one or both tutors. *Nan needn't worry about me*, she thought, *I wouldn't have the nerve.*

After she had enjoyed Nan's steak, kidney and mushroom pie for dinner, Nan reminded Sunny about the letter. 'You don't have to tell me what it says,' Nan said tactfully. 'I put it in your bedside table drawer.'

Sunny actually waited until she got into bed at ten o'clock before she opened the letter.

Dear Sunny,

I have put off writing to you, in case you changed your mind about our relationship. This is obviously not the case. While I agree we both need to concentrate on our future careers, I wish you had told me your thoughts face to face. It seems you had doubts about my feelings for you. I admit I let you down on several occasions, but perhaps it is because you think I took advantage of you when we spent the night together. If this is so, I can only say I am sorry, although I can't regret what happened.

You may decide to ignore this letter, but please continue your friendship with Grandfather, even if you feel contempt for me. I'm glad he and Nan keep in touch. I'm afraid he was right to point out I am not the marrying kind, but I came nearer to it with you than I ever would with anyone else.

I wish you every good fortune in the future.

Alec

PS Is it ironical to say as they do in films – 'It was nice knowing you.'

She knuckled the tears away from her eyes and tore the letter in half. She replaced the pieces in the envelope and tucked it under her pillow. She said aloud, 'I love you, Alec; I have ever since I first met you in the alley on the way to the Rowland Printing Press. But I'm not going to answer this letter.'

*   *   *

Ravi took the steps two at a time. Mrs Ford had said, 'Go up! She's been very poorly, but you'll know what to do, after all you're a doctor.'

Chrissie had combed her hair and wore her mother's bed jacket over her nightie. She smiled at Ravi, but her lips trembled. 'You came back,' she said.

'Of course I did and if I'd known you were ill, I would have left the conference earlier! Oh, Chrissie, what's wrong?'

'Can't you guess?' she asked. 'I'm expecting a baby, I think, but I don't know for sure.'

'You must get an independent opinion, but I'm sure you're right if you think so,' he said.

'I'm sorry, this must be a shock for you.'

'Chrissie, we love each other, don't we? Things are looking up. I have a permanent position at the surgery and we have the chance to buy a place of our own to live, thanks to my parents. It'll just happen earlier than we thought. We'll get married as soon as we can arrange it.'

She threw back the bedclothes and he helped her out of bed so they could sit together in the chair.

'Can you pass me my dressing gown please? It's hanging on the back of the door,' she said. 'Then you can help me downstairs and we'll talk to Mum and Dad about all this.'

'Let me give you a kiss and a hug first. I've missed you so much,' he said.

*   *   *

Sunny had some important news to impart to Nan. 'I'm going to be a bridesmaid on Boxing Day – Chrissie and Ravi are getting married in the church then. You'll get an invitation I know, but it'll be a small affair. Unfortunately, Ravi's parents can't come, but they plan to visit in June.'

'When the baby arrives?' Nan asked.

'Oh, Nan, how did you know?' Sunny exclaimed. She'd promised Chrissie she wouldn't tell anyone as hopefully it wasn't noticeable yet. She had lost weight when she was sick, but she was feeling better now and back at work in the bank. She was hoping to carry on there until the sixth month, she said.

Nan said, 'Oh, Sunny, it happened to young women before they came to the Mother and Baby Home, of course, but nowadays it's not the problem it was. I felt so much then for those who had to give their babies up; we kept them together as long as we could.'

'If it had happened to me and Alec, would you have felt the same?'

'Yes, I would. But I would have worried about you, of course.' *Would Alec have married Sunny then?* Nan thought. She changed the subject. 'May I ask Alexander to join us for Christmas dinner this year, Sunny? Eleanor and her friend have booked a week's holiday in Rome, as he thought they might.'

'Well, of course you can – though not if Alec is with him,' Sunny said.

'No, apparently Alec will be away too. I don't know where,' Nan told her. 'Have you heard if Rodney will be back at Christmas?' She was aware of the weekly airmails from Rodney in Germany, of course.

'He hopes to be home for four days from Christmas Eve,' Sunny said. 'Don't read too much into that, Nan, please. We're best friends, that's all.'

'If you say so,' Nan commented wisely.

* * *

Two weeks before Christmas, Nan had her final driving lesson. When they drew up outside the Mother and Baby Home, the Major had a word or two with her before he escorted her to her front door as usual. 'Miss Cato, I say this with some reluctance, for I have enjoyed these sessions with you, but all good things come to an end. You are ready, I feel, to take your driving test. That will be in the New Year.'

'What about Sunny? Is she ready too?' Nan asked.

'Ah – your daughter . . . I'm afraid she has not concentrated so much lately, and I believe she needs a few more lessons, if that is possible. I expect she is preoccupied with her art; very understandable.'

'I think you are right,' Nan agreed. *Of course, he doesn't know about the upset over Sunny's breakup with Alec,* she thought.

'Your daughter did mention earlier that she intended to visit Cambridge in the New Year.'

'I think she has given up that idea,' Nan said, indicating she was ready to leave the car.

Usually, he would drive straight off but he said, 'I would like to issue an invitation to attend the Mayor's Christmas lunch as my guest, tomorrow week. It wouldn't have been proper to have asked you while I was teaching you to drive.'

Nan was surprised. 'Why me?' she wanted to know.

'May I call you Nanette?' he said and, taking a deep breath, 'I would be happy if you would call me Walter. I – well, felt we had a lot in common the day we met at the church and would like to get to know you better.

I would be honoured if you said yes.' He smiled, and as he usually looked so serious, she suddenly agreed. 'I would be delighted to accompany you, Walter.' She hesitated. 'Will it be formal dress?'

'No, it's lunch, not dinner. I will wear a suit, and perhaps you might wear a hat with your outfit?'

Nan thought immediately of the blue silk outfit that she had worn at the birthday party in September. Perhaps she could buy a hat to match.

'I will telephone you later with the details. Goodbye for now, Nanette.' He helped her out of the driving seat and escorted her to the door as usual.

She met Sunny in the hall, with Zosia in her arms. 'Serena and Jan were tired, so they're having a rest in their bedroom, and they asked me if I would amuse the baby, as she's awake.'

Nan surprised her by commenting: 'Having a rest – is that what they call it? Ah well, give me the baby and make us a cup of tea, please.'

'How did you get on with the lesson?' Sunny asked, as they went into the warm kitchen.

'I'm ready for the test,' Nan told her. 'So, no more lessons. You appear not too interested in driving now, Sunny.'

'I suppose that's how it seems. I won't be visiting Cambridge, anyway.'

'Believe it or not,' Nan said, trying to sound casual, 'The Major has invited me to be his partner at the Mayor's Christmas lunch in the Town Hall, on Sunday week.'

'Nan – I do believe he's hopeful, if you know what I mean.'

'Maybe he is.' Nan surprised her. 'And I don't mind at all!'

TWENTY-TWO

Sunny said, 'Keep still, Nan, I'm trying to get your hat on at the right angle – and don't move your hands about, you'll smudge your nail varnish. It takes time to dry, you know . . .'

Nan was seated before her dressing table mirror with Sunny bending over her, making sure she looked her best for the big occasion. 'He'll be here in five minutes,' she told Sunny. 'And don't say I need some lipstick, because it's not me!'

'Oh, Nan, I'm sorry, I didn't mean to fuss! Was that a car pulling up outside? I'll go and see, but be ready to scoot!'

'Scoot – where *do* you hear these expressions?' Nan murmured, but she looked out of the window, saw Sunny greeting the Major, and smiled ruefully.

The Major looked resplendent in a smart navy blue suit and a bow tie. He gazed at Nan in her blue costume with the lovely cream shawl, Sunny's birthday gift from Chrissie, draped round her shoulders. Sunny had insisted she must wear because it was December, and cold outside. He had a twinkle in his eye as he said, 'Better duck your head when you get in the car, Nanette, or you might bend the feather in your hat!'

He's actually got a sense of humour, she thought. Sunny waved them off, and Serena, holding Zosia up to see her Nana depart, watched from the front upstairs window.

'I feel a bit nervous,' Nan confessed.

'You're not the only one,' he assured her. 'This is the first time I have been honoured with an invitation. I became a councillor earlier in the year, you see.'

Nan nodded. She recalled reading of his election in the local paper.

'Have a look in the glove compartment,' he told her. 'Something I thought you might like.'

Nan discovered a fragrant yellow rosebud wrapped in tissue paper. The stem was covered with silver paper, with a small safety pin attached. She inhaled the scent. 'Oh, it's lovely, thank you!'

The Town Hall was part of an imposing red brick building embellished with patterns of Portland stone and a roof of Westmorland green slates. During the week, buses ran at intervals along this busy road, but today several cars that had arrived earlier had already parked outside and the Major had to find a space. Nan didn't speak to him while he manoeuvred the car. This was one of the rules pupil drivers had to learn.

'Here we are,' he said. 'I'll come around and help you alight, then pin the rose on your lapel.' When that was done, they stood for a long moment gazing at the line of people filing through the main entrance to the building. the Major indicated she should take his arm, and when she faltered at the steps, he said: 'Hold tight!' and looked concerned.

'It's my shoes,' she told him, 'I'm afraid I'm not used to high heels.'

'My wife was the same,' he assured her.

When Sunny and Serena wanted to know what the meal was like, Nan said simply: 'Oh, I couldn't eat much, but I did enjoy the Black Forest Trifle! I had a glass of sherry too; I didn't like to tell the Major I don't imbibe – well not much.'

They smiled at the old-fashioned term she used, and Sunny exclaimed, 'Oh, Nan, you know you like a glass of Burgundy and lemon at Christmas!'

'I prefer the lemon!' Nan said, but she was smiling too. 'Let's say I had an interesting time and – the Major is a real gentleman. Would you put my rose in water for me please, Sunny?'

* * *

Serena asked Sunny if she would be able to babysit the following Saturday evening, because she and Jan were going to his firm's annual dinner and dance in London. 'We'll be back after midnight, as there's the drive home afterwards. I hope that's all right. I did ask Nan first, because I thought you might be at Chrissie's, helping with the wedding plans.'

'Well, I will be out in the morning, helping Chrissie choose her outfit. Mrs Ford is coming with us and says I can advise her too. She didn't tell Auntie Beryl, otherwise she would have wanted to come too. Chrissie said Auntie Beryl had hinted she would like to be a bridesmaid, but she told her it was going to be a modest affair. Chrissie's not wearing a long white dress; anyway, shorter wedding gowns are all the fashion now.' She added, 'Did Nan say she couldn't help, then?'

'She just said a friend was coming to supper.'

'Oh, do you think that's the Major?'

'Well, it's up to her to tell you really, but – she said Alexander.'

Sunny bit her lip. 'I haven't been in touch with him, since, you know . . . Nor has Nan, I believe. But of course I don't mind, because he is her friend as well as mine. Perhaps it's just as well I won't be around downstairs, Serena. I know I should have made it up with him by now, though.'

'I'm sure he didn't mean to upset you. He was telling Nan how it was, with him and with his grandson. I assume you haven't heard from Alec either?'

'Only once, and I don't want to think about that letter, Serena.'

'I didn't mean to pry,' Serena said. She gave Sunny a hug. 'Saturday evening at five o'clock, is that all right? Zosia usually settles down in her cot after her evening bottle.'

Zosia had recently been weaned and taken to this without any problems, though she was not too keen on some of the baby food her mother tried to tempt her with. 'She likes cereal, Farex best, but Jan had a taste and said he didn't think much of it!' Serena smiled.

'What will you wear?' Sunny asked.

'Well, I had a pleasant surprise. My dear husband had a look in my wardrobe and checked the size of my clothes, then called in at Richard Shops and chose a beautiful red velvet dress; very smart.'

'Sounds just right for you!' Sunny said.

* * *

On Saturday morning, Sunny caught the bus to Streatham with Chrissie and Mrs Ford. They walked towards their favourite shop, Pratt's, with Chrissie between them, each holding an arm. She had protested, 'I'm not an invalid, you know! I feel much better than I did, thank goodness.'

It had rained most of the night and the pavements were still wet. 'You've got to think of the baby you know. You don't want to fall over, do you?' Mrs Ford said.

'Oh, Mum, stop worrying! Ravi's just as bad, though, he won't let me tidy his flat when I'm there. What you'll all be like later on I don't know.'

They paused at the main window of the store, beautifully decorated for Christmas. Sunny mentioned Serena's new red dress, which she'd proudly wear tonight as it was a special occasion.

'Oh, I don't think red would be right for a wedding,' Mrs Ford put in.

'Let's go inside, it's cold out here and drizzling again.' Sunny propelled Chrissie into the shop and a disgruntled Mrs Ford followed behind.

A sales assistant came over, smiling, asking if they needed help to find what they wanted.

Chrissie said, 'My mother would be glad to have your advice, she needs a smart outfit for a Christmas wedding. My friend and I will have a look around, and will call you when we've seen something, we like.'

'Oh, you are going to the wedding too? Is it in church or a register office?'

'Church,' Sunny said, steering her friend away, and they began to look through the rails of outfits. Mrs Ford gave her a reproachful look when she was escorted in the opposite direction where there was a sign proclaiming, 'Lovely outfits for the mature figure.'

'Most ladies of your age like neutral colours – beige, for instance?' the assistant prompted.

However, Mrs Ford had spotted something interesting on the sale rail. 'What colour would you call this?' she asked. The material had a silver thread running through it, which sparkled when the light caught it.

'Gunmetal grey,' the assistant sighed. 'You'd need a bright scarf to wear with that,' she added hopefully, pointing out a plethora of silk scarves on a stand. These cost almost as much as the costume her prospective customer had her eye on.

'This is just right for Christmas; the longer skirt, and the fitted jacket with velvet on the collar. I wonder if it's my size,' Mrs Ford said, adding, 'It looks as if it will be. And comfortable too.' What she liked best of all was the sticker which read: 'REDUCED TO £3.' 'May I try it on please?'

'Of course, madam,' the assistant said, steering her towards the scarves en route to the changing cubicle. 'Cornflower blue would be perfect with grey.'

The outfits the girls were exclaiming over were much more expensive, and fashionable. Chrissie glanced ruefully down at the slight swelling of her stomach. 'It isn't obvious at the moment,' Sunny reassured her. She was concentrating on helping her friend choose something special for her wedding; *I can wear my birthday dress and the shawl to keep me cosy*, she thought. 'How about this shift dress?' she asked. 'It skims the waistline, and you'd be able to wear it afterwards too.' This was labelled: mohair – colour, rose. There was the usual 'dry clean only' instruction, which meant you wouldn't wear it every day. Skirts were shorter for younger women; the New Look was now the Old Look. This dress fastened on the shoulders with small gold buttons and there was matching gold trim round the neckline and on the cuffs of the three-quarter-length balloon sleeves, fashionable this year. There was a long matching stole, that she could drape round herself. The assistant said, 'You throw one end over your shoulder, like this – see?'

Sunny and Chrissie looked at each other. 'This is the one, ten guineas, but Dad said don't worry about the price,' Chrissie said. 'It's a size larger than I usually buy, but it's perfect! What can I wear on my head?'

Another assistant had watched their progress and now came up to them. 'I understand this is for a wedding? Are you the bride? Try it on and look in the long mirror. Your mother has just bought her dress, and she looks like your sister in it. It's a very youthful style.' She steered the two girls to a display of hair ornaments. 'A wreath of tiny roses, a glittering band, one with a veil?'

It was a satisfying morning's shopping. When they emerged from the shop, although the sun wasn't shining, the drizzle had ceased and they were in good time for the bus back to Grove Lane.

*   *   *

Nan was downstairs in her kitchen preparing supper for her guest and herself. Sunny was told there was ham salad and banana and custard in Serena's small kitchen-cum-scullery upstairs for her to tuck into when she felt hungry.

Her first task was to give the baby her bedtime bottle and then put her in her cot in her parents' bedroom. Serena had bathed Zosia earlier and the baby was in her night clothes. 'The baby alarm is on the table in the sitting room and the number you can contact in an emergency is by the telephone. She's usually fast asleep by six o'clock. See you later!' Serena said when they left.

She wore a faux fur coat over her bright dress, another impulse buy by Jan who insisted she must keep warm in an English winter. 'He likes to spoil me,' she said fondly.

'You deserve it,' he had told her.

Sunny tiptoed away from the baby's cot and went into the small sitting room next door. There was a long settee covered in black leather, a pile of cushions and a rug to put over knees on a chilly night such as this. *The gas fire gives off a warm glow but it's not the same as a proper fireplace*, she thought. There was a small television set, but she didn't turn it on as, despite the baby alarm, she was listening out for a cry from the baby. Sunny settled on the settee and reached for the rug. She would eat her supper later she decided. She thought that really Serena and Jan had very little space up here since the day nursery had taken over the bigger rooms. In contrast, she and Nan had more rooms than they really needed. She would suggest to Nan that Serena and Jan might have use of the drawing room when they had friends round. They shared the garden, of course, during the summer months.

Sunny yawned. She was tired after the shopping expedition, and before she knew it, she was asleep.

Nan's visitor arrived. He had come by taxi, and was laden with Christmas presents. 'These small gifts are to go under the tree ahead of Christmas, of course,' he said to Nan and then he handed over packages for Christmas Day for the family – for Nan, Sunny, Serena, Jan and the baby.

It seemed as if there had never been a rift between them. Nan and Alexander sat down to a supper of gammon and pease pudding. 'Your grandson's favourite. I always used to make it for him when . . .' She didn't finish the sentence.

He reached out and covered both her hands with his large gnarled ones. 'I'm sorry. He has a car now. Eleanor and I decided we should have helped in this way before, then he would have been able to see Sunny and us, of course, more often, so that is our Christmas present to him.'

'He's gone away, hasn't he, on a working holiday?'

'I'm not sure. He didn't say he'd be coming home.'

'I'm sorry, Alexander, for being, well, cool towards you since . . .'

'Dear Nan, it wasn't your fault. I said some stupid things. I upset dear Sunny, and I'm so sorry about that. Will you forgive me?'

'Not if you let your supper congeal on the plate!' she said.

'I have something to ask you tonight, if I can get my courage up,' he said, 'But you're right, I must eat all this before you hit me with a rolling pin.'

'Stop teasing,' she said.

After they had eaten and washed the plates, they retired to the drawing room with the coffee pot and Nan's favourite blue and white mugs.

Mr Rowland stirred the fire into a blaze. He cleared his throat and said tentatively, 'Nanette, will you marry me? I wish I had met you when we were younger, and I admit I am some years older than you, but I think we would be very comfortable together . . .'

Although Nan had once considered this might be a possibility, it was before she'd heard his views on marriage.

She said slowly, 'I have to tell you I could never leave my home or my family. This is still the Mother and Baby Home, where women are predominant. Could you live with that? Jan is the only man around, and wisely, he goes off to work every day.'

'I wouldn't expect anything else from you. I feel involved with all of them too. Could you put up with me here with you? I plan to make my place over to Alec, after ensuring the living accommodation is brought up to date. The workshop could become a studio for Sunny, when she has finished her course – but first Alec has to convince her that they are meant to be together . . .'

'Please give me time to consider all this,' she said softly.

He nodded. 'No announcement yet,' he said. 'I'll be patient. Shall I turn on the television? By the way, I've booked a taxi to collect me at ten.'

*　*　*

Sunny woke with a start, to a rapping on the door. 'Come in,' she called, realising at the same time that she was sitting in the dark, with just the glow from the gas fire.

There was the click of the light switch, and as she swung her legs down, she heard a familiar voice. 'Sorry for disturbing you,' Alec said. 'Nan said you were babysitting and that Serena and Jan won't be back until the early hours.

She had just gone to bed when I arrived. Grandfather left an hour ago.'

'Have you come from Cambridge tonight?' She ran her fingers through her rumpled hair.

'Yes, I came because I couldn't bear the thought of not seeing you this Christmas,' he said. He sat on the end of the settee, put his head in his hands and his shoulders shook as he tried to control his sobs. 'You mustn't feel – sorry for me. It's all my fault. I should never have posted that last letter to you.'

Sunny stood up. She was wide awake now, and she said, 'You put your feet up. Here's the blanket. I'll put the kettle on. Are you hungry?'

He nodded. 'Starving,' he admitted. 'I haven't eaten since breakfast.'

'My supper is still on the table, I'll cut some more bread and we'll share it,' she said.

'You are a wonderful girl,' he said humbly, 'I don't deserve you.'

'I must just check on Zosia now, and by then the kettle will have boiled, so try and stay awake for a bit. Oh, did Grandfather know you were on your way?'

'No, I didn't want to worry him,' Alec said.

When she returned from checking on Zosia, he was asleep. At that moment, there was another knock on the door. Sunny opened it and Nan stood there in her dressing gown. 'Everything all right, Sunny? I've put a hot water bottle in your bed. Alec looked shattered when he arrived, so he needs a good night's sleep.'

'Come in, Nan. Would you like a cup of tea? I've just made a pot. I'll have to wake him as he needs some sustenance first!'

'Not for me, dear, I had my cocoa with Alexander. I'll stay here in case the baby is disturbed when you take Alec downstairs. Use the lift. I moved his bag into your room, too.'

'I must wait for the partygoers to arrive back.'

'Of course, dear. Sunday tomorrow, we can all have a lie-in. I expect the baby will be the only chirpy one,' Nan said.

Sunny guided Alec into her room. 'That's your bed,' he said, 'I'm capable of undressing myself you know, the couch will do for me.'

'You need the bed tonight,' she said firmly. 'I must go back to my duties upstairs, not that I've done anything so far, apart from looking after you.'

She shut the door before he could say anymore and climbed the stairs, before she remembered she could have returned by the lift.

Nan kissed her goodnight. 'It's nearly midnight, they'll be on the way home soon.'

Serena and Jan arrived home before one in the morning Serena said, 'We'll tell you all about it in the morning. We had a lovely time. Was the baby good?'

'Oh, yes, she's such a darling,' Sunny said. 'Goodnight, sleep tight!'

She went into her room, tiptoeing about. She changed into her pyjamas, and observed Alec was asleep. She didn't stop to think about it as she slipped into the warm bed beside him and put her arm cautiously round his waist. 'Goodnight,' she whispered. 'I love you, Alec.' Then she snuggled up to him. There would be no love-making that night, but they were together again.

TWENTY-THREE

Sunny's first term at art school was over, and as the new term would not begin until mid-January, she was back and forth from the Mother and Baby Home helping Mrs Ford with the wedding arrangements. Chrissie worked until Christmas Eve, like Ravi. She was taking the week after off for her wedding. There was no time for a honeymoon. Chrissie had decided she would tell the bank manager about her condition when she returned in the New Year, when she and Ravi would need to begin house-hunting, with a view to a spring move.

Alec was back at his grandfather's place, but he had studying to do, and Nan and Serena were looking after their charges in the day nursery until two days before Christmas. 'Fortunately,' Nan said, 'I kept a Christmas pudding from last year. It should taste even better as it will have matured.'

The extended family at the Mother and Baby Home were spending Christmas Day together and Mr Rowland and Alec would join them.

Jan was at home to look after the baby, so Serena and Nan drove to Croydon in the little car on Christmas Eve morning to buy the food supplies and visited the market to buy pink grapefruits, Jaffa oranges, tangerines, and other fresh fruit, as well as mistletoe and holly with berries, to decorate the drawing room. The bakery had taken their order over the telephone this morning, but they still had to queue patiently for the crusty loaves of bread. The butcher had already delivered the turkey, cooked ham, bacon and sausages. Serena and Jan had contributed generously this year.

The boot of the car was packed full after all their shopping and Nan remarked, 'I hope the milkman brought my big order today, at least we'll have plenty of milk, eggs, butter and cream to see us through Christmas! We couldn't have fitted all that in the car, could we?'

'You're going to church tonight, aren't you?' Serena asked.

'The service begins at half past eleven – all right if I take the car?'

'Of course it is. Is Alec coming around to see Sunny?'

'Yes, and Rodney rang to say he was home, and could he come and see her too as he has a surprise for her.'

'Won't Alec mind?'

'Why should he? Sunny and Rodney are good friends. Rodney will be invited to the wedding on Boxing Day I expect. I'll have the turkey ready to go in the oven over-night, before I go to the church,' Nan said.

* * *

Alec arrived around teatime. 'Don't look so hopeful,' Nan teased. 'All this baking is for tomorrow onwards! How about a cup of tea and a mince pie? Join Sunny in the drawing room, she's on the stepladder fixing the decora-tions, that's why I answered the door.'

Sunny, who had tinsel in her hair, was on the top rung of the ladder. She called out to Alec, 'Fetch the dustpan and brush, I just knocked an ornament off the tree and it shattered to pieces on the floor. Watch out, it's glass and sharp. What are you eating?' she asked suspiciously.

'Mince pie,' he said with his mouth full.

'I made those for tomorrow, don't you dare eat them all, and help me down, will you?'

'Say please, but I'll get the brush and pan first, or you'll likely tread on the bits,' he said, and made a quick retreat.

Nan passed over the item requested, then said, 'Did you see the mistletoe in the alcove?'

'Yes, but she looks too cross at the moment.' He grinned.

Just then, Rodney knocked at the door and Alec went to open it. He was not alone, but was accompanied by a young woman wearing a woolly hat, which she pulled off to reveal braided blonde hair. She said, 'Hello,' and smiled at Alec. Rodney and Alec shook hands solemnly. 'Is Sunny around?' Rodney asked.

'She's in the drawing room, you can go in, but let me lead the way, I have a spot of sweeping up to do,' Rodney said.

Sunny had heard their voices and was descending the stepladder. 'Rodney, you're earlier than we expected,' she said, feeling flustered.

'This is Magdalene, but she is called Magda. She was eager to meet you,' Rodney said.

'I come from Germany,' she said shyly. 'I am an interpreter in the Pay Corps. I translate the letters and speak on the telephone. I have no family, so Rodney invited me to come to his home for Christmas. We had to travel separately, but he waited for me at the airport.'

'It's lovely to see you again,' Rodney said to Sunny, after settling Magda in Nan's armchair. 'Oh, mistletoe, have you been kissed under it yet?' he asked Sunny.

She looked at Alec apologetically. 'No, I haven't. Do you mind, Alec?'

'Of course not,' he said. 'Go ahead.'

Nan and Serena came in the room at that moment and there was much laughing, as Rodney gallantly kissed both of them under the mistletoe too, and then they were introduced to Magda.

Sunny whispered to Rodney, 'I thought you said you weren't allowed to fraternise!'

'Oh, I said that because I thought you might be jealous. The war ended thirteen years ago, you know! But we are told to respect the local girls . . . or else. Actually, Magda's mother was English, she met her future husband, who was from Berlin, when they were both studying at university over here. He was Jewish. Magda was their only child. She was sent away to live with her grandmother in the Black Forest at the outbreak of war when she was five years old and didn't see her parents again. Well, I can see Alec's back in the picture. He seems a nice guy, and I know you have chosen him, not me, so . . .'

'I do care for you, Rodney, you know that. I always will,' Sunny said.

'Magda and I – well she's a few years older than me, but at the moment, we are good friends, nothing more.'

'You never know,' she said. 'Well, she's gazing over here, so go and look after her!'

*   *   *

It was seven o'clock and their visitors were leaving. 'We are going to pop in on Chrissie and find out all about this wedding – unexpected, but exciting,' Rodney observed. 'The first of we three to be married!'

'Then we will help Rodney's mother make ready for Christmas Day,' Magda said. 'They have a small tree. My grandfather always brought us one that size from the forest. Later, we planted it in our garden. So, we had a little forest of our own, but my grandparents are gone now, of course.'

There were hugs and promises of 'See you soon' and Rodney and Magda departed.

At quarter past eleven, Nan went off to the Midnight Mass, and Sunny and Alec decided to call it a day. 'Don't wait up!' Nan said as she left. 'But leave the hall light on for me! You're staying the night, I presume, Alec? Don't forget to ring Alexander and tell him, and say we are looking forward to seeing him tomorrow.'

Sunny was sitting at the dressing table brushing her hair; she looked at her reflection, remembering her sad face last September before she and Alec had their one night of love. He had been much more restrained since they had finally made the decision to be together. She wondered if he was waiting for her to make the first move.

He was obviously thinking the same. He indicated the couch. 'Where do I sleep tonight?' he asked softly.

She was shivering in her new nylon nightie and jumped into bed. 'Come and warm me up!' she invited.

'Are you sure?' This was the outcome he had hoped and prepared for. But she was the one who must decide.

'Alec, come on do, we've only got an hour before Nan comes home,' she murmured.

Then she was in his arms, and in the distance, they could hear the church bells, welcoming the faithful to the midnight service. Christmas Day was almost here, and two young people were about to confirm their love.

* * *

The church was packed, and Nan squeezed into a pew at the back. A hand touched her arm and she turned slightly to see Mrs Perkins. They had always kept in touch.

'How nice to see you,' Nan whispered. 'I didn't know you still came to this church.'

'I do sometimes, hoping to meet up with friends,' Mrs Perkins whispered back.

'How did you get here?' Nan wondered. She realised her neighbour on the other side was giving them a reproving look, but there were still a few minutes to go before the service began.

'My Patsy – well her boys, have a friend, another boy, who lives near us with his dad. I had been helping out by taking him back to our place until his father fetched him after he finished work at six o'clock. He met Patsy one afternoon when she arrived home, and – well, it was love at first sight, she says, and they're getting married – here – in the spring. We'll all live in his house, then, as one big family. Jack drove me here tonight!'

'Oh, Mrs Perkins, how wonderful for you all!'

'It's a relief too, as Patsy's job comes to an end soon. Mr Rowland is packing it all in. I expect you know that.'

Nan nodded, because others were now shushing them, and the organ music swelled as they all rose to greet the clergy as they progressed down the aisle between the pews.

After the service, the recital of the Nativity, they all rose to sing joyously 'Hark the Herald Angels Sing', then the bells rang out and the congregation filed out from the church. Nan lingered in the porch, hoping to see The Major. It was very chilly outside, and after ten minutes she decided to drive home. She heard hurried footsteps behind her, and The Major caught up with her. 'Happy Christmas, Nanette,' he said. He sounded wistful. She wondered if he had been hoping to see her, or to be invited for Christmas dinner.

He must have read her thoughts because he said, as he helped her into the Mini, 'Don't worry about me, I have been invited to the vicarage, along with a couple of others who have no family. I will ring the bells in church for the morning service, and for the wedding on Boxing Day. I hope to see you then – happy Christmas!' and he saluted her, as she drove off.

She thought, *I might have asked him to come to us, but then, Alexander will be there.*

* * *

It was Christmas morning, and presents were being opened and exclaimed over, upstairs and downstairs in the Mother and Baby Home. Sunny was in the kitchen with Alec, they were making the early morning tea, and she was about to take a cup to Nan, who appeared still to be asleep. She had left a note on the kitchen table which read: *Check the turkey, and turn the heat from low to moderate, please!* Alec opened the oven door and sniffed appreciatively. 'Lovely smell of cooking!'

He opened the door for Sunny and gave her waist a quick squeeze as she went through. 'Don't do that!' she said. 'You nearly made me drop the tray!'

'Hurry up,' he said, 'I'll take our cups into our room. We haven't opened our presents yet.'

Our room. She blushed at the thought. 'We mustn't be too long, it's already seven o'clock, and I need to help with the breakfast. I'm sure you're hungry as usual.'

Nan was sitting up in bed and smiled at Sunny. 'Thanks, dear. I looked in on you last night when I got back from church, but you were both asleep. I've got some exciting news to tell you – sit down for a moment – about Patsy and her family.'

Sunny clutched her dressing gown round her. She didn't want to reveal the flimsy nightdress. 'I haven't drunk my tea yet, and then I was hoping to be first in the bathroom. I'll tell Alec he'll have to be after you! We can talk while we are making breakfast, eh? And open our presents later.'

'What's the weather like? Did you look out?'

'Well, it wasn't snowing, but there was a frost, and Alec has instructions to get the fire going in the drawing room,'

Drinking her tea and sitting on the side of the bed, she told Alec, 'Nan said she looked in on us last night!'

'I know, but luckily you'd nodded off – how romantic is that? And she might have thought it was just me in your bed, and you were on the couch,' he said. 'She didn't turn the light on of course.'

'I think she knew we were together, but she didn't look disapproving.'

'She never does,' Alec said. 'Your Nan is the kindest person I have ever met.'

*   *   *

Later, at breakfast, where they were joined by the family from upstairs, they enjoyed the sweet pink grapefruit halves, then bacon and eggs. They didn't toast the bread, because Nan said it was too new and soft, and best eaten like that – and nowadays they could spread the butter, not scrape it on and off like they did in the war. Sunny enjoyed spooning baby food into Zosia's mouth and glimpsed two top teeth coming through.

Then Serena and Jan took the baby upstairs again for her bath and promised to be back soon to help with preparing all the vegetables. Nan said to Sunny, 'I'm teaching Alec how to cook. My mother always said if there is a man around, put him on bacon and egg duty. My father, well I don't remember him being helpful in the kitchen, but I was only young when we lost him.'

After spud bashing, as he termed it, recalling his National Service days, Alec drove over to Croydon to collect his grandfather. He looked doubtfully at the cat basket, which Mr Rowland carried out to the car. The car was not smart and showy like the yellow Mini, but a useful estate car. 'Grandfather, does Nan know you are bringing Pilchie?' he queried.

'No, but she has to get used to having a cat around the house,' Mr Rowland said enigmatically. He held the basket on his lap. 'We won't be back until late, and it's too long to leave her by herself. I see you've got your feet under the table, my lad.'

Alec grinned when he realised what his grandfather was hinting at.

There was a wonderful smell of festive cooking wafting from the kitchen when they arrived. Nan gave the basket 'a look' but merely said, 'Keep an eye on her, Alexander, don't let her climb up the Christmas tree.'

Sunny hugged Mr Rowland, and said, 'Come and sit by the fire.'

'What about me?' Alec said, tongue-in-cheek. 'Don't I get a hug?'

'You've had one already,' she returned smartly. 'We're going to open up the presents now, while everything is bubbling on the stove – and the table's laid. Serena's filled the coffee pot, and the lift has just arrived downstairs, so you three can play with the baby.' She opened the drawing room door and ushered them all inside.

Slippers seemed to be the favoured gift that year; Nan had a pair with pompoms, which Pilchie immediately pounced upon, and she gave a little scream. Serena had some bootees with zips up the sides and Sunny had a pair of slipper socks, knitted in a Scandinavian pattern. She was instructed by Mr Rowland, 'Don't wear'em outside!' Jan and Mr Rowland each had a pair of moccasins, which Sunny had spotted in the Bata shoe shop.

'What about me?' Alec joked. 'Is the humming top for me?'

'You know it's for the baby, you just have to keep it going, eh?' Serena said. Sunny handed him a bulky package, 'From me,' she said simply. Alec unwrapped a long warm scarf which she had knitted in alternate blue and white stripes. 'Nan helped me make the fringe,' she said. She wondered what his gift to her would be.

When she unwrapped it, she was very surprised. 'A guitar!' she cried. 'Who is going to teach me how to play it?'

'I am,' he said, 'then you can play beside me when I'm at the piano here, eh?'

He cleared his throat then and said, 'I have an announcement to make, and you are all invited to hear it.'

Everyone gathered round, expectantly. 'Sunny, will you marry me? I know we are engaged, though that's been on and off, and I am aware it will be eighteen months before I hopefully graduate, and that you have a lot more studying to do, too, but I can't wait that long before we tie the knot. We'd still be mostly living apart, but now I have the car it will be easier to see you much more often. What do you think?'

They were all waiting for Sunny's answer. She took a deep breath. 'When?' she asked.

'How about during the Easter break? I'd prefer to have a simple wedding, just family and a few friends like Chrissie and Ravi, and we'd have to wait some time before we are able to live together.'

Sunny said softly, 'It sounds wonderful.'

Serena whispered something in her husband's ear and he nodded. 'Sunny and Alec, Serena and I would fund a trip to Trinidad for your honeymoon, if you would like that?'

Sunny and Alec looked at one and other and agreed, 'We would.'

Nan made a sudden move. *No one seems to have realised how this unexpected news will affect me*, she thought, but all she wanted of course was for her daughter to be happy.

'Must check on the Christmas dinner,' she said, and just then, as she turned, Sunny hurried after her. She waited until they were in the kitchen then she hugged Nan close and said, 'Be happy for us, dear Nan, it won't be a conventional marriage to begin with, but it means a lot to know that he wants to commit himself to me. I'll still be living here, if you'll have me, until we finish our education.'

'Maybe I'll have someone else to look after then,' Nan said. 'We must get busy . . . all sorts to do before we serve up.'

It wasn't the austerity meal it would have been in the years after the war, until 1954, when rationing at last ended. Mr Rowland was invited to carve the turkey, but admitted that Eleanor had preferred a capon, which was smaller and easier to slice. Zosia had her first taste of unfamiliar food too. Boiled potatoes glazed with butter, Brussel sprouts (they'd drawn straws on who would prepare these, as it was a tedious task), home-grown runner beans, which had been preserved in brine, crunchy roast potatoes and parsnips in covered dishes, sausage meat and chipolatas, stuffing, streaky bacon, and gravy, made in the pan in which the turkey had been cooked.

A cheer went up as the Christmas pudding flared when the brandy was lit, and it was served with custard and cream. Jan poured the Burgundy and lemon in the best pink glasses and they toasted Christmas and each other. There were more presents to open round the tree at teatime.

Sunny and Alec agreed it was a happy family day they would always remember, the day when he made a pledge which she had not expected. But tomorrow was Chrissie and Ravi's special day.

TWENTY-FOUR

It was Boxing Day, and Chrissie returned to her bedroom after a leisurely bath. Her mother had been unable to persuade her to eat more than a small bowl of porridge for breakfast. 'You must keep your strength up!' Mrs Ford kept saying. 'We don't want you fainting at the altar.'

'Don't be so dramatic, Mum, and please, can you keep Auntie Beryl out of here? She's more excited than I am!' Chrissie said ruefully. 'Thank goodness Sunny is coming around to help me dress and do my hair.'

'Don't let her persuade you to wear it up, dear; Ravi says he loves your long hair. As for Beryl, anyone would think she was the bride! She's disappointed you're not wearing a bridal gown. I think she envies you, because she never found the right man, and she says time is running out for her to have children. She's over forty now, you know.'

'She told me she would be thirty-eight soon.' They smiled at each other. Despite her 'flutterings', as Mrs Ford referred to them, Auntie Beryl was family, after all.

Mr Ford poked his head round the bedroom door. He'd obviously nicked his chin shaving and employed the usual remedy, a piece of tissue paper over the spot. 'Sunny's here, shall I send her up? Mother, you'd better go in the bathroom before Beryl decides to spend the morning in there.'

'Send Sunny up but keep Auntie Beryl at bay!' Chrissie entreated him. 'Hurry up, Mum, as Dad says, once *she's* in the bathroom, no one else gets a chance. It's lucky we have a separate loo!'

Sunny came in smiling. 'I collected your posy and half a dozen buttonholes from Rodney's mum – she spent over an hour making them all up. She says it's her contribution to the wedding. She was ironing a shirt for Rodney when I arrived, and Magda was in the kitchen washing up.' She saw that Chrissie was sitting on the edge of the bed, clutching her dressing gown round her. 'You look pale,' Sunny said, concerned.

'I feel sick,' Chrissie said faintly, 'I thought I was over that, though some things like coffee and cabbage cooking still make me – heave—' With that, she reached for the chamber pot which her mother had put under the bed as a precaution and Sunny supported her, although it made her feel squeamish herself. 'Feel better?' she asked. 'I'll take this to your mum, and bring back a bowl of warm water and a flannel – and a jug of fresh water with a glass.'

Ten minutes later, Chrissie felt better and was able to get dressed. 'Thank goodness I don't have to wear a roll-on now. Auntie Beryl bought me some new tights, so I don't need stockings and suspenders. She asked me what colour I'd like, and I chose white, not black as she suggested.'

A hand towel was draped round her shoulders to guard against mishaps while applying makeup, which included a new pink lipstick to match her lovely rose frock. Chrissie wanted the makeup to be understated, because she said, 'I'm not in a beauty contest!'

'You'd win, if you were,' Sunny told her. She picked up the hairbrush. 'Now to arrange your hair. It's still a bit damp, Chrissie, from washing it earlier. Then I'll put the rose headband in place, and all you need then is the stole to keep you warm, your white kid ankle boots, white gloves and handbag.'

'Don't forget the perfume. Just a squirt. My favourite Lily of the Valley,' Chrissie said.

Sunny took off the pinafore Mrs Ford had lent her to keep her own outfit safe from spills and face powder and looked out of the window. 'Your dad is tinkering with the car – in his new suit . . .'

'Typical man,' Chrissie sighed, but happily. 'It was good of Jan to volunteer to be best man. Ravi hadn't thought of that! I wonder if he has arrived at the Mother and Baby Home yet? Jan's driving him to the church in his company car, but the rest of your family are coming in the Mini I understand. Rod and Magda are coming on foot, I think.' She added, 'Dad's taking Mum and Auntie Beryl there first, and coming back for us, the bride and bridesmaid. Only half an hour to go now until eleven o'clock.'

Sunny took her turn to look in the cheval mirror and arranged her soft warm shawl round her shoulders. She hoped Alec would get there in time. The plan was for him to drive her back to the celebration here, a modest affair as Chrissie and Ravi requested, and the bride and groom would travel together. Later, they would go back to Ravi's flat, now the marital home.

'Look,' Chrissie exclaimed, watching from the front window and spotting her mother and Auntie Beryl waving as her father drove away. The neighbours in the terrace had hung bunting between the lamp posts in the street outside. Coloured lights flickered on Christmas trees and a dog paused by their gate post; Chrissie banged on the window and it disappeared quickly.

Chrissie and Sunny were the only ones still in the house. 'Are you all right?' Sunny asked anxiously. 'Your dad will be back soon.'

'Everything seems to have happened so quickly,' Chrissie said.

'You still want to get married, don't you?'

'Of course I do, but – oh, Sunny, it's a big step to take.'

'You won't regret it, I know,' Sunny said. She wondered how she'd feel on her own wedding day. Would

Alec change his mind? They'd been together on Christmas night, so she supposed she could call it, *two nights of love,* but nothing had been said about a wedding after the announcement he had made. He was returning to Cambridge the day after the New Year. The jazz band had several bookings before they returned to their studies, which would be intensified this year. 'Back to the Classics,' as Alec termed it: 'Serious stuff.'

Chrissie walked down the aisle on her father's arm, with Sunny following, ready to take her posy when she joined Ravi, who was standing in front of the alter with Jan. They turned their heads as she progressed towards them, and the organist pulled out all the stops, after the muted background music ceased, like the bells which welcomed the small congregation. Alec arrived at the last minute and joined Rodney and Magda in the third pew; Nan sat beside Serena with the baby in the second pew; Mrs Ford and Auntie Beryl were in the front pew. Auntie Beryl's opulent hat somewhat obscured the view of those sitting behind. She had to move along to make room for Sunny when her escorting duties were done.

Sunny glanced back and saw to her relief that Alec was there. Rodney raised his hand to her and smiled, but Alec was preoccupied with finding the wedding service in the prayer book. She wondered if he had been to church much before. She felt rather guilty herself in that respect, because she'd attended regularly when she, Chrissie and Rodney belonged to the Church Youth Club.

It was not a long-drawn-out service. Sunny could only see the back view of the young couple, not their faces: Chrissie's long, glossy black hair contrasted with the rose colour of her wedding dress, and Ravi stood straight and tall beside her in a new dark suit. Vows and rings were exchanged, the vicar gave his homily with the expected touch of humour, 'May all your troubles be little ones,' and Sunny wondered if Chrissie was blushing at that.

The last hymn was a Christmas carol, which seemed appropriate, chosen by the bride and groom: 'Away in a manger'.

Then they were filing slowly out of the church, when Nan was greeted by The Major. 'I hoped to see you,' he said, shaking her hand. 'Did you have a good Christmas?'

She said, 'Yes,' and then, she didn't know why, as she hadn't thought of it before, she asked, 'Would you be able to join me and my family for New Year's Eve?'

'I should be delighted to,' he said immediately. 'Though I will be ringing the New Year in at the church at midnight.'

'Of course, I hadn't thought of that – but come to lunch, and supper. I hope we will be entertained by Alec, Sunny's young man, on the piano.'

'I look forward to it,' he said. 'Oh, I am keeping you – your family is waiting for you.'

Cameras clicked, recording the occasion, and then they drove in convoy to the refreshments waiting for them back at the Fords' house.

'Wedding cake and a cup of tea,' that's what Chrissie had requested, but Mr Ford had splashed out on two bottles of champagne. The cake, with pink and white icing, had been a surprise gift from her former employers at the bakery. There were two tiny figures on top, the bride and groom, holding hands and smiling. The wedding break-fast ended before lunchtime and the bride and groom were duly waved off by family and friends as they drove to the apartment near the surgery where Ravi was a junior doc-tor. The following Monday they'd both be back at work. A three-day honeymoon, that's all.

'Leave the luggage to me,' Ravi said, when they arrived. 'Put your feet up on the settee and have a rest. What do you fancy for lunch?'

'Nothing,' Chrissie said, 'after that rich cake.'

'That's a relief, but I'll make something you fancy for dinner tonight.'

Chrissie yawned. 'I can't believe we were married two hours ago. I'm glad it went well.'

'So am I,' he agreed.

The telephone shrilled. He glanced at his watch. 'That'll be my parents, I hope. Would you like to speak to them?'

'You answer it and talk first, and then pass the phone to me,' she said. She sat up. *I must compose myself,* she thought, *and tell them it has been a wonderful day.*

*   *   *

Alec and Jan took Nan and the family back to the Mother and Baby Home and then Alec drove off again to collect his grandfather, who would spend the rest of the day with them. He passed Rodney and Magda walking home after the wedding breakfast, and they waved to him.

'He and Sunny are to marry soon, too,' Magda said, glancing at Rodney. 'Does that make you sad, Rod?'

'In some ways,' he said slowly. 'But I hope it will turn out for the best.'

'You hoped it would be you she chose, didn't you?'

'I suppose I did. But I have a good friend now, in you, Magda.'

'That's all I will be; I haven't changed my mind about becoming a nun. It took me a long time to realise that was the way I should go. I thank you and your parents for your kindness in asking me to stay with you this Christmas. I have seen something of the country where my mother grew up.'

'I'm glad you feel like that,' he told her. 'We'll return to Germany shortly, but I will be coming home for good in six months' time.'

'To the bank?' she asked.

He nodded. 'My travelling days are numbered,' he said. 'But I have learned a lot about life in other places and I feel I'm a man now, not a boy.'

Mr Rowland waited until Nan was on her own for a few minutes and seized the chance to ask her, 'Have you thought about my – suggestion, Nan?'

She said slowly, 'I have, Alexander. I'm afraid I've come to the conclusion we are both too set in our ways to change. I am working again now, too, and enjoying it. I think you should wind down your business slowly, because what would you find to do here, with babies around all day and me concentrating on seeing to their needs, not yours? I hope we'll always be close, though, and that you regard us as family, as I do you, Alec and Eleanor. Sunny thinks of you as her grandfather, and I hope she will jump at the chance of one day having a studio at your place, but she would still need you to be around to encourage her. Go ahead with the modernisation! However, I have to say that I don't think a marriage between Alec and Sunny will come about.'

'You are right, in every respect,' Mr Rowland agreed. 'Do you want me to ask him before he goes back to Cambridge if he intends to honour his pledge to Sunny?'

'I think they must decide themselves; we can't do anything about it,' Nan said.

*　*　*

Sunny changed out of her wedding outfit – the dress had been just what she needed on her birthday, she thought, but now it was Christmas and the home fires had burned low while they were out, so she needed something warmer to wear. Out came the tartan trews, not so fashionable as they were, but comfortable with her chunky-knit jumper and the slipper socks on her feet. She wondered how Chrissie was feeling at this moment; she'd looked radiant in the church of course.

She emerged from her bedroom to find Alec hovering outside. 'Why didn't you come in?' she asked. 'I didn't know you were back.'

'Grandfather's having a conflab with Nan in the kitchen. I thought I'd be discreet and disappear. Serena and Jan are upstairs with the baby, I suppose.'

'Well, we need to have a conflab too, Alec. Let's go into the drawing room.'

He poked at the fire and added a fresh log. Sunny wondered, *is he trying to put off any awkward questions?* 'Sit down, Alec, please,' she said.

'I think I know what's coming,' he said slowly, but he sat down opposite her in one of the fireside chairs.

'Please be honest with me, Alec. It may hurt, but I must know. You've said nothing more about getting married. It wouldn't be ideal, living apart, would it? We both want to succeed with our studies. I know that, but I feel that isn't the answer. If we are married, I want us to be together – I know it won't be possible all the time, but . . .'

'Sunny, I feel the same. I shouldn't have made that proposal in front of everyone, I know that.'

'It's like in your letter Alec, it hurt, but it's true, isn't it? "It was nice knowing you . . ." It was more than that for me, I have to say, but tell me the truth, please . . .'

'The truth is, I am not worthy of your love. I – cheated on you again not so long ago. It wasn't planned and I apologise. It wasn't anything like the nights we spent together.'

'Sometimes I think we shouldn't have made love, but it was only twice, and – it won't happen again,' she said firmly. 'Was it the same girl as before?'

'Yes. She plays saxophone in my band. Her fiancée rejected her when she told him what happened. She came to me sobbing, and said it was me she loved anyway, and we . . .'

'You made love,' she said flatly.

He flinched at that. 'You've made me feel a cad.'

'No, you aren't, Alec. I felt you loved me at the time we were together like that,' she said.

'I did, that's the truth – I do love you, but I'm not ready to settle down. I hope to have the opportunity to travel, to play grand pianos all over the world.'

'Then do that, with my blessing,' she said huskily. 'Perhaps this girl – you have more in common with her than me – may turn out to be the one for you.'

'Will you keep in touch?' he asked.

'Better not,' she said, and she felt as if her heart was breaking.

'You'll still think of my grandfather as yours too?'

'Of course I will. Nan and I will keep an eye on him!'

The door opened and Nan ushered Mr Rowland inside before she followed. 'Is everything all right?' she asked, trying to sound casual.

Sunny answered, 'I hope so. I don't feel like talking about – things – at the moment. How about a board game?'

'Good idea,' said Mr Rowland, clearing his throat, and glancing at his grandson. 'You and I, Alec, against the ladies?'

* * *

Chrissie and Ravi decided on an early night. It had been a long, exciting, but tiring day for them both. 'It's lucky you have a double bed,' Chrissie said. 'Which side shall I be?'

'Take your pick, but you usually decide to be on the left, don't you?' he teased. 'Before you nod off, I've some good news for you; my father told me they had transferred £2,000 to my account. We can go ahead with finding our new home. House prices are rising all the time, they say the average cost will soon be £2,500, so we need to buy as soon as we can.'

Chrissie sat up and said, 'I can't get to sleep now, I'm so excited! How kind of your parents.'

Ravi said, 'There is a new estate of small family homes being built on the outskirts of the village, but within walking distance of all the amenities. Shall we find out about it in the New Year?'

'Oh, yes we will!' Chrissie said. She felt under her pillow and the little keepsakes were there; the tiny bride and groom that had been on top of the wedding cake.

TWENTY-FIVE

It was New Year's Eve and tomorrow would be the first day of 1959. The Major was expected at noon for lunch; Serena and Jan thought it would be diplomatic to stay upstairs with the baby, who was rather grizzly as she was teething. 'We'll join you for supper later, though,' Serena told Nan. 'If Sunny doesn't mind, Zosia could sleep during the evening in Sunny's room in the Moses basket – she is top to toe in that now, so I guess she won't be able to fit into it soon.'

Nan agreed. 'It'll be easier than going up and down the stairs, even with the lift, if we hear the baby alarm.' She added, 'Alec will come later in the afternoon with his grandfather, and Eleanor is back from Rome, so she will bring Miss Brooke. I felt we couldn't ask one without the other.'

'Sunny looks very solemn, she hasn't said anything to me, but I gather there will be no wedding?'

'No wedding. This appears to be the parting of ways for them,' Nan said. 'Which is sad, because I know how much she cares for him.'

'Some things are not meant to be,' Serena said. 'But let's be cheerful for her sake. I understand it'll be a buffet supper, easier to manage than a large cooked meal. What are you having for lunch with The Major?'

Nan smiled. 'Pease pudding and gammon, my well-tried standby! But he'll be here for supper too, though he has to leave before midnight.'

The Major arrived 'on the dot' as Nan knew he would, and she took him straight into the kitchen, which she and Sunny had tidied up in his honour, and he said approvingly, 'Obviously this is the hub of your home, a real family room. Something smells good, I am looking forward to lunch! Is Sunny joining us?'

'She'll be here this afternoon when more friends arrive – it's just you and me for lunch,' Nan said. 'Take a seat, and would you like a glass of something – sherry perhaps?'

'That would be most acceptable, thank you.'

They raised their glasses and wished each other a happy, prosperous New Year. Then, there was just the parsley sauce to make and after this had been poured into a jug, Nan took the Royal Crown Derby plates from the warming oven and laid thick slices of cooked gammon onto the plates, with a mound of pease pudding. She passed the parsley sauce, and he observed, 'I haven't had a meal like this since I was a boy; my mother was a good cook like you!'

Nan's face was already flushed from bending over the hot stove, but she thought, *I'm blushing, I haven't done that for years!* They enjoyed their lunch, with crusty bread and Stilton to follow. Nan had recalled him saying he preferred cheese to dessert, at the Mayor's Christmas lunch. She thought, *the treacle tart can be eaten at supper. He obviously hasn't got a sweet tooth.*

Sunny appeared when it was time to wash the dishes. She looked pale, but she smiled at The Major and said, 'I've decided to carry on with the driving lessons, if that's all right?'

'Of course it is. You will be a good driver, like your mother, I believe.'

'You both go in the drawing room and I'll manage this,' Sunny offered. 'I'll bring the coffee through in about fifteen minutes. There should be some good programmes on the TV this afternoon, I hope.'

When Nan and The Major were ensconced in the warmth of the drawing room, with the crackling fire, he observed, 'This is a very comfortable room. Let's have a chat before we turn on the television. Didn't Sunny have any lunch? She looks a bit wan.'

Wan, Nan thought, *an old-fashioned word I haven't heard for ages.* She said, 'She's tired that's all. She'll perk up, I expect, when our company arrives.'

'Ah, young people; burning the candle at both ends.' He sighed. 'I joined the army when I was eighteen, married when I was twenty-five, went to war, and returned to – an empty life. What about you?'

'I think I was more fortunate, because although I never married, and lived with my mother until she passed away, I was always concerned with the needs of others and glad to support them. When I adopted my daughter, I felt complete and now – well, I suppose, she is grown up and I'm not sure what the future holds.'

'It's good to have friends; you are more gregarious than me, Nanette. I enjoy your company.'

'Thank you,' she said, relieved because friendship was important to her, and she put away the thought that he might have hoped for more.

There was a rattle of cups outside and The Major rose and opened the door for Sunny. 'Allow me to take the tray,' he offered. 'The coffee smells good!' There was also a wrapped chocolate placed in each saucer; sweets selected from a large tin of Quality Street, a gift from Rodney.

Sunny switched the television on. *It is better to be watching that,* she thought, *than talking. I must try to look happy, but oh, I feel as if I'll never get over losing Alec, and I've got to face him this afternoon.*

Alec didn't speak as he drove along with Mr Rowland beside him; the cat in its basket on his lap. His grandfather knew that Alec would leave tomorrow and that it would probably be some time before they saw him again. He eventually said, as they drew up outside the Mother and Baby Home, 'You are sure you want to come in?'

Alec turned to look at him. 'I must, Grandfather. I know how much I have hurt Sunny, but it really is for the best, that we part now. I can tell her I love her, and that's true, but I can't promise to be faithful, and she's younger than me, and more vulnerable. Please keep in touch with her.'

'I will,' Mr Rowland promised.

*   *   *

Sunny and Serena wheeled the trolley, which usually held all the nursery equipment, into the drawing room at eight. The top tray was laden with buffet food, including chicken drumsticks, small savoury pies, Scotch eggs and ham sandwiches, packets of Smith's crisps, which contained the little blue bags of salt, a large bowl of salad mixed with chopped walnuts, cheese scones and freshly made mayonnaise. The lower tray had a pile of plates, cutlery and serviettes, and a large fruit pie with a bowl of double cream, as well as the treacle tart.

The television was turned off while they enjoyed their supper, and Pilchie was given titbits surreptitiously by Mr Rowland. Later, cups of tea arrived and the bottles of wine, gifts from the guests, would be uncorked at midnight for toasting the New Year.

After supper, the trolley was wheeled back into the kitchen, 'We'll tackle the washing-up later,' Nan said, shutting the door firmly behind her.

Alec sat down at the piano, and Sunny was persuaded to fetch her guitar, and to strum it now and then. She was learning from a manual entitled *Play in a Day!* written by the popular guitarist Bert Weedon. Some guitarists had already achieved fame from following Bert's advice but Sunny didn't believe she was musical. Sunny stood beside Alec, but not close, unlike on earlier occasions.

The Major smiled ruefully, when 'The Galloping Major' was requested, but sang with gusto, like everyone else. After several rousing songs, Alec announced: 'Some Gershwin, I think . . . Despite the time of year, I hope you'll enjoy "Summertime".' He didn't look at Sunny, as he began to play and sing.

Tears pricking her eyes, she moved away from the piano, clutching her guitar, to sit next to Nan on the set-tee. Nan placed a comforting arm round her hunched shoulders.

At around eleven, The Major announced he must leave to join the bell ringers at church. He thanked Nan for a lovely day and wished them all a happy New Year.

Mr Rowland said, 'I have to admit I think it's time for me to depart with the cat, and if Alec could run me home,

I would be grateful – I don't want to embarrass the ladies with my snoring!'

'You'll be back, Alec, won't you? To see the New Year in?' Nan asked.

'Of course I will.' He looked over at Sunny. 'Will you come along for the ride?'

Nan gave her a gentle nudge. 'Why don't you go, Sunny?' She nodded. 'Wrap up warmly,' Nan advised. 'What about your red coat with the hood?'

Sunny thought, *with the hood up, my face is half-hidden, which is how I want it, tonight.*

Serena and Jan, who had collected their fretful baby, said a regretful goodnight too and went upstairs to their flat.

Then it was just Nan, Eleanor and Helena, as she had suggested they call her. 'Time for the television, Eve Boswell will be singing,' Nan said. She thought, *it's been a long day, but it's forty minutes to midnight now. Andy Stewart will be hosting the celebrations from Scotland as usual; the Scots know how to celebrate the New Year!*

After Mr Rowland and Pilchie had been delivered home safely, Alec said diffidently to Sunny, who had been quiet throughout the short journey, 'I'm glad we've half an hour to say goodbye properly, Sunny. And I know the best place for that . . .'

They drove along to The Grove, parked the car and made their way to the big tree where they had last looked up at the evening sky and embraced in what Sunny thought of nostalgically as innocent, magical times. She'd been there with Rodney too, before that. It was not a starry night, but it was mild for December, though misty. *What happens now*? she wondered.

'We won't see the aurora like they did in Scotland for several nights,' Alec said softly. She didn't resist when his arms went around her and her face was pressed to his chest. 'Aren't you going to say anything?' he asked.

'What can I say?' Her voice was muffled. 'We said it all, didn't we? I – I can't stop loving you yet, but I must carry on, if I want to succeed in my studies, as you do. But you'll become famous, I just know you will. All I ask is to enjoy life again – without you. It's hard, Alec, it's very hard.'

He tilted her face upwards and bent over her. 'Will you allow me to kiss you goodbye?' he whispered.

She took a deep breath then said, 'I suppose so.'

It was a brief kiss. Sunny wanted to say, 'Don't go, Alec!' but soon they returned to the car. They arrived at the Mother and Baby Home just in time to hear the church bells ringing in the distance, and to toast the New Year with the three ladies.

'We'll leave the washing-up soaking in the sink,' Nan insisted. 'Let's get to bed, eh?'

Later, Nan could hear smothered sobbing from Sunny's room. She made her way there but didn't switch on the light. She thought, *Sunny won't want me to see how much she has been crying.* She had her torch, but she turned the beam away from Sunny. 'It's all right, dear, let it all out. Alec will regret this, I'm sure.'

'He won't, Nan! He's got another girlfriend. He thinks I'm too young for him, anyway – he always has.'

'He doesn't appear to be grown-up either,' Nan said. 'But Rodney is nearer your age—'

'Oh, Nan, I'm not ready for that; and what about Magda?'

'She's hoping to become a nun and live in a convent, Sunny. She is a friend and colleague, that's all. Rodney thinks a lot of you.'

'I feel the same about him; but I'm going to steer clear of romance now and concentrate on becoming an artist,' Sunny said. 'See you in the morning, dear Nan, thank you for caring.' She turned her face to the pillow.

Nan went back to her own room. *I'm the one who won't sleep tonight,* she thought. *Maybe I should have suggested that Sunny might confide in Serena, who also lost the one she considered the love of her life. At least that never happened to me.*

* * *

A month later, Nan took her driving test, and passed first time, which The Major said was very good indeed, as older drivers usually took longer to learn than she had. Sunny took Nan's photograph sitting at the wheel of the Mini, and waving 'like the Queen'. Sunny was determined to follow suit and booked another six lessons on Saturday mornings as she was back at art school during the week.

Jen had plenty to tell her about the way her Christmas break had gone. 'Lachlan invited me to lunch on Boxing Day! I discovered then that he lived with his grandmother, who brought him up and she gave me a grilling, I can tell you. She obviously doesn't want him to leave home, and she even said she didn't think he was interested in the opposite sex, so she hoped I hadn't been pestering him! Pestering! What a cheek!' Jen said indignantly.

'He's a drip,' Sunny said. 'What about the potter?'

'He's too old!' Jen sighed. 'What about you, Sunny, did you see much of your fiancé?'

Sunny had prepared herself for this question. 'Actually, we're not together any more, Jen. I really don't want to talk about it. We must both concentrate on being ready for our first year assessment in May.'

'You're right,' Jen said, 'and I'm aiming to lose at least a stone in weight!'

* * *

The bank manager had taken Chrissie's news philosophically, although he said he would be sorry to lose an employee whom he considered had potential. The female staff were excited about the prospect of a baby in June and offered to knit little garments. All being well, Chrissie planned to work on until April. By then she hoped she and Ravi would be moving into the modern semi-detached house they were in the process of buying. Belatedly, at her mother's insistence, she was adding to her 'bottom drawer'. They applied for a small mortgage, with furniture to buy, and the baby needing, of course, a cot and a pram, as well as all the other things. A layette, as Mrs Ford called it.

Chrissie didn't see a lot of Ravi, because he was often called out to patients overnight, as well as seeing them daily in the surgery. There were clinic days too, including the pre-natal sessions, but Chrissie saw the nurse there, or another doctor. As it was her first baby, she was booked in at the hospital to give birth. She didn't relish the thought of two weeks away from home then.

* * *

Sunny practised strumming on her guitar. Bert Weedon smiled encouragingly at her from his picture in the book. She thought, *I've no one to go out and about with now. I can't go to dances or the cinema on my own. I visit Chrissie every*

Friday evening for supper, but she hasn't had the energy to cook anything, so she always says, 'How about some fish and chips?' and I say, 'OK' and nip around the corner to the shop. We don't talk about old times, and she's always busy knitting, and telling me what fun it is to go to the pre-natal classes with other mums-to-be and lying on the floor doing deep breathing and learning to relax. She has to rest a lot, because she is still working at the bank every day, so she often nods off to sleep when I'm there. When Ravi comes in, if he's been out on a call, he makes his own supper, poor chap, and I say cheerio, and go home to my bed.

However, Sunny had two targets to meet. One was passing her driving test, and the other was an art project; she had taken photographs of Pilchie in action, as she thought of it, and she was designing a poster featuring the little cat advertising a favourite brand of tinned pilchards – *after all, David Hockney was captivating the world,* she thought, *with his striking pictures of familiar commodities. My experience at the Rowland Printing Press on the posters is proving invaluable. Simple outlines, bold colour; wouldn't it be wonderful,* she mused, *if Pilchie proved to be as popular as the young Sunny in Mr Rowland's portrait.*

* * *

Nan was about to make an important decision: she had discussed with Jan and Serena the proposal they had made recently. Serena said, 'You won't want to go on working forever, Nan, but this is your home and we realise that unfortunately it is becoming a burden to keep up. We would like to buy the business and the house. That would give you financial security, but of course, we would want things to remain as they are: you would be here, in this part of the house, also as Matron, and head of our family. Any changes would only be with your agreement.'

'What about Sunny? I did know that at some point the Mother and Baby Home would have to be sold, and if you take it on, I must have your assurance she can still think of it as her home, until she decides to go her own way.'

'You have our word on that,' Serena said. 'You should both think of it as home, because as Jan says, we are one family now.'

'I will tell Sunny, when the time is right. She is still coming to terms with losing Alec,' Nan said.

TWENTY-SIX

Time seems to pass more quickly when people are busy and enjoying being so; it was coming up to Easter before Sunny realised that something was happening at home. Nan intimated that changes were ahead but Sunny assumed she was referring to the nursery.

Serena and Jan were now often with them in the drawing room in the evenings, and at weekends enjoying the sunshine in the garden with the baby, when Nan would usually join them. Jan kept the grass under control, which made a lot of difference. Weather forecasts were good; it looked like the balmy weather might continue all summer.

Sunny had just arrived back from her driving lesson on the Saturday before Easter Sunday. The family upstairs had taken the baby to The Grove; Zosia was toddling now, she would be one next Tuesday. As it was just the two of them chatting in the kitchen before lunch, Nan decided to tell Sunny what was happening regarding the Mother and Baby Home.

'Why didn't you tell me before?' asked Sunny, and Nan floundered a bit trying to explain that she thought Sunny might feel it was something else to cope with when she was not over her broken relationship with Alec.

Sunny listened in silence, then said, 'This is your home, Nan, and I thought it was mine, too.'

'It still is,' Nan insisted. 'Sunny, we can't afford to stay on here much longer as things are, even with me working again. Most of the money we earn goes back into the business, it's not a profit-making venture, but a service to the community. The original home was like that, too. We are one family now, and this gives me security, and you, too. You really won't notice that much difference, honestly, but I don't think it's fair to expect them to stay upstairs all the time, now that most of the rooms up there are taken over by the nursery. Isn't it good to be part of a bigger family now, not just the two of us?'

Sunny looked near to tears. 'I thought I was getting married and that one day Alec and I would be together all the time. I would have felt guilty, though, to think of you on your own – yes, you are right, we're a family now, five of us with Zosia. When – if – I do leave home, I will have somewhere to come back to, won't I?'

'Of course you will, but you're not going anywhere yet, are you?'

'No, Nan – and please don't worry about how I am coping, because now I am concentrating on becoming a real artist and making you all proud of me,' Sunny said.

'I've always been proud of you,' Nan told her. 'And Serena and Jan are too, I know.'

* * *

The postman had delivered a box that morning and above the address were printed the words: OPEN AT EASTER. It was easy enough to guess what was inside, because it was addressed to Sunny and the sender's name on the back revealed it was from Rodney.

Sunny was looking at the parcel speculatively, and Nan took it from her and put it inside a cupboard. 'Open it tomorrow,' she said. 'But there are all these Easter cards – oh dear, more than I sent out. You can arrange these on the mantlepiece in the drawing room instead.'

'What is this other pile of cards?' Sunny enquired.

'They're for Zosia's birthday. She likes tearing paper so I thought I'd hang on to them and keep them safe for now. It looks like some are from the mums of babies who come to the nursery. Have you bought a present for her yet?'

'I have, Nan, it's in my dressing table drawer. A couple of weeks ago Chrissie and I went to Marks & Spencer and looked at children's clothes. Chrissie said to buy something practical, not a frilly dress for Zosia, so I bought a pair of baby dungarees with snap fastenings round the legs, because of nappies, you know, and a little T-shirt with Bugs Bunny on the front. Chrissie knows all the answers now about baby clothes, and she advised me to get a larger size so they will fit for longer.'

'Is Chrissie keeping well?' Nan asked. Sunny never said much about her weekly visits.

'She seems to be. Fed up with wearing smocks, she says, not being an artist like me! Their house seems very small compared with this, but she's got a lovely kitchen with a yellow enamel sink and a Formica table with four stools. Upstairs there are two big bedrooms and one small one for the baby, and a bathroom and loo. There's an immersion heater for hot water. Downstairs is a large living room with a fireplace with a back boiler. They have a settee; they can't afford the matching chairs yet.'

'Sounds nice.' Nan smiled. 'Is there a garden?'

'It's very small, and Ravi is hoping to dig it over soon and plant potatoes.'

'Why not flowers and shrubs?' Nan asked. 'Potatoes are cheap enough at the greengrocer's.'

'Well, their neighbour, who is quite old, well, in his forties, told Ravi, if he planted potatoes it would make the soil right the following year for plants, and laying down turf for a small lawn.'

'Is this old chap, as they call him, a keen gardener?'

'I don't think so. But he reads the gardening column in the local paper, he says.' Just then they heard voices and laughter in the hall. The kitchen door opened and Zosia, followed closely by her mother, walked in unsteadily, and said hopefully to Nan, 'Choc-choc?' but Serena picked her up and said, 'Upstairs with you; Nana and Sunny are about to have their lunch. You must wait for a treat until after you've had yours too.' She added, to Nan, 'I bought you a pair of kippers for supper on my way home. I'll put them in the fridge.'

When they had gone, Nan said, 'Not the weather for kippers, and they'll make everything else smell fishy, but . . .'

'Pity Rodney's not here.' Sunny smiled. 'He loves kippers!'

Nan looked at her hopefully. *Rodney appears to be in the picture again,* she thought.

* * *

They had their usual breakfast on Easter Sunday morning; boiled eggs, with funny faces painted on them by Sunny, sitting in egg-cups which dated back to Nan's childhood. They were shaped like chickens, and Sunny remarked, 'They look more like cockerels, Nan!'

'Oh, well,' Nan said. 'They only come out once a year, eh?'

She went to the cupboard and took out some Easter surprises. 'You aren't too old for these are you, Sunny?'

''Course not,' Sunny said, 'but I can restrain myself from eating all these delights nowadays until this afternoon.'

Nan pushed the box nearer to her. 'Go on, open up!'

This egg was a work of art: a large, two-sided chocolate oval embellished with edible flowers. When opened up, it was full of assorted sweets. The card read: *To my friends at the Mother and Baby Home, with best wishes for a happy Easter. From Rodney.*

'I sent him a nice card from all of us,' Sunny said defensively as she guessed Nan found the message disappointing.

'Don't forget I'm attending the morning service in church at 11 o'clock,' Nan reminded her. 'I promised Walter I would. Serena is providing lunch today, she says, so don't touch any chocolate until after we've eaten!'

'Oh, Nan, don't tell me you and The Major are courting!'

'No, he's far too cautious – and so am I!' Nan scolded her, but fondly.

Then they heard the patter of small feet, and Zosia was beaming at them and saying hopefully, 'choc-choc', while Serena laughed and said, 'Nan, please hide that egg you're displaying on the table!'

* * *

Sunny was back at art school. Miss Guyatt put a card beside her poster of the cat and the tin of pilchards which read: *NOW PRODUCE SOME COPIES ON THE SILK SCREEN!* There was also a second card, as there was beside all the other exhibits. Sunny's said: *Sunny Cato: Top of the class!* Jen's had a query on it: *Is this Lachlan?* regarding Jen's pottery piece of a man in a crouching position on a motorcycle with the comment: *Jennifer Jackson: This would be improved by colour!*

Jen sighed. 'Lachlan said he didn't want anyone to know it was him.'

Sunny could hardly wait to tell Nan the good news about her modest success, but Nan had something important to tell her, too. 'Alexander rang. He said he was sorry not to be in touch over Easter but he and Eleanor had a call from a hospital in Cambridge to inform them that Alec was a patient there, and hoped his grandfather and his mother would be able to visit him. They have only just returned. Alexander said they had to take Pilchie to the holiday home for pets, as he thought I wasn't that keen on cats.'

'Nan,' Sunny interrupted. 'Why is Alec in hospital. Did Grandfather say?'

'He didn't give details, but said it was to do with his eyes, I think,' Nan said.

'What does that mean?' Sunny demanded.

'You'll have to ask Alexander; he would like to see you this evening if possible.'

'Can I take the car?' Sunny sat down abruptly. She added, 'I had some wonderful news for you, my poster design got top marks, but this is a shock, Nan.'

'Of course, it would be. You must have something to eat before you go, dear, never hear bad news on an empty stomach.'

'A sandwich will do, but it's already six o'clock. I might be late home tonight, which doesn't matter as it's Friday. Oh, Nan, I've got a bad feeling about this, please can you make the sandwich now, and I'll get changed.'

'I'll tell Serena where you've gone, and that you've taken the car,' Nan told her.

Sunny parked the car outside the Rowland Printing Press, and the door opened immediately, as Mr Rowland had been looking out for her arrival. Before she could say anything, she was engulfed in his arms, and hugged tightly. They went upstairs to his sitting room, and he held on to her hand as he sat beside her on the old settee with the groaning springs.

'Please tell me, what's wrong with Alec?' she prompted him.

'He didn't say anything at Christmas, but he had been suffering bad headaches, migraines he called them, and disturbed vision, mainly in the left eye. Did he tell you that he was born with a cataract on that eye, which had to be operated on when he was a few weeks old?'

She shook her head. Mr Rowland continued, 'I thought he had kept it to himself. Yet he was considered physically fit for National Service a few years ago, although like Rodney, he ended up doing office work in the army. He was short-sighted too, like me and his mother, with severe astigmatism. His glasses didn't seem to help the problems he developed. When he went to the optician in Cambridge, he was immediately referred to the hospital for on-going treatment.'

Sunny interrupted, 'Why didn't he tell me this at Christmas – why did he ask me to marry him as soon as possible, without telling me something as important as this?'

Mr Rowland said slowly, 'I suppose he thought he had time to get better, Sunny. I can tell you that the confession he made to you, after he learned his condition could only be controlled, not cured, was untrue. The young woman he referred to left Cambridge, returned to her fiancé – she was forgiven for the one mistake she had made and is about to be married. Please believe this, my dear.'

After a long moment Sunny said, 'Why didn't he write me another letter about all this?'

'Because, there is no easy way to say this – he is blind now in the left eye, and he will eventually probably only have limited sight in the right eye.'

'Will – will he be able to continue his music?'

'There are blind pianists and composers; disabled ones, like those who play one-handed. I always think you can do anything if you are determined enough – and have real talent. Yes, he will continue – he is concentrating on the classics, learning the scores by heart. He loves his jazz too, but won't lead the band again, I think.'

'I need to see him.' Sunny was openly weeping now. 'Oh, Grandfather, could I see him this weekend? I've passed my driving test, but if I can't take the car – it is jointly owned by Nan and Serena you see – you could tell me how to get there by train, couldn't you?'

'I'll come with you,' he said instantly. 'You must see him on your own, of course, and I hope you will take him on.'

'Take him on. Of course I will,' she cried. 'I'll wear my ring again, but we must meet up more often, and think of the future when we can be together like Chrissie is with Ravi.'

'Shall we go tomorrow and return Sunday evening?' he asked. 'I will let Eleanor know and she can come round and feed Pilchie.'

'Does Eleanor know you're telling me all this tonight?' Sunny asked.

'Yes. She said, "Sunny may be young, but she's more sensible than Alec! Or you, for that matter, Father! They are right for each other, and that's that."'

*   *   *

It was just past nine o'clock as they boarded the train, and Sunny had a flashback to when she and Eleanor had stood on the same platform ready to wave Alec off to Cambridge for the first time. Doors had clanged and folk climbed aboard. Alec had kissed his mother, and then he turned to Sunny, who was then sixteen years old, confused as she hardly knew him but was already aware of her feelings for him. It had just been a brief kiss. Now, she was nineteen and it had been a topsy-turvy relationship all along. She thought, *why can't I settle for Rodney, who is a true friend to me?*

Some hours later she walked down a long, echoing corridor with Mr Rowland, who pointed out the ward ahead. There was a waiting area, and the local volunteers were making tea and offering biscuits to those who had travelled a long way. He sat on one of the chairs and joined the throng. He had a newspaper in his bag to read while he waited. He said to Sunny, 'It's just on visiting time: you'll find Alec in the bed at the end of the ward. Good luck. I'll stay here until you return.'

Sunny walked down the corridor and pushed open the swing doors. Some of the beds were curtained off, including the end one on the right. A nurse swished by in her starched uniform, carrying a folder. She smiled at Sunny. 'Visiting a patient?'

'Yes,' Sunny said. 'Alec Rowland.'

'Ah, I gather you are his fiancée? I was told you were coming. He's having a nap, like some of the other patients.

You can leave the curtains closed if you would rather talk privately.'

'Thank you,' Sunny said, and they went their different ways. She peeped through the curtains. Alec appeared to be asleep. Even as she wondered what she should do, he opened his eyes and saw her face. He sat up and called, 'Come inside my tent!'

Sunny suddenly felt tearful. Alec had a bandage over his left eye, and his glasses sat crookedly on his nose, but that was not unusual. He held out his arms. 'My darling, I knew you would come!' She went to him without hesitation and he held her close and whispered, 'You're wearing your ring, Sunny. Do you forgive me, and do you still love me, even looking like this?'

'Of course I do,' she murmured, before he kissed her.

He whispered, 'Pity you can't get under the covers with me . . .'

Sunny reproved him mildly. 'Fancy thinking of that, Alec Rowland!'

'I was actually thinking how you aren't a little girl anymore, and how much I've missed you.'

TWENTY-SEVEN

June 1959

Chrissie moved slowly around her kitchen one morning. She found the yellow theme made her feel nauseous. The twin tub washing machine was noisy, but she had turned up the volume of the little radio, and was listening to John Dunn. Chrissie glanced down at her distended stomach and sighed heavily. 'Why are you taking so long to come?' she asked the baby, who the midwife said had 'dropped into position nicely'. All Chrissie could think of at the moment was that her tummy was so stretched, it was bound to be flabby, like Terry said, and she wasn't up to lying on the floor and trying to exercise along with the music. She hauled herself up and sat in the wicker chair, with the plump cushion her mother had made, that she'd spotted in a junk shop, and Ravi had painted yellow, of course. 'You must rest more, dear,' she'd said anxiously. The chair was more comfortable than the stools, which wobbled when she perched on them.

The Beverley Sisters were singing in harmony, but Chrissie's feet were too swollen to tap in time to the tune. Chrissie sighed, then gasped and gripped the arms of the chair as a wave of pain struck her lower back and shifted round to the front. *I must get up*, she thought, *go to the phone in the hall and ring Ravi as he told me to. He's in the surgery this morning though . . .*

She gasped again, as another pain engulfed her and she became aware that the doorbell was ringing; someone was obviously pressing it as it didn't stop, but then the caller, whoever he or she was, banged on the door with his or her free hand.

Chrissie made her way unsteadily along the hall, but as she paused when another contraction doubled her up, she heard a voice she knew well. 'Chrissie, I can see you are in trouble – I just managed to look through the letterbox. Is the back door open?'

'Yes,' Chrissie managed. 'I was – going – to hang the washing – out . . .' She collapsed in a heap on the floor and closed her eyes.

The next thing she knew, Sunny was leaning over her, and saying, 'Hang on – I must ring Ravi before I try to move you. Just tell me the number.' There was no answer, so Sunny opened a diary she found on the hall table, and discovered the surgery number on the flyleaf inside. Trembling, she dialled the number and waited for a reply. The receptionist answered and told her that Ravi was out on a call. 'I'll put you through to one of the other doctors who will help,' Sunny was informed. While she waited, she glanced fearfully at Chrissie. Her eyes were closed and she was moaning.

It seemed an eternity before a doctor came to the phone. 'Can you move the patient to a settee? Don't attempt to get her upstairs. A colleague is going now to tell her husband and take over his patient. He should be with you in about twenty minutes, I hope.'

Sunny said anxiously, 'What can I do to help, if I am able to move her, that is?'

'Just do your best to keep her calm. Talk to her, even if she doesn't answer, and sponging her forehead will help. Good luck! I have to go now,' said the doctor. 'I am with a patient myself right now.'

'Thank you,' Sunny managed. The door to the sitting room was ajar. It was easier to move Chrissie in there, she decided, to the settee under the window.

She managed to help Chrissie to her feet, then stood behind her, gripped her under the arms and guided her step by dragging step to the settee. 'Easy does it,' Sunny said, suddenly remembering Nan saying that to her when she was a child and feeling frustrated when trying to lift the wheels of her doll's pram over the back step.

'Why are you here and not at college?' Chrissie asked faintly.

'It's half-term, I'm off this week. I – I just had a feeling this morning that you needed me, so I came.' Sunny thought it wasn't the time to tell Chrissie she was off to Cambridge tomorrow for a few days. Alec would hopefully be back at university the following week.

Chrissie's face contorted, then she was clutching at Sunny's arm and crying out, 'Help me, please help me!'

At that moment Ravi arrived, rushing through the front door. He took one look at his wife and disappeared again, upstairs to the airing cupboard to return with an armful of towels. Together he and Sunny managed to lift Chrissie and put them under her. Then Ravi asked Sunny to fetch a bundle of old newspapers stowed in the cupboard under the stairs. 'Hopefully, they will protect the settee cushions,' he said.

'Are you going to send for the ambulance?' Sunny asked.

'I've already alerted them; it's not far for them to come,' he said. 'You'll help me, Sunny, won't you? If there are complications, Chrissie will have to be moved right away to the hospital. She was booked to go there anyway.'

Sunny swallowed hard. 'Of course I'll help, but I don't know, you see – what will happen . . .'

'Chrissie will be comforted to have you here,' he said. 'Now, boil up water in the biggest saucepans, please, while I see how things are progressing.'

'Shall I ring Chrissie's mother?' she asked.

'Let's bring the baby into the world first,' he said wisely. He took off his jacket and rolled up his sleeves. Then opened his black bag. He had everything he needed, a doctor must be ready for any emergency,

How calm he is, Sunny thought. *Chrissie is so fortunate to have married him.*

The ambulance arrived with siren blaring, and Sunny let them in. Chrissie was crying out and the doctor who'd come with the crew went straight into the sitting room, closing the door behind him. Two other men had accompanied him to the door and returned to the ambulance to fetch a stretcher and a bundle of red hospital blankets.

They propped these up in the hall and the older of the two asked Sunny, 'Any chance of a cup of tea, my love? This is the third time we've been out this morning.'

'Come into the kitchen,' she managed. 'How many cups shall I make?'

'Make a big pot and keep it in on the hob, in case the others want one. Just pour out for us three – and boil the kettle up again please,' the same man advised her.

Ten minutes later, they sprang into action when Ravi called out, 'It's a boy!' while Chrissie managed, 'Sunny – where is Sunny?'

Sunny was just behind the door. She opened it and went in. Ravi looked up and smiled. 'Here's the baby's godmother, Chrissie – your best friend!'

Sunny went slowly across the room. Chrissie, sitting up now still cloaked in towels, and cuddling a tiny baby in her arms, she urged Sunny, 'Don't be shy! Come and see what you think of little Ravi!'

'Is that his name?' Sunny asked as she gazed down at the baby.

'Of course,' Chrissie said. 'The eldest son in Ravi's family is always named after his father.'

'He's very small, isn't he?' Sunny noted the little dark head. 'He's got hair!' she exclaimed.

Ravi laughed then. 'Our son,' he said firmly, 'is like both of us, don't you think? Here comes the stretcher, Chrissie, the hospital midwife will clean you up and see that all is as it should be.'

'Do you want a cup of tea?' Sunny remembered belatedly.

'We won't delay the men any more. Will you hold the baby while we transfer Chrissie to the ambulance, Sunny? Oh, and after we've gone, please will you ring my mother-in-law?'

Sunny nodded. She looked down at the tiny newcomer in her arms. He was wrinkled and red, his eyes closed. A sudden thought came to her. *Will I ever have a baby like this? One day perhaps, one day. Even though Alec said when*

I sat with him in the hospital, 'They told me this is probably an inherited condition and I ought to consider that, if I decide to have a family.'

'Do you want that?' she had to know.

'I've put you through enough worry, Sunny, already,' he said simply. 'At the moment I can only think how fortunate I am that you are still willing to take me on.'

'I won't let you go again,' she'd told him. 'I won't, *I won't!*'

Now Sunny gave the little dark head a quick kiss. 'Ravi, I'm going to be your godmother, and I wouldn't mind betting that Rodney will be your godfather.' The baby was gently taken from her arms and given back to his mother. Then the ambulance drove off. Ravi followed in his car. He wound down his window and called to Sunny, 'Ring Mrs Ford from here, and close the door to the sitting room. I'll see to everything. I've got my key. I'll be in touch.' Then he left.

* * *

Ravi was already at their daughter's bedside when Chrissie's parents visited her that evening. Chrissie was in the maternity ward, midway along a long line of iron-framed hospital beds. Mrs Ford was shocked to see the mother in the next bed receiving a bottle of stout from her husband and concealing it under her pillow. The woman saw her looking over at her and called out, 'Full of iron, dear. But don't let on to the nurse, will you?'

Ravi whispered, 'Sorry, Chrissie, I didn't think – I'll bring you some flowers tomorrow.'

'I'd rather have a box of Bassett's,' she whispered in return.

She was overheard by a passing nurse. 'My dear, your baby will pay for it if you eat anything like that!' But this was said with a smile.

Chrissie's eyes suddenly filled with tears, and she gripped Ravi's hand. 'I'm not sure, Ravi – if I'm old enough to be a mum.'

'You'll be wonderful, you are anyway,' he said. 'You're a good wife, and being a good mother will follow, you'll see.' He glanced at Mrs Ford. Her husband had gone to get them all a cup of tea from the canteen. She was trying to look as if she was not listening in to this personal conversation.

'And you're a good husband,' Mrs Ford said. 'Oh, here comes Dad with the tea!' Visiting hour seemed to go by very quickly. Before Mrs Ford went, she said, 'Oh, Auntie Beryl said if it had been a girl, she would have suggested you use her name.'

'Did she?' Chrissie sounded amused. 'No, Mum, we thought of Susanna, after you.'

Mr Ford, who usually let his wife do all the talking, said, 'Next time, eh?' and he gave a roguish grin.

'Come on, Dad, anyone would think you'd had a glass of beer, not a cup of tea,' his wife said disapprovingly. She kissed Chrissie and said, 'Thank you for our darling little grandson, Chrissie.' Then they departed as the bell rang to signal the end of the hour.

'You'd better go too, Ravi,' Chrissie sighed.

'I'll tuck you up,' he offered. 'You must be tired.'

'I am, but, Ravi, I'm so happy. We're a family now, aren't we?'

'We are,' he agreed.

* * *

Sunny passed on the good news back home. Suddenly, she was crying, and Nan was hugging her tight as she wept. 'I didn't know that having a baby was like that – things won't be the same now between Chrissie and me now she's a mother. We had a lot of fun growing up together, didn't we?'

'Of course you did, Sunny. And one day you'll get married and have a baby yourself, I hope.' Nan sounded wistful.

'It all depends . . .' Sunny didn't finish the sentence.

'On Alec; I know, dear, I know.'

* * *

Chrissie was fed up, she had been in hospital for nearly two weeks, as was expected of new mothers. She wanted to go home and look after her baby herself. In the hospital he was only brought to her for feeds and taken away to the night nursery after six. She could hear babies crying in the night, but the night nurse told her not to worry and go back to sleep.

She was allowed to get out of bed, have a bath, and get dressed on the last two days there. All the new mothers went to the nursery in turn to watch the babies being bathed by the nurses. They took it in turns to put a clean nappy on their own baby when he or she was handed to them. Baby boys had a large blue safety pin, and baby girls had a pink one. Chrissie was worried she would prick little Ravi's skin with the pin, and make him cry, but she managed to fasten the nappy so that it didn't fall down round his ankles. He kicked quite vigorously and waved his arms about. 'An active baby,' a nurse told her.

Chrissie looked down at him lovingly as he lay on her lap. She had brushed his damp black hair into a little quiff, and now his eyes were open, they were bright and he appeared to be looking around. *Such a lot for me to remember*, she thought: *test bath water with your elbow, always put cold water in the tub before you gradually add hot. Use cotton wool to clean nostrils, they were told, and never allow a baby to lay in a wet or soiled nappy, or there was a danger of nappy rash.*

Her mother had already made her a baby box for toiletries; lining an apple box from the greengrocer's with padding, then covering the box with blue material, patterned with white ducks. In the box nestled baby powder, Vaseline, a cake of soap, cotton wool, a baby hair brush, toothbrush for when it was needed, muslin pieces to line nappies, bibs, and a small glass feeding bottle for juice or boiled water. In the bathroom there would soon be a collection of rubber ducks along the windowsill.

Presents for the baby were accumulating at home. Ravi had wisely left these for his wife to unwrap. His parents were due to arrive from Ceylon the weekend after Chrissie was due home and Ravi was hoping his mother would not fuss over the baby like Chrissie's mother. He was dreading the first visit by Auntie Beryl, who wrote she was bringing a 'smart new outfit for my first great, nephew'. He would be taking a week of his annual leave to help settle his wife and baby into the new house. He was thankful that dry cleaning the settee had been successful, for Chrissie seemed to cry at every little setback.

He needn't have worried. When his parents arrived, his mother sang lullabies to little Ravi, and had a calming effect on them all. Ravi relaxed and talked to his father, who was a retired doctor himself. Chrissie relaxed too and didn't notice there was one new cushion on her beloved settee.

* * *

Rodney had been demobbed. He came home, but he was not alone. Magda had decided not to go into the convent, but to move to England and train as a nurse. 'I might decide later to go home and work in a hospital there,' she said to Rodney. Meanwhile, Rodney's parents invited her to think of their home as the place she could come to whenever she had a few days off from the hospital. Nan and Serena helped her find the right place to train.

Perhaps Sunny felt a little neglected because Nan was so enthusiastic about 'Rodney's young lady', as she thought her to be. Magda herself was aware that Rodney was still hoping that one day Sunny would turn to him if things did not work out with Alec.

Sunny was going out occasionally with a new companion – Jen, her fellow student at art school. As she had with Chrissie, she enjoyed visits to the theatre, the cinema, and once or twice to a local dance. She saw Mr Rowland now and again, when he was invited to supper by Nan. The Major seemed to be in the same groove, she thought. Nan had no intention of marrying either of them.

Serena reminded her about the promised honeymoon to Trinidad, but Sunny said, 'No firm plans yet, Serena. We both want to graduate first.' She couldn't afford to keep driving to Cambridge, she realised.

I'm almost twenty, she thought, *and have to accept my dreams may not all come true, but my poster is on lots of bill-boards, so Pilchie, at any rate, is famous and Grandfather is proud of me.*

TWENTY-EIGHT

Sunny didn't see Alec during the summer holidays: her only break was when she and Jen went on a walking holiday in Surrey, staying at youth hostels along the way. They wore baggy khaki shorts bought from the Army Surplus Store in Brixton and T-shirts which they customised with silk-screened slogans like *We're Arty-Crafty*. They carried their painting gear in knapsacks, also from the store, on their backs. They couldn't afford a tent or sleeping bags, but Nan, for one, was relieved, as she thought the YHA hostels were safer for young, unaccompanied girls. Miss Guyatt told her students: 'Sketchbooks at the ready!'

Sunny enclosed some thumbnail pictures in the letters she wrote to Alec now and then. Nowadays, he telephoned her at home once a week. He was in and out of hospital, receiving further treatment. His condition was now stable, he reported, which was encouraging, but he didn't mention their future together.

The baby was christened in the church where Chrissie and Ravi were married, while Ravi's parents were staying in a hotel near the young family. They'd return to Ceylon at the end of July. Little Ravi was a very vocal baby; he was smiling most of the time but he let his mother know when he wanted a feed, and when he woke from his afternoon nap he expected to be amused.

Godmother Sunny stood alongside Rodney, who, as she had expected, was her co-godparent. Later the party went to The Grove and they had a picnic celebration. Zosia was very taken with the baby; she talked to him and made him chortle when she leaned over his carrycot and blew a raspberry on his tummy.

Sunny remembered the last time she was here, on a cold Christmas night, when Alec broke her heart by telling her their relationship was over. She closed her eyes, as she recalled those words. Rodney, who was stretched out beside her on the grass, tickled her bare leg with a blade of grass to make her aware he was there, while the rest of the party chattered away and held little Ravi in turn.

'Stop that,' she responded, but didn't sound cross. She sat up and smoothed her skirt down.

'Little Miss Prim and Proper,' he teased. 'I was admiring your legs!'

'I'll get you for that,' she cried in mock anger, jumping on him. They rolled away down the grassy slope, laughing all the way. Now they were out of earshot of family and guests, they were able to talk. It was like old times, and

Sunny suddenly remembered how often he'd caught her, when they were young, and stolen a kiss, when no one was around.

Rodney sounded out of breath. He brushed her hair out of her eyes, and she didn't resist when he kissed her. *This was a warm, experienced kiss*, she thought. Then she pushed him away. 'Enough of that, Rod!'

'You liked it, admit it!' he said triumphantly. Then he stood up and said, 'Race you to the bottom of the hill!' Like the two kids they once were, they both took up the challenge, and Rodney allowed her to win, which he hadn't when she was sixteen. They leaned against the tree, the same one they had sheltered under looking up at the stars as the young Sunny had done, first with Rodney and later with Alec. Suddenly, she was crying and Rodney put an arm round her, saying, 'What's wrong, Sunny? Have I upset you?'

'No,' she managed, 'it's just that I said goodbye forever to Alec here, but later I found out why he had said what he did; because he knew he was in trouble with his eyes.'

'You got together again, though, didn't you? Nan told my mum that you intend to marry after you both finish your courses.'

'That hasn't been mentioned again,' she said sadly. 'But I can understand why, Rod.'

'Can I dare to hope?'

She took a deep breath. 'You may have a long wait,' she said finally.

'Well, I've got ambitions to fulfil too, with the bank. But it's good to be back, Sunny.'

*   *   *

It was September 1959 and Sunny's second and final year at the art school was beginning. Alec would shortly be back at Cambridge, and feeling the same, she thought. They both needed to 'work their socks off', as Miss Guyatt told her students. Her twentieth birthday was almost here, too. She didn't expect Alec to come home. He went around Cambridge by bicycle now, as he had in his first years there, along with all the other students. The car had been sold, for his eyesight was not good enough for driving.

They really were a family now at the Mother and Baby Home. The bedroom, bathroom, kitchen and sitting room upstairs was now Sunny's domain; somewhere she could entertain her friends at the weekend or in the evening after the day nursery babies were collected by their parents. It was time, Nan decided, for her to enjoy her independence. She could join the family downstairs whenever she felt like it, of course, Nan said.

Serena and Jan now had Sunny's old bedroom, and the spare room next door had been cleared of clutter and become Zosia's nursery. It was their house now after all, Nan said, but they reminded her she was still in charge of everything, in particular of her kitchen.

None of them commented when Rodney became a regular visitor to the flat upstairs. Nan knew what had happened between Sunny and Alec but, she said to Serena, 'Our girl is an adult now, and we have to realise that.'

'I don't think you need to worry on that score,' Serena said. 'Sunny says they are just good friends and I believe her. She finds it hard to let go of Alec, I think.'

'She is still in touch with him – Alexander told me. He would be delighted if they did marry eventually. However, should Alec's condition suddenly deteriorate, I think he would release her from any commitment they have made,' Nan said.

* * *

'Another birthday been and gone.' Sunny gave a sigh but she was smiling, as she jigged little Ravi up and down on her knees. It was Saturday morning, the day after her birthday, and she was in Chrissie's kitchen, no longer yellow, but painted pale blue.

Matching the sky today, she thought, *but there are just a few clouds which obscure the sun in passing. Like my life, I think. A bouquet of red roses arrived yesterday, but beautiful as they are, they don't have the heady scent of the old rose bushes in The Grove. The roses were from Alec, but I think Grandfather bought and sent them; the florist's van was from Croydon.*

'Any plans for tonight? Are you going out with Rodney?' Chrissie asked, sitting down at last at the table after she'd poured homemade soup into blue bowls, matching the kitchen colour scheme. 'I hope you heard from Alec? Oh, let me put Ravi in his pram, before we eat.' She was on her feet again. Sunny thought, it's a busy life being a mum.

Sunny dipped her spoon in the soup, and Chrissie indicated the plate of what she described as 'roughly hewn bread'. 'I hope you like leek and potato, I've got a Marguerite Patten cookbook,' she added proudly. 'Well – you haven't answered my question, have you?'

'About the soup?' It was rather watery, but of course, Sunny wouldn't say.

'Don't prevaricate!' Chrissie flicked back her hair, worn in a long plait over her shoulder these days, before it dipped in her bowl.

'Did I hear from Alec? He sent some roses, with a card. "Still in love with love, Alec", it said.'

'Is he back here this weekend?' Chrissie probed.

'Not as far as I know. Rodney is taking me out tonight, don't ask me where, because it's a surprise, he says.' She wiped her bowl clean with the last chunk of bread. 'Well, I must be off, I know you have to feed the baby, and Ravi will be home soon, eh? Rod is working this Saturday morning too. I'll come again soon.'

'I miss you, Sunny,' Chrissie said. 'Enjoy your freedom while you have it! Oh, don't get me wrong, Ravi is the man

I dreamed of meeting one day, and I did, and I love my baby, of course, but sometimes I look back and remember us growing up together, making mistakes. It was fun, wasn't it?'

'It was,' Sunny said simply. 'But things aren't so easy for me. Thank you for your present, I'll treasure that pretty compact and will powder my nose tonight!'

* * *

Nan popped upstairs to see whether Sunny was ready for her evening out. Sunny cooked for herself at weekends, but still had supper with Nan during the week, after she arrived home from the art studio. Tonight, she would be eating out with Rodney, but he had not divulged where they were going or what was planned for afterwards.

Nan admired the pretty silver compact and watched as Sunny applied a little peach powder to her forehead, nose and chin. 'Is that mascara?' she asked, as Sunny applied it; it made her eyes look even more lustrous and dark.

'Mmm,' Sunny murmured. She was rather put off by Nan's interest. *I need a steady hand, to avoid dark rings round my eyes*, she thought. She'd covered her shoulders with a clean towel, before applying her makeup.

'Not too heavy with the lipstick,' Nan advised, and then wished she hadn't for Sunny turned and said, 'I know what I'm doing, Nan!'

'Sorry,' Nan said, 'I didn't mean to criticise; it's just that you are beautiful as you are.' She turned to leave.

'No, don't go, Nan – I'm sorry if I snapped, it's just that I hoped – you know – to see Alec today.'

'My dear, I understand. But you have Rodney.'

'Yes, I have Rodney, as you say, but I don't want to give him false hopes, Nan. I think, I don't know why, that Magda might have changed her mind about the nunnery, when she realised she might not see him again. Is she like me, longing for the impossible?'

'I think you could well be right,' Nan agreed. 'You are wearing last year's birthday dress I see.'

'I believe it might bring me luck,' Sunny said, as she brushed her hair. 'I am thinking of wearing my ring too.'

'Because it would signal to Rodney that you still consider yourself engaged to Alec?' Nan asked.

'Oh, Nan, you know me inside out, you really do!'

Rodney had recently changed his motorcycle for a car. He could afford to run one now he was being promoted rapidly in the bank. He had his own office space now, and clients had to book to see him and discuss the possibility of mortgages or loans. He had done the right thing, the manager told him, joining the Pay Corps for his National Service with the army. He could see, he said, that Rodney was now a very confident young man and an asset to the bank.

He didn't have to toot the horn for Sunny came out directly she heard the car arrive. Nan was behind her, and waved them off, calling, 'Have a good time! Have you got your key?' Sunny nodded, as the engine was already throbbing. 'She says that, when she thinks I am going to be late,' Sunny said. 'Where are we going, Rod? Streatham?'

'Further than that . . . wait and see,' he said.

'Will I like it?' she persisted.

'I hope so. First stop will be Lyons Corner House, have you been there?'

'I have to say I haven't.'

'Nor have I. We are going on from there.'

Sunny was entranced by the art deco facade and gold lettering: J. LYONS & CO. LTD., and was eager to go inside. The restaurant was full, and buzzing with talk. Sunny was a little disappointed that the Nippy girls, as the waitresses were called in the 1920s, were no longer nipping around smartly with orders for customers.

Inside there were Formica tables and bright lights and laughter from people sitting nearby. After the smoked salmon and Waldorf salad, with a glass of wine, they drank Lyons famous own brand of coffee and sampled delicious gateaux.

Sunny excused herself to wash her sticky fingers after the meal and discovered that the facilities had obviously not changed from twenties styling. There were marble basins, shiny red mahogany woodwork, brightly polished taps, gilded mirrors reflecting it all and a pleasant whiff of floral disinfectant.

She emerged to find Rodney waiting at a discreet distance, and they went out into the street, but she had no idea where they might be going. The Regent cinema was nearby, she realised, but they walked past that. The streetlights were on, but there were brighter lights from shop windows, although the shops were closed, and from a big cinema. There were plenty of people out and about.

'This way I think,' Rodney said, as they turned down a side street. They went down some steps and arrived at a small theatre. There was a queue outside, but Rodney had tickets in his pocket and they were soon inside the foyer. There was a large poster on the wall and Sunny had a funny feeling inside when she read:

A Night with Gershwin. Guest Pianist Alec Rowland. Singers from the Broadway.

They were settled in their seats, not plush and posh, Sunny thought, but linked along the row. The curtains were still drawn, the lights on, as others arrived and soon the theatre was full. She looked up. Not so grand as the Albert Hall, where she had dreamed of one day seeing Alec perform, recalling the promenade concert he had taken her to. That seemed a long time ago.

'Comfortable?' Rodney asked and she nodded. Then she said, 'Did you plan this surprise for me, Rodney, or did Grandfather have something to do with it?'

'He gave me the tickets, told me not to tell you – I have to admit Nan and Serena knew too.'

'Where is he staying?'

'With Mr Rowland,' Rodney said. 'Sunny, I can't answer all your questions, because I don't know the answers. Just sit back and enjoy the evening. You'll see Alec afterwards; we are taking him home. Shush, the curtain is rising, and the orchestra is tuning up.'

As the lights dimmed, there was an expectant hush from the audience. Rodney held Sunny's hand. He sensed she was trembling slightly, but she didn't question him further.

Alec came on stage and bowed to the audience, then sat down at the grand piano, flanked by the orchestra. There was a short introduction by the compere. Sunny blinked tears from her eyes. Alec wore evening dress with a bow tie, but she had immediately focused on the tinted glasses he wore. He didn't look like the Alec she knew. His hair was tidy, for one thing.

Sunny felt she must be dreaming as the music began with 'Rhapsody in Blue' with what was termed a clarinet glissando – she thought, *I must look that up in the dictionary*! – then Alec's fingers were poised over the piano keys, the conductor raised his baton and the rhapsody began. At the end there was rapturous applause. Alec took another bow. *Is he looking in my direction, can he see that well?* she wondered. Rodney's grip tightened on her hand. He wanted her to know he understood how she was feeling.

The music went on, but Sunny had to wait for the last piece, the one she knew Alec would play. There were singers backing him and a backcloth of a cotton-picking scene. Rich, resonant voices, some deep, some soaring sopranos. Singing from the heart; heart-breaking, Sunny thought.

'Summertime', the audience joined in with the chorus. Rodney lifted Sunny's hand to his lips and kissed it. 'Don't cry,' he whispered, 'this one is for *you,* I believe.'

They waited some time in the theatre at the end of the show, before Alec joined them. He shook hands with Rodney and said simply, 'Thanks for bringing Sunny. It meant so much to me to know she was here.'

'You two sit in the back,' Rodney suggested, as they located the parked car and he opened the doors. He knew they must want to say so much to each other. He concentrated on driving while they did just that.

'I thought you were in Cambridge,' she began.

'Mother brought me back home yesterday – to Grandfather – with all my baggage,' he said. 'I won't be going back to university, Sunny.'

'Oh, why not!' she cried. 'We agreed to carry on with studying, you, music and me, art.'

'I know that I'd considered my future and thought I could manage somehow to travel to faraway concerts and play classical music, even if my eyesight deteriorated, but my professor sat me down and we talked it over, and his advice was that it would prove impossible, and that I was talented enough to play my music nearer home. There were plenty of London venues, he said, and I would have family around to support me. He told me, "Don't put off your marriage any longer. A partner in life is just what you need."'

'You mean—' she faltered.

'I mean you, of course. If you agree, we'll get a special licence, and marry as soon as possible. You must carry on with your art, of course. Nan and Grandfather want that too.'

'Where would we live?' she asked.

'Nan and Serena say I can join you in the flat – tonight, if you're willing! Grandfather has a plan, I believe, to get on with the rooms and studio improvement at the Printing Press, and that will be his wedding present to us. I think the bargain will be we look after the cat. We will have enough money to live on for a while, thanks to the sale of *Sans Souci*.'

'But where will he go?'

Alec's arms went around her and his voice was muffled as he said, 'He asked Nan and Serena if he could take over the flat in the Mother and Baby Home and Nan in particular seemed very happy at the thought of having him there. Do you agree?'

'You haven't said you love me yet,' she said, 'but it seems you do.'

'We're here, Grove Lane!' Rodney said, drawing up outside the house. 'I won't come in,' he said. 'Good luck!'

'Oh, Rodney, thank you for making all this possible,' Sunny said.

'Don't worry about me,' he said. 'Magda knows. I think she hopes to piece my broken heart together. Well, I'll say goodnight, and await some good news soon, eh?'

Sunny opened the front door with her key and they tiptoed cautiously over to the stairs. 'They'll hear the lift humming if we go up in it,' Sunny whispered. Actually, both Nan and Serena were lying awake in their beds, waiting to hear the key turn in the lock, and two coming in, not one.

He opened his bag. 'Music scores mingling with pyjamas.' He tried to make her smile. 'Where do I sleep – on the couch?'

'Someone's added another pillow to the bed,' she said, ignoring that remark. 'Excuse me, I must have a wash before I get into bed. The bathroom is next door.' She picked up her nightie and decided to get undressed in there.

When she returned, he was already on the far side of the bed, which was big enough for two, as it was originally used by Serena and Jan. 'Shall I turn the light out?' he asked. The lamp was on his bedside cabinet. 'Oh, you'd better have this on your side,' he added, handing over the china pig Rodney had bought her in Rye. The little black bear Serena had knitted so long ago leaned against the pig. 'He needs some new stuffing, like me, I suppose,' he told her ruefully.

It would be easier to talk in the dark, she thought, although she usually read for a while when she got into bed. She settled in beside him. They didn't do much talking, though. Summertime was almost over, but it had brought them back together.

EPILOGUE

September, 1960

On Saturday, 9th September, 1960, a day before her twenty-first birthday, Sunny and Alec were married in a short ceremony at the register office. They decided on a quiet wedding, and Alec asked if she would wear the pretty dress she'd chosen for her eighteenth birthday party. She hadn't worn it since they were reunited, but often fingered the material lovingly when she opened her wardrobe. Would it still fit her? she wondered. She hoped that Alec's grandfather would insist Alec wear a suit and a tie for this special day.

There had been a celebration when she graduated from the art school that year and it was then that they moved into the refurbished Rowland Press accommodation. Sunny had her studio, and the bedroom was transformed, also the kitchen, which Alec's mother and grandfather had generously furnished for them, with a refrigerator, boiler, washing machine and dryer and a new stove. Friends gave them cutlery, crockery and saucepans. They also bought a red Formica-topped table, two stools, and a tall cupboard for packets and tins of food, and, of course, a large packet of dried peas!

The sitting room had a long couch and a couple of matching chairs, but most of the space was taken up by their gift from Nan – her father's grand piano. Mr Rowland had persuaded her to allow him to make prints of the picture Sunny had painted (which won her a trophy from the art college). Patsy framed them as before, and the revenue was shared between Nan and Sunny.

Mr Rowland took over their rooms at The Mother and Baby Home. He was not the only one interested in Nan of course. The Major thought he might be in with a chance, however, Mr Rowland thought smugly: *I'm the one with my feet under the table!* Nan included meals within the modest rent. She also persuaded him to invest in some new clothes and to wear slippers without his big toes peeping out.

Eleanor and her friend Helena were enjoying life with holidays several times a year. Eleanor was freed from feeling responsible for her son and her elderly father, but both attended Alec's concerts whenever He was playing at a jazz venue in London.

Alec stayed in an hotel with his grandfather, the night before the wedding, and Sunny was at home with Nan and Serena, Jan and three-year-old Zosia, who was furious because she was not allowed to go to bed in her brides-maid's frock.

Mr Rowland and Nan were witnesses at the wedding ceremony, and the best man was Jan. Serena and Chrissie were occupied with keeping their small children quiet. The wedding breakfast was back at the Mother and Baby Home, and the bridegroom asked Nan to make his favourite meal; gammon and pease pudding with parsley sauce, while Sunny wished for treacle tart.

Later, they went to the village hall and were joined for the evening by close friends, including Chrissie's mum and dad. Rodney came with his fiancée, Magda, and his parents. The Perkins were all there, too. Ravi came after he finished work, but The Major regretted he had a previous engagement. Eleanor and Helena came home a day early from one of their trips abroad. Jan had to meet them at the airport. Jen was also invited, as she and Sunny had remained good friends after leaving college.

There was the traditional cutting of the wedding cake, which Chrissie had ordered from her friendly bakery, and she placed the tiny china bride and bridegroom on top with the proviso she would like them returned later. Champagne was now allowed.

It was Eleanor who sat down at the piano, so this time Sunny was able to have the last dance of the evening with her new husband.

The newlyweds had decided to spend the night in their own little home and have a honeymoon later. Alec was returning to hospital the following week for an operation on his left eye, to remove a second cataract he'd had for several years, in the hope of restoring some sight.

Sunny was determined to be cheerful about this, and their wedding night was blissful.

They had never discussed whether they should have children or not, but Alec had been told that the short sight he had obviously inherited from his mother and grandfather was not connected to problems he had now.

A year later, Chrissie and Ravi had a second baby, a brother for young Ravi. Rodney and Magda were married around the same time, and were delighted to be parents the following year, but as Alec had further treatment and a long convalescence, it seemed unlikely he and Sunny would be ready to have a baby in the near future. She worked hard at her art projects and was gaining recognition for this, and she concealed her longing for a baby to make life even more perfect.

*　　*　　*

June, 1964

'We are going back to the jazz club where we found each other again,' Alec told her, after opening a letter from the manager there. 'You must wear your lucky dress, Sunny darling!'

'I'm not sure I will be able to get into it,' Sunny said demurely. 'We are going to have a Christmas baby!'

'What? Does Nan know?' he asked, wondering why she hadn't told him before.

'Not yet – but they'll all be delighted back at the Mother and Baby Home. Wouldn't it be lovely to have our first baby there?'

'I suppose it would,' he said, but he was bemused by the unexpected announcement.

'Are you happy about it?' she asked.

'Of course I am – if it's a girl we'll call her after you.'

She said firmly, 'It will be Nanette, if it's a girl, and Alexander after Grandfather – and you of course – if it's a boy.'

He took his glasses off and wiped his eyes. 'There, you've made me blub for the second time in my life.'

*   *   *

It was Christmas Day and Nan cradled the tiny dark-haired baby in her arms. 'She looks like you, Sunny – why don't you name her after yourself?'

'Nan, we are calling her after you. You are her nana, and she will be Nanette.'

It had been a quick and easy birth, and Serena had delivered the baby in the Mother and Baby Home as Sunny and Alec had wished. Nan was about to cook the Christmas dinner for the evening meal. *Too much going on earlier*, she'd thought.

Alec had sat by his wife since she woke in the early morning and said, 'I think the baby is on its way!' However, he was sent out of the room when the birth was imminent and he and Jan were put on vegetable preparation duty and were keeping an eye on mischievous Zosia. Serena and Nan couldn't be dealing with husbands fainting at this time, they said. 'And keep Alexander occupied,' they added.

They heard the Christmas bells ringing, The Major was busy as usual, but was invited to dinner in the evening. Eleanor and Helena were waiting for the news, too. Chrissie and Ravi were with her family, together with Auntie Beryl, and they were also listening out for the phone to ring. Rodney, Magda and their small daughter, Isabel, were spending Christmas with his parents.

Nan said firmly, 'No visitors, Sunny, until after Boxing Day, eh?'

'Oh, Nan, let them all come – but not today!' Sunny said. 'You can't put The Major off this evening though; *two* suitors – you are a dark horse, Nan.'

'I'm nothing of the sort,' Nan said firmly. She smiled. 'Life begins at sixty-plus,' she said.

ACKNOWLEDGEMENTS

Remembering a little abandoned cat called Pilchie who found a home with Glenys and Eric.

Nanette is named after a lovely ambulance driver, who reassures patients.

My thanks to my sister-in-law, Margaret, for her memories of dancing with my late brother in the Orchid Ballroom, Purley.

Welcome to the world of *Sheila Newberry*!

Keep reading for more from Sheila Newberry, to discover a recipe that features in this novel, to find out more about Sheila Newberry's inspiration for the book and for a chapter of the next book . . .

We'd also like to welcome you to Memory Lane, a place to discuss the very best saga stories from authors you know and love with other readers, plus get recommendations for new books we think you'll enjoy. Read on and join our club!

www.MemoryLane.Club
f /MemoryLaneClub

Meet Sheila Newberry

I've been writing since I was three years old, and even told myself stories in my cot. So it came as a shock when I was whacked round the head by my volatile kindergarten teacher for daydreaming about stories when I was supposed to be chanting the phonetic alphabet. My mother received a letter from my teacher saying, 'Sheila will not speak. Why?' Mum told her that it was because I was scared stiff in class. I was immediately moved up two classes. Here I was given the task of encouraging the slow readers. This was something I was good at but still felt that I didn't fit in. Later, I learned that another teacher had saved all my compositions saying they inspired many children in later years.

I had scarlet fever in the spring of 1939, and when I returned to our home near Croydon, I saw changes which puzzled me – sandbags, shelters in back gardens, camouflaged by moss and daisies, and windows reinforced with criss-crossed tape. Children had iron rations in Oxo tins – we ate the contents during rehearsals for air-raids – and gas masks were given out. I especially recall the stifling rubber. We spent the summer holiday, as usual, in Suffolk and I remember being puzzled when my father left us there, as the Admiralty staff was moving to Bath. 'War' was not mentioned but we were now officially evacuees, living with relatives in a small cottage in a sleepy village.

On and off, we returned to London at the wrong times. We were bombed out in 1940 and dodging doodlebugs in 1943. I thought of Suffolk as my home. I was still writing – on flyleaves of books cut out by friends – and every Friday I told stories about Black-eyed Bill the Pirate to the whole school in the village hut. I wrote my first pantomime at nine years old, and was awarded the part of Puss in Boots. I wore a costume made from blackout curtains. We were back in our patched-up London home to celebrate VE night and dancing in the street. Lights blazed – it was very exciting.

I had a moment of glory when I won an essay compe-tition that 3000 schoolchildren had entered. The subject was waste paper, which we all collected avidly! At my new school, I was encouraged by my teachers to concentrate on English Literature and Language, History and Art, and I did well in my final exams. I wanted to be a writer, but was told there was a shortage of paper! True. I wrote sto-ries all the time and read many books. I was useless at games like netball as I was so short-sighted – I didn't see the ball until it hit me. I still loved acting, and my favour-ite Shakespearian parts were Shylock and Lady Macbeth.

When I left school, I worked in London at an academic publisher. I had wanted to be a reporter, but I couldn't ride a bike! Two years after school, I met my husband John. We had nine children and lived on a smallholding in Kent with many pets (and pests). I wrote the whole time. The children did, too, but they were also artistic like John. We were all very happy. I acquired a typewriter and wrote short stories for children, articles on family life and romance for magazines. I received wonderful feedback. I soon graduated to writing novels and joined the Romantic Novelists' Association. I have had many books published over the years and am over the moon to see my books out in the world once again.

Dear readers,

I so enjoyed returning to a place I knew well in my youth. It is so different there now, I know, no longer in Surrey but now part of Greater London, but I always promised myself I would write a book about those halcyon days in the 1950s and now I have . . .

The Grove is based on a favourite haunt of me and my friends; we rolled down the grassy slopes, played our version of tennis with ancient rackets and dud balls, explored the old gardens, still fragrant with roses in the summer, and yes, later on, walking home from the Grandison ballroom with our escorts on a Saturday night, after we had enjoyed dancing to Kenny Ball and his Jazzmen, we paused under the big tree and gazed up at the stars. I am the only one left of that group now, but I don't forget my salad days . . .

I was able to revisit all my favourite places by sending Sunny and friends to them – the promenade concerts, the zoo, Madame Tussauds, the National Gallery and yes, I was entranced by Turner's pictures. I also enjoyed recalling our favourite clothes of the era, and dear old C & A! Like Sunny and Rodney, I went on a 'float' tour with my friends, and have the embarrassing pictures tucked away somewhere . . . It is sad to reflect that our all-girls Lady

Edridge School was demolished some years ago, and a huge estate built on the site. We had inspiring teachers like our form mistress, 'Auntie' Capell – English Language and English Lit; Freda Feasey – 'Miss Fizz-Bang' – History; Helen Brook – Art; – we were very impressed by her fish net stockings and makeup! and yes, the volatile Mademoiselle Mallett (who shouted naughty words in French at us, so we looked them up . . .) 'Auntie' would read our essays to the class and ask, 'Who wrote that?' I dreaded the response when she read mine, and they chorused, 'Sheila!' and I blushed like mad. Although I loved the school, I was unfortunately bullied by two older girls, just because I was 'dreamy'. However, I sat next to Diane Pearson, who became a great editor, president of the RNA, wrote wonderful books, and we kept in touch. After hearing my brother had passed away, she wrote how she'd enjoyed dancing with him as he'd won a cup for ballroom dancing! I rode pillion on my future husband's motorcycle, like Sunny did on Rod's machine . . . and loved visiting Rye.

Love,

Sheila

A Recipe for Gammon and Pease Pudding

Nan's gammon and pease pudding was a favourite – particularly of Alec's – and one she cooked often.

Ingredients

For the pease pudding:
300g/10oz dried yellow split peas
50g/2oz butter
1 onion, roughly chopped
½ tsp dried thyme
1 bay leaf
1 tsp sea salt flakes
½ tsp finely grated nutmeg
1 free-range egg, beaten
Freshly ground black pepper

For the gammon:
1kg/2¼lb smoked or unsmoked gammon joint, tied
1 medium onion, peeled
4 cloves
1 large carrot, roughly chopped
2 celery sticks, roughly chopped
2 bay leaves
10 black peppercorns

For the parsley sauce:
25g/1oz butter
25g/1oz plain flour
600ml/1 pint milk
Salt and white pepper
4 tbsp finely chopped parsley

Method

1. Rinse the peas in a sieve under cold running water and drain. Put the peas in a bowl and cover with hot water. Leave to stand for 20 minutes.
2. Heat 25g/1oz of the butter in a heavy-based frying pan and cook the onion, thyme and bay leaf very gently for 15 minutes, or until softened and only just beginning to colour. Stir regularly.
3. Drain the peas and add to the pan. Pour over 1 litre/1¾ pints water and bring to the boil. Reduce the heat slightly and simmer for 30–40 minutes, or until the peas soften and start falling apart. The liquid should be well reduced by this time.
4. Meanwhile, put the gammon in a large lidded saucepan and cover with cold water. Bring to the boil then discard the water (be careful as it will create a lot of steam). Cut the onion in half and stud each piece with cloves.

5. Take the peas off the heat, remove the bay leaf and blend with a hand blender until a thick purée. Beat in the remaining butter, nutmeg and the egg. Season with salt and freshly ground black pepper.

6. Spoon the pea mixture into the centre of a piece of muslin. Tie the ends tightly with kitchen string just above the peas, allowing a little room for expansion.

7. Tuck the pease pudding and onion into the pan beside the gammon. Add the carrot, celery, bay leaves and peppercorns. Fill the pan with enough cold water to cover the gammon and return to the hob. Bring to a simmer, cover loosely with a lid and cook for 1–1¼ hours.

8. Remove the gammon and place on a board. Cover with foil and a couple of tea towels. Leave to stand for 10 minutes before carving. Ladle 300ml/10fl oz of the gammon stock into a heatproof jug.

9. For the parsley sauce, melt the butter in a saucepan over a medium heat. Stir in the flour and cook for 1–2 minutes. Take the pan off the heat and gradually stir in the milk to get a smooth sauce. Return to the heat and, stirring all the time, bring to the boil. Simmer gently for 8–10 minutes and season with salt and white pepper. Stir in the parsley.

10. Carve the gammon into thick slices. Unwrap the pease pudding and transfer to a warmed serving bowl. Serve a spoonful of pease pudding with a slice of gammon and drizzle over the sauce.

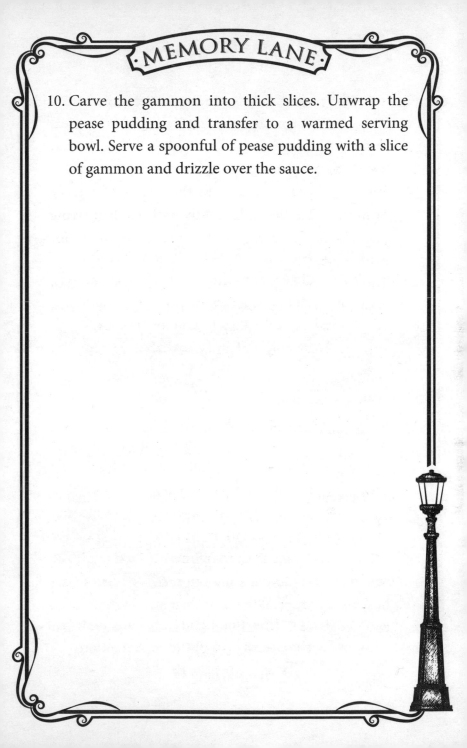

Don't miss Sheila Newberry's next book,
coming May 2021 . . .

THE CANAL BOAT GIRL

Wales, 1883

Young Ruth Owen, a talented musician with a scholarship to a prestigious music school, has a sparkling career
ahead of her. But after a run-in with her mysterious
tutor, Drago, she flees to London, leaving
everything and everyone behind.

London, 1897

Fourteen years later, Ruth, now married with two
children, finds herself struggling for money and a place
to live. Left with no other option, they decide to return
to Wales and live on a canal boat. Life on the canals
may seem idyllic, but what troubles await her return?
And can the past ever truly be forgotten?

Read on for an extract

**Sign up to Memory Lane to find out more and do follow
us on Facebook and join in the conversation**
MemoryLaneClub

PROLOGUE

She remembered another chapel, another time. Not a simple meeting place like the mission, with flowers picked by the boat children in jam jars along the windowsills and sunlight streaming through the plain glass in the high windows, but a place with a great, arched roof, dark panelled walls, glorious stained glass and high-backed pews. On the lectern was a carved eagle with spread wings; on the altar a blue cloth overspread with fine, creamy lace.

This was Ruth Owen's first service at the College of Music, the first time she actually met Drago, although, of course, she knew him by sight and reputation as they both came from Brynbach, both lived alongside the canal, though in very different circumstances. Ruth lived with her elder sister, Rachel Hughes, and her husband Davey: he was the lock keeper then and they had cared for her since she was six years old when her parents died of typhoid fever. Drago lived at that big house with all the steps down to the water's edge.

She was less than five feet tall with a childlike figure that belied her seventeen years, and amazing dark eyes in that glowing little face. She had tiny hands with such a span over the piano keys.

Then, as always, Drago played the organ and Ruth Owen, the young student of music, was lost in the beauty of it all as the music soared to the rafters. She felt rising excitement within, for wasn't she, the scholarship girl, about to study piano with this marvellous teacher? This man was a living local legend.

She would have been amazed if she had known that the man so absorbed in his playing was also vibrantly aware of her presence, for she was but one student among many dutifully attending morning service.

'Don't be too much in awe of him,' Rachel had advised quietly. 'He has gifts, yes, but so do *you*. Remember that.'

'But to be taught by *Drago*, Rachel – that's always been my dream! Oh, but I'm going to miss you all ... ' She caught Meg's sulky sidelong glance – all this fuss! But she thought wryly that now Meg, Rachel's daughter, not far from her in age really, would be pleased to have the small bedroom all to herself. Could Meg actually be jealous of her success? She hoped not, being a kind-hearted girl.

They spoke briefly, after the service, when he warmly gripped the hands of the new intake in turn and wished them well.

'I am—' she began breathlessly, as the others had done.

'You are Ruth Owen, of course. We are neighbours, give or take a mile or two of water between us ... So, we are already friends, I hope?' He had a deep voice, an almost shy smile.

She was flattered, he was completely without side, so ... nice. Middle-aged and married for many years, she knew that, but surely she could keep her hero worship hidden? She had this burning ambition, not only to play piano, but also to sing, for she had a lyrical Welsh voice; she intended to leave quiet Brynbach before too long and make her mark in a wider world. Drago, despite returning dutifully home at the end of each term, would, she knew, be the one to help her fulfil all her hopes and dreams. Who knows what heights he might have risen to himself, if he had not had the responsibility of an invalid wife?

In turn, the students were invited to Sunday tea in Drago's rooms. All very proper, the girls were always in pairs with a lady tutor to chaperone, the boys, unaccompanied, in a group. Drago's manservant toasted muffins, served tea, and Ruth Owen sat fascinated, hardly saying a word, listening to Drago talking. He was always called 'Drago', never 'Mister Drago' or even 'Sir' and his darkness was as Welsh as that of Ruth Owen and many of the local young men and women whom he encouraged and inspired. Yet Ruth knew what they did not: that

Drago had a foreign side to him. His paternal grandfather, a Spaniard, had been an engineer involved with the canal from its conception. He had married and settled in Brynbach, risen high in his profession and had built that beautiful house for his growing family. Drago, childless, was the last of that line.

Long letters home, she wrote to her family, for she dearly loved them, even though she intended to leave them. She did not often mention Drago, remembering Rachel's words. In any case how could she explain the bond she felt between the two of them?

They were never alone together until the end of Ruth's first year was approaching. She had been his bright star at the end of term concert, singing to her own accompaniment, aware of his presence between the dignitaries seated in the front row of the audience. Such applause! The first of her dreams realised.

It was a day of mists and she walked by the lake in the college grounds, alone with her happy thoughts. He caught up with her, walked quietly beside her, merely catching her arm in his, respecting her daydreaming.

It was then that the words were said: 'I have patiently waited for this moment, Miss Ruth Owen – I have something I *must* say to you . . . '

That same night, full of anguish, Ruth had taken flight, her very first moonlight flit – though there were many to follow – back to Brynbach, given a lift by a kindly carrier who knew her elder brother, Ivor. She went back home to sob her heart out in Rachel Hughes's arms. 'How *could* he?' wept her sister, hugging her so tight.

Three years passed and there was no time for daydreaming. Ruth Owen was found a job in the canal office: quite the business lady she was with her hair piled high and her sober clothes. Rachel and Davey said they were proud of her making a success of her life despite the bitter disappointment she had suffered.

There was Meg growing up now, almost fourteen, still resentful of her mother's fondness for her younger sister which made for awkwardness between the two of them and quarrels over lack of privacy in their shared bedroom – '*Why* did you have to come home like that?' Meg raged once.

But there was also little Alun, born after Ruth's return, the surprise baby who brought such joy to them all.

I'll never be happy sitting behind a desk, but he makes it bearable . . . Ruth thought. She loved to let her hair down at the end of a tiring day, to whoop about the meadow at the back with the little boy on her back, to smother him in kisses when they tumbled, as they inevitably did, even though Rachel told her gently that she was spoiling him. Meg resented *that* closeness too. 'I have to wash up the dishes while you're playing with Alun, Ruth,' she said, lips compressed, eyes flashing.

Later, when things went wrong, she would wonder how she could have run away from her family, after all they had done for her to ease the shock and despair after Drago. Yet leave them she did, very early one morning; knowing how hurt Rachel would be, she couldn't even bring herself to write a note.

She had fled in her naivety to London, trusting in that well-thumbed introductory card concealed in her purse, which had been presented to her by a musical impresario after that never-to-be-forgotten triumph at the college concert.

Amazingly, her hopes and faith in strangers were rewarded. Within a year she was enjoying modest acclaim on the concert circuit. Then she met the man she would eventually marry, Bayly Barley.

He was a handsome man with an imposing tall fig-ure, a fine head of iron-grey hair, waving at the back over his collar. As her career was beginning to take off, his was fading. He was quite a few years her sen-ior. He had been married to Anne, who died following childbirth; he had a young daughter, Daisy, who lived with her maternal grandmother, who blamed him for the loss of her only daughter, and whom, it seemed, he never saw.

She had so quickly fallen in love with him, despite his initial lack of interest in her. There was a distant look in those narrowed, light-blue eyes. She had tried so hard, but she could never become remotely close to him and was unable to understand why he behaved as he did. Of course she was aware that Anne, tall and beautiful, had been the great passion of his life so she supposed that her loss had triggered Bay's instability, his excessive drinking. He was not cut out for responsibilities, but she loved him nevertheless even though *this* love, too, had feet of clay.

She was destined, when she cast her lot in with his, to be classed as a third-rate performer. When at last she married Bay, her agent cut their ties. It was all-downhill from there.

Would he have married her if she had not become pregnant with their daughter, Clemmie? Ruth doubted it. Soon after Clemmie's birth she had taken on Daisy when her grandmother died. 'Of course she must come to us!' she cried to Bay, silencing his doubts.

In that gloomy house with dustsheets already covering the furniture, Ruth Owen met Daisy for the first time. There were debts to be met from the sale of the property – Daisy's grandmother had lived beyond her means. Daisy had been bequeathed merely a few of her late mother's childhood possessions. Ruth learned that she

and Anne had had something in common beside their love for a feckless man. Anne had also left home without a word or a forwarding address. The first her unfortunate mother knew of Daisy's existence was when Bay brought the baby to this house.

Ruth Owen held out her arms impulsively to the bright-haired silent child, offering love and comfort to one who had grown up so far lacking both.

Over the years since, Ruth had discovered how very different Daisy was to her own Clemmie, who was the lively young Ruth Owen all over again, yet to her they were equally her daughters. She protected Daisy fiercely from the unkind indifference of her father. She had not bargained for the fact, she often thought ruefully, that Bay would become like a tiresome third child.

Those dreams, the ones that Drago had so cruelly shattered, they were long past. Yet often at night she would dream of Brynbach. Would she ever go back?

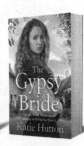